HIDDEN YOUTH

SPECULATIVE FICTION FROM THE MARGINS OF HISTORY

EDITED BY MIKKI KENDALL AND CHESYA BURKE

Crossed
Genres
Publications

Framingham, MA

HIDDEN YOUTH: Speculative Fiction from the Margins of History

Print ISBN-13: 978-0-9913921-2-4 / Print ISBN-10: 0-9913921-2-4
Ebook ISBN-13: 978-0-9913921-3-1 / Ebook ISBN-10: 0-9913921-3-2

FIRST EDITION: November 2016

Edited by Mikki Kendall and Chesya Burke

Cover design by Kay T. Holt
Interior layout by Bart R. Leib

Cover art copyright © 2015-2016 by Julie Dillon
http://juliedillonart.com

Interior art copyright © 2016 by:

    Kaley Bales (http://kaley-bales.squarespace.com)

    Jay Bendt (http://jaybendt.com)

    Anna D'Amico (adamicoart.com)

    Lindsay Ishihiro (http://chaoslindsay.ca)

    Amy Kwan (https://www.behance.net/aKwan)

    Alice Meichi Li (http://alicemeichi.com)

    Charis Loke (http://charisloke.com)

    Ellen Million (http://ellenmillion.com)

    Kim Miranda (http://www.isaia-arts.com)

    Ivonne K. Moran (http://ikm218.tumblr.com)

    Wina Oktavia (http://kreavi.com/veleries)

    Eric Orchard (http://patreon.com/ericorchard)

    Mirelle Ortega (http://mirelleortega.com)

    Paula Arwen Owen (http://arwendesigns.net)

    Patrick Thicklin (https://pdillathegreat.wordpress.com)

    Kathryn Weaver (http://kathrynmweaver.com)

TABLE OF CONTENTS

Art by Wina Oktavia

THROWAWAY CHILDREN
JESSI COLE JACKSON

1860
New York City, NY, USA

When the aid societies rounded up all of the orphaned street kids of New York City and shoved us onto a train headed West, I was a teenager – a girl hovering somewhere between late childhood and true adulthood. Technically, I was not an orphan, as my parents were alive.

I saw them sometimes as I huddled on the corner of Vesey Street and sang for change. They would toss a penny and hurry on their way, dragging their guilt behind. They had thrown me out, to make room at the dinner table for three younger sisters. Supposedly without large, lumbering me, they had more food to go around, but they and I both knew the real cause of my exile.

I was ejected from my family's home and put on that train West for the very same reason – I had a dangerous magic, and no longer belonged.

***

I met Charlotte the first night we rode the orphan train. She was crying when she crawled into my bunk.

"What ails you?" I asked the whimpering child.

I did not ask why she had sought shelter with a stranger rather than with Mrs. Wright, the aid societies' female chaperone on the train. The woman was tall and frigid and terrifying. I would not seek her help either.

"It's dark," she said.

I agreed. The constant flickering of the streets' gaslights was a comfort not present on the train. All lamps went out at nine o'clock, Mrs. Wright said.

This was the darkest night of my life.

"I'm scared," she said.

"Here," I said, "climb over, beside the wall."

When she settled, I turned on my side so my broad shoulders would hide the light from Mrs. Wright and the others, then I made a teeny flame in the palm of my right hand, held between our faces. I did not consider the danger of introducing fire to a train car full bed linens, wooden bunks, and sleeping girls. Nor did I wonder if she would find my magic more terrifying than the nighttime.

Thankfully neither were a problem that night.

"What's your name?" I asked.

"Charlotte," she said, her eyes were large with wonder and her tears forgotten as she watched the little, dancing flame.

1

"I'm Marcella."

She reached out a finger and I extinguished my flame.

She gasped. "Oh!"

Having known the comfort of that small light, the darkness seemed heavier for us both, I think.

"I will bring it back, but you must promise not to try to touch it. It's a real flame, no trick of your eyes. It will burn whatever it touches, the same as any fire."

"I promise," she said, and I brought it back to life. She giggled. "You have magic."

"I do indeed."

"But how did you put out the flame a moment ago?" she asked. "Did you snuff it with your own hand? Did that not hurt?"

"I just called the fire back inside myself."

She bit her lip and furrowed her pale brow. "I thought once magic is out in the world, it's there. It can't be undone."

"You knew other magic workers?"

She nodded, still watching the flame. I took joy from her awe.

"Mama could make flowers bloom," she said, "Papa would bring home small closed buds he found in parks or bought for cheap from the flower stall, and she would bring them to life, bright and smelling sweet like spring. But she could never close them back up or prolong their life. I'd ask and ask, but she said once she put her magic into the world, it was no longer hers to bring back."

"That is a lovely magic," I said, "and your mama is right, that's how it most often works."

"Was right," Charlotte said, "She's gone now. Her and my Papa caught the fever."

So Charlotte was an orphan due to God, not her parents' cruel choice. I couldn't be sure which was harder to bear.

"Could I sleep here with you?" Charlotte asked after long minutes of watching the tiny fire dance in my palm.

Before I agreed, she was asleep.

***

Three days later I combed Charlotte's hair as she stared listlessly out the dingy train windows. The daytime view remained the same since we left the city – bare trees, white ground, rolling hills. Charlotte shrank further into herself with each passing night. I had not heard her giggle or seen a smile since the first time she saw my magic.

I yanked the comb through her knots. She never flinched, so I pressed on through thick tangles, determined to get her hair in a braid for our first stop, a mere day away. We would not look like street urchins. If we were clean and dressed properly, Charlotte and I would have our best hope for finding a place in a proper family. A small, secret part of me began to hope it may be in the same home, as two new additions to the same family.

"Charlotte, what would you like to do today?" I asked.

She turned, a small glint in the corner of her eye.

She whispered so the others couldn't hear. "Would you make fire again, Marcella?"

I set down the comb. I worried this would be the request. She'd asked me to produce it every night since the first, and I had put it off. Mrs. Wright had given us a long lecture about the use of magic on the train. Any and all magic working was limited to the last train car, with the most dangerous magics prohibited entirely.

Working fire definitely fell within the forbidden category, and I was not one to risk a caning.

"It's not allowed, Lottie."

Even her wheedling was sweet sounding. "Perhaps if we went to the caboose and none of the others were around...."

I was glad to see mischief in Charlotte's small face. I sighed and packed the comb back into my small valise. "But later we'll fix your hair."

She waved a hand, swatting my concern aside and bounced impatiently while I stashed the valise in a compartment.

"Alright," I said, "Let's go."

Charlotte needed no further permission. She ran toward the back of the car, skirts swirling around her shins.

"Meet you there!"

She dashed through the dining area, over and under and around obstacles, and I half understood how this slender, quiet child survived on the streets of New York City on her own.

She was fast.

I followed at a subdued pace. As a young woman, I was far too old for running to be charming and it jiggled parts of me I'd rather not jiggle. I may have lived on the streets for a time, but I still had hope of growing up to be a lady.

Charlotte waited for me in the second to last train car, just before the connecting doors.

"Marcella, you took forever!"

"Before we go in there," I began but Charlotte was through before I could finish my warning.

I followed immediately.

Many eyes turned to stare at us, most of them belonging to young men. None of them smiled.

Charlotte reached up for my left hand and I squeezed reassurance.

There were no adult chaperones nearby, no Mrs. Wright and her ilk, but we were in a car full of orphaned children who had lived on the streets same as us. If they saw we were the same sort, they would leave us be. For the first time since bathing, I wished the grime back on my cheeks.

A kid rough and dirty stood up from the game of cards and sauntered over to us.

"This is our car, and you're not welcome," the girl said. She looked close to my age, up close.

"Turn around a go back from whence you came and your trespassing will be forgot."

"Trespassing? Says who?" Charlotte let go of my hand and squared her scrawny hips and shoulders. She had spunk. And a large mouth.

"Says Esther. Me."

The girl was not intimidating per se. She was all smooth curves with light brown skin and a halo of brown curls which she wore loose. Her beauty made her seem soft, but I knew well enough that a person could be beautiful and dangerous.

"How'd you get them to let you wear trousers?" Charlotte asked. "I really miss my trousers. You can't run in these." She held a fistful of skirt and stared wistfully at Esther's canvas-clad legs.

Esther held out her right hand. On her thumb, stretching up to her wrist was a crudely tattooed lightning bolt. As if to emphasize the mark and the danger it represented, small blue sparks crackled across her palm.

"I said I was wearing trousers and Mrs. Wright didn't ask twice."

"That supposed to scare us?" Charlotte asked, but she'd stepped slightly behind me.

I was a little scared too. I'd never seen anyone with the ability to work lightning before. She was a feminine Zeus standing before us, and we'd invaded her train car.

"It's not supposed to scare you," she said, "it's supposed to make you leave."

"Alright. We did not mean to disrupt you," I said, "we didn't think anyone would be—"

"We have as much right to be here as you!" Charlotte interrupted.

Esther laughed and goosepimples popped out down my arms.

"Let's see your tats then," she said to both of us, but our hands were clearly visible and held no marring ink.

I turned to go. I did not want to tussle. This girl was prickly and powerful and I had no need to prove I belonged.

I believed her that I did not.

I did not belong in my parents' home, or on the streets of my city, or in this train car of dangerous magic workers. I may have a dangerous magic, but I had never used it to do damage or to threaten. If I had, I would also bear a tattoo warning others of my ability. But my hands and my conscience were clean and I had no desire to fight. Wherever I belonged lay ahead of me, somewhere on these tracks.

Charlotte, however, seemed to like the fight.

"She may have no tattoo, but Marcella does too have magic! Magic as powerful as yours," she said.

Esther snorted, eyeing my unmarked thumb. "Tell us, Lady Marcella. What is the magic you work so well? Can you talk to the birds? Make them peck out my eyes? So sad that there are no birds inside the train. Or maybe you have an even more useless magic. Can you make flowers bloom on command?"

She laughed and the boys around them, still seated at their various games, laughed along. Her words and laugh were cruel, but they only bothered me because of Charlotte.

I saw her wilt slightly.

I held my right hand out and it burst into high flames – much, much larger than Charlotte had previously seen. The fire was hot and multi-hued as it skittered across my palm.

Esther leapt back and one boy overturned his seat in order to scramble as far away from me as the enclosed car allowed.

Charlotte laughed and clapped and I wondered slightly if the little girl craved danger. Her face held none of the fear that was written plainly across the others' expressions.

"Never seen a fire worker?" Charlotte said.

Her words betrayed her innocence. If she'd known another before me, she would be huddling with the boy in the corner.

A young man with long dark hair that hung in his face stepped around Esther.

"I'm Jeremiah," he said. "I work water. Now that you've made your point, would you like me to put that out?"

I smiled at the young man whose voice and offer were both kind, but shook my head.

"No need," I said and closed my right hand. In my fist, the fire extinguished. Gasps echoed around the car.

Jeremiah ran forward and took my hand in his, opening it. He ran a finger against my palm.

It tickled and was more than presumptuous, but I knew why he was checking. My hand remained whole, unburnt, and the fire was gone.

"How did you do that?" he asked.

"I simply called it back inside myself."

"Impossible," Esther said.

"Not impossible," I said, "How do we blink? We just do. It is how God made us to be. I was made with the ability to extinguish my own flames."

A giant of a boy stood up. "Some say the devil bestowed our gifts, not God," he said. "Especially the fire workers' curse."

He was very tall and very broad and wore the tight, shiny, wrinkled skin of a burn victim.

"From my baby sister," he said when he saw my eyes on his face, "God rest her soul. She never meant to hurt me, or our parents, but when her womanhood came and her powers spiked, she burned the house around us all. You're telling me, you can control your curse?"

"I am."

They tested me then.

I lit small things on fire whilst Jeremiah stood by, prepared to douse them in water, but Jeremiah and his magic was unnecessary. When a thing was sufficiently burnt, I would call the fire back to myself and it would come, same as it always had. The thing would smolder and smoke, but not alight again. The fire was gone.

After an hour of testing, Harland, the giant boy with the scars, gave me a hug so tight he lifted me off my feet.

"Welcome to the madhouse," Esther said and kissed my cheek.

***

I wandered over to Esther's bunk, my corset in hand. I woke her with a gentle shake.

"I need you to lace me up," I said. I kept my voice low so as not to wake the other girls who slept near, snug in their tiny bunks.

Esther rubbed her eyes. "Not again. It's been weeks of this, Marcella. Why do you torture yourself so?"

"It is not torture to hope."

Esther swung her legs off the edge of the bunk and hopped down. She landed lightly. "I meant the corset. In truth, I understand neither the corset nor the hope."

"I wear a corset because all proper young ladies wear corsets. And I will never find a proper family if they do not think I am a lady."

Esther's mouth quirked, but she didn't say anything. She took the corset from me and motioned for me to turn around. "And you want to find a family," she said. "You could come back to the city with us. At the end of the tracks those who haven't been adopted are going back."

When I didn't reply, she continued, "Or you could live on your own in whichever po-dunk town we come across that strikes your fancy."

I looked back over our shoulders to where Charlotte lay still curled up in sleep, tangled up in the covers of our bunk.

"I don't have skills enough to keep us both fed," I said. "In the city, I begged. That is no life for a child like Lottie."

"It is no life for you, either." Esther threaded the laces through their eyelets slowly, her fingers occasionally brushing my back through the thin cotton of my chemise and sending tingles up my spine. "You could learn a trade, or use your fire–"

"Never."

I knew how magic workers with dangerous gifts used them to take money. It may have been enough of a life for Esther, but I would not be a hired thug. I wanted no tattoo on my thumb, announcing to the world I was a threat.

"She'll be chosen, you know." Esther spoke low after a long moment, her breath warm against my neck. "If you give her space and do not play the elder sister, a family will take her home. If she's lucky, it'll be a good, kind family."

"Families will take a beautiful child, if she's not attached to an oaf, is what you mean," I said.

Esther yanked the laces, less gentle. "Few families can afford to add two children to their table at once is what I meant."

By the time Esther was done, I could barely breathe, but I had a narrower waist and a made up mind.

I stood apart from Charlotte on the train platform that afternoon while the ladies and gentlemen examined us. I did not hold her hand, and made her promise not to claim me as her sister. She shed a few small tears, but agreed to my request.

It was not even noon before Charlotte ran over to me with her gap-toothed smile wide. "Marcella. They chose me! I'm going to have a family! Aren't they fine? Isn't she beautiful and doesn't he look strong? Do you think they'll be kind? Oh, but I hope so! I hope they are kind. And I hope they like flowers. Do you think they will, Marcella? Do you think they will love flowers?"

I crouched down and she wrapped her arms around my neck and almost knocked us both into a heap on the dirty platform floor.

"I'm sure they will love flowers because you love flowers," I said.

I hid my tears in her braid, and said my goodbye without showing her my face.

"Oh, but I'll miss you," she said. "Will you come to visit me? When you're a woman, will you come see me here, with my new family?"

I lied and assured her I would so her frown would disappear.

She glowed when she smiled.

"Goodbye!" she called over her shoulder, skipping off into the town hand-in-hand with a beautiful lady in a very fine dress.

I thought for one brief moment about my conversation with Esther, about how easy it would be to walk away from the orphan train, and about how hard it would be to set up a life for myself, by myself. I may be able to do it, but at what cost? My first family might have thrown me away, but I still hoped there was somewhere ahead I belonged.

I turned and reboarded the train. I did not go back and face my friends, but instead went to my bunk and curled up under the thin sheet, dressed down to my boots. Sometime in the evening, long after the train had resumed its westward trip, I heard the door open and shut and the sound of heavy footsteps. They stopped behind me.

"What's happened?" Jeremiah said. I spun around. Harland and Esther stood with him in the small walkway between the bunks.

"You cannot be in here!" I pulled the sheet up under my chin. "If Mrs. Wright catches you..."

Jeremiah chuckled and knocked on the heel of my boot. "Your modesty is preserved, my lady. You have every stitch possible yet on your person. Besides, Mrs. Wright is already well into the wine this evening."

"Where's our little sister?" Harland asked.

My eyes found Esther's, but I could not hold her gaze.

"Charlotte has found a family," I managed to get out before my tears began falling once again.

Jeremiah placed a hand on my ankle through the sheet. It was a small comfort.

Harland's next words came like a cut. "Why didn't you stop them?"

"What do you think I should have done?" I asked.

"Used your power," Harland said. "Just to scare them a little. They would have left her alone."

"I'm no thug! I don't use my magic to threaten innocent people."

"You don't use your magic at all," Esther said.

"Would you rob Charlotte of a family and a chance at happiness, and by such vile means?"

Esther raised an eyebrow. "I've used my magic for much worse means, playing the *thug*. But no, I'd not take Charlotte's joy away from her if a family what's best. Neither would I stifle my gifts."

She shot a spark of lightning onto a nearby gas lamp and it flared to life with a violent pop, chasing away the shadows of early evening.

"Neither your magic nor your body are as vile as you believe them," she said. "I trust you can find help to remove your corset tonight?"

With an exaggerated wink at Jeremiah, she and Harland left.

***

Station after station after station went by. Each time I would carefully prepare. I would wear my cleanest, prettiest blouse and put my hair up in elaborate styles. Once I even nicked a pinch of Esther's rouge to paint my cheeks, but scrubbed it off immediately after Jeremiah whistled a wolf call. I wanted a family, not a job as a common tavern girl.

Finally the train rolled into Council Bluffs, Iowa. The last stop. The last station. My last chance.

This time even Esther, Jeremiah and Harland joined me in the scraggly line of leftover children on the platform. Some us were still hanging tight to our bits of hope that we may find a home with kind parental figures and warm bread on the table. My friends were there because Mrs. Wright forced them out of the caboose, slapping her stiff caning switch on her palm as a threat.

She'd insisted on little else on our train trip West, preferring the company of a bottle to us.

Despite my friends' presence on the platform, they did not willingly participate in the procedures.

"They just want a farm hand," Harland said of a broad-backed couple, their faces tan from long hours in the sun.

Esther growled at an old woman with soft gray curls under a cap. "I'm no nursemaid," Esther said.

The woman hobbled off down the line.

At the end of the long day, not one townsperson had even spoken to me, possibly out of fear my companions may bite if they drew too near.

I did not blame the townsfolk.

"Now that's over, let's go home," Jeremiah said when the platform stood empty of all but us orphans.

A few townsfolk stood around, perhaps buying tickets or completing other business, but they paid no mind to us orphans.

The little kids went aboard first with bent heads and heavy, plodding feet. Jeremiah practically bounced behind them, he was so pleased to finally return home.

Before he could board the train, Mrs. Wright stepped into the doorway, barring his way. "Not so fast."

"Excuse me, ma'am," Jeremiah said, honey in his voice, "but no one else is here. We didn't get chosen by any fine families, and I believe it's time to head back home, if I'm not mistaken?"

"I'm afraid you are. Mistaken. You three," she pointed to Jeremiah, Harland, and Esther, "will not be returning to New York. Marcella, though, is welcome to board."

She shifted slightly to the side so I could get past her, but I was rooted to the spot.

I could not comprehend her words. She would not allow my friends back on the train? All they'd longed for the entire way West was the chance to turn around and head back to their beloved city.

"Mrs. Wright," I said, taking a slight step forward, to explain the situation.

I could bear my own heartbreak at not finding a family and having to return to a city full of unpleasant memories and sorrow, if I had my friends' happiness to buoy me.

Mrs. Wright held up her left hand. In her right her caning switch shivered.

"I'm sorry, but before we even left New York, the city government decided that whichever of the dangerous orphans had not found a permanent place by the end of our journey would remain at our final destination and not return with the others. You three each have a tattoo on your thumbs. You're dangerous. Your trunks have already been unboarded. You will find them in the station with a few coins for each of you to help ease your transition to independence."

"But ma'am—" Harland said and stepped forward. Whatever he was going to say, was cut off with a sickening crack. He fell to his knees. Harland moaned and held his hand over the scarred portion of his face. When he removed his hand, his palm came away with a streak of blood.

Mrs. Wright shrieked. "Stay back, you ugly beast! I will not have you threaten me!"

My mouth fell open.

I could not believe Mrs. Wright would hit Harland and with absolutely no provocation. He had not threatened her – only spoken her name. And he was the gentlest, kindest soul of us all, despite his intimidating size and fearsome scars.

Further up and down the train, doors closed.

Jeremiah hurried to attend to Harland while Esther stepped forward, legs and shoulders squared and right hand twitching.

I worried she would attack. Her hand already bore its tattoo. If she harmed another person or did damage to the train, she'd face serious repercussions. In Iowa, possibly even a hanging.

With few other options, I stepped up to her and took her right hand in my left. I clasped it as hard as I could. She would have to kill me to use her lightning now.

"Marcella, let me go."

9

She tried to shake me off, but I held tight and ignored her.

"Mrs. Wright," I said, "There was no need to harm Harland. Please, just let us all back on the train."

"Yes, let us on the train." Esther whispered her words, but this was not the scare tactic she used with the old woman earlier. These words had real threat behind them. And if I could sense the threat, so could Mrs. Wright.

The older woman took a small step back.

"Marcella," she said, "You have thirty seconds to get on this train before I seal this door. Or we could leave you behind with these sewer rats, if you'd prefer?"

I'm ashamed to admit I considered it, however briefly.

The thought flitted through my mind that if I returned, I could ride the orphan train again. I may have a second chance of finding my family.

"Or perhaps you've already found the family you sought so desperately?" Mrs. Wright said. "They're rather a pathetic substitute for a true family. Tell me, who would be the mother figure? Jeremiah?"

Esther lunged forward, her left hand outstretched. What she had planned to do, I could not know.

Before she came near enough to touch the woman, Mrs. Wright hit her with the switch.

Esther recoiled, but Mrs. Wright stepped forward and hit Esther further up her arm, then on her shoulder, neck and across her cheek. Still holding her right hand, I prevented Esther's retaliation, but I also prevented her escape.

"Stop!" I screamed and to my own horror, flames shot from my right hand. A wall of fire exploded between Esther and Mrs. Wright just long enough for the older woman to throw herself back and slam the train door shut.

I called the fire back as the train slowly pulled away, taking with it all hope of returning home. It would take months, possibly years, to earn the fare to NYC ourselves, and that was if we could even find paying work. I, for one, had no worthwhile skills.

"Excuse me miss," a man said behind me.

I turned, startled anyone had stuck near enough to witness the last moments.

"Yes?" I said.

He tipped his hat to me.

"I'm the sheriff here in Council Bluffs. I couldn't help but see what just happened, and I'm afraid I'm going to have to take you for a branding miss."

Esther stepped forward. "Branding?"

He shrugged, slow and lazy.

"Don't have much call for those fancy tattoo artists way out here, but cattle brands we have plenty of. It'll hurt for a long while, I'm afraid, but in time..." he held out his own right hand, which had a thick puckered scar the shape of an X. "It'll heal well enough. I figure 'bout half the town has a similar mark, so you'll all be welcome right enough. Especially with that handy talent you have."

"Handy?" I asked.

He nodded. "I've never seen anyone else who could call back their fire in all my years of knowing magic workers, but if you can repeat the trick, I suppose you'll have steady work for a long while."

He removed his hat and fidgeted with the brim.

"Personally, I could use some help clearing brush on my back forty. I'd pay you well for your time and talents," he said.

I opened and closed my mouth like a land-trapped fish.

Jeremiah wrapped his arm around my waist, as forward as he ever was. "Take the job, Marcella."

Harland stood beside him, bloody but smiling, while Esther remained holding my hand. Mrs. Wright must not have hit her as hard as she'd hit Harland, for she did not bleed, though she was bruised and had welts.

"Take it," Jeremiah urged, "and you'll buy your new family all dinner tonight."

***

As long as it paid us coin and hurt no one, we used our powers however, whenever, we could after that evening. We were not too proud to complete any small task.

In time, we saved enough to build a home in town for other children who reached the end of the tracks with no place to stay. We'd wait on the tracks and those Mrs. Wright and her ilk left behind, we'd bundle up and take home. We'd give them work and food for the bellies and if they wanted it, our love. Some left, when they earned the coin to make leaving possible, but some stayed and built their own homes near ours.

We lived in a small apartment off the back, which caused no end of gossip. Some say we lived together, all four as lovers. Some say Esther and I loved one another, and Jeremiah and Harland shared unnatural affection. Over the years, that sort of talk blew away in the tumbles. No one wanted to think about the sex lives of us old folk.

They talked instead of our true work. For sixty-five years the orphan trains kept coming from New York or Philadelphia or DC or Boston and we kept taking in the leftovers – dozens of sad, lost, angry orphans with tiny black tattoos. In my selfishness I thanked God for misguided aid societies and hoity eastern cities that would throwaway children, so I may scoop them up. They became our sons and daughters and nieces and nephews and grandchildren. In the end, I had my family after all.

Art by Alice Meichi Li

A NAME TO ASHES
JAYMEE GOH

1874
Cuba

"Thousands of words are under the sweep of our brushes, but they are too many to be put down in words. Whips lash our backs; shackles chain our bodies. The young and strong can merely live with starvation; the old and weak die with unrighted wrong. From now on, if we remain alive, we will be cold and hungry men; if we die, we will be ghosts of the starved."
– trans. Lisa Yun, The Coolie Speaks

My father died when I was very small, and my mother could not afford to take care of us all, so she gave me to the local temple to raise. The priests were very gracious about it, and appreciated one more pair of hands to help keep everything tidy. They taught me to read that I may answer the petitions of the people who came to our temple, taught me to cook for the beggars that sought succor, taught me to chant the sutras that would calm souls both dead and living. To read and write was more than what my brothers could do. Only our eldest brother, Kheng, had had such an education.

Still, I was very close to my brothers, and my mother also, and they visited me at the temple often. It was very inappropriate, according to the neighbours, but the priests didn't seem to mind. We were a happy family, except for one sadness: the unknown fate of Kheng. He disappeared a little after I was born, so I have no memories of him. The last letter he sent said he was boarding a ship to a place called Cuba, to work there as a clerk. My mother refused to believe he was dead, so he did not have a tablet on our small family shrine.

It was part of my temple duties to attend to the ghosts that drifted around the village. We didn't have many lost spirits, but ancestors often visited. During the seventh month, I would see them in the empty chairs we set out for them at feasts, enjoying the ambience. Whenever I visited homes, I would hear them muttering by their altars. The priests, when they finally realized out why I would talk to empty air, cautioned me to not tell anyone else, because it would open me to requests far beyond my ability to fulfill.

Master Wong in particular was very adamant about it. Before he retired to our temple, he had been an exorcist, and he warned me that unless I was truly committed to that path, indulging in my sight would bring no good. Then he taught me a few sutras, to alleviate the pain of ghosts, or to chase them away, so that I could calm them, and thus calm my own fears.

I came to know my deceased father through this ability. He was a quiet spirit, a shadow of the man my mother and brothers described him as. Still, in and out of ghost month, he would visit. He looked on me kindly, was by my bedside if I woke up from a nightmare, and laughed with us when Third Brother, the joker of our family, said something funny. I would find him often at the edge of the village, gazing off into the distance, waiting for something, or someone.

Master Wong took me with him to Heong Kong many times a year. He shaved the front of my head and braided my hair into a queue, so that no one would ask questions. When I returned, my family would teasingly ask what new language I had learned on my latest trip. I used these languages to ask stevedores if they had seen my brother, gave them his name and home village. Always, they shook their heads.

Perhaps it was fate, perhaps it was karma; I learned of an imperial commission that required servants and clerks who could handle long journeys. I was able to read and write, which raised me in the commissioner's esteem. When I demonstrated my facility in language, I was engaged immediately, with less than a week to prepare.

There was an uproar over this. My mother had lost her eldest; she did not want to lose her youngest, too. Half of my extended family took her side, both Father and Mother's relations. The other half was all for my going. I turned to the family altar for an appeal. *Go*, my father insisted, his voice less in my ears than in my head. *Come home safe.*

Thus was I engaged with the Educational Mission abroad, assistant to Commissioner Chen Lanpin. I copied documents, and sorted and stored them. I cleaned and cooked when needed. I wrote home often, and sent home money when I could. I was the youngest of the staff, but not bothersome, so my cleverness was tolerated. There were also no spirits in Master Chen's offices, so it was quite peaceful work. Master Chen was a kindly man who taught me guan-hwa, the court language, and spoke to me often in Gongtung-hwa, so that we both would not lose our tongue away from home. Doubtless I would have passed several years this way, and gone home to let my hair grow out and get married.

Then came the edict that would determine the rest of my life, on the tenth day of the tenth moon of the twelve year of Tungchih: the Son of Heaven tasked Commissioner Chen with investigating our countrymen who were sold into bondage in the place called Cuba.

> *"His Majesty's kindness is like a wide ocean, extending to the corner*
> *of the world. We are like grass and trees that benefit from his*
> *rain-like generosity, which is a rare grace in thousands of years."*
> – trans. Lisa Yun, *The Coolie Speaks*

We arrived in Havana on the second day of the second moon. Commissioner Macpherson, one of Master Chen's companions on this inquiry, had already arrived, and had arranged apartments for us in the hotel he stayed in.

At first, they left me in the hotel room to look after their belongings while they conducted their inquiry. In the evenings, I would sort through the depositions and petitions they brought back, and transcribe and categorize them carefully. The petitions, in particular, were challenging to sort, since they were written on all sorts of paper: scraps, the backs of receipts, old yellowing pieces. It was only on the fourth night, as the commissioners were conducting their enquiries in the Havana jail, that I thought to read them carefully, rather than simply copy every stroke I saw.

"*Only our hearts look forward to our country as sunflowers look forward to the sun,*" I read aloud, relishing the poetry on my tongue as I transcribed the petition. "*Voices crying wrong and bearing pain, shapes of broken skin and flesh, suicides are not isolated cases here.*"

I flipped another, and another. My heart beat hard but slow, and every character, every stroke etched anguish onto the petitions. "Come home safe," my father had told me, and he surely must have told my brother the same.

Such words, I realized, would never be fulfilled by these men, far away from home. A fear gripped my heart – if my brother had truly reached this place, he would have been trapped here, unable to write home. I took stock of the pile of papers on my table. If this hundred was just a sliver of the number of Chinese here, then how could I find Kheng?

I went through the pile. Every petition mentioned at least a few names of the men who either wrote it or men they knew. Every name seemed precious and necessary to record – their home villages, their occupations before, how they came to be here. To every name clung an unspoken hope that the wrongs they suffered would be righted.

Petition after petition after petition, and no sign of my brother's name. I tried very hard, that night, to console myself that it was just the start of the journey. Perhaps the depot would have a roster of coolies registered with them.

> "*We are now more than 100,000 Chinese in this island,*
> *whose daily existence is that of criminals confined in jail.*"
> – trans. Lisa Yun, The Coolie Speaks

After the first day at the depot, the commissioners were already overwhelmed with the number of petitions and depositions they had to handle. So I was asked to go with them, to the Havana jail. Outside, the roads were clear, but within, I heard the familiar mutterings of ghosts.

"My name is Chen A'Ren! My cedula is real and I demand it back!" something shrieked from the corner of the room.

"I have done nothing! Nothing!"

"I am Hong A'Jin from Guangzhou! My name is not Julio!"

What were they doing here? It was months before the gates of the afterlife would be open, although, perhaps, there were no such gates here. I didn't ponder the metaphysics of the problem, because the noise was so loud.

I looked around and found a man knocking his head on the wall rhythmically. "Abah! Abah! Abah! Abah!" he moaned. No one else noticed him, and Commissioner Chen walked right through him.

A ghost, then. I swallowed and gripped the box of paper tighter. I ducked my head under the rafters from which men hung, their spirits overlapping each other in blithe disrespect for the laws of physical space. I told myself, of course, it is to be expected that the jail would have many ghosts.

When we spoke to the Chinese prisoners, and when they mentioned a suicide, a death, or a disappearance, the ghosts would take an interest in the matter. When I glanced up, they had an air of waiting. And when they heard a name they recognized, they beat their breast and wailed. I was never sure if it was because they had heard their own name.

Under my breath, I whispered the sutra that Master Wong had taught me. The ghosts did not disappear, nor did they fall silent.

My only consolation was that Kheng was clearly not in the jail, among the dead or the living. Yet, it was small comfort, because I didn't know where else to look.

> "I was whipped many times; my name was changed."
> – trans., Denise Kelly, *The Cuba Commission Report:*
> *A Hidden History of the Chinese in Cuba*

Las Cañas plantation was the only plantation in Havana that would assent to the inquiry. We took the depositions in the back of the house where the plantation owner had prepared a shed for us to meet with workers. Labourers came from other plantations as well, having heard of our commission. I was sent out to ensure the lines were orderly. This was an easy task, not because we Chinese apparently keep our manners when abroad, although certainly we do and must, but because no one had the strength to fight my authority about it. The novelty of being able to tell grown men twice my size what to do wore off quickly, because their faces were so worn, and so sad.

The sun was high. I didn't see a living soul in the sugarcane field, just the sea of green, swaying softly with the heat. The workers had a day off, because of the commission, even though we had to ask questions as swiftly as possible. Behind me, in the line of men, I heard mutterings that having the one day off from the work was the best thing they could hope for.

I began to hum softly to myself, and then saw.

In the leaves of the tall grasses, faces.

I stopped humming, and then heard.

In the rustle of the leaves, whispers.

They gazed at me, these green faces put together – their eyes in the blades, their mouths in the spaces between, yawning lamentations. When I blinked, they were still there, insistent on my gaze. They were everywhere.

How many were there? I couldn't count.

Hastily, I ran back to the shed, hot and stuffy, but quiet. A man stood in front of Commissioner Chen. "Who is Gui Chen and why was I forced to sign his contract?" he was asking. He looked baffled, as if he expected us to have an answer.

I must have looked restless, because Master Chen thrust some papers into my hands to sort. "Don't go too far without an escort," he warned me in a hush. "It's dangerous." I sat down by his feet to work, listening to the interviews with half an ear.

Coolie after coolie corroborated that they had been asked to take on another man's contract, or sign under a different name. Then, after finishing the terms of that contract, they would sign another one, under their own name, assuming they survived.

Maybe my brother was still alive, and he had been forced to take another person's contract, too. If so, then my work was harder than I expected. I would not be able to simply look at the lists of names of workers.

"Something's wrong with that young fellow," Commissioner Macpherson declared, in English, as we made our way back to the Havana hotel.

"Probably overwhelmed by the heat and the work," Commissioner Huber replied in my defense. "It's a lot to take in, you know. Jia's very little."

Master Chen glanced at me. I didn't have to pretend to look tired.

I took dinner with the few other helpers who were part of Master Chen's entourage, and one of them offered me a local newspaper. "So you can practice your Spanish," he sniggered.

Out of curiosity, I flipped through the newspaper, glancing across the articles. My eyes chanced on a column. "Runaways," I translated aloud. "There's a column about our people!"

My Spanish was slow, but I had an old dictionary from our United States mission. Carefully, I translated a section, and frowned. "What kind of name is Fernando? Why would any jongkok-yan have that name?"

Suddenly, the cries of ghosts insisting on their names made sense. My shoulders felt heavier than before. Not only were workers forced to take someone else's contract, but they weren't even called by their own names. Lim Kheng wouldn't even be Lim Kheng, here.

> *"Looking at the sky, I cannot reach it. Looking at the ground,*
> *I cannot rest in peace. How sad and desperate I feel."*
> *- trans. Lisa Yun, The Coolie Speaks*

Over the next several days, we went to Matanzas, then to Cardenas, and at each, we stopped at the depot, the jail, and maybe a plantation or two, or three.

Against Master Chen's wishes, Commissioners Macpherson and Huber sent me out to spread the word about the inquiries they were conducting. The local officials were not always cooperative. They set the hours for visiting the depots and jails, and we were lucky if we managed to visit more than two plantations at each town we stopped, knowing full well there were tens more we were not permitted to visit. I was the lightest of the entourage, thus would tire the horse less, so I could cover wider ground.

The nights before beginning work in a new town, I copied information about the commission's visits onto multiple sheets of paper, working late into the night. The ink on my hands would still be drying even when I set out early in the morning, in advance of the commissioners, to distribute the papers to any Chinaman I saw. They would do the rest of work in spreading the word. I would turn back in the middle of the morning, returning to my master's side by lunchtime.

On these mornings, I would see that Chinese ghosts were not the only ones wandering the roads. They often would sit by the ghosts of black slaves, gesturing to each other as if they could, in life and death, try to communicate. Perhaps they got on better in death than in life, considering the antipathy I saw between the living workers on the field. There were also the ghosts of the Spaniards, but if I focused on them, they would abstract themselves out of my apprehension disdainfully.

If I looked out into the streets, the winds blew the sands up against the silhouettes of dead men walking, eyes sunken in despair and mouths wide open in hunger. If I looked to the trees, I saw the trails of the dead in the bark, their arms the branches reaching out in supplication. The most disturbing sights I saw when I served the commissioners at breakfast. The English commissioners liked to have tea in the morning, and with their tea, milk and sugar. In the sugar bowl, there would be spirits, drowning.

I understood, or thought I did. In many of the depositions and petitions, at every single plantation we visited, at every sugar refinery, there was at least one report of a suicide by jumping into the sugar cauldron. Death by boiling sugar, chosen over suffering, and their spirits were trapped in the sugar. Their forms were disintegrated beyond human recognition, and I winced as Macpherson and Huber stabbed their teaspoons in and out of the bowls.

One of the commission's concerns was how employers handled affairs when a man dies. The answers: there were no graves, or just shallow ones. There was no coffin, or proper cremation with the ashes sent home to waiting families. Master Wong had always insisted on proper funeral rites; the lack of them made spirits malevolent, and added to a ghost's pain tenfold. There is no reason for anyone to suffer after death even more.

One day, my mouth itched too much. "What happens to the bones?" I asked, interrupting Commissioner Huber before he could ask the next question. I ignored Master Chen's frown.

The men they were questioning glanced at each other. One of them, Lo A'Chi, said shortly, "they are used for fuel."

"What do you mean?"

He shrugged. "They use the bones of oxen for fuel sometimes. And they will mix in the bones of dead men."

Commissioner Chen sat up, his brows knitted together. "What? Why do they do that?" he asked sharply, in Gongtung-hwa.

"Because, your honour, if you use the bones of men, the sugar will be a purer white."

"And if they don't use the bones as fuel?"

Chi shrugged again. "They scatter the ashes to the wind. Especially if the man committed suicide in the sugar cauldron."

Another coolie added, "Hu A'Jing died like that. So did Yue A'Er. And their bones were used under the same sugar cauldron they killed themselves in."

The other men supplied further names of coolies whose bodies were burned without ceremony. Then they gave us several more names of men who

18

were simply left to rot, in the fields. As we left the plantation, my gaze glazed past the crying leaves and praying trees, and saw overhead how the crows perched on the trees, the signposts, the fences, black eyes waiting for the next man's death.

I have never been able to bear the sight of white sugar since.

> *"You could die easily like an ant."*
> *- trans. Lisa Yun, The Coolie Speaks*

It was the fifth town, or the sixth, that I was attacked on my route. My master was due to interview at a store owned by a Chinaman before visiting the depot. It was one of the very few places owned by Chinese, and the commissioners had been given so little time at the depot, they agreed that Commissioner Huber would go with his secretary to the depot to inquire there.

I was knocked off my horse with a bag of heavy grain. Someone hooted from the side of the road, and when I scrambled to get up, another voice shouted, in Spanish, "be careful!" They threw another bag at me, soft to not damage me, heavy enough to smack me back down.

I leapt to my feet. Five Cuban men, sweat shining on their sandy skin, surrounded me. A sixth was trying to capture my horse, which bucked wildly.

"I am the assistant to Commissioner Chen Lanpin, here on the orders of the Emperor of China!" I yelled at them in Spanish, one of the first things I had learned to say.

A couple of the men glanced at each other, then to their leader, who didn't take his eyes off me.

Glancing around, I saw that ghosts had gathered at the side of the road. One of them approached, and then jumped threateningly towards us. My horse shrieked in response, and I slapped its rump to make it run away, back to where we had come from. The men jumped out of my horse's way to avoid being run over, and I sprinted past them after it. Then I ran off the road, and vaulted over the first fence I saw into a sugarcane field.

The leaves sliced across my cheeks and forehead, and sweat and blood streaked across my face as I dashed towards the first group of workers I saw. They were both black and Chinese, and I ducked amidst them as my pursuers behind me shouted at them to stop me. I didn't hear anyone shout anything against them, but I heard men trip behind me, even as I kept running.

Finally, in a tiny clearing among tall sugarcane grasses, I crashed to the ground, panting heavily. My knees knocked against each other as I curled up. I lay there a long while, contemplating what had almost happened.

Shadows hovered over me, and I didn't have to look up to tell that they were ghosts. Overexposure to the multitudes of ghosts here had taught me by now how they felt: a prickling under my skin, a new thickness in the air. They patted me, maybe to determine whether I had joined their ranks yet, and they sat around me. In the distance, I heard the shouts of angry men, and knew that my pursuers were still looking for me.

I lay still, murmuring sutras under my breath over and over. The rustling passing me grew louder, and I saw the leaves of the sugarcane trees around me weave into a protective barrier. Soon, the danger moment lifted, and I was left alone in my hiding place save for one ghost who was staring at my face hungrily when I finally focused on him.

Even on his ghostly form his face was pale, but there was something about it I knew immediately – Ah Kheng! He had my father's long face, but my mother's eyes. Fourth Brother had a very similar face; my siblings and I were known in our village for our distinctive looks.

Breathless, my words tumbled forth. "It's me. I've come for you. I am Lim Jia, our father was Lim Sung. From Red Leaf Village. Don't you recognize me?" It was a stupid question; he had left when I was an infant. Yet I couldn't help myself, in my rush to make the connection.

His hands reached out for my face, and the remains of a spider web drifted across his face, the dew his tears. Then he stepped away, and I peered closely at him – perhaps I was mistaken. He shook his head, and began to walk away towards a copse of trees at the corner of the plantation.

When I did not follow, he stopped, turned to me, and beckoned.

Something in me grew cold. I didn't want to go.

He stood in the corner of the field, and gazed down at the root of a sugarcane tree. Tears ran down his face, and he gestured to it.

I blinked, then bent down to the plant. It didn't look anything out of the ordinary.

He gestured again, even more insistently, and emitted a grunting sound. It should not have felt like a shriek, but it did, and I covered my ears and crouched down. When I opened my eyes, I noticed a rock at the bottom of the sugarcane.

They burned the bodies and scattered the ashes across the field.

I had heard that two towns ago! Why was I thinking of it now? But trembling, I reached down for the stone, and dug around the corners to pull it up.

The fragment of a skull, black as charcoal, smudged grey by the earth.

The singing of blood, the certainty of tears, the clenching of the heart – these are ways the mind expresses its grasp on truth when logical explanation will do no accounting for itself. This is how I knew I had found my brother.

I curled up around it, pressing it to my chest. "First Brother, how can I take this home to our family?" I wept. "You are scattered across the fields and your ashes have been pounded into the dirt. Even Mother wouldn't be able to recognize you."

I scrubbed my eyes with my sleeve, and then saw an ant on the edge of my robe. We are like ants, and can be crushed any minute like one, I recalled. Several of the petitions wrote on the same theme.

"Friend in the soil," I murmured to it, "all my countrymen are just like you in this land. Please, let me recite a sutra for you, that you all may be reborn in a better life."

When the words tumbled from my mouth, I meant every syllable. The ant waved its antennae at me, and when I was finished, it seemed satisfied at my offering, and began to walk again. I set my robe against a leaf, and let it walk off.

I looked up at my brother, his face sallow with the suffering he had borne before dying. I felt like I had to say something, so I babbled about Mother keeping faith that he was still alive, and the women who had married our Second and Third Brothers. I told him about Father's ghost still keeping watch over the family, and about growing up in the temple. He squatted down to listen to me.

A prickling at my feet made me glance down, and I found a line of ants, each with a black speck of dust in their pincers. I blinked, then looked at Kheng, who was starting to smile. His form sharpened around the edges, and as the ants dropped their burdens at my feet, he seemed to become more solid, although I knew he wasn't.

His ashes. I cried again in relief and gratitude, and mumbled all the prayers of thanksgiving I could think of, for the ants, for the earth, for the spirits and living men in the field who had helped me. I reached into a pocket for a handkerchief and carefully swept Kheng's ashes into it, then tied it up.

I made my way out of the sugarcane field, and stood on the fence to look around, making sure there wasn't another group waiting to ambush me before I headed back. The walk back took a while, but I happily babbled at Kheng's ghost, walking next to me. Labourers who saw me stopped to look at me curiously, because I must have appeared completely mad, talking to empty air. My clothes were muddy, my face a mess, and my queue probably looked as terrible as the rest of me. I didn't care. In my arms I cradled the cloth with my brother's ashes. For the first time since arriving on this island of complete misery, I had something to be happy about.

When I stumbled into the small dry-goods shop where the commissioners were conducting their inquiry, Master Chen was just finishing with a group of men. Their eyes were dull when I looked in, but one of them turned to face me, and began to stare.

As they filed out to let the next group in, the coolie stopped to talk to me just outside the door. "You look like one of the men who worked here."

"Lim Kheng?" I whispered.

He nodded.

I closed my eyes, trying not to cry. Again. "Did you see him die?"

He hesitated. "Yes."

"How?"

He didn't want to answer.

"How," I hissed.

He swallowed. "He was a foreman. He beat us. So we killed him." He licked his mouth nervously. "I'm sorry. We didn't want to, but it was already too much. We had already killed all the other overseers, and we thought a countryman would understand, but he beat us all the same." His words fell out in a waterfall rush. "We thought we would just beat him to teach him a lesson, but he was sick and we didn't know. I'm sorry."

I couldn't say anything for a long time. It seemed so impossible that a family member of mine could have been cruel — no one in our family was cruel! But I had seen so many such impossible things here, so I bit my tongue.

The coolie's eyes were very still, waiting for my reaction. He knew the wrong, a wrong among so many other wrongs.

"Thank you for telling me," I told the man. I took a deep breath. "I'm also sorry." Then I turned to enter the room where the commissioners had begun to question the new group of men.

But my brother's ghost stood in front of me, stern and grim. He gestured back at the men who killed him. I blinked. Did he want me to punish them? Did he want me to beat them, blow for each blow he had been dealt? He shook his head, and pressed a hand over his heart. He cupped my cheek with the other one, and looked over my head at his killers, who were also his countrymen, who were also my countrymen.

I turned back and ran after the coolie. He seemed frightened by me, and shrank back.

Instead, I bowed low. "Sir, on behalf of my brother, please accept my humblest apologies for the pain he has caused you."

He was confused.

"In this place, you all are suffering so much. Even in death, you may not be able to go home. I am only a small clerk, but I hope you will give me the opportunity to help you. If you tell me your names and your hometown, I will make sure I send home word to your families. That is the only merciful thing to do, and my brother would have done the same for you, if he had been able."

I kept myself bowed, waiting for the man's answer. He licked his lips uneasily.

Finally, he bowed. "We would be honoured."

Later, the commissioners exclaimed a bit over my condition, and Master Chen was furious that a servant of his had been attacked by Cubans. But the rest of the day, I would feel the bundle of ashes in my sleeve pocket, and see my brother's ghost, now close to me.

The stinging of my face and the aches I felt the rest of the trip were, I thought, worthwhile.

> "There are hundreds of thousands of Chinese labourers in Luasong,
> while there are hundreds of thousands of sorrowful families in China."
> – trans., Denise Kelly, The Cuba Commission Report:
> A Hidden History of the Chinese in Cuba

Master Chen did not raise the incident again and soon, we were on the way back to Havana. We would stop there one more time, visit yet another nearby town, and return to China from after. He had not sent me on any further errands by myself, and, when Macpherson and Huber had suggested I ride out again, given them such a terrible glare it made their faces, usually red from heat, pale. I even got to ride in the carriage with them, rather than on the wagon behind.

At a rest stop, while the other commissioners had gone to take some air before continuing, he leaned forward. "What are your thoughts, Ah Jia?"

I pondered the question, thrown by the guan-hwa. At that moment, I hadn't been thinking about anything in particular. "About what, master?"

"This mission we are on."

22

"Oh." I frowned. It was a question that could easily draw an offensive answer. "I think that it is.... going as well as could be expected."

Commissioner Chen's eyebrow twitched – a small gesture, but indicative of when he felt he was being lied to. "How do you feel about it?"

"It is distressing to see so many of my own countrymen in such states of suffering, with so little recourse to justice."

"It is good that you are so honest, Ah Jia. Perhaps I remember wrongly, but you once mentioned your eldest brother?"

I nodded, pleased he remembered. "Lim Kheng. The last we heard of him... the last we heard of him, he said he was coming to Cuba."

"And have you found any sign of him?"

"I met a man at one of the plantations who said he saw the family resemblance."

"And what are you holding so tightly in your pockets?"

I hadn't realized that my hands, which I had tucked into my sleeves, had been trembling as I gripped onto my brother's ashes. I swallowed. "The man gave me these ashes, and said they were the last of my brother."

Again, the small twitch of his eyebrow. "And you believe him."

I turned my head to look through the window. "There are three zhongguo-ren on the railing, watching this conveyance, your eminence," I remarked. "They sit on the stile by the side of the road beside the building that your honourable colleagues have entered."

Master Chen had a look, then leaned back. His eyebrow, however, did not twitch. "There are no countrymen of ours on the railing, and if there were, that would give credence to the idea that those who are trapped here are lazy and should be at work."

I kept silent a moment. "One of them has half his head ripped open by blows, and the other two have twisted arms and necks. They are all hungry, but no one will feed them in this land, because those who know our traditions cannot, and those who don't will never feel their vengeance. Their spirits are disintegrating, and will never know justice."

He contemplated what I told him. "I had rather thought your secret a bit more mundane, Ah Jia," he said at last.

I managed a small smile at him. "I entered your service under no false pretenses, your honour. You requested a servant and a clerk, and I have served you in both capacities."

"You have done it well. You will make fine sons, Lim Jia."

Master Chen patted the front of my head, where I had shaved away my hair for a queue. It was one of the rare times he ever touched me.

I might have replied him, but Commissioners Huber and Macpherson returned then from their cigar, and we continued our way to Havana.

Like every night, I copied the petitions and deposition transcriptions. My wrist began to ache with every stroke of my brush, and eventually I set it down to consider the stacks before me. I heard the commissioners at work in the next room, their guan-hwa soft beneath the wind that signaled a storm.

My brother's ashes were a small bundle, taking up a fraction of my table. If I had had lost all four brothers, the pile would be higher, wider. If I had lost my cousin brothers, the ashes would spill over and fall to the floor. If even a tenth of my village had been lost, the ashes would cover the floor. The windows clapped open, and I was lost on a sea of ashes and brittle white bones. The flecks blew on the wind, bone shards cutting my skin. Howling in the distance were the cries of men who would never see their homes again, unclaimed by family and country.

Thunder jolted me awake, and I hurriedly rose to close the windows. Some rain had got in, and the wind had blown my work all over the place. Commissioner Huber came in to check on me, and found me picking up papers, ink stains on my hands and face.

"What's wrong? What's the matter? What happened?" he kept asking, his bad Gongtung-hwa grating on my ears.

Nothing. Everything. All the papers in my hands, and all the words that could have been written, all the names that would never be anymore. No one would ever be able to bring home this sea of ashes, much less lay to rest all their souls. Yet, to never try seemed worst of all.

> "We beg your honor to show pity on our ant-like lives.
> Save us and right this injustice!"
> - trans. Lisa Yun, The Coolie Speaks

After we had returned to the Tsung-li Yamen, Commissioner Chen released me from my service, and rewarded me generously. I paid him my final obeisance and took my leave, riding home on just a horse for a swifter journey. It was not like returning with a new rank, but it was no less glorious a return, because my brother's ghost finally touched the soil of our homeland.

When I reached my village, my family welcomed me home with a great hubbub. I presented to them Kheng's ashes, now in a proper urn, and instated them into the family shrine. We agreed on a date for the funeral, and I left for the temple.

The temple was quiet, and most of the monks had gone to sleep by the time I arrived. Master Wong, however, I found sitting in the hall, contemplating the face of the Goddess of Mercy. We exchanged news, our whispers bouncing off the walls gently; he told me of what had happened in my absence, and I told him of my service to Commissioner Chen.

Then, he asked me the question I itched to answer. "So, does your sight work in the lands abroad?"

I threw myself at his feet, weeping, and told him of the ghosts I saw, the thousands upon thousands fading in the wind, souls trapped in sugarcane trees and sweet grains transported across the world. I tallied them against the souls of the living, trapped by the laws of men which enmesh them further, and the helplessness of the Emperor's reach. I doubted I could have brought my brother home alive, and the spirits I had to leave behind weighed heavy on my conscience.

"Teach me," I begged. "Teach me how to bring them home."

Art by Anna D'Amico

THE BREAD-THING IN THE BASKET
K.T. KATZMANN

1750
Poland

There would be screaming and terror later, wide eyes and dark smiles, but first, it started with the bagels.

The street corner where it began wasn't optimal for bagel selling, but that was why Yussel was there. A block north lurked a boy in the same business, one twice Yussel's size. Economic struggles there had already cost Yussel a tooth. One block south lay the burnt synagogue, not exactly a friendly place for Jews. East and west lay gentile bakeries who responded to competition with rocks. It wasn't so bad, all in all; his friend's cousin had been knifed over a discussion of the bagel-selling rights outside the University of Krakow.

With a pole across his arms to hang bagels on and a basket of extras at his feet, Yussel resigned himself to his usual spot on the cobblestones amongst the ancient stone houses. He also resigned himself to the policeman, who showed up promptly at noon.

Officer Kozlow was much like a bagel himself. He had a hard crust, a round body, and an emptiness inside him. Kozlow had been run out of university for something. Yussel had repeatedly asked his parents why, but they'd only swore to explain when Yussel was older. That seemed less likely now, considering the stern border policy in both Poland and Heaven.

"Yussel!" Kozlow stopped in front of Yussel's basket, an anticipatory gleam in his sunken eyes. "How is the business today?" He tapped Yussel's pole with his club just hard enough to make Yussel stumble. "You look like you have quite a cross to bear there." Leaning in, Kozlow gave a smile that a stranger might've thought was friendly. "Careful. I hear that really riles your people up."

"I wouldn't know," Yussel said, softly and without heart. Trial and error had taught him which responses made Kozlow merciful, or as least as close to it as he ever got.

With a nod, Kozlow inclined his club towards the basket at his feet. "I see that you're selling bagels today, Yussel."

Yussel could hear the policeman's words before they were spoken, and had once earned himself a beating by mouthing along with them. Like morning prayers at grandfather's old temple, the repetition was constant, the order fixed, the ending always inevitable.

"Yes, Officer."

"Do you have a permit?" As Kozlow spoke, he swished his club over

Yussel's head, knocking the bagels back and forth along the pole like soft abacus beads.

Yussel's eyes jumped from one passerby to another. Strangers stared and people who knew him averted their eyes. He managed to spot the guilty blue eyes of Kazia, the vegetable merchant's daughter. She had a cross around her neck and a dress that swelled more with each season; she'd never need fear Kozlow's club. Still, she was the only one that, day after day, always watched but never laughed.

If he held back his line, Yussel wondered, could the play go on? As Kozlow's eye twitched in the ensuing silence, Yussel sighed as the fear in him boiled over.

"No, sir."

"I'm surprised. To my mind, an educated boy like you should know that is, frankly, unlawful."

"Yes, sir." Permits were expensive; Yussel doubted that half the city's street vendors had one. He grit his teeth, knowing what was coming.

"Why, I'd think your old kook of a grandfather would have something in his books about following laws."

A nod was all Yussel could manage. He held his hot, trembling heart very tightly inside his chest, the lid ratting as it barely contained the contents.

Finally, all the usual niceties having been followed, Kozlow raised his hand. "The basket."

If there was a beating bought from the policeman, it would usually be paid for here. Yussel couldn't help himself. Like one of the magicians from Grandfather's books, Yussel sculpted words together and hoped to will reality into something different. "That's twenty-five bagels, sir. Could I keep twelve?"

Kozlow's smile widened. "Lawbreaking needs a swift penalty. Thus, societies continue. Why, Aristotle said–"

"Could I come to the station later for the basket?"

Shortly afterwards, Yussel steadied himself, pushing off the floor with one hand and wiping his mouth as Kozlow rubbed his club clean on Yussel's shoulder.

"You know," the policeman said with raised eyebrows, picking up the basket, "just to be a Good Samaritan, I have a suggestion. You could leave. I hear the Tsar knows what to do with Jews."

As Kazia ran over and dabbled Yussel's face with the hem of her dress, Yussel's eyes tracked his basket until it vanished down the street.

***

"I wish all those Polish pigs would choke."

In the sweltering heat of the kitchen, Yussel's grandfather sighed, his thin and boney fingers sliding a worn old bookmark into his book. "Of course," he agreed amiably. "That would somewhat cut into our business, though."

"Yes, Grandpa." Yussel glanced into the coals of the magnificent stone oven that took up a whole wall. Fire was much more interesting than Grandfather's reproaches.

"Oh!" Snapping his fingers, Yussel's grandfather continued. "What about Kazia? The nice *shiksa* who always gives you an extra carrot? She should choke as well?"

"Okay. I get it, Grandpa." Yussel stood up and turned away from his grandfather completely, staring into the fire. He could spend hours there, but his grandfather never joined him. He'd lost the taste for fire.

"And that nice–"

"I get it!" Yussel looked at his feet. "I just wish that rotten cop would choke on our bagels."

His grandfather nodded. "That, I have less specific reservations against." He sighed. "These are not the days of good King Sobieski, indeed. They will never forgive us for the coming of the Cossacks."

"We didn't bring the Cossacks!"

"Really?" The old man waved dismissively. "*Nu*, this should matter to them? I would hope so. Some people need a scapegoat, Yussel."

The words hung in the air as a stooping giant shambled into the room. Esau was the largest man in town, but he must have traded for that height with all of his words. The baked and ruddy skin of his mute face rarely showed emotion or even sweat; he was the only baker in town who tended the oven fully-clothed. One day long ago, Yussel's life had consisted of his mother and father, his grandfather's synagogue, and the old rabbi himself. A week later, flames had taken everything but Yussel and the old man; Esau had arrived shortly afterwards.

As Esau fed a long tray of twisted dough into the oven, his gigantic hands wrapped around the six-foot long handle of the baking pan, boyish thoughts ran through the thickets of Yussel's mind.

"I should bring Esau with me. I bet if I asked, he'd knock that policeman's teeth out."

The pole clattered out of Esau's hand, as he turned towards Yussel and his grandfather, his fingers clenching. Before Yussel could respond, his grandfather leapt to his feet and exploded with wrath.

"You will not suggest violence to my Esau!"

If the sky had switched places with the ground, it would be less strange to Yussel than the angry bellow of his grandfather.

"No," the old rabbi muttered, wiping the sheen of sweat on his forehead away with his scarecrow arms. "No, Yussel. That is too great a risk. Esau is a peaceful man. He stays here, to work and guard the bakery. I, however, might be willing to help you find a solution for your legal issues."

Laughter in the face of the ridiculous is the oldest Jewish cure for melancholy, and Yussel found plenty of it while picturing his grandfather lecturing Kozlow. Surprisingly, the old man didn't crack a smile, but only waited patiently for his grandson's attention.

"You're serious, Grandpa. You against Kozlow?"

"Absolutely. I know a recipe."

"Grandfather, I doubt another bagel recipe–"

"Hush!"

Yussel flinched. There was something in the old man's voice, like an old tree straightening before it crashed down on someone.

"Hush, boy. Hush, and listen for once. I know a recipe. It was taught to me by a holy man of Prague, under circumstances you'd never believe. It's a little bit on the miraculous side, but it should work. If you're willing, that is."

Yussel spent long moments staring into the old man's eyes while Esau watched mutely on. Only the crackling of the stove would tell a witness to the scene that he was looking at real life instead of a detailed painting. The silence finally broke when the old rabbi tiredly muttered, "You don't believe me."

"I do."

The grandfather blinked.

"I do," Yussel continued, "and that's why I'm angry. You were a great rabbi, Grandpa. I'd believe you can heal the sick and fight werewolves like the *Bal Shem Tov* himself if you said so."

The old man wisely waited for the other shoe to drop.

"So, why'd you wait until now to say something?"

Yussel's grandfather sighed and fell into a chair.

"Maybe our finances are finally bad enough. Perhaps, in my foolishness, I had hoped that God would send us a miracle before I resorted to mysticism." With Esau's gaze upon him the rabbi gave out a long, struggling breath. "Walking backwards so much also does a number on my back. Or," he said in a low, embarrassed voice, "it just might be that a man can only watch his grandson be beaten so many times. But, yes. There is a way to fight this."

"Is there a risk?"

The old man snorted. "Is having a baby a risk? A little at the beginning, and more so as it grows. Yes, it's a risk, and we should use my solution for as short a time as possible. Otherwise, the whole town will be in danger."

He waited until Yussel nodded to gesture at Esau. The mute laborer had been staring at the former rabbi the entire time, nearly allowing the bagels to burn.

"Esau," the old man said gently, "my grandson and I will not be eating for three days."

"What?"

"Shut up, *boychik*. You want power, you need sacrifice." Ignoring the crestfallen youth, the rabbi continued. "This is how a Jew fights, my grandson. We suffer, we adapt, and we think of a way. A cautious head is better than a quick sword. Esau! You may cease the cooking of our food for three days and focus solely on the business."

The old man and Esau stared into each other's eyes long enough for a silent conversation to pass between them before the mute nodded.

In all the talk of revenge, rebellion, and mysticism, Yussel kept the traditional priorities of a teenager well in sight. "Three days without food?"

The old man struck his cane against the ground with a fury not seen since Moses' staff had shattered stone. "This is the recipe! If you want my help, I will not be argued with, and you will do all that I say!" He gave in to a flurry of coughing, expelling some of his fight with the wetness inside him.

"Of course, I could drop the whole matter. Hell, maybe I'm just a crazy old *meshuggeneh*." For just a moment, the spark in his eyes dimmed before flaring up. "Or you could listen for once, Yussel."

Yussel looked to Esau, who responded with a nod.

"All right." Yussel shrugged, throwing his hands up. "I'll get beat up for three days without food. How could things get any worse?"

"A body," his grandfather said, staring into the fire. "One morning, a body could show up on the lawn, drained of blood. Of course, every good Christian knows that we bake blood into our Matzah, so their path becomes clear. 'The Jews are coming for our children,' someone will declare." He coughed. "'Light the torches.'"

The only sound in the bakery was crackling of the oven.

"Alternately, we might run out of poppy seeds, but that's too horrible to contemplate."

Yussel breathed out, and his grandfather was already smiling before he had even spoken.

"Three days, Grandpa?"

"Three days of fasting while we bake the most delicious bagels in town, yes."

"And then?"

"Then we cook up a dish that Officer Kozlow will never forget."

***

The next day, Kozlow felt a wet, sticky eruption of disquiet inside him that normally only the threat of Cossacks could cause. The natural order had been upset, and he felt a cold shiver run up his spine, like a witch was at his home counting spoons.

As he approached that day, the boy was smiling.

Kozlow was familiar with smiles like that. The conversations they heralded usually began with a greeting and ended with a knife fight. Club out, Kozlow kept an extra foot or two distant from the boy than usually, hoping he wouldn't notice.

Yussel noticed, and the unnerving smile grew. "Good morning, Officer!"

A wary Kozlow tried to recite the lines that gave him so much joy every morning. "Good morning, Yussel. I see you're, uh, selling bagels today."

"Yes, sir," Yussel said with pride. "Without a permit, sir!"

A giggle floated to Kozlow's ears, and it rang like the trumpets of Jericho against his resolve. Obstinacy and aggression could be met by the law and the club, but humor left a sting that authority rarely forgot. The tried and true script of extortion broke down in Kozlow's mind. Still, even without the niceties, Kozlow was nothing if not pragmatic. "Bagels, boy."

"All yours, sir." Yussel gestured to towards the basket.

Tentatively, Kozlow poked his wooden truncheon under the blanket of the bagel basket, using the club to reveal the breaded bounty inside.

"I almost thought..." Kozlow shook his head. Any of his fears, if spoken, would only serve to make him sound ridiculous, something his soul lived in

31

terror of. He left the street with a film of disquiet clinging to him. Still, there was other evil afoot in his city than just this one Jew, so he went to find himself other crusades.

Kozlow lost only fifteen minutes of sleep over Yussel that night. As his eyes searched the ceiling, he berated himself for his useless fears.

The next day, Yussel look more haggard yet was still in excellent spirits. "Good day, Officer Kozlow!"

Hands behind his back, head held high in the air, Kozlow approached Yussel while trying to affect an easy and casual air. He attracted the stares of half the market, several of whom thought he had become suddenly separated from some parade.

"Expect," Kozlow said with solemnity, "no difference in treatment for being affable. Inside, you are yet a ravenous wolf." Tentatively, he smiled. "The Bible says that."

The twelve-year merely shrugged in reply. "Do as you see fit, Officer."

"I always do," Kozlow said, whipping his club into the air to knock a bagel into the street. It landed face down in a puddle, a few poppy seeds floating away while the rest resolved to stick together and see things through.

In the hush of the watching crowd, Kozlow cocked his head and wooden stick at the puddle. "Eat it, Yussel. No need to waste it."

Yussel swallowed, his throat parched and ravenous. "I'm fasting, Officer. I apologize—"

"Eat it." The club was raised.

Every passer-by along the street stopped in morbid wonder.

Yussel stared at the bagel with more fear than he regarded Kozlow's club. Drawing his breath, his thoughts flashed to his people's history. Yussel was the grandson of a rabbi, a profession that, if stories could be trusted, had won arguments about Jewish law against the very Lord himself. The demands of Officer Kozlow were just like another interesting page of Talmudic rules to interpret.

Carefully, Yussel held his shoulder pole with one hand while reaching the other to the despoiled bagel. He held it up for the crowd like a wandering conjurer. "I cannot break my fast, Officer Kozlow, but I think I can make you happy."

He licked it, every surface, inside and out, before carefully placing it back on the ground.

He was still smiling. Within a stone's throw of crying, yes, but still smiling. "Will you hit me now?"

"You'd like that, wouldn't you," Kozlow said before grabbing the basket and walking away, disturbed and unsure. The rest of his shift passed in a blur, except for the extra minutes he spent screaming invectives upon the Gypsy camp outside town. There was a certain amount of Kozlow he had to give, after all, and the fact that Yussel took less that day meant that someone else must make up the quota.

The day after found Kozlow at police headquarters, stewing in his own angry juices. For several hours, he actually managed to convince himself (though not his fellow officers) that he was actually accomplishing something, but such self-delusion can only sustain a man for so long. While intently staring into the wooden knothole of a mess hall table, fingers clutching his own hair, the florid gesturing of a nearby policeman caught his eye. The man was animatedly regaling his fellow men with a story that was causing great shows of glee.

Kozlow knew deep in his bones that they were discussing none other than himself and the Jewish boy. This could not be allowed.

On the fourth day, Kozlow marched to Yussel's corner as soon as his cudgel was strapped on. Taking care that his uniform was immaculate, Kozlow stopped along the way several times to offer guidance to his constituents.

"Authority cannot allow itself to be mocked," he reminded a bewildered man on crutches.

"After all," he told a hurrying turnip vendor, "even compliance can be disrespectful if given wrongly."

By the time he found Yussel, Kozlow had worked himself into a state of physical agitation usually reserved for biblical prophets on the verge of spouting prophecy. Catching sight of the boy, he instantly unsheathed his club and pointed it at Yussel's thin, pale, yet excited face. With the solemnity of the Tsar, he intoned the word, "You."

Everyone on the two surrounding blocks suddenly pretended to be busy.

Yussel was young, but he had walked the streets long enough to smell the change in the wind. "Yes, sir," he said as he straightened himself to attention, his smile disappearing.

Drawing himself closer with small steps, Kozlow's mind felt all of its prepared speeches trickled away. As he stared at the boy, the very silence seemed to be insubordinate, and he desperately flung words into the terrifying quiet of the street. "You seem better today," he said, speaking as if it were a stern rebuke.

Nodding respectfully, Yussel said with caution and care, "I had my first meal in three days today. Very little sleep last night, but at least one of my bagels is inside me. Sir."

The *hmmph* that slid out of Kozlow conveyed his general skepticism at everything, even the very concept of a blue sky. "And your shoes?" He gestured towards Yussel's clay-caked feet with the cudgel. "What's with your shoes?"

Yussel shrugged, his bagel pole nearly tipping off his tired shoulders. "I was at the river last night."

"A shame you returned." Kozlow licked his lips, disconcerted. The traditional speech and jokes had left him, but a dramatic gesture always worked wonders in the policeman's experience. "The bagels," he said, thumping the blanket-covered basket with his club. "They're mine."

At Kozlow's words, Yussel's heart nearly stopped from the effort of containing a smile. "Absolutely," he replied.

Snapping his fingers twice, Kozlow pointed at the pole across Yussel's shoulders. "That, as well."

Not quite as surprised as he thought he would've been, Yussel handed over his pole to the sound of the crowd's whispers.

Kozlow accepted the burden with a grunt before walking off. Having only walked a few feet away, he spun on his heels, offering Yussel a snarl as the bagels on his shoulder pole bounced around. "I'm onto you, boy."

Yussel blinked. "Of course, sir."

"I know," Kozlow said, jabbing a finger through the air, "that there is a mountain range with a single gate as an opening, and behind it lays all the tribes of Jews that Alexander the Great imprisoned there, along with the giants and monsters. All of you are just waiting for a little fox to open that gate, and your people will swarm out and slaughter anyone that doesn't speak Hebrew." Kozlow laughed, high and rapidly. "I'm an educated man. I've read Sir Mandeville, and he was onto you. You can't fool me."

Yussel stared back and said nothing, and they looked at each other in silence until a man, having seen none of the confrontation, approached Kozlow and tried to buy a bagel off of him.

The words Kozlow uttered were not fit for Yussel's ears. Toting his bagel-bearing pole on his shoulder while slumping to the side under the weight of the basket, grim-faced and determined, Kozlow walked off, presenting the most ridiculous sight the Polish peasantry had seen in generations. Still, no one laughed until he was well out of earshot. Yussel followed him, expectantly and from a distance, smiling the whole way.

***

The pole entered through the door of the police station first, drawing stares until it became clear that there was a Kozlow behind it. The desk sergeant eyed the shoulder-mounted display of lean bread products that dangled across Kozlow's shoulders, regarding them with an unnerved curiosity. "Is it Lent already?"

Kozlow, grinning for the first time in days, loudly announced to the handful of officers in the room, "I have confiscated the bread of a criminal!"

No one clapped, and this dismayed Kozlow.

The desk sergeant squinted. "A criminal?"

"Well, a Jew," Kozlow admitted, being a man convinced since childhood of the importance of honesty in all things. "Still, a criminal down to his bones." He turned around to survey the room, wondering why there was not more joy on the faces of his companions. Indeed, the desk sergeant was quite irate, having ducked his head to dodge Kozlow's spinning bagel pole twice already.

Still, Kozlow was no rookie. He knew how things work in the station house. "Gentlemen," he intoned cheerfully.

The desk sergeant ducked as Kozlow spun around again.

"Who wants bagels?"

This time, the men smiled. As they pulled the bagels off of Kozlow's pole, one of them asked him jokingly about the price of his bagels. The stare the policeman earned in return sent him walking away.

All throughout the food and festivity, Kozlow saw Yussel through the window, standing across the street from the station. *Good*, he thought. *Let the boy see what law and order is like.* Leaning the significantly lighter bagel pole against the wall, Kozlow settled into one of the office desks with his basket, ready to taste himself the rewards of justice.

He pulled the blanket off the basket and nearly fainted. Inside was a baby.

Not a baby made of flesh, blood, and bones, mind you. No, this baby, curled up in a fetal position and taking up the entirety of the basket, had a boiled crust and poppy seeds. Carefully, Kozlow's trembling hands lifted it out of the basket. It was easily the size of a toddler at least, its soft arms hanging at its side. The bagel-thing lacked a face, and Kozlow thanked the Lord for that mercy. Still there was something on the head. Across the forehead, someone had painstakingly cut out a word or phrase in Hebrew. Haltingly, Kozlow raised a finger towards the mysterious writing, but the head slumped away as his touch grew closer. The bread-thing made a soft thud as Kozlow dropped it onto the desk. The moment stretched on for him, the world seemingly silent as he stared at the incomprehensible manikin spread across the table.

Then he heard the laughter.

Kozlow's head jerked up, making eye contact with Yussel through the window. Across the street, the boy was in hysterics.

Picking up his club, Kozlow stormed out of the building. "You! You think this is funny, don't you?"

"Sir," Yussel said as he pulled himself to his feet, wiping the dirt off of his clothing. He bore the solemnity only possible where staring down a policeman's club. "In all seriousness, I will bake you another one if you wish, gladly." His smile reappeared. "I will bake as many of them as you want."

Eyes narrowed, Kozlow whispered, "You're testing me. Stay right there, Jew, or I'll beat the bones out of you." He disappeared into the station only to rush back out, nearly being hit by a horse and carriage in the process. In one raised hand, he held a chunk of poppy-coated baby. "I'll eat your damn bread! Just watch me."

Yussel did, barely containing his tears of joy.

Kozlow stuffed the bread into his mouth, chewing as if upon the neck of the Jewish nation. As he continued, he started to become aware of the crowd that had gathered. This was nothing new, but normally they seemed friendlier to him, he thought. Uncomfortable ideas swirled in his head as he finally swallowed.

"Don't . . . loiter." Kozlow glancing behind him, Kozlow noticed some of his spectators were fellow policeman. After all these years, they were finally whispering about Kozlow loud enough for him to take notice. "Go about your business, boy."

"You took my whole business, sir."

Making sure to leave an extra bruise on the now-prone boy, Kozlow nodded and walked back towards the station. The sergeant was waiting at the doorway, offering a deceptively-friendly smile as he snaked his arm around Kozlow's shoulder.

"I believe it's time we had a talk, Kozlow. A talk about professionalism, propriety, and the use of the club."

Kozlow nodded. "I support all of those things."

"As do I," the sergeant said with a sigh, "As do I. Now, the good folk of this town expect us to bear clubs against the unrighteous. Why, it's one of the greatest tools of the policeman's trade."

"Of course, sir. In fact—"

"Kozlow." The sergeant's voice was barely above a whisper. "The good folk of this town, however, do not expect to have to watch."

Kozlow nodded, the knuckles of his fist a bloodless white.

***

Outside, Yussel sat down against a cobblestone wall, staring with an expectant focus into the station window. His gaze never wavered until a carrot was lowered into it.

"Thank you," he said, shining the first friendly smile he'd used all day. Yussel scooted over as Kazia sat down next to him. He broke the carrot in half, but she shook her head.

"You look like you need it more," she said with a grin that filled Yussel's empty stomach with butterflies. "What are you doing here?"

He aimed the stub of the rapidly disappearing carrot across the street. "Officer Kozlow."

"He's crazy."

Yussel snorted. "Because he hate Jews? How could he be considered sane in Poland if he was otherwise?"

She looked away, fiddling with the hem of her dress. "My father says Kozlow's mind is like a clock running down. Intricate and clicky."

He laughed, and she smiled back. Kazia was three years older than Yussel, but in that moment, he'd have sworn she was easily ten or more years ahead, a mature and refined lady.

A bluster rose within Yussel. "Just watch. I bet we're going to see our clockwork watchmen chime rather loudly by the end of the day."

***

Leaving the out-of-breath sergeant at his desk, Kozlow's eyes didn't lift from the floor until he slumped into the desk chair, trying not to think without caring why. Idly, he reached to tear another piece off of the bread child. He could not think of it as a man, the way a doll might be of an adult. It was, to his mind, definitely a child.

It was also gone.

Ridiculously, he slid his hand across the desk, as if the gigantic foodstuff could have been moved to one of the corners. Slowly and reluctantly, Kozlow turned his head to the inescapable truth. The bread-thing was gone.

By nature, Kozlow was a suspicious individual. The existence of Jews and Gypsies gave an easy and constant source of release for his overflowing cauldron of paranoia. In a pinch, he gladly turned his suspicion to novel targets.

"Someone," he said as he shakily rose to his feet, "some so-called officer of the law has stolen my bread!"

Glances were cast his way, but the half-dozen other policemen went about their business, only stopping to make eye contact with each other. Kozlow, staggered at the inattention, shouted towards the sergeant, now facing away from Kozlow with his head in his hands.

"There is confiscated food somewhere in this precinct, Sir, and I intend to find it!"

The sergeant turned around with a raised eyebrow. "I am overjoyed to inform you of the existence of many other Jewish street vendors from which food could be easily attained. I suggest you do so. Quietly."

"But–"

"Now."

Seconds later, Kozlow walked through the station hallway with slumped shoulders, measuring the unfairness of life against the goodness of the Lord.

A waist-high shadow rushed across his vision.

By this point in his day, Kozlow's mind, however running down it may have been, still tried to defend him from the impossible. What he thought he saw was too bizarre to contemplate, so he skipped over the "why" part and skipped right to the "where."

"You there, in the armory! Surrender immediately!"

His face red, teeth gritted, Kozlow still stepped slowly and carefully into the room. Rows of shields, swords, and muskets lined the walls, paid for by nobles and expected to defend nobles. More weapons and armor covered the many tables that wrapped around the edges room, an arms collection large enough by itself to put down a peasant revolt. The last officer who tripped and caused a mess in this room was drummed out officially. Kozlow shivered as he remembered the unofficial part that followed. "Show yourself," he said as he barred the door behind him. "There's no way out."

Kozlow jumped as something jingled under a table.

It's a child, he thought as plucked a lantern of the wall and lit it. *A child, or some stunted, drunken dwarf.* "You can't hide," he bellowed while lowering himself to his knees. A bag of musket balls rattled from the far corner of the room, bringing a smile to Kozlow's face. This arrest would show the sergeant. This was something he could handle.

Then the bread-thing stepped out of the shadows, and it took Kozlow stunned seconds to realize he was whimpering.

When he was young, Kozlow's grandmother had told him stories before bed. No matter how many ugly witches, child-eating ogres, or crafty Jews he heard about, the scariest creature was Kolobok, the dough boy. Sure, she had described him as a hero, but the idea of a severed head of living bread rolling around always terrified Kozlow. It was the face; he would lie awake at nights, wondering what lips made of dough looked like when they moved.

The nightmares of a hundred childhood nights rushed to the front of Kozlow's mind as the bread-thing approached. The faceless thing had human form, but no bones; it moved as if controlled by a puppeteer who'd heard of people walking but had never seen it, flowing and bending inhumanly. The face was still blank but now lit up, the suggestion of smoldering coals simmering inside the Hebrew letters. It was staring at him, he knew absolutely from the ice water running down his spine.

It stepped further into the lamplight, and his eyes were drawn to a discoloration. There was a wound in it. Something had pierced its side.

Kozlow covered his mouth and very dearly wished to throw up.

The bread-thing took a single step towards him and Kozlow kicked it across the room. His shaking fingers nearly dropped the lamp as he rushed to the bar of the door. He heard rustlings and jangling behind him, but any imagination he might've used was overridden by panic as he strained to lift the bar with a single hand. His sweaty fingers danced along the irregular, rusted iron, feeling it slip upwards time and time again only to falls back down. A fear that smothered all reason grabbed hold of him as he put the lantern down and grabbed the bar with both hands. A second more and he'd be free.

The light vanished.

He could've tried to leave; the bar was right there. Still Kozlow was paralyzed. If he tried to concentrate on anything more than keeping his heart beating, it just might give out. A stronger man could have escaped, would have fought through the fear and lifted the bar. Kozlow had always lived his life by bearing (and misusing, some other officers would surely say) a badge and a club. He had never faced a threat that couldn't be avoided with the judicious use of either of those items. Now Kozlow faced danger as a man rather than a policeman, and his knees gave out as he feel to the floor as a sobbing wreck.

It was bread, Kozlow tried to reassure himself. If he was hunted by an inhuman thing, surely it was made of the most yielding material known to man. If it came towards him, even stealthily, all that could result was . . .

The carriage of Kozlow's thoughts overturned on a road slick with horror.

For the life of him, Kozlow could not contemplate a confrontation with the creature. Any attempt to downplay things in his mind would be halted by the awful immensity of the gap between his existence and the bread-thing's. A man trying to kill him would be understandable, a being of similar desires, who ate, loved, and belched like any other human. The creature could not approach the mental life of a man; regardless of its almost laughable components, the staggering immensity of the gulf between the bread-thing's mind and his made bile rise up in his throat. A simpler man would have been better equipped for battle, but hours of debating seemingly inconsequential subjects at university had left Kozlow specifically vulnerable to the crushing dread of the unknown.

Ask a man to fight a living pillow and he will laugh with abandon. Tell the same man that any pillow could be alive, willing to wrap around his unconscious face, and he will never sleep again.

After a few seconds had passed, Kozlow realized that he was not dead. True, there was no reason to yet suspect mortal danger, but he was not applying his much vaunted (by him, primarily) reason and education. With a moment's breather, Kozlow finally tried to think his way out of the situation. He'd fallen away from the door; he didn't know which way lay freedom and safety. Gingerly, he reached out a hand, hoping to touch a table leg or a wall, anything that he could use to reorient himself. Officer Kozlow reached out, only to make contact with a pliable mass of warm dough that shifted its seed-covered body under his touch.

The thing's forehead letters flared, illuminating the room with four Hebrew bonfires held inside a container of bread that did not burn, and it was probably that moment when Officer Kozlow finally went mad.

The next thing he remembered was standing in the hallway. He would remember it for the rest of his life, for he did not choose to stand, but his legs refused to run. Kozlow felt a fire burning in his stomach as his limbs moved of their own volition, turning him back towards the armory. The going was slow; he fought for every inch, but a man is only given so much willpower at birth and Kozlow had used his supply up years ago. As he walked involuntarily back to the bread-thing, a flame of agony in his stomach, his ears, still his own, detected the sound of crinkling paper.

Wadding paper, he thought. *Dear God, the thing knows how to use wadding paper and gunpowder.*

Before he stiffly reentered the room, ineffectively trying to scream the entire time, his mind had created dozens of versions of the scene to which he was dragging himself. None of them compared to the actual terror of entering the room, closing the door behind him, and seeing the bread-thing aiming a loaded musket at him.

Neither of them moved for a while.

"How," Kozlow finally panted, his mouth back in his control, "how did you do this to me?"

The bread-thing, still holding the musket, pointed one of its doughy hands at the wound in its side, then pointed to the policeman's stomach.

He swallowed, but something was preventing him from throwing up.

The bread-thing raised its gun.

"No!" Tears ran down Kozlow's face. "Don't hurt me! Please, don't shoot!"

His breath finally escaped as the gun lowered.

"Thank you," Kozlow said. He could feel his limbs shifting back to his control, and tried to make calming gestures towards the creature. "Good boy. Good bread. Look, why don't—"

It raised the musket again, pointing it across the room at the station's supply of gunpowder.

Kozlow was never sure afterwards if the bread-thing let him run away or it just found his overwhelming terror impossible to force its will upon.

"Fire!" He ran screaming out of the room, causing shrieks and policeman to follow in his wake. "Fire in the powder room! Abandon the station!"

Like a conscientious monster, the bread-thing waited for the retreating sound of shouting to end. It finally decided that no human remained in the station house, then fired.

Outside, Yussel and Kazia clapped their hands as the police station vomited a full police force onto the streets right before a fireworks show that would be talked about for as long as either of them would live.

***

Just before sundown the next day, caked with rubble and made of mostly ash, the bread-thing shambled through the bakery's back door, bringing joy and relief to the old man's face.

"Our little golem has returned to us, Esau!"

It bonelessly shambled into the ancient rabbi's arms, where he cradled it like a real child.

"You did good work, little bread-thing. You hurt no one."

He'd always swear afterwards to himself that the creature in his arms, a mass of undifferentiated dough with one exception, approximated a sigh of relief at his words. He stared at his creature in the firelight, memories flowing back to him, before turning to Esau.

"My old friend, I believe that if anyone here is capable of the task ahead, it should be you."

Wordlessly, with bright, unblinking eyes, Esau nodded. Gently, he took the bread-thing and raised it into the air. It twitched and flapped, only calming down as Esau's gigantic hand began stroking the remains of its face. Suddenly, carefully, Esau's finger flashed out, ripping out the first dimly glowing letter on its forehead. The bread golem instantly fell limp in his hand, nothing more than a pile of burnt dough. Esau stared at it for a long time before turning to the old man.

"You decide, my friend."

Nodding, Esau reverently placed the lifeless body of the small golem inside the bagel stove and closed the grate. He stood there for many minutes, letting the escaping smoke cling to him.

Esau gave the old man one last philosophical look before he returning to his task of twisting the day's dough into rings.

The old man said nothing, his eyes full of flame and doubt. He only smiled again when Yussel returned with an undecorated pole and empty basket. If there was one thing the old man had learned over the years, it was to smile when children are around. They'd pick up on life's troubles later.

"Doing good business, I see!" His smile shrunk. "The new policeman? How is he?"

Yussel shrugged as he plopped down into a chair like a poured liquid, the way only teenagers can. "Not bad. He mentioned that he would check for permits someday, then asked for a bagel."

The old man leaned forward. "And then?"

"I gave him one. And then he shrugged, said, 'Someday,' and walked off."

"Good." Yussel's grandfather slapped the table. "Good. A bagel bribe a day we can deal with. It's not a contract and he may yet ask for more, but God willing, we'll have some good times between the bad. That's all a Jew can hold for sometimes. I heard about Kozlow from the miller."

Yussel sat up straighter than he had ever done in his life. "Oh?"

"Ran away. They're blaming the explosion on his incompetence. Last I heard, he intended to join a religious order near Warsaw." The old man allowed a smile to slowly cook on his face. "A strict one. The monks eat only vegetables." He continued speaking over Yussel's laughter. "I expect him to live a long, fearful time. A man who fears his food coming to life is one who never grapples with a weight problem again."

Yussel's laughter slowed to a stop. "And the . . . child?"

The old man's eyes flickered to Esau. "Dead. Buried in a place where no one curious will even find its clay heart, much less read the inscriptions written therein." As Yussel's eyes widened, the old man raised his hand. "Don't worry, it didn't feel any fear. I had to give it a very simple mind. Bread's no use for golems, Yussel."

"That's a shame."

"That's a good thing." Grandfather leaned forward solemnly, and even Esau paused in his baking to surreptitiously listen. "A golem is created as a protector, not a trickster. Give it too much violence and the poor thing begins a rampage you would not believe. No," the old man said with a cough, his eyes moving back and forth from Yussel to Esau. "No, better to keep them away from violence as long as possible. The bread child has tasted of that well, and it's a good *mitzvah* for the entire city that we destroyed it."

The conversation paused for a while until Yussel's curiosity flared up again.

"What are you reading, Grandpa?"

"This? Oh, nothing. An idle fantasy, nothing more."

Evasiveness has never, in the history of the human species, dissuaded a teenage boy. Perhaps his grandfather knew that and was counting on this very result. In any case, Yussel charged around the table, only to break out in an immediate sweat.

"G-grandpa, t-that's–"

"The Talmudic laws on women converting to Judaism in case of marriage, yes, I'm aware." While he had the advantage, he risk a full coup-de-grace. "So, eaten any good carrots today?"

With Yussel disappearing from the room in a red-faced haze, his grandfather laughed. "Let that dough cook inside his head for a bit. That leaves just the two of us, right, Esau?"

The larger man said nothing. The old rabbi let that sit awhile before deciding that he owed Esau something more.

"Bread is too temporary, you know? Meant to be used up." With effort, he rose from the table, crossing the room carefully to rest his hand on Esau's shoulder. "Not like clay, of course. Clay mixed with ash, now, that's quite a number. You could make a fine golem with that, a brilliant worker, a great protector. A good friend."

Esau, smiling, tipped his cap to the old man, taking care as he slipped it back onto his clay forehead not to wipe out any of the Hebrew letters etched there.

Art by Eric Orchard

THE JINN'S ONLY SON
MOMTAZA MEHRI

1910
Mauritania

The milk of the afternoon is beginning to fade. Air stiff with heat as it clutches at the soft fabric around her shoulders. She watches the sheep make their usual languorous noises, picking at the shrubbery with clamped jaws. Their bleats mark an appreciation, or perhaps a plea to be left out for just a little longer. The smallest is still caught in the whirlwind of infancy, its downy coat rippled onto small bones. It bounds over, teetering over fallen branches and nibbling at a fresher growth. Her hands will find its back, the warm arch of each ear and the humming-bird whirs of a heartbeat. A heartbeat that always surges to the touch.

She decides this already. He is her favourite.

***

"Ever since her son bought her that gold necklace, she thinks she's Sheba."

Her mother's words clinked against the glass. Under the flicker of kerosene lamps, she could see a sadness settle on the aging woman's features. This wasn't jealousy. Her mother did not envy Halimat, the tailor's wife who sold dates and palm milk outside her mud-daubed home. It was the prospect of a living, breathing son who made it big elsewhere without having to sign his own death warrant. Saleh, her only brother, was across the border now, a guard at the palatial home of a Kabyle official. He worked for the kind of man whose own people wanted to see with a cut throat.

"Saleh could buy you the moon but you would never accept a thing..." She couldn't help pointing this out, how her brother would angle his questions at every visit, only to be shot down and told that everything was alright. The flock would feed them; father's irregular tanning work would keep the pots bubbling.

"I don't even know how he is living and you want me to make demands? He lies to me, Zeina. If he wanted to please me, he would not have put himself in harm's way." She rubbed her temples, letting out a sigh into the room's hush.

The eldest and only son was living a thread-bare existence. He worked for a man who spoke to the lame alley cats with more kindness than the guard he trusted with his own life. Saleh spent his days protecting this man only to return home and protect a weakening father from such truths. Zeina would

43

often listen at the door; hear a voice choked with something she knew she hadn't lived to understand yet. A borrowed French that littered his speech like someone else's raided heirlooms. Harsh syllables that landed heavy on the knuckles like her old teacher's thin asa. She had seen one of these Frenchmen once. A russet-haired man in uniform at the market, tying his horse to the gate. His companion, a Serer with the five-pointed star amulet draped on his chest, accompanied him, haggling on his behalf. The Frenchmen had smiled at her, given her a handful of grapes. She still remembered wanting to touch his skin and the papery smell she imagined it would emanate. These strange men had made a mockery of the famed horse-men in all her milk-mother's poems. They had claimed entire cities for their own; at least that's what the worldly uncles said, exhaling into their sweet tea.

"Umma, it's for the best. There is nothing for him here." Zeina kneaded the dough, leaving pockmarks the size of thumbs. Khobz for tomorrow and the day after.

"This is his home. Where else should he be?" Her mother sounded offended at the mere suggestion that their small town, with its humble soil and humbler inhabitants, did not mean the world to her children. "You don't understand. A woman can make home out of ruins but a man needs solid ground under his feet." Another one of her truisms. Her mother's mouth grew thick with them, only plucked when the time was right.

Zeina simply pressed her palms into the dough, teased it into another distraction. What about women like her? Would they ever find a home? A fruit-seller had once scolded her for pushing against his stand. "Watch your step, ahradan girl. Or I'll have your fingers." He'd hissed this, scowling as if this wasn't her land too. It had stung. She knew who she was, but also knew just as well they were those who would never see anything but enslaved bloodlines and the wet clay of her skin. She knew why the older women rubbed turmeric dust into their faces, hoping its yellow glow would wash off a lineage. *Haratin.* People of the gardens, they had named themselves. There was power in that. This small town of theirs held an oasis in its centre, a landscape dotted with freshwater streams and the dip of ravines. It was all theirs. Zeina contented herself with this. She made her own kind of peace.

***

A whisper carried over into the thatched mouth of her window. Zeina's room was low-roofed with a diwan pressed against stone walls that made nights like this torture. She heard the same urgent murmur again. It was Rayan, her wide-eyed, small-palmed friend. She'd never known a time without the compass of her companionship. The sound of padding footsteps grew ever more impatient.

"Wake up, y'allah! I have a little something for you." Her shadow flitted near the wall, casting itself on the peeling rails.

Zeina rose up, in the blue cotton of her mulafa and slipped on sandaled leather. Tapping the arched shutters, she played at annoyance. Truth was, tonight's unforgiving heat had left her tossing and turning to the hum of moths.

Rayan's gap-toothed smirk greeted her as soon as she stepped foot outside. Her face was already ruddy. The dusky maroon wrapped around her neck did little to disguise this flush of excitement. With the slight hand of a magician, Rayan lowered her stick and reached into a basket, plucking out the smooth curve of a plum. Its ripe blush was visible, even under the moon.

"Let's just say, Juwairiya's kitchen is a little barer." Her grin grew wider at the thought of that least favoured aunt with the pinching fingers. This was typical of her. This kohl-lined mirth shining liquid in her eyes to melt the elders and tempt the young. A bad example given flesh. For her, forgiveness always came as quickly as anger did. Zeina simply shook her head in mock disapproval. This was their well-practiced dance. Neither would stray from it.

They walked, linked through the nook of elbows. The tinkle of hushed laughs matched the hiss of their silver anklets. Their usual haunt was a circular clearing atop a hill. It was empty now. Sitting, they crouched low and let the sand graze the bareness of legs underneath them. From here, Zeina could see the stretch of valley ahead of them for what seemed like a lifetime. Chegga was half a day's journey away, maybe more if the camel was older. Further still were the cities she'd only overheard in conversations at the marsa, glowing like hot coals from the mouths of the well-educated and well-heeled. *Oran, Tumbutu, Tanjah.* She remembered tracing their letters as a young child, her father sitting cross-legged as he guided small fingers over the curve of vowels. As if pressing hard enough would transport them both. There, again, was this flare of resentment at this woman-body that meant she should be content only with what was in her reach. The bare stone of four walls, the frayed edges of woven rugs and the familiarity of a life measured in the few children who tottered into adulthood. No-one except Rayan understood this feeling. Both with chests as expansive as the arid spaces they were born into. Somewhere in this was a curse, surely.

Overlooking the pen, they listened to the gentle braying of sheep.

"Here they go again. Never a minute's rest." Rayan rolled her eyes, licking baobab juice off her thumb. She, too, spent her days tending to her father's flock under the sun's glare. Her father who had passed away before the month's blood had even visited her. Since then, even the herding had become her responsibility. Afternoons spent milking and feeding then scraping hide into parchment for the zawiyya to inscribe holy verses onto. The hardest task yet had been becoming a mother's backbone. Zeina thought this meant something, their shared troubles. Fate had aligned their lives and joined them together like beads in a necklace. Or perhaps this was her being selfish, knowing a friendship couldn't hold the weight of only one person's duty without keening over.

The sheep's bleating grew louder, their figures shifting apart. This felt strange. The huddle they now formed, leaning against the makeshift barriers. Even from their sitting place, Zeina could see the dark rings of their eyes against the cloudy wool.

"There's something in there – with them." She tapped Rayan, pointing to the spot.

45

"Yes. A fat-bottomed jackal. Stop worrying yourself and eat while we can."

"I swear by the dust under me, there is something scaring them." Her eyes scanned the flock, the unease quickening their movements. Zeina rose to her feet, grabbing the length of her friend's stick.

"At least wait for me. Ya rabbi." Rayan's unimpressed tone rang behind her.

As they drew closer, they were struck by the sight of a tall figure draped in white. Leaning over the flock, its back was turned. There was something undeniably male, and eerie, about this silhouette.

Zeina felt the grip of a hand. She flinched, turning back. It was Rayan's expression awash with warning. Facing forwards again, she felt her breath catch.

The figure was now a hand-span away. In what had seemed like a second, it was now outside the pen. It was a man. A luminous face shrouded in thick, inky hair brushing the nape of an unusually long neck. His eyes were twin well pits, the pupils sitting vertical like the glare of mountain goats. The gash of his lips was set against alabaster, resembling a slit rather than a mouth. Zeina had never seen this man before, and he was the kind of man you'd remember meeting.

It was then, right then, that his features thawed into a smile. Rayan's grip on Zeina's wrist tightened. They had both seen the unusually sharp tips of teeth. Zeina had heard of some desert tribes filing their teeth into pointed, almost feline canine, but this man did not seem like a weather-beaten traveller. His spotless robes gave this away like the looseness of gossip.

"Salaam to you both. This barren place holds beauty, after all." His voice seemed to come from elsewhere whilst enveloping them at the same time. They could feel it graze their clavicles. Zeina grounded herself, resisting the urge to take a step back.

"This is our barren place. Travellers come and pass. They honour us with their names."

He chuckled, a cavernous laugh that made the animals prick their ears upwards.

"I am no traveller, but you already know that. My name matters not, least of all to a young shepherdess."

"A young shepherdess whose herd you were planning to steal. Even the night doesn't hide dishonour." Zeina began to regret her words almost as soon as they had left her. This was not the time or place for her mother's sayings. She saw the spectre of amusement visit his smooth features, the clench of jaw. Though those eyes were now seeing right through her.

"Stranger or friend. We do not take what isn't ours." Saidou's voice visibly jolted both his friends. There was a full-throated threat loaded into each word. He had intended this. Slipping into view, he cut a lean figure next to Rayan. This boy-turned-man who had earned Zeina's friendship from childhood and Rayan's heart a few summers ago. How long had he been there, watching this scene unfold from afar?

"Ya raajil, every day you take from this earth what isn't yours. I am no thief. If I were, I would be an honest one."

"Who are you?" Saidou's hand fell to his side, clasping the cold iron of the muss he always hid in sirwaal pockets.

"I am but a messenger, from my king to yours." The stranger said this with mock flourish, splaying long fingers upwards.

"We have no king. You've come to the wrong place. Even the Aznag chiefs have nothing now. You must have lost your way."

"I have been here before when you were suckling at your mother's breast and I will be here long after your last days. It is true then. The fair-haired visitors rule over you now."

Saidou visibly tensed. The stranger's knowing tone carried a softness that left you bewildered, uncertain. He moved like sin.

"Not us. We answer only to our elders and hardly travel north. Some have made their way here, but never more than a few."

"Laa, they are too busy for this dust-patch. Cursing the angels with every step. They will not stop until their own blood runs thick through the streets."

"How do you know this?" Zeina felt a chill in her lungs. She did not really want an answer.

"I have seen it. The dogs gnawing at their still flesh. Rags hanging from empty pockets. Stay where you are. That is my advice. The desert will see less death." He spoke of coming death, of an unbearable loss, with the easy air of someone far removed from it all. Of tribesmen who would defeat fire and gunpowder and lay siege to the invaders. It seemed an unlikely tale. Zeina thought of her brother in all of this. Suppose this man knew something they didn't, would Saleh be safe in the midst of carnage? She decided on hating this man.

Rayan spoke at long last. "What do you want? The townspeople are sleeping. Pass through in the morning and—"

"I want only this. A gift for my youngest."

The knowledge that this other-worldly dream of a man had a child brought comfort. There, between the translucence of his veins, the same blood flowed. Perhaps he was a travelling gnawa, guided by the unseen. *Ghayb*. Once, she had seen healer-men care for a local woman's half-crazed son. The young man had thrashed wildly, biting his tongue until bloody spittle ran down his chin. The gnawa steadied his head and smeared red dirt and prayer on his cheeks, chanting into the whorl of a left ear. Zeina could see her child self now, clinging to her mother as the young man rose, his bare chest aflame. They said he was cured. Perhaps he was. Zeina herself could smell the change on him.

"You have a child? Have you left him alone? He might lose his way."

"He is with me. Right here."

Zeina's words were cut short by that barely hidden grin. The man's entire being seemed to gloat, basking in a secret they would never know. Rayan's anxious gaze met hers. What did he mean? Ahead, all around, there was no-one else. Nothing but the night air's quiet.

Nothing but four grounded shapes in the clearing's brazen openness.

"Do not fear what you don't understand. How intolerably human." He continued, leaning over the gate to pet a nervous ewe.

"Have you come here to speak only in riddles? There will be time for that in the morning." Saidou's shoulders were taut, his back arched like a harp. Even in the dimness, the fuzz on his chin could be seen. Rayan touched the small of his back, a silent plea to swallow any wounded pride that would cost them more than livestock.

"I want that one. For my child."

Yann. Zeina's favourite. Sleek-eared and nimble, his young legs already covered in a fine, fawn-brown. The stranger was pointing at him. His eyes had grown murky.

"Do you offer a price? Even the weakest hold a worth of their own." Zeina heard herself respond.

"You will receive your payment. Have patience and it will be fair, I promise you."

"Sidi, we cannot trust the word of a stranger."

"Ya bint." This was sneered. "Your word lasts only as long as your flimsy heartbeats. My people seal their deals in fire."

Stillness. It spilled itself all over them. Zeina lowered her stick and strode forwards, ignoring Rayan's frantic hisses. She unlocked the entrance to the pen, ensuring her back was never turned away. The closer she was, the more his presence unsettled her. Walk. Steady your hands. She reminded herself that they, in fact, outnumbered him. The sheep jostled around her, their gaze fixed on something only they could see, or even make sense of.

"Bass, bass. Come here." The lamb paced tentatively towards her embrace. She held its writhing form close to her chest, stroking the smooth under its chin. Yann, the gentle one. This was bigger than him. She knew loss as intimately as the blood in her jugular vein. She had trained herself to only feel its afterglow. It still wouldn't hurt any less. This stranger whose silent fury seemed capable of singeing the ground beneath him. To anger him would be to bring danger to the town. Throw cursed bones into the peace of her people's courtyards. She imagined umma's sleeping face, sharing the same air as her father's laboured breaths. Yann would have to save them all. Even Ibrahim's blade had found a ram's neck to spare his beloved son, Ishaaq.

Blood dries faster when it isn't human. She knew this much, at least.

"Take him. Take him and leave us."

The stranger's hooded eyed studied the girl's face. Its soft edges curved into hushed brownness, the steadiness of lips. He should have seen fear, there, tugging at the corners. She was a brave one.

"Mashkoor. You have decided wisely." His arms wrapped around the now squirming animal. Placing it beside him, he watched it scurry away to a safer distance. In that moment, Zeina knew. All doubt left her in a flutter. Yann's shrinking bleats told her this was no man. She thought of the *ghilan*; jinn who burrowed deep into graves and ate the dead. Only the men would meet at funerals, yell in horror at the sight of upturned earth and bones shrivelled by the sun. Ubba's teasing warnings not to stand under trees after sunset. These, along with drains and waterlogged streams, were the homes of *afareet.* Death or madness would await you there. Once, she had been carrying a pail of milk into the house when she saw a freshly killed ratel by the brook. She told her mother and was told to wash her hair thrice to ward off evil. Saidou had seen it too and Rayan had been quick to comb her fingers through his hair, perfuming it laboriously.

She watched as the stranger lifted Yann in his arms and walked away, heading into nothingness. The white of his garment dragged behind him in the dirt, remaining oddly unsoiled. He left as suddenly as he had appeared.

The three did not utter a word. Even when he was nothing more than a veiled speck in the horizon. Tonight, sleep would come with even less ease.

***

Morning broke with the sound of a mother's hoarse cries and a promise held at the tip of the day's finger. Light streamed in through the netted curtains lining the hangar. The hours before rushed in flashes, awakening Zeina with a tug. She hurried barefoot, flinging the wooden door open and making her way outside. The sight of her mother stopped her in her tracks.

The pen was open. The flock still present. Along with what seemed like fifty more unruly animals. Goats, rams, lambs barely weaned. Three she-camels had planted themselves in the middle of the clearing, chewing at the dry undergrowth. Their gleaming hides almost blinded her.

"Ya rabb! Look at all this! No one knows where they've come from, no-one!" Her mother's face shone with warmth, her hands raised to the skies. A fat-bellied ewe padded around her, touching Zeina's feet with its wet nose. Her father leant on his cane and watched them both from the doorway, his smile wider than a valley's opening. It had been years since she'd seen such joy line his tired face. Her mouth stumbled over itself. Little could be said. Instead, she held on to umma's neck and took comfort in this moment. She could feel duty sliding off her shoulders like a sheet of snow. It was this, she knew, that brought tears to a father's eye.

Rayan entered her vision, equally barefoot and surrounded by the clamour of animals.

"A dozen camels! You should have seen Saidou! He woke up and they were eating his tent!"

"You too?" Zeina could barely hear herself amidst the noise. She knew the answer like she knew her friend.

Saidou loped towards them, out of breath, knotted curls bouncing like a mad-man. He threw himself on Rayan, playfully covering her head with her shawl and grabbing her waist. There, in front of the gathering women, his lips found the inside of Rayan's wrists. Zeina laughed at their careless abandon, knowing Saidou could now afford a dowry and earn the approval of shrewd aunts. Rayan would have all the freedom she wanted with a man who would never curtail it. Saleh, too, could come home. They could nurse their father together; send him to medicine men in suits who would ease his pain.

The three hollered, ululating over the heads of elders. The air hung heavy with animal stench but this did not matter. Not now. When the only thing Zeina wanted to concern herself with was how to bottle this delight for later days. She wanted to hold this moment in the warm lap of memories.

There, too, was the small matter of a flicker of white she could have sworn she had just seen. In the dying mist, an outline of a man glided across the sand, a hilltop away. A lucent face revealed itself, under the cover of sky-line. Was that a smaller figure clinging to his side? A young, night-haired boy, now waving.

We seal our deals in fire.

In the stifling morning heat, she did not doubt this for a minute longer.

He had paid.

Well enough.

Art by Ellen Million

NOT A WITCH
DANIEL BREWER

April 1693
New England

Wake up.

I groaned, rolling over in bed.

Wake up.

I muttered a curse, and screwed my eyes shut tighter.

"Wake up!" A shrill voice shouted in my ear. It was at that moment that I realized the voice was not in my head, but the voice of someone standing over me. My eyes shot open as I bolted upright, throwing aside my sheets, and sending a small form crashing into the opposite wall.

I quickly looked about the dark room. Nothing moved as I struggled to keep my breathing steady. I swung my legs over the bed and rose, keeping my gaze trained on the wall. As I slowly crossed the room, the form began to rise.

A pair of iridescent eyes appeared in the darkness. I crouched down, frowning.

"Oh," I spat. "'Tis you."

"A good morning to you, too," Seri grumbled in response.

"Why is it that you woke me?" I asked, returning to my bed. Seri pulled herself up next to me.

"It is four o'clock in the morning," Seri said sternly. "Therefore, it is time to practice."

"Very well," I sighed, and shifted further away, crossing my legs when I had enough room. "I feel this might be unwise."

"Why is that, Celia?"

"Other local girls have been arrested for suspicion of witchcraft," I explained. "And you are telling me I should actually perform it myself."

"This has not disturbed you for many months," Seri retorted. "What brought on this change of heart?"

"Emma," I said, my voice growing soft. "She was my friend."

"And did not have a lick of magic to her," Seri mused. "Though if she did, she probably would not have been suspected."

"How does that make sense?"

"Has anyone suspected you?"

"No."

"Then that is your answer."

"So by practicing magic, I am decreasing my risk of being hung?"

"Enough," Seri's tone was impatient. "We are cutting into our already limited time."

"Very well. What shall I attempt this time?"

"A bit of light would be welcome," Seri said. I nodded, closing my eyes.

Seri had taken the time in the past year I'd known her to go through how it all worked, explaining matters of mana, spells, and rituals. Mana was as a coin to magic, and spells where what you bought. Unlike coins, all mortals had a steady influx of mana, and thus – given time – regain spent mana.

Spells – being a service purchased with mana – caused all manner of things to happen. Spells could be a lot of things, given the whimsical nature of magic. Maybe the spell would become light, or perhaps drain all the light from a room, or silence the words of everyone within it. Spells were odd like that, fluid, just as mana is.

Of course, nothing comes without a price. Even fairly simple spells still drew heavily on me despite a year of regular practice.

Light was easy enough to conjure, but keeping it around was tricky. I found my focus, and slowly opened my eyes, extending my left hand in front of me, palm up.

And then, a tiny speck of light floating a couple of inches above my hand winked into existence. It grew quickly, first to the size of the tip of my pinky, then an acorn, stopping when it reached the size of a potato. The light was soft, and warm, illuminating the bed but fading out as it approached the door.

"Good," Seri nodded, her form now in full view. Seri was about the size of a squirrel, with a flat muzzle and canted eyes surrounded by black spots dotting her otherwise brown fur. Thin gold rings pierced her bat-like ears, and green scales covered her four sharply clawed feet, and her long swaying tail.

"'Tis easier than before," I mumbled, sweat dripping down my brow.

"A sign that you are improving," Seri said. "It shall not be long before you become more in tune with your magic."

I didn't respond at first, too focused on maintaining the light.

"May I dispel it yet?" I mumbled through gritted teeth.

"A few more seconds."

I didn't let the light fade quite yet. It felt as though ages passed as I poured all of my focus into the light, sweat beading down my face.

"You may release it," Seri stated.

I leaned back, dropping my arms to my sides and breathing deeply.

When the light did not disappear, I felt a twinge of worry. When the light began to expand, so too did the twinge.

"Seri?" Fear was creeping into my voice.

"Relax. It is but a light."

When it became bigger than Seri, a searing pain struck my body. The light's shape became unstable, growing and shrinking erratically.

"Cover your eyes!" Seri barked.

My body was unwilling to move. I mustered what little strength I had left and rolled to the floor.

The next instant, blazing light filled the room.

***

I was still rubbing my eyes every few seconds as I left my home carrying a basket, Seri riding along on my shoulder. I could see, but bright spots filled the majority of my vision.

"I still say you should be resting," Seri muttered as I began the walk into town.

"The pantry is barren, and it's market day," I hissed. "We can't not go into town today; you know there would be questions."

"The townspeople do seem rather eager to throw accusations of witchcraft of late. On the other hand, you drained every bit of your mana. How do you intend to defend yourself if something happens?"

"I... I do not know."

I continued walking, not breaking my pace.

As we drew close to town, Seri vanished, yet I knew she remained nearby.

Upon arriving at market, I was able to swiftly make my usual purchases, but before heading home, I was struck with an overwhelming feeling that something was off, something was terribly wrong.

Market was far too quiet. Instead of the usual gossip and bartering, people were simply passing through, all heading for the same place.

Against my better judgment, I began to follow them, ignoring the whispers that rose among people whenever I seemed to draw near. I suppose when your entire family dies of plague it raises some questions.

If there was a bright side to the death of my kin, it would be that it happened before all this talk of witches arose.

The people from market led me to a nearby home, though I could not quite remember whose. A glance at the crowd revealed that nearly the whole town was present. The mayor guarded the front door, refusing entry to all.

I could hear one word being muttered among the crowd. *Murder.* A shiver ran down my spine and I quietly slipped away from the crowd. I walked normally for a few streets before turning onto an alleyway, heading for the back door of the house.

Seri was on my shoulder as soon as I was alone, but she stayed quiet. Leaving my filled basket at the threshold, I slipped inside the ajar back door.

"This is unwise," she whispered.

I nodded.

"They will not hesitate to hang you," Seri reminded. I continued inside.

The curtains were drawn, but there was no lack of light. In the center of the sitting room there was a collapsed table, and on it, a body covered with only a thin sheet. I could hear the mayor still outside trying to calm the crowd. I had a few minutes at most.

I got closer, and kneeled down. My hand was shaking as it approached the sheet.

"Some things are better left unseen," Seri spoke softly. I took a deep breath, and pulled the covering down.

The woman's eyes were open and unseeing. I dared not touch her, feeling all the hair on my body stand on end.

"There should be more blood," Seri leapt from my shoulder, prodding the corpse with her feet. I nearly retched when Seri's actions drew attention to what little remained of the victim's neck.

"What do you mean?" I could barely speak, desperately wanting to tear my gaze away, but finding myself unable.

"Still warm, but her blood has been drained."

"Why?"

My question hung in the air

"No," Seri muttered. "No, no. We're leaving."

"What?" I demanded, needing some kind of answer after all of this. Before Seri could respond, the sound of the door creaking rang out.

Neither of us spoke as Seri mounted my shoulder while I pulled up the sheet. I darted for the back door, sweeping up my basket. I sprinted through the alley, swallowing bile as the images of the dead woman hung in my mind.

***

I returned to the market, putting on a false smile as I bought a few other things to last the week. After that I turned toward home. I needed to speak with Seri.

When I was nearly home, Seri appeared on my shoulder.

"Speak," I whispered as I shut the door behind me.

"We must leave town," Seri's voice was distraught. "Pack your things now."

"What happened back there?"

"It was a Bloodcursed that murdered that woman. Former humans that travel in packs. They will wipe out this entire town, so please. Pack your things, and run."

"Former humans?"

"Practitioners of blood magic, those who burn their own lifeforce in place of mana to perform magic."

"How is that different from me?"

"Utilizing mana is natural. Forgotten, but natural. Using blood in place of it is...horrific. It can easily kill the user, but the strength is unquestionable."

"So, they killed that woman for her blood?"

"It certainly was not the only reason, but drinking their victim's blood is not unusual. Though their bodies can still create blood, they can also assimilate the blood of others directly."

"That's..." I suppressed a shudder, trying desperately not to think of the woman's corpse.

"Appalling?" Seri offered. "Disgusting? Monstrous? I could go on."

"Why will they kill everyone?"

"They lost any humanity they once had when they fell to the Curse. They need no reason for slaughter."

"Can we do anything about them?"

"We can run."

"What about everyone else?"

"You know what will become of them."

"Can't we at least warn someone?"

"Warn them of what, pray tell? That blood-seeking beasts are hunting them? It's pointless. Even if everyone picked up their life and left, the Bloodcursed would hunt them down. We can only hope they do not notice your departure."

"But..." I trailed off. "Can we truly just let these people die?"

"And why not? I would think you understand most of all. You see them slaughter innocent girls while you know yourself to be the true witch. A witch who would never raise a finger to harm any of them."

"I know. I know and yet..."

Seri let out a sigh.

"The only way to stop them would be to kill the entire pack," Seri's spoke slowly. "If their first kill was today, they likely plan a full attack in a few days. Before that, the body count will rise slowly."

"The entire pack?"

"One Bloodcursed can slaughter a village," Seri clarified. "And it's likely to be upwards of six."

I didn't respond, and Seri continued on.

"There are three forms of Bloodcursed, and we have no way of knowing in advance which these will be. There are the Darkhunters, barely alive in sunlight, but unrivaled at night when it comes to physical prowess. Fortunately, their affinity for magic is weak. Darkhunters are predictable. If all were Darkhunters, there's a slim hope."

"And if they were fought during the day?"

"If they could be found, I alone could destroy a pack of Darkhunters during the day."

"And the catch?"

"The second type are Daystalkers. A bit weaker than Darkhunters, but the day does not weaken them. They tend to rely on strength, but their magic is deadly enough. Something of the wild cards and less predictable than either other type. And yet, it is better than fighting the third type," Seri shuddered, her fur rising on end.

"The third type," she began. "Are the Bloodletters. Unhindered by sunlight, they are an unstoppable force of destruction. Physically, they're weaker than the other two, but do not misunderstand. They will tear you apart without having to raise a finger. Their magic is... overwhelming. They're as strong as the mages of legend, when magic was abundant. Please, Celia, swear to me that if any of them are Bloodletters, *any* of them, that you will run."

"You make it sound as though I'll fight them," I replied. If Seri had proper lips, they'd certainly be pursed.

"I have known you for an entire year," Seri said a few seconds later. "I have seen your curious faith in humanity. You are a martyr, Celia, and we both know it."

I let out a soft, grim chuckle. Seri was right. I was far too eager to throw myself in harm's way for others. Had Seri not come into my life, I have no doubt I would be dead.

"Do you intend to stop me?" I asked.

"I am your familiar. I intend to keep you alive."

"How do I fight them?"

"Darkhunters are weak in sunlight. Daystalkers detest water and are seared by it. Bloodletters are frail compared to the other two. And lastly, all of them share two major weaknesses."

"And they are?" I said.

"Mutilation," Seri began. "And fire."

***

Learning the weaknesses of the Bloodcursed did not do much to comfort me. I shook my head and refocused on the task at hand. I looked to Seri in the darkness of my room and let out a breath.

"May we go over this once more?" I asked.

"As many times as you wish," Seri replied. "This is working under the assumption that if you had years to train, you might be able to defeat a pack of Bloodcursed."

"Time being the limiting factor."

"Yes, in a matter of days you will go through a large growth in magic. Even if we had the time to wait, that alone would not be enough, but, there is still one option left."

"If it fails?"

"We run. Your magic would be damaged, but that can heal with time."

"And if it succeeds?"

"I would have to start learning from you."

"And there's no risk?"

"I should have been clear. If this fails, the best case scenario is that it only damages your magic."

"Of course," I sighed, nodding.

"Are you certain you want to go through with this?" Seri's voice was firm. There would be no turning back after this.

"How do we begin?"

"By opening a rift into the Aether," Seri said. "That will—"

"Aether?" I interrupted.

"Magic once used to reside in this realm. It now resides in another known as the Aether. As I was saying, by opening a tear into the Aether it will let us harvest both mana and knowledge."

"What do you mean?"

"Mortals forget things, mana does not. If you are willing, in theory we can grant you memories."

"Memories of what?"

"The experiences of heroes with names lost to the ages," Seri said. "That will let you learn how to fight, and we can increase your muscle tone with magic, but..."

"But what?"

"It may change you. You will retain your memories, but gain the life of another, as if it had been your own."

"I might become someone else?"

"I fear so. But I suppose you will go through with it regardless?"

"You know me well."

"Very well. As long as you are certain, then I am as well."

"How do we begin?" I swallowed my fear, rising to my feet.

"Follow me," Seri said. She leapt off the bed, heading for the door.

Seri led me out into the night, away from the town. It was not far until Seri came to a halt at a nearby hill with an ancient tree.

From up here I could see the entire town set against the horizon.

"Here," Seri said. "It is not much, but it will have to suffice."

"What's here?" I asked.

"A slight weakening in the fabric of the universe. It is faint, very faint."

"Will it be enough?"

"We will see. I recommend you sit."

I took a breath, sitting down and crossing my legs.

"Close your eyes," Seri instructed. As soon as the words left her, my eyes were shut.

"I have taught you to look inward for magic. You must look out now. Reach out to the world around you."

Turning my attention outward was surprisingly difficult, and moments passed with nothing.

Then I felt it. At the end of my patience I sensed it. Just the slightest difference. Everything in that one small spot felt... weak.

I reached out to it with my magic, mind, and hands, my body moving faster than my mind. Seri barked a warning, but I barely noticed as a vibrating hum began to fill my ears. As my hands touched the weakness, it felt fluid, as though I dipped my hands into a flowing stream.

The buzzing faded, and a feeling of clarity washed over me.

"I'm going to open it," I said softly. Seri said nothing.

I pulled against air, trying to separate it from the center. Meeting resistance, I pulled as hard as my arms allowed. The air fought against me. The flow did not wish to be disrupted. And yet, somehow, I knew that it could be. Giving up had never been an option. And it was that I poured what little mana I had into the air around my hands.

I felt lightheaded, but did not falter. I could feel that I had reached a point of no return. If I failed now, I would not get away unscathed.

With every fiber in my being, I pulled against the fabric of the universe, desperately trying to pry it open so that a small town might be spared.

A horrendous shriek filled the air. Unable to cover my ears, I listened to the cry of pain as my hands sundered the air in front of me.

My eyes shot open. Inside the rift was a different world, lit by a near blinding bluish light.

My ears were ringing but I could still make out Seri's words.

"You did it," Seri said. "A rift to the Aether. In this mundane age."

I could see the mana filling the air, a feat Seri has wistfully spoke of. I could understand why, having been able to sense mana for some time, but seeing it was awe inspiring. My skin tingled as the mana brushed against me, spilling out around us.

A loud *crack* drew my attention to the tree. But when I looked, I lost my breath. It had turned to milky crystal, trunk and all. Jagged purple "leaves" filled the branches, whistling in the wind.

I took a deep breath to stay focused on why we opened the rift. I looked to Seri and she to me. No words passed between us, but she nodded, and leapt into the rift without a word.

She emerged a moment later, mana of a more vibrant shade than the all encompassing blue of the aether pouring off her small form. Her iridescent eyes were glowing more brightly than I'd ever seen and the gold rings on her body sparked and crackled with every step she took.

Her mouth opened and a screech filled the air, the mana surrounding her body latching onto me.

I felt a blow to my chest, knocking the wind out of me as I fell flat on my back.

Images rushed before my eyes, voices of people I didn't know, and were yet familiar. I could feel myself being swallowed by memories that were not my own, drifting deeper into a mire that would soon suffocate me. Threatening to change who I was.

I did not give in, clenching my hands, I kept myself afloat in the sea of my mind. I would not become someone I was not. I would not let myself become them. Her... A hero.

Elencera was her name. And in some ways, it seemed now to be mine as well. Yet despite this, I knew I was still me. Celia, the lonely witch.

And that was what made it hard. My life had never been special, and it had been painful. I could become the hero by just giving myself to the long-dead Elencera.

But I wasn't truly alone. Now more than ever. I did not love my life, but it was mine. No memories from the past would change that.

I slowly gained my breath back, and sat up, looking to Seri.

"Are you, you?" Seri had fear in her eyes. I smiled at her concern.

"I'm still me," I confirmed. "Just a bit more so."

"Then we did it," Seri said. "We actually did it."

"I think you're forgetting. This was half of it."

"Then you still intend to fight the pack? We did not speak of combat strategy."

"I think... I think I know what to do."

***

I strolled down the street with Seri on my shoulder.

"You remain certain of this, Celia?" she whispered to me.

"Of course," I replied. "Do you doubt me?"

"I doubt your memories."

"I'm not asking you to trust them. I'm asking you to trust me."

"And I do."

"Thank you."

The two of us continued on our path, the plan clear.

I could see tainted sources of mana when we got to the town. Tracking them when they were on the move was going to be impossible, but once they stopped, I knew they had found their prey. It would take them some time before they moved again, and I could only hope I would arrive before it was too late.

Their target was a fairly small home to a kind couple I saw regularly at market. While they oft had visitors, seven standing outside in the dead of night was clearly unusual.

Bloodcursed. Seven outside, and I could see five more mana sources from within. As the house came into sight, the ones outside noticed me. Too late to back down, I got closer.

"I'm sorry," was the first thing I said as I approached. The words came without warning, and surprised me.

All seven Bloodcursed's attention was on me. They looked like average people, to a degree, but they were oddly muscular, three in particular.

"I guess that's an old habit," I chuckled grimly to myself. "A very, very old habit. But I am sorry. I can't let you have this town."

"I don't like this," the nearest Bloodcursed growled. "She knows something."

"'Course she does," another said. "Something smells funny about this one. And that thing on her shoulder?"

"Idiots!" a brutish one began approaching at a breakneck pace. "She's just a human!"

"Actually," I began as I sidestepped, and struck his kidney with my palm. He howled in pain but did not fall. I extended my hand and felt magic spill forth, forming a thin blade. He tried to strike me, but he went high and I went low. I thrust my hand forward, driving the blade into his gut. I yanked the blade to one side, disemboweling him.

"A witch," I finished as his body crumpled, falling to the side.

Oddly enough, despite cutting him down, I was not nearly as sickened as I had been by the corpse just this morning. In the time it took to entertain that thought, I felt a searing pain. I realized I had been distracted just a second too long. I looked down and saw a hand had been driven through my stomach, but instead of blood, light pooled forth.

I looked up at the second Bloodcursed and grit my teeth, raising my hands and driving two blades of mana into him before my body shattered into dust.

I darted in from the side, tapping him with my hand, a bright glyph forming on his clothes just before it burst into flame. He dissolved to ash.

I looked to the remaining Bloodcursed, not speaking a word as their eyes widened. I'd died before their eyes, and then returned unscathed. Anyone would be confused.

Two sets of footsteps approached from behind, but I did not fret. The cavalry was here. Now standing back and to my sides were myself. Each a copy made of mana, a so called "mirror image."

"You three going to start talking in unison?" one of the Bloodcursed called out.

"Please," I spoke alone. "Let us not glorify this for more than it is."

"And what do you think this is?" a different Bloodcursed taunted.

"Mercy."

I dashed forward, ready to strike.

I was expecting the Bloodcursed to assault all three of me together, but their agility and coordination was more than I expected. They moved as a wave, crowding one of me. I didn't have any more images ready, as I had hoped three would be enough.

I could feel their blows on my second self, and knew it wouldn't last long. I took a breath, stepping back along with my third self. My second image exploded, alighting the night with flame, destroying itself as well as three Bloodcursed. And yet, two Bloodcursed remained.

I kept my other image back, and darted forward in an attempted feint. When I reached the Bloodcursed, their forms dissipated, naught but smoke. I felt a blow of pain land on my other self, and cursed myself for my haste. Daystalkers, they'd fooled me.

I pivoted, and began rushing back. With that set, I diverted my attention to reacting to their assault with my other self. I could tell it was already too late to save it, the Bloodcursed worked fast and light was pouring out of multiple spots.

I altered my earlier tactic, and instead of bursting, I had the nearly shattered image simply reach out and touch them, glyphs appearing on their bodies upon contact. The image shattered as they burned, their death cries piercing my ears.

And those two Bloodcursed fell.

My heart was racing as I looked to the five remaining sources of tainted mana still within their target's home. They had begun to move, quickly approaching the door.

I was without reinforcements, and out of time to conjure more. The thought of being on my own was dispelled when I felt Seri appear on my shoulder.

"Our last resort is ready, if you need it," she said softly. I nodded, looking up just in time to see a door hurtling towards me.

I dove to the side, and it hit the ground, breaking apart on impact.

One Bloodcursed alone stepped forward from the other four as they poured out into the open. When I saw her, I thought my mind was playing tricks on me.

"My, my; you're quicker than I remember," Her voice lacked the emotion it once held, but her face was just as I remembered. Emma, the one friend I'd had left. Accused of witchcraft and executed. And yet she stood before me, Bloodcursed.

"I... I saw you hang," My voice was hoarse. "They left you up for days."

Emma took one step forward, flashing a smile of pointed daggers. I shuddered under the weight of her gaze. Her eyes lacked the laughter, the humanity they once had. I knew, even though we were once friends, this...

abomination, would not hesitate to kill me.

"How strong you've grown," Emma licked her lips. "I'm eager to know the taste of a witch's blood."

I needed to follow through with the plan. I knew I couldn't afford to waste time here, lest all this be for naught. And yet...

"Why?" I asked, truly wishing I could understand her.

Emma's eyes narrowed, just a hint of some emotion other than bloodlust playing across her lips.

"Accused of crimes I couldn't have committed, about to die, and desperate for a miracle. And then, I'm presented with a wonderful gift. A gift of life, and power. You're surprised I take it?"

"But—!"

"Pray tell, what would you have done in my situation?" Emma interrupted. "Though, I suppose you wouldn't have needed to sacrifice anything for the power to live. You had it all along. So don't speak as if you understand me, as if you could."

Her words cut deep. All humanity she once had was gone, claimed as the price for power. I took a deep breath. I wouldn't let her incite me into a direct fight, not like this.

Desperately wanting to end this right here and now, I took stock of the situation. I couldn't attack from afar; their reflexes were too sharp. Five to one were odds I couldn't afford to risk, because if even one survived, it was all over. I was outnumbered and outclassed, so why hadn't they moved? Something was clearly wrong.

The answer hit me. None of them looked unusually muscular, unlike the Bloodcursed from before. That, and none cared to try and smash my face in.

"You're all Bloodletters," It was only after saying it that the horror of the statement sunk in. I hadn't been able to tell from their mana, as it was tainted the same as the Darkhunters and Daystalkers.

Finding myself face to face with five people with enough power to raze the town in a matter of hours made my blood run cold.

"Run," Seri whispered to me. "Run!"

I sprinted away toward the town hall. If I could make it there...

"Oh, a hunt is it?" Emma called. "How fun!"

I shuddered as I sensed all of the Bloodletters running after me. I didn't let the fear slow me. Lights flashed from behind me, and I had to dart side to side to avoid bolts of energy. I heard panicked cries, and saw lights appearing in windows. The town was waking up.

I kept running, only barely outpacing the Bloodcursed. I just had to hope that they continued after me, and weren't tempted by the townspeople.

I raised a shield an instant before a bolt hit me, causing it to fizzle just in time.

Town hall was only a few feet away. I dove in inside, rounding a hallway and stopping at a pair of double doors. All five had followed me, stalking ever closer.

"You're far more entertaining than the rest," Emma said. "A shame we won't be able to do this again. That is, unless you care to join us? Imagine, we could play this game for eternity."

I gave a sad smile, shaking my head.

"Goodbye, Emma," I said softly, pushing the doors open.

Inside, the true me was seated on the floor in the center of the room, eyes closed, muttering.

As the spell began, the draw it had on me started to eat away at my form, light beginning to leak from within.

"Another fake!" Emma shouted, barking orders to the other Bloodcursed.

"I'm sorry," I whispered as they charged past my shattering form. "You don't deserve what they did to you."

"But you did!" Emma shrieked. "You were the witch!"

I responded with a faint, pitying smile.

"Kill her!" she shouted. The other Bloodletters prepared to launch an attack, but my body opened her eyes. Eyes that were not my own.

"*Hellfire*," her voice, *my* voice, resounded through the town hall. She drove her hands down in front of her, plunging them toward the floor.

Before they reached the earth, they struck an invisible boundary, sliding into it and fading from sight.

My body wrenched the air apart, and a rift opened. A screech roared in my ears as the fabric of reality cried out.

This was not like the tear into the Aether. It did not depict a blue world of mana, but a hellish land instead. All of the Bloodletters barraged my body with magic, but seas of flame rose from the tear, serving as both an attack and defense. Their magic was engulfed by the inferno. The blazing wave swallowed the Bloodcursed, searing them to ash.

All but one of them had burned when my form finally shattered.

***

Emma dove at me. I couldn't control the flames any more, and I wouldn't be able to dodge in time.

Seri was a blur out of nowhere, latching onto Emma. I watched as my familiar raked her claws across Emma's eyes.

Emma's cries of pain drowned out the roar of flame. She collapsed to the ground as Seri darted back to me.

The air had grown heavy with smoke, but I took a deep breath all the same. Emma stumbled to her feet, blood streaming down her face. Still, I didn't let my concentration break as I attempted my escape.

Emma lunged at me. Her hands mere inches from my face when everything disappeared.

Everything rushed back all at once, my ears popping and blood gushing from my nose. I fell to my knees, exhausted, but alive.

Teleportation, an ability recalled from Elencera's memory. A wonder I had pulled it off.

I rose to my feet, standing next to the rift and crystalline tree. I watched as the town hall continued to burn. In my absence, the tear I'd opened there would close, and the fire would die out. One building was a small sacrifice to save the rest of town.

The town to which I could never return; too many people had seen me. Even if they hadn't seen me using magic, there would be too many questions as to how I escaped the inferno.

Knowing Emma would die blind and alone would have saddened me if not for the fact that my friend didn't die this night. She died when she gave in to her curse.

I felt no guilt or remorse for my actions. Killing what those people had become truly was a mercy; none of them more than beasts wearing human skin.

I glanced to the rift, one question on my mind. How would this power change me? Closing the rift was easy enough, nothing was keeping it open any longer. Already it was slowly stitching itself shut. But I knew that wouldn't return things to how they were.

"They saw us," Seri said flatly.

I nodded, glancing skyward.

The home I'd had all my life was no longer mine. Everyone in my life was either dead or convinced I was one of the monsters. And they weren't exactly wrong. To them I was something to be feared. To them, was I any different than the Bloodcursed?

Part of me did want to use my magic to stay here, to be the hero, even if only from the shadows. But I knew that was a fantasy. I didn't belong in their world. Magic did not fit in with this mundane age. An overwhelming power held by far too few people.

Of course I couldn't stay. Humanity wasn't ready for magic. Maybe someday, but not today.

Wordlessly, I walked toward the Aether.

"No one has ever lived in the Aether before. It may kill you," Seri warned. I only smiled in response, eliciting a chuckle from her. "Of course you are. The first witch to live in the Aether."

"Not a witch," I said softly, as I crossed the threshold of the rift. "A human, don't let me forget that."

And the rift closed.

Art by Mirelle Ortega

TRENCHES
SIOBHAN KRZYWICKI

1917
USA and France

I never felt quite right. Though I was what they called a "strapping young lad" of around 6 feet in height, broad of shoulder and thick through and through, strong as an ox my pa said, I always thought this was wrong. I was proud of my size and strength. Well, not really. Proud of what I could do with it, but I always felt like I should be more delicate. I got jollied often about my graceful movement, the care I showed for the space I took up and in my appearance. I got called dapper on a good day and nancy on most. I'd always been like this, even when I was small.

The other children seemed to sense something wasn't quite right about me and I was picked on throughout my childhood, beaten by other boys during the day and given a hiding by my father on any excuse. I got to be a decent brawler thanks to it, but it was never something I liked, even when I won.

By my 15th year I was well and truly sick of schooling. Not of learning, I loved that, more than pa said was truly proper, but of schooling. I wanted to be rid of the other children, or at least the boys and get on to adulthood, the main show. I knew there were plenty my age who were making their own way, but I had my eyes set on college. Learning among adults. All the tortures of school and schoolchildren left behind, but for that I needed a diploma.

It was a beautiful spring day and I was sitting in the park on a rock, reading a book and occasionally retrieving some food from the basket my mother had prepared for me. It was warm, sunny and quiet and I hadn't a care in the world. At least not until Roy showed up.

He entered the park, spotted me and strode straight for me, menace in his posture.

"Hey nancy," he called.

I ignored him, pretending to be lost in the book that I was now completely unable to focus on.

"Hey! I'm talking to you," he said and knocked the book from my hand. I was bewildered. He'd picked a fight with me the month before and I'd thrashed him. He was slight and around 5' 8", but he'd been picking on me for years. That kind of habit dies hard.

I rose slowly to my feet, still standing on the rock and seemed head and shoulders taller than him. "Leave me alone," I said. "I have nothing to say to you. I just want to be left alone."

"I want to be left alone," he said, mocking my higher tone.

I lowered my voice in an attempt to sound tougher. "Go away. You remember what happened last time you tried."

"Yeah, I do," he said and raised his right hand over his head. Four other boys stepped up from all around me. "That's exactly why I wanna talk to you."

The way he said "talk" made me think no words would be used.

Three of the other boys were spread out behind me with one behind Roy. I took two steps towards him, fists clenched & when he took a step back I ran to my left, out of the park. That's what I always did. I ran.

I didn't want to go home in this situation, but I didn't know where else to go. I bolted through the front door with them a few steps behind and slammed the door. I heard them come to a stop & heard muttering for a moment before I heard them walk away.

As I stood there leaning against the door, the reason I didn't want to come home walked up.

"Running away again, boy?" Growled my father.

I knew what was coming. Despite myself I protested.

"There were five of them, father!" I knew it wouldn't do any good.

"No wonder they're always after you," he said, not even listening, "You're a coward and they see it. I swear I'll make a man of you yet."

And with that he walked out of the room. I didn't relax, I knew he'd be back in a moment with a switch. Father thought using a switch was how the better class disciplined their children, only poor people used bare hands.

***

The next day I was sitting gingerly in class, trying not to show pain, and dreading the taunts after school. Trying to decide if I would rather take a beating from the gang of boys or from my father. It'd probably be from my father again since if I lost a fight I'd face the switch anyway.

Not wanting to face either, I snuck out from school early and headed downtown. I stopped at a newsstand and picked up a newspaper, intending to read until chased away. All the headlines were about the war. When I was little I'd read about the great empires in Europe and dream about traveling there when I was older. Now it looked like the Great War would never end and Europe was in ruins. We'd entered the war a month ago, but it wasn't looking like we'd change much with our small army despite what Wilson and the newspapers said.

I made it through almost the entire front page before I was noticed & had to leave, the newsstand guy yelling at me as I walked away. I walked aimlessly through downtown past shop fronts, ads and the occasional recruiting poster. They sure made it look heroic.

I turned a corner & saw Sam. He was my friend, but I really didn't want to talk to anyone. He saw me before I could turn away.

"Jesse!" He called

"Hey Sam." I sullenly replied.

He walked over to me.

"Where'd you go? I was looking for you after school. Me and the fellas were going to walk home with you. You don't deserve the crap Roy's been putting you through."

"I can take care of myself," I grumbled.

"I know, I know," he said softly, "but we have to watch out for each other, you know?"

Sam was one of the only people who knew my secret and I knew his. It made our friendship a little closer, but a little needier and more desperate too. I found out his because, well, he liked me. I mean *liked* me. He sensed there was something different about me and thought it was the same thing that was different about him. I told him I wasn't like that, that yes I was different, but not in that way. Not exactly. He was frequently exasperated by my insistence on this because my explanations didn't make sense to him. He couldn't understand that what made it impossible for me to appreciate his attraction was the very reason he was attracted to me.

I'm sure I didn't explain it well, I never did. It was confusing to me, so why should it be clear to anyone else?

"Yeah Sam, I know," I said. I turned to walk home with him and let him briefly put his arm around my shoulder.

We soon arrived at my home and as we walked in the front door I saw my father seething in the foyer. Sam realized he should beat a hasty retreat, so he slapped my upper arm and said "I should get home, thanks for talking me through that stuff about Roman emperors. I could never keep them straight!"

And he hurried out the door, down the steps and out of range, leaving me to face the storm myself.

"What was that all about?" My father asked, flat and hard.

"Oh, Sam was just jollying me. He knows I'm not much on history." I would have gotten a quiz on Roman emperors had I said anything else.

"Then where the hell have you been?" he demanded. "You're almost an hour late getting home. You have chores to do!"

"I'm sorry father! I... I took the long way home. So I could think!"

"What do you have to think about?" The scorn he poured into "you" hurt. Such a short word and he filled it with so much disdain.

"School!" I improvised, "and what comes after. What will I do when I'm done? It isn't that long until graduation."

"You know what you'll do. You'll work for me. God knows you don't have the brains to do anything I don't hand you." He started to turn away and I should have left it there, glad to avoid another beating, but I didn't.

"I was hoping to go to college, father. My grades are good and..."

"College? College?! Don't be an idiot. I can't afford to send you off and you can't possibly get in anywhere worthwhile anyway. Why do I want you to waste another four years of your life? No, you'll work for me and that's final. Go do your chores."

"But father..."

"I said go do your chores." Each word was a sentence unto itself and I could see his hand start to clench.

I muttered "Sorry father, I'll go," and hurried away to carry the upstairs rugs out back for mother.

I dreaded getting up in the morning. I did every morning. The same torture from the boys that kept me from paying attention to my classes, the same knowledge that though I love learning it will be taken from me, the awkwardness with girls I like and admire who pity me at best. I got up and prepared as though I was going to go to school, but on the walk there I took a turn and went to town instead. If my father found out I was missing the day, he'd beat me like the last time I did this, complaining all the while that I never learned my lessons.

I wandered aimlessly through the town for some hours, but kept finding myself in front of the army recruiting office. I'd been brooding about my torments all morning, but now I started to feel angry.

"I'll show them!" I thought, and with that I strode into the office.

A tall, older man stood from behind a desk. He was in a worn, but neat uniform with lots of stripes on his sleeve. I knew a sergeant was three, but his other stripes baffled me.

"A new recruit!" He said enthusiastically. "Come to have the army make a man of you? Good thing you came in today! With the US in the war, it'll be over soon. If you're lucky, you can still see some of the action."

He motioned for me to take a seat. I did.

"So, let's get some quick questions out of the way first. Healthy?"

"Yes, sir."

He started making notes on a piece of paper in front of him.

"Height?"

"Six foot, sir."

"Enough of that 'sir', just the answers will be enough. Are you on the run from someone? From the law?"

I hesitated. Am I? School, my father, the bullies, myself? No! I'm here because I'm going to show them all. I'm not running from them, I'm running at them!

"No," I said firmly.

Now it was his turn to hesitate. I saw him glance down at some other papers on his desk.

"Good enough for me. Last question for you. Age?"

I looked up quickly and saw a recruitment posted that said "18 to 35" on the wall.

"18," I said

He looked me up and down.

"18? You sure?"

"Yes sir," I said, "My birthday was just last week." One small lie easily begat others.

"Very well then. Who am I to question the brave souls who come in here and need no persuading? Sign here!" and he thrust a piece of paper in front of me on the desk with a pen beside it.

I picked up the pen, glanced at the paper and signed.

"Very good! Report here Friday and you'll be off to boot camp! They'll teach you all you need to know to knock the Huns in the jaw and finish the war."

He stood from his desk and offered his hand. I stood and shook it, turned and left. Once I was outside I slumped against the building. What had I done?

I couldn't go to school this late, I didn't want to wander in town any more, so I went home. I walked in and my mother came out from the kitchen to see who'd come in, worry on her face. When I told her what I'd done, she started crying and it took all I had not to cry along with her. I'd thrown away college, but at least I wouldn't have to work for my father.

"It'll be ok mum. You'll see."

I spent the afternoon helping mother around the house with her daily work. We talked gently to one another as though nothing had happened, as though nothing was different. I knew this might be the last time I could spend time with my mother. I dreaded the storm when father came home.

But I was stunned. When I told him, he broke into a broad grin, clasped me on the shoulders and said "This will make a man out of you, my boy! You foundered in school, you never knew how to stand for yourself, you'll get that out of this!"

My mother cried "But he's only 15! We can get him out of this, they can only take him if he's 18! Claudette got her boy out just last week!"

"Nonsense!" he responded, "This is just what he needs! And a bold, brave action it was to skip school and sign up on his own! A promising portent of things to come! Come with me, son!"

He led me into his study, poured two glasses of scotch and handed me one.

"You've decided to be a man instead of a cowering boy, this calls for a drink with your father." He raised his glass. "To growing the hell up!" and we drank together on it.

Friday came all too quickly. Sam was aghast. He tried to talk me out of it, but there was nothing to be done. I said goodbye to my few other friends and the greater gathering of kids who stuck together for protection at the bottom of the school's social ladder and went off to boot camp.

Before I knew it, I was in France. We'd gotten off the ship and they sent us almost immediately to the front. I got to see the trenches first hand. I saw the looks on the men who'd been here and fought for years. Some looked haunted, others incredibly tired, some resentful and a few just looked like they'd died long ago, but their bodies kept up their routine. It was ghastly. I knew the war hadn't gone well, but I wasn't expecting this.

Months of time with all the men in basic training and on the ship had made me quieter, more shy than I'd been before. I tried to keep to myself as best I could, terribly uncomfortable in the close quarters. There were a few other boys in our group around my age, but they played at being adults as best they could. Honestly I didn't see much difference between their playing at adulthood and that of many of the older fellows.

A few Americans tried to talk to the French soldiers before they moved down to reinforce other parts of the line, but they pretended to have no English or just glared at us in contempt. One did respond with a harsh "Fuck Off!" to our lieutenant who probably deserved it. These men all looked like they'd seen their own ghosts and we come in and, well, the ones who tried to talk to the French anyway, started cheerily talking about how the Huns would be routed in days now that we're here. I caught one of the last French soldiers to leave glancing over his shoulder with what looked like pity. He shook his head in disbelief and trudged out of sight.

We got busy setting up in the just vacated trenches, sergeants screaming at us to do the things we were already doing.

"Don't get too homey boys! We won't be here long!" Sgt. Thomson yelled in between more yelling about how we weren't working fast enough or well enough. I'd long ago given up trying to understand them and just did what I was told. I was really hoping they were right at this point and that we'd be home quickly. Army life was mind-numbingly boring.

We'd been there four days and were wondering what the sergeant had meant when I heard a strange, high-pitched noise. Someone yelled "TAKE COVER!" and I fell forward to a little dugout in the forward trench wall just before explosions rang out around me. I heard someone screaming and another yell "I thought the Huns were about done!" One fellow tried loudly bantering about something, but stopped when a shell went off nearby, whether because he was dead or terrified I never found out.

I tried to make myself as small as I could, hands gripping my helmet to my head until it felt like I'd pull it down around my shoulders. It went on for hours and in-between blasts I heard whimpering, some if it might have been mine.

When it finally seemed like it was letting up I heard someone shout "UP! UP! HERE THEY COME!" I grabbed my rifle as I'd been trained and started to stand to look over the edge. The guy to my left was a little quicker than I was and immediately toppled back into the trench, blood pouring from his eye. I had no idea what hit him, but I was a lot more cautious after that.

I poked my eyes up over the edge and saw a wave of men coming at us, crouched low and firing as they went. I shot at them a few times before I felt something ping off my helmet. I reached up to feel my head and my helmet was gone. I dropped down into the trench to grab it and started to scramble up again, terrified that if I didn't get there in time we'd be overrun, but someone fell on me. Someone who was writhing in pain and screaming. I turned to look and had to wipe his blood from my eyes. I found myself looking at where his shoulder used to be.

I collapsed to the ground with him on top of me and started crying. I was trying to claw my way into the dirt at the bottom of the trench, desperate to get away. After a few seconds I just curled into a ball, rifle clutched to my side, pinned to the muddy ground by a dying man. I was thinking frantically to myself.

"What have I done? How did I end up here? What is this going to show anyone? That I died like they all expected? Why couldn't I have been normal? I'd still be at school! Why couldn't they all just have accepted me for who I am? Why couldn't they even see who I really am? I'm going to die and no one will ever know! I wish people would see me as who I'm supposed to be!"

The air grew thick, the sound of the guns started to quiet & I thought the fighting was letting up when I realized there weren't fewer shots, everything just seemed to be getting quieter like someone turning down a radio. I hesitantly opened my eyes and saw no-one around me was moving. I looked down the trench in front of me and saw a glow coming toward me. As the glow approached I saw the trench sprouted grass where the glow touched and the people, weapons and trench "improvements" disappeared. I couldn't move to get away and the glow enveloped me. I felt peaceful and well. I saw little wings flitting about me. I tried to reach out toward them and something smacked down on my head and I lost consciousness.

As I groggily woke up I heard someone directing people, his voice coming closer.

"Get a medic over here! Someone see if he's unconscious or dead. You two, watch the Huns, make sure they're really pulling back. Get a litter for this poor bastard... What in the... How'd a nurse get down here?! Someone give her a hand, make sure she's alright! You two, you're detailed to get her back to where she belongs. She must have come up from the hospital tent thinking she could help."

I felt a man grab one of my arms and another grab the other. They lifted me from the ground, put an arm around each of them and started towards the rear.

"What? What are you doing? I'm no nurse!"

"She's shell shocked." One said. "Out of her gourd. Maybe some bed rest will get her back, this sure as hell is no place for a woman."

"She?" I thought, "What the hell are they playing at?" I was too weak to do anything about it, so I let them carry me away. Every time I tried to protest, they shushed me and before I knew it I was back at the local HQ and being led into the medical tent.

They laid me down on a cot and went over to talk to a doctor. I raised my hands, they looked normal to me. My boots and pants were caked with mud, they'd crouched low the whole way back for some reason and ended up dragging me. I was lying here in army fatigues, but they kept insisting I was a nurse. I'd dropped my gun back in the trenches, but I still had everything else, even my helmet. My helmet had a dent in it, but no hole. I must have been dazed when I saw that glow.

I tried to sit up with a "Hey!" and felt a hand on my shoulder pushing me back down. I looked over and it was a nurse.

"It's OK honey, you can rest. You're as safe here as you can be. What nursing unit are you from? What's your name?"

I just looked at her, astonished. Couldn't she see? Was I delirious? Was I hallucinating that I was a woman at last? At last? Where did that thought come from?

"You've seen some hell huh?" The nurse continued when I didn't answer. "Sleep. Get some rest. We'll be here when you wake up. Then you can tell me and the other girls what it's really like at the front."

She gave me a wink and walked away. I lay back in the bed and tried to figure out what was happening. I fell asleep while trying to puzzle it out.

I woke at dawn, 18 hours later. I had a compress on my head and had been cleaned up. I was in some kind of robe or hospital gown. Maybe it was more than 18 hours! I looked around. I was in a building in a medium-sized room with large, high windows. All I could see was sky. There were a dozen beds in here, but only 4 or 5 were occupied. All women. I was in a women's ward. What the hell was happening?

I looked down at myself, under the robe. It was still my body in every way that mattered; I was definitely a man. I was cut here and there, but that was all. I reached up to my head and felt a bandage. I felt around a little more and it hurt like hell. I'd been hit hard in the head twice, maybe I was hallucinating all this, but what a weird vision to be having.

I swung my feet over the edge of the cot and went to stand up and heard a nurse walk quickly up behind me. "Awake at last, honey?"

I turned. It was the nurse from the tent.

"I'm just glad I'm the one on duty when you came to. You've been asleep for three days, must have been one hell of a party." She had a smirk on her lips and a twinkle in her eyes.

"Party?" I started. "Three days!" I thought.

"I'm just kidding, kid," she said. "You should lie back down. Something rang your bell pretty good up in the trenches and you're going to need time before you're ok again. What ever possessed you to go up there? Did some idiot brass have a bright idea that you could help some way? Men always seem ready to throw us in harm's way when they think they need us and shelter us when we can actually help. Officers around here are a special group of bastards."

I stared at her, baffled. I was doing that a lot.

"I'm sorry," I whispered to her, "I know this is going to sound odd, but can you describe me to me?"

She stepped back and gave me one of those looks. The kind where you know you're being judged, all of you.

"Sure, kid," she said "You're around 5'7", light-brown eyes, light-brown hair, hazel & auburn some would say. Big eyes too, & good cheekbones, like my little sister back home. I put a little makeup on you so you won't feel so naked." She smiled. I put my fingers to my lips and saw a little red when I pulled them away. "Hair's shoulder length, not in a style I'd pick, but that's war-time nursing duty for you! Most importantly," and she leaned in, "you're what, 14? 15? You've started putting on womanly curves, sure, but you've got a lot of 'girl' about you still. How'd you manage to get over here anyway?"

"I lied about my age."

"That all?" She said, measuring me with her eyes again. "You found one gullible mark, kid. Well, good for you, you made it here, now let's put you to work. What do you know about nursing?"

I hesitated. "Nothing really. You tend to the sick and injured."

"There's a hell of a lot more to it than that! Come on, I'll show you the basics. We'll start you on bedpans and I'll show you how to change a wound dressing." She turned and went into the second men's ward. I stood there for a second and followed.

Over the next few weeks and months I learned a lot about nursing and even more about myself. Was this really how I wanted people to see me? Is this who I really was? I'd never let myself think of it this way before. I always stopped any thoughts that might lead to this because what could I do? It could only make things worse. The rotten kids at school would be even worse. I don't think even Sam would understand and my father might actually kill me. Always best to squash it down and be miserable.

But now? With whatever this gift was? I still had no idea what was happening, but everyone saw me as a girl. I talked to soldiers as I tended them, those who were awake and lucid, and they talked to me like a kid sister. Some made rude sexual comments, but as they were incapacitated I ignored it. I'd been flirted with by many soldiers who saw me as a small woman. They'd move to put a hand on my shoulder and adjust to where it actually was, but never seemed to notice their hand was higher. While I found myself enjoying a lot of being a woman, there was a lot I didn't enjoy either and fending off the attentions of lonely soldiers was a big one of those. The patients weren't usually any serious trouble, but the soldiers who came in to visit their wounded buddies could be. Fortunately, there weren't a lot of those. Most of the time taking a strong grip on their arm was enough to get them to leave me alone. Most seemed to just think they had somewhere else to be, but a few held their arm where I'd squeezed and gave a backward glance as they left.

The rest of the time it felt good, right somehow, to be considered a woman, but it still wasn't quite right. I was slowly realizing that it wasn't being seen as a woman that I wanted as much as being a woman. I'd managed to find a nurse's uniform in my size (though it didn't seem to matter what I wore, others saw a nurse's uniform) and a bunch of the nurses were treating me like a kid sister, so I was learning a lot of things about being a woman that a girl wasn't expected to know yet, but I wanted more. I was finally admitting to myself that my body felt wrong, that it had always felt wrong. Now that I was letting myself think about it, or was being prodded into thinking about it honestly, it was becoming clear.

In some ways being seen as a woman and being treated as one without actually being one was even worse than when everyone saw me as a man. Sure, I appreciated not being in the trenches. I'd give almost anything to not go through that ever again, but it was like having something you'd never realized you wanted dangled inches out of your grasp.

We were sent from hospital to hospital to help where the need was greatest. I think I liked the traveling the best, the camaraderie of the nurses as we went from town to town on our own was wonderful. I'd been here well over a year and could almost forget I was anything but a young, idealistic woman helping care for wounded soldiers. Almost, but for my body. Obvious to me and only me, it was nonetheless something that kept me from believing, from happiness.

I was sitting at the bedside of a black American soldier in a French hospital, changing his dressing, when Elizabeth, the woman who'd first talked to me and helped me through my "amnesia" after I got brought back from the front, ran into the room, searched quickly until she found me and yelled my "name".

"Alice!" she cried with joy in her voice. She'd named me after her little sister back home who was around my age. I liked it, so I kept it.

I looked up at her expectantly.

"It's over!" she yelled, "The war is done! Germany surrendered yesterday!"

I leapt up and we hugged and jumped up and down together for a moment, grinning. The soldiers within earshot who were able, cheered and passed on the news. We stopped jumping after a moment and I glanced down at the soldier who's arm was partly bandaged and then back to Elizabeth.

"Of course, kiddo." She said, "The war may be over, but I think our work will continue for quite awhile."

I sat back down to finish changing the dressing of the now grinning soldier while Elizabeth started trying to keep excited soldiers from jumping around and re-injuring themselves. After maybe 10 minutes of elation I stopped short and thought, "What now? Home? Back to my old self? What if I stayed like this? How would my parents, what would my parents, where would I..."

"Miss? Miss?" The soldier I was tending to said.

I snapped out of it. "Yes?" I said, once again paying attention to what I was doing.

"Are you alright? All of a sudden you looked like someone walked over your grave." He looked worried about me. Bandaged all over, but he looked worried about me.

"Oh. Yes. I'm fine." I said, embarrassed. "Just realizing everything this means. This is wonderful!" I put on the best smile I had, wondering for the thousandth time what the smile looked like to other people.

"It sure is." He said, mollified. "Of course, I'd be happier if it happened two weeks ago." And directed his smile right at me.

I smiled right back, "I bet you would, I bet you would."

Six months later I stood at the docks with Elizabeth, waiting for our turn to board our ship home. The remaining nurses came along to see us off. We stood on the deck at the railing, waving to the others and Elizabeth said to me "So where are you going?"

"What do you mean?" I said, pangs of several different fears hitting me at once. "Home."

"Where is home for you? Do you remember that now?" she asked. She was very protective of me.

"I think I do." I said. "Some of my memory has been coming back bit by bit since you found me. I'm going to go where I think home is and see if I'm right."

"Good for you, kiddo." She said, chucking me on the arm. "Anywhere near me? Troy's not too much of a backwater."

"No. New Jersey," I said.

"Aw, well. You have my address. You come see me if you're wrong, or hell if you need anything at all. Far as I'm concerned you're my kid sister now and I'm gonna look out for you. You remember to write me as soon as you're settled so I know where you are and that you're ok, right?"

"I will, I promise," I said, smiling "up" at her. "But don't worry, you have a week to nag me on the high seas."

She grinned back, threw an arm around my neck and we started toward our berths as the ship started to move. "Come on, wiseacre. Let's go get settled in and then find some chow."

I couldn't sleep that night. I lay in my bunk and fretted. I tossed and turned, wondering what I should do. Do my parents think I'm their daughter now? Will they recognize me at all? Will they be confused and horrified? Worst of all, am I trapped in this in-between state? Forever doomed to be in this clunky body wandering through the world of womanhood?

"I wish," I said aloud, quietly as I could, "I wish to be fully who I am. Who I'm meant to be. Who I feel myself to be."

That strange thickening of the air happened again and the ship began to glow. I saw tiny wings again and suddenly I could sleep.

I woke late the next morning, Elizabeth shaking my shoulder.

"Come on kiddo," She said, "Let's get some breakfast before it's all gone."

I felt weird. I lay there groggily for a moment, taking stock. I'm not sick, not seasick. I feel... different. I'm... shorter? No! It couldn't be! I quickly ran my hands over myself and screamed at the top of my lungs in a joyous, high-pitched voice that was alien and utterly familiar all at once.

"I'M A WOMAN!!" I think I screamed that 3 or 4 times with Elizabeth looking startled, then amused, then worried.

"Woah, woah, kiddo. Shhh. Let's not get carried away. Most people would still say 'girl' for someone your age, but given what you've been through this last year, sure. You're a woman. Now would you stop screaming?"

That sobered me right up. I must sound like a crazy person.

"I'm sorry, Liz," I said, looking every bit as mortified as I felt. "Bad dream, you know?"

She got that motherly look I'd become so familiar with.

"Yeah kiddo. I know. We all get those for sure."

But the kind of dream she was talking about was from the horrors of war. I had no idea what this was, just that it was right.

The rest of the voyage went quickly with me stealing whatever private moments I could to make sure this was really happening. They weren't many and they weren't long, but as far as I could tell it was real. I spent as much of those moments as I could staring into a mirror. I couldn't believe it. I looked how Liz had always described me, but I still saw my old self in there too. I was definitely still me, but blessedly not.

I tried putting lipstick on for the first time when Liz mentioned I'd stopped. I guess her just seeing what she expected to see was gone. Liz laughed at me when she saw it.

"What is wrong with you hon? You've never had problems with this before."

"I'm just a little dazed," I said. "Peace is so strange, like I'm walking through a dream."

"I know what you mean, kid," she said, "I find myself daydreaming through a lot of things too." And gave me that familiar, indulgent smile.

We docked in NYC and Liz and I said our goodbyes at Grand Central, getting on different trains.

"Remember," she said.

"I've got it, sis," I said. "I'll write as soon as I'm settled and we'll work out a visit soon, I promise!"

"You'd better," she said, smiling.

We hugged, stepped back from each other, wiping tears from our eyes, and made our ways home.

I stood with my bag in front of my house, terrified of what was about to happen. I kept focusing on the bag to keep myself from running away. I had no idea where the clothing inside had come from, but it was clearly mine. Part of the magic I've experienced, I supposed. I clung to the idea that that same magic had fixed everything at home for me too. I was steeling myself for the walk up the steps to the door when I heard my mother scream.

The front door flew open, she ran down the steps, threw her arms around me and screamed over and over "My baby! You're alive! You've come home!" and other variants, all the while sobbing. I tried to comfort her best I could, patting her back and saying "Yes mum, I'm fine. I'm alright. I'm home. I've missed you too." And with that I started weeping as well.

After what seemed like an hour, with neighbors coming out to stare or welcome me home or comfort my mother, she shooed them away and we went in and she made us tea in the kitchen. She insisted on me telling her everything, even the horrible parts and I did, leaving out anything about before the hospital. I had to stop a few times so she could compose herself after some of the truly horrible parts, but she made it through it all. She was much stronger than I'd ever expected. She broke in every so often to scold me for running off and for not writing, but ended every one with "but I'm so glad you're home!" I was so happy the magic had made home still my home and mom still my mom that I was as contrite as I could muster for every scolding.

Then father came home and it all went to shit.

He walked into the kitchen and looked at the two of us sitting at the table. Mom said "She's home! She's well! It's a miracle!"

He looked straight at me and said, as though he hadn't heard a word. "You're home." Flatly. And he turned and walked out.

I looked at mom, confused. She looked back, worried. I stood and went after father, realizing he was the same horrible man whether I was a boy or a girl. "Woman," I corrected myself. I'd been through horrors of war enough to make me an adult and I'd use this in confronting him.

He'd gone into his study and I followed.

"Father," I started.

"Father, is it?" He said, looking up from the drink he was pouring. "No more papa, eh? All 'grown' now?" he said with scorn before yelling.

"Do you know the hell you've put your mother through? You vanish one day and not so much as a letter home? We thought you'd died! Then we heard from a neighbor's boy that he'd seen you in France in a hospital where he was visiting wounded soldiers from his unit. But we still heard nothing for weeks and your mother went from thinking you'd died to knowing you were alive, but worrying you'd be killed every day. Frankly I think it would have been better if she'd continued thinking you were dead."

"Yes, father, I know I was wrong, but I'm home now."

"Home? You still want to call this your home? As far as I'm concerned, you threw that away with your wretched behavior! Why should I let you come back? Do you know what it'd do to your mother if you did this again?"

"But I won't."

"Damn right you won't! If I allow you back you will do as I say! It's too late for school for you, so you will help your mother at home until we find you a proper husband. You will not go out unattended, your mother will be your escort whenever you do leave the home until you are courting. If we are unable to find a suitable husband for you quickly, you will come work for me. Now that that's settled, go find what your mother needs help with and I'll let you know in the morning if I'll allow you to stay." And he started to turn away from me, drink in hand.

"No." I heard myself say.

"What did you say?" he said, turning back.

"I said 'no'. I am a woman, I have been through a war. I have tended to wounded, comforted the dying and made my way. I will not be dictated to like I'm a child!"

I noticed I was standing ramrod straight with fists clenched at my sides.

He stood staring at me for a second and then said.

"Very well. You may stay the night, but in the morning you are to leave. You say you can make your own way, then do so. Now get out of my study."

I stood there in shock for a moment, then turned on my heel and left.

I went back to the kitchen to tell mom and to spend one last night with her, but she passed me on the way, heading into the study, closing the door behind her. I stopped and heard her start to speak and father angrily retort. I realized I didn't want to hear any of this so I went to the kitchen, drank my tea and thought about what I would do.

Mother came back in after around an hour looking exhausted and defeated. She sat down at the table and slumped in her seat. I took her hand and said "It's ok mum. I'll be ok."

She started to quietly cry.

"I promise mom, I'll write. I'll stay in touch this time. I'm not running away any more, I'm just moving out."

We hugged again for a long while and when we stopped, I freshened our tea and we talked. We relaxed more as the night went on and had a much better time. I made us dinner and she brought some to father. We stayed up until mom couldn't keep her eyes open any more.

In the morning I'd packed as much of my things as I could carry and gave mom Elizabeth's address as a way to stay in contact while I figured out where I'd go. Mom promised to send the rest of my things on to me and I thanked her, but most of it was from a past I didn't really experience. It was a cover story made from fairy webs.

I made my way back to Grand Central and tried to decide where I'd go. I had enough money to last awhile, I'd drawn pay while a nurse and had very little opportunity to spend it. Sure, there'd been a little drunken carousing, but not often and it was cheap. Add in my worries something would happen and I'd be found out, and I hadn't drunk much at all. I thought about going to ask Liz if I could stay with her for awhile, but decided against it. A visit was one thing, but I wasn't about to burden her. I found myself going to a ticket counter and purchasing a ticket to Springfield, MA. I wasn't sure why I was doing this, it felt partly like I was being guided and partly like a long-buried memory urging me on.

I spent the night in Springfield and then went on to Holyoke. When I'd arrived at Holyoke I realized what the "memory" was urging me toward, and I made my way to Mt. Holyoke college a little further north in South Hadley. I went in to the office of the Dean of Admissions and scheduled a meeting for later that day. I booked a hotel room nearby and wandered the campus and small town, relaxing and enjoying myself.

I told the dean I had just returned from nursing in the war and I'd heard that they had a program for women who'd done that and wanted to attend college. I was jumping blindly here, the "memory" told me this was true, but I had nothing else to go by. The dean said they did, but that classes wouldn't start for months. I filled out applications, had another long talk with the dean when they found I didn't have a high school diploma and arranged to have a "make-up" year where I'd get my education to the point where I could be a regular student.

I wasn't sure I could afford the college without getting a job, but they told me not to worry. Veteran Nurses got scholarships, part of what they called their "Mary Lyon Scholarship Series." The dean said they wanted to make sure independent women stayed independent.

I had my dream of going to college. I had my dream of myself come true. Now I had the chance to make new dreams for my future.

Art by Amy Kwan

FEET OF CLAY
A.J. ODASSO

First Century
Byzantium

Kleia studied the lumps of earth in their cool, dark tubs, plucking up the damp cloths that covered each one. She wrinkled her nose at the musty smell, which varied a little from tub to tub – here reminding her of the fungus on Master Andros's rotting boat, there reminding her of the copper ore mined out in the countryside by Laksa's husband. She flinched at the thought of her mistress's strict body-servant, who would not be pleased with how long she had lingered in the market. No one had warned Kleia that she would be so spoiled for choice. She bit her thumbnail.

The merchant, a gaunt man with chin bristles and an unpleasant demeanor, had been watching her for quite some time. Idly fanning himself with a tightly woven reed mat, he frowned.

"Out of your price range, little slave," he muttered.

Kleia clutched defensively at her gold neck plate, and then rummaged in the folds of her sash, producing three bronze coins.

"Lady Ireni sent me," she lied. A trip to the market had been her own idea, and Laksa had given her the coins.

The merchant rose with a huff and strode over to her, leaning across the tubs to examine Kleia's neck plate. His frown deepened as he fingered the grooves in the gold. *I am Kleia, property of Ireni, who is the wife of Andros Nicosia. Return me without harm.*

"They do say your master is soft," said the merchant, finally, letting the plate drop back against Kleia's chest. A slight breeze rippled the lean-to above their heads, and Kleia tried not to look smug. "What's the Lady after?"

"Clay," Kleia said. "Nothing expensive. It's so Laksa can make a votive offering for her at the temple. See, she's been–"

"Ill, lame, suffering from headaches," said the merchant, already hefting a lump of coarse-looking clay out of its tub and onto a stone slab. "I've heard it all. How much?"

"Um..." Kleia bit her thumbnail again. Her mistress *had* been suffering from headaches, as well as sharp pains behind her eyes. This was the least she could do. "Enough to make a head?"

"To what scale? Miniature, doll-sized, true to life–"

"She's not very big," Kleia said. "Half that lump would do."

The merchant snorted, raising a large, curved blade with a wooden handle on each end. "Little slave," he chuckled, "with those coins, you can only afford a third."

"Fine," said Kleia, drawing herself up as tall and proud as she could. "A third." The head would be slightly small, but for Lady Ireni's sake, she would swallow her dignity.

"You'll want to work with it quickly," explained the merchant, lopping off the portion in one smooth stroke. "Failing that, an old kitchen pot with a lid would do for storage. You've got to keep it wrapped – like this," he added, pulling a dripping wet strip of linen out of a tub hidden somewhere near his feet. He wound it around Kleia's clay and hefted it in both crusty hands. He cleared his throat.

"Here," Kleia said, placing the coins on the edge of the nearest tub. "Now, give it to me. Please."

"It's heavy," said the merchant, placing the parcel carefully in Kleia's small, outstretched hands. "Can you manage?"

"Yes," said Kleia defiantly, staggering a little as she turned from him without so much as offering thanks.

Laksa was grumpy when Kleia returned, but that was hardly unexpected. She found the old woman laboring over a steaming pot of rose petals in the kitchen. Sweetened rosewater was Lady Ireni's favorite, and the cooling process would take hours.

"It took you long enough, child!" she scolded, stirring with one weathered hand and wiping the other on her cloth-bound brow. "I suppose you'll be needing a pot to keep that in?"

"Yes," Kleia said as she deposited the messy bundle on a wooden stool. It had ruined the front of her dress, and her bare arms were a patchwork of slip-smears and mild sunburn. "I won't have time to do anything with it until after dark."

"Best you not get caught," Laksa said, beckoning Kleia nearer. "Stir this for a moment. I'll find you something."

Several minutes and a lot of clatter later, Laksa returned with a copper stew pot and a lid that, although mismatched, fit.

"You'd better run along and change," Laksa said, depositing the clay in the pot with an unceremonious thump. She covered it and set it aside on the packed-earth floor in one dusty corner, and then took over the stirring. "My poor Ireni is worse today."

Kleia sighed and nodded, pausing briefly at the foot of the staircase. She couldn't contain the question burning at the back of her throat. "Laksa, why do grown men have nothing better to do than remind me that I'm a slave? Andros and Ireni don't."

"*Master* and *Mistress* don't," Laksa corrected, dipping one pinkie into the pot to take a surreptitious taste. "As for why – well, they're men. *That's* why. Even my Zakarias likes to remind me I was once no better than you. No offense, child."

Kleia lowered her eyes.

"Why did you stay?"

"Because I've known nothing else," she said, lifting the pot off the heat and onto the stool. "Because I raised Ireni from a babe, and because she married a gentleman as kind as you please."

"If my mother had survived, would she have been freed?"

Laksa's eyes darkened as she stared into the depths of the pot.

"Not very likely," she said. "Child, I am sorry, but you must remember that your father is an honorable man. He would not hurt Ireni so. And yes, he is fond of you – but fondest of her."

"I know," Kleia said, fighting back tears as she climbed.

By the time she reached the villa's bright atrium, her eyes were dry.

***

"Enter," said Ireni in a thin, strained voice.

The room was cast entirely in shadow, except for an oil lamp on the night stand and a smouldering plume of frankincense beside it. Kleia closed the door as quietly as she could, averting her eyes. Ireni lay propped up against a pile of silk cushions, dressed in a rumpled linen gown, her eyes gleaming with fever.

"I have not seen you all morning," she said. "My darling, I am *very* displeased. But come, sit beside me," she continued, patting the mattress. "Tell me all about the market."

Obediently, Kleia crossed the room and climbed up beside her mistress, noting the way she flinched with every shift until Kleia had settled. Ireni slid one soft, lotus-scented arm across Kleia's shoulders, drawing her close. The linen at Ireni's breast smelled of sweat, perfume, and sleeplessness. Ireni kissed the top of Kleia's head and pinched her arm impatiently.

"Ah!" Kleia gasped, feigning excitement as the sting subsided. "Well, everyone was saying that the fishmonger had caught some kind of monster – sort of like an octopus, only bigger, with twelve legs and two heads. They said it was covered in dark red spots, so I went to take a look. By the time I had gotten there, though, it was gone. Some rich man's cook had bought it."

"I suppose it won't have been Laksa," said Ireni, sounding disappointed. She stroked Kleia's arm, absently humming.

"No, Mistress," Kleia said. "She's making rosewater."

"Good," said Ireni, her fingers digging in hard enough to bruise. "*Mother*. When we are alone. How many times must I remind you, Kleia?"

"Mother," Kleia murmured, willingly letting Ireni's hand guide her head to rest in the curve of her neck. Her heart ached, but so did her arm.

"What else did you see, my treasure? Were there horses?"

"No," Kleia sighed. "I didn't see any horses. But I saw some glass beads that I thought would look pretty as a necklace for you, and I saw some rare flowers brought all the way from–"

"Did you buy any of the beads?"

"No. Laksa only gave me enough to buy figs," she lied.

"Then I suppose we're having stewed figs for supper?"

"I don't know," Kleia admitted, forcing her breathing to steady. "I didn't ask. I can go ask her, though, if you like."

"No, my sweet one," Ireni crooned, folding Kleia closer still, rocking her as if she were an infant. "I will give you some money for those beads, and tomorrow morning you shall go buy them and we'll braid them into your hair. How's that?"

"Wonderful," said Kleia, closing her eyes. "Mother."

***

"The nose is wrong," said Laksa, leaning on the rough wooden tabletop. "Ireni's is more delicate. Pointed." She frowned, running her fingers across the marks on Kleia's arm. "Again?"

Kleia dipped her fingers in the bowl of water, obediently pinching and smoothing the nose until Laksa seemed to approve.

"Mistress is ill, and she's not sleeping well," she insisted, schooling her expression. "It distresses her so. She doesn't realize that she—"

"She was such a pretty child," Laksa mused. "Dark curls, pale skin, blue-gray eyes. She's so faded now, my blossom! I can scarce stand how ashen she looks. And her lovely long hair, all cut down to nothing! You should have seen her at your age."

"She's still very pretty," Kleia said, running her clay-caked palms down the planes of the model's cheeks. "Beautiful, even," she added, letting her fingertips trail down to the gently curved neck, which was where the model ended. "Like a muse."

"You've got the forehead right, though. And the eyes." Laksa offered Kleia a sip from her beaker of rosewater. "Good?"

"Yes," said Kleia, wiping a drop from her lips and smearing it across the model's mouth. It seemed to smile at her.

"Surely Mistress must be thinking of buying you a match. Two more years and you'll be nigh on marrying age, isn't that so?"

"I'm only ten summers," said Kleia, stubbornly.

Laksa only nodded, slurping the rest of her rosewater with satisfaction. "Two years if it's a day, three at most. We're in need of help around here, so your children will be welcome."

Kleia gave her a hard look and picked up the scrap of copper wire she'd been using to detail the ears. "I don't want children," she said. "*You* didn't have any."

"No, alas, they all died," Laksa said. "But I had Ireni."

"She — I mean, Mistress — doesn't, either."

"True enough," said Laksa, frowning. "But I think sometimes she feels it. If I didn't know better, I'd say she dotes on you."

"Mistress is kind," Kleia said. Most other slaves she knew of wore neck plates of copper, but hers had always been gold. "She sees to it I'm provided for. Makes me pretty."

"Your father — your master — is kinder."

Kleia ignored the regret in Laksa's voice, concentrating on some last-minute additions: fine lines to the forehead, crinkles at the corners of the eyes. Perhaps she'd set blue beads in them. Kleia yawned, pressing the back of her hand to her mouth.

"Get off to bed, child," Laksa said, draping a freshly dampened cloth over the head like a veil. "This will keep."

That night, on her pallet in the corner of the atrium, Kleia clutched Ireni's coins to her chest and listened to the new, painful sound of coughing that echoed from the end of the corridor.

***

"Kleia, where are you going?"

"Out, sir," she said, turning to face Andros with a bow.

Her master's smile was stern, but good-natured. "Has Laksa sent you on a wild goose-chase again, minus the goose?"

"Yes, sir. I believe it's duck tonight."

"Lady Ireni has worsened," said Andros, without preamble. He held up a silver coin, indicating that Kleia should take it. "The sweet wine that they make out in mining country would soothe her if served hot. I hereby charge you with finding some."

"That will be easy," Kleia said. "Thank you, Master."

Andros nodded, his smile vanishing.

"Find some bauble for her with what's left over. I trust you know her tastes."

Kleia's heart skipped a beat.

"Yes, sir," she said, taking her leave quickly as two men she didn't recognize entered the atrium. Perhaps one was a doctor. She could still hear Ireni.

In the marketplace, Kleia purchased the beads first, tying them safely inside the sash at her waist. Finding a suitable wine merchant proved considerably more difficult. Most of the ones present were local, selling bitter swill that Andros would never permit at his table, much less give to his ailing wife. She found a Greek olive oil merchant whose table also boasted some impressive-looking wine flasks. They were painted with elaborate scenes in shades of red, tan , and dark brown. Kleia ran her finger from one vessel's slender neck down to its tapered, rounded bottom. It could not stand on its own, so the merchant had put it on a rough linen pillow. The scene depicted a seated woman with Etruscan-dark curls and piercing eyes. A child sat in her lap.

"It's too much for you, girl," said the man. "Run along!"

Kleia said nothing, but held up the silver coin.

The merchant's eyes rounded a little before settling into a pleasant, crinkling accompaniment to his smile. He snatched it.

"Take the cloth as well," he said. "It's a sack."

Kleia wrapped the flask well and cradled it in her arms.

"Thank you, sir," she said.

Upon her arrival back at the villa, Kleia avoided the atrium in favor of the back kitchen entrance. Ireni's shouting matches with Andros and her various physicians, though impressive given her fragile condition, upset Kleia. She preferred not to hear such phrases as *Just give me those drugs for pain and have done with it!* and *There's nothing you can do for me, you old quack!* shouted at the top of her mistress's failing voice.

Granted, Ireni did seem to have a point about the doctors. Regardless of how much Andros paid them, they all averted their eyes and said the same thing: *Some kind of fever, some kind of exhaustion, some kind of wasting away – very curious, indeed.* Kleia was quite convinced that they knew little of what ailed her.

"What's this?" Laksa asked, taking the linen-wrapped bundle from Kleia's arms. "Shaped like olive oil, but sloshes too much."

"Sweet country wine," Kleia said, busy unwrapping the model of Ireni's head. "Andros says to serve it to her hot, with spices." Kleia selected two of the clearest blue beads from the lot she'd purchased and pressed them in carefully with her thumbs.

"Gives me the chills, that does," Laksa said, breaking the wax seal on the flask with a knife. "Now it's staring at us."

"It's staring at nothing," Kleia said. "It can't see."

Laksa made a sign against bad luck and popped out the cork with her teeth. "You're summoning spirits, child. Tread softly."

"I'm asking the gods to make my mistress well," said Kleia, and propped the head up to dry.

"I'll have you take some of this to Mistress when it's done heating," Laksa said, pouring the wine into a pot.

Kleia toyed absently with the remaining beads.

***

"Such a pity there aren't more blue ones," said Ireni, carefully slipping a green bead onto one of the fine braids that she intended to frame Kleia's face. "I should like you in blue."

"The vendor didn't have many," Kleia lied. She held the cup up to Ireni's lips, tipping it just *so* as her mistress took a sip.

"This is good wine," Ireni murmured, reaching for a yellow bead. "Sweet. Whatever Laksa has put in it soothes my throat."

"Is your coughing very bad, Mis– Mother?" Kleia winced as the slip earned her a slight tug on the braid.

Ireni smiled.

"No, my beauty. Besides, it only comes in the evening."

Kleia nodded, staring down into the cup of wine. For a moment, she couldn't help but imagine that it was blood.

"Although my chest and my belly *do* ache," continued Ireni, adding a few more green and yellow beads before tying off the braid with a twist of gold wire. "Those stupid men have no idea as to what may be causing it. The one I just threw out said it may be demons. Can you imagine, Kleia? *Demons!*"

"Laksa says they exist. They live in wells and in deep, damp earth."

Ireni's hand at her elbow tightened, fingernails digging in hard.

"Well, Laksa is an old fool. There! Aren't you beautiful, sweeting? Have a look."

Kleia inspected her reflection, nodding mechanically.

"Beautiful, Mother," she agreed, blinking back tears.

***

"Kleia!" called Andros, waving from across the courtyard.

Kleia looked up from her spinning and nodded. "Sir?"

"That wine was well-chosen," he said, striding towards her. "I tasted some for myself. Ireni is much improved this morning."

"I am glad to hear it, sir," Kleia said, bending her head.

Andros took hold of one of her beaded braids, running his fingers over it curiously. "Did Laksa do this? It's childish."

"No," Kleia said. "Mistress did. I bought her some beads with the leftover money," she lied. "She put them in my hair."

Andros sighed and let go of the braid.

"So indulgent."

"Others have said so, sir," Kleia ventured tentatively, turning the wool carefully between her fingers. "Even of you."

"I wouldn't pass that on if I were you," Andros said with a chuckle, tousling her hair. He set two silver coins on her thigh.

"Sir?" Kleia asked, glancing up in startled confusion.

Andros chewed his lip.

"Go get some more of that wine."

***

"Have mercy, child," Laksa said, frowning at the large block of clay as Kleia hefted it onto the table. "You'll have all our necks wringed for wasting the master's silver!"

"I've come back with wine, too," Kleia said, gingerly unshouldering another linen sack. "Two bottles. The man must like me, because he gave me change enough to afford this."

"Good for repeat business," Laksa muttered, taking the wine to one side. "Tell me, what will you make this time?"

"Well," Kleia said, "the head's not fully dried out yet, and since Mistress has got pain in her chest and belly now, I thought I'd make a body and attach it to the neck with slip. You know."

"A doll without limbs," Laksa clucked. "Kleia, you could have said that you wanted a doll. Ireni would permit it."

"I don't want a doll," said Kleia, stubbornly beginning to shape the clay with all the strength her hands could muster. "I want Mistress to be well again. That's all."

"Don't we all," Laksa sighed. "It would do the entire house a world of good."

Her eyes flicked down to the fresh marks on Kleia's arm, but she said nothing.

Kleia's palms lingered over the tentative mounds of the figure's small breasts, wondering if Ireni would have nursed her if Laksa had not been there to do the job.

***

"Be sure to hold the knife steady," Zakarias said, folding his big, calloused hand gently around Kleia's as she worked. "Like this. Always cut away from yourself. Swiftly."

Kleia nodded and did as she was told. She had always liked Zakarias, not least because he taught her to do *useful* things, like spit fruit pits at pigeons and skip stones across the fishpond. Today's lesson was on carving acacia branches.

"That's very good, anyway," he said, scratching his whiskery nose. "Are you making yourself a doll? Laksa says you'd like one."

"Well, not exactly," Kleia said. "It's Mistress."

"I see. You have a ways to go before it'll resemble her."

"This one doesn't need to look *exactly* like her," Kleia explained. "I just need the spirits to get the right idea."

"I see," Zakarias mused. "What temple will you leave it in?"

"I don't know," she said, pausing. "One for healing."

"Perhaps you ought to scratch her name on the back."

"Yes, I had thought of that," Kleia lied, squaring her shoulders proudly. She dug the knife-point into the figure's face, notching out divots for eyes. She hadn't any beads that small, and even if she had, she didn't know how to attach them.

"You've finished learning your letters?" Zakarias asked, as if lost in thought. "I never did."

"Mistress taught me," Kleia said. "I can write my name, hers, Master's, and Laksa's. Shall I carve you after this?"

Zakarias chuckled, shaking his shaggy white head.

"You'd best learn to write my name first!"

***

"Gods, but my bones ache," Ireni rasped.

Kleia re-dampened the strip of linen she'd been using to mop her mistress's face and neck for the better part of an hour. Ireni's naked body shimmered in the lamplight, covered in a thin sheen of rosewater and sweat. Kleia swabbed her throat.

"Which bones?" she asked, concealing her fear.

Ireni sighed, making a feeble gesture at the frescoed ceiling. Her arm flopped helplessly back onto the pillow above her head, and her brows knit as if the movement had hurt her.

"My arms and my legs," she said. "Every joint in this cursed body – my shoulders, my elbows, my hips, my knees."

Kleia frowned, passing the cool cloth over one shoulder, then the other.

"What about your ankles?"

Ireni laughed weakly. "No, not yet. My feet are all I have left. I suppose I shall at least be able to *walk* in the afterlife. But the rest of me is useless, my darling."

Kleia steeled herself and rubbed Ireni's elbows.

"In the afterlife, Mother?"

"Surely I'll die soon," Ireni breathed, her gaze meeting Kleia's with still, grave certainty. "I've told Andros to keep those quacks and bastards away from me for now on."

Kleia lowered her head and moved down her mistress's body, tenderly draping the cloth across her abdomen. She couldn't imagine those slim hips too wracked to function, too wasted to propel her through the atrium on slender legs to hurl cups at the doctors.

"But what if they discover a cure for your sickness?"

"There is no sickness like mine," said Ireni fiercely, taking hold of Kleia's wrist. She tugged Kleia upward until they lay side by side, the damp linen half crushed between them. "You wouldn't understand. Failure has driven me to this. Andros would say otherwise, but I know better. I *know*."

Kleia hiccuped against Ireni's shoulder, locking the sob deep in her belly.

"Failure, Mother?"

"I so wanted a child," she whispered, threading her trembling fingers through Kleia's beaded braids. "A girl. You."

Kleia nuzzled her neck.

"But you have me."

"No," Ireni muttered. "Only when we're alone, only in secret. Andros would never have permitted it. He never would have–" Ireni's eyes hardened, full of old, cold fury.

"Wouldn't have what?" Kleia asked, unable to breathe.

"Freed your mother. If he'd had any heart, he'd have done it as she lay there bleeding to death in the wake of your birth."

"He thought he'd hurt you if he did," Kleia murmured, hesitantly stroking Ireni's hair. "Laksa says so."

"Laksa doesn't know him," said Ireni, her voice bitter. "Doesn't know why. But I know, *oh*. Do I ever know."

"Know what?" Kleia begged, turning Ireni's head so that they faced each other once more. "Know *what*, Mother?"

"Don't call me that!" Ireni sobbed, curling in on herself, away from Kleia. "Too painful."

Kleia fled the room in tears, but not before she'd grabbed a small handful of coins out of the basket on the bedside table.

***

"Heavens, child," Laksa said, clutching at her sweat-stained tunic. "It's growing more ghastly by the day."

Kleia shrugged and continued to carefully shape the slender arms, pausing to compare them now and again. If not perfect, they at least had to be symmetrical. The hands would be easier.

"Does anybody know what you're on about?"

"Zakarias," Kleia said indifferently.

Laksa sighed. "Forgive me, I ought not to have said."

"He taught me how to carve last week," Kleia said, setting the finished arms aside carefully before breaking off two more lumps to roll out for legs. "I made a figure and put her name on it. He took it to a temple for me. I don't know which one. I told him to make sure it was a place where they're good healers."

"Dear, you may have noticed that Andros won't let any of the priestly sort set foot in this house, whether they're considered excellent healers or not."

Kleia looked up. It hadn't even occurred to her.

"Why not?"

"He doesn't believe in that sort of thing."

"What, in gods? Or spirits?"

"Neither," said Laksa, shrugging.

"Since the doctors haven't worked, hasn't it occurred to him to *try* a priest? Or a priestess? Maybe a priestess would know better. Mistress told me that she thinks she's ill because—"

"Hush your tongue," snapped Laksa. "You wouldn't know."

I know too much, Kleia thought, *but it's not enough.*

***

The next day, as Kleia sat at her spinning, Andros wandered into the courtyard and stood watching her for what felt like an age or more. Finally, when the spool was finished, he spoke.

"Tell me," he said casually, "has Ireni's illness lately made a liar of her?"

Kleia blinked, setting the spool aside in her basket.

"Sir?"

"Lies," he said. "Lies conjured by her fever-addled brain. Does she tell them, or have you known her to be truthful?"

"Master, she is as truthful as ever I knew her to be."

Andros nodded, biting his lip. Ireni had always said that's what first caught her eye about him: the unguarded, almost vulnerable look that doubt lent him.

"I see," he said.

"Is there something troubling you?" Kleia asked, keeping her tone as mild as she could. "Shall I fetch you some wine?"

"No, Kleia," he said, raising a hand. "It is merely that I've noticed that some of Ireni's coins have gone missing, but she insists she sent them to market with you to buy figs. Figs, however, do not cost so much as that."

"I see," Kleia said, her eyes wide. *Shit.*

"Did she, in fact, send them with you to the market?"

"Yes, sir," Kleia said, lowering her eyes. "She wanted figs and some wine. Cheap wine, sir. We ate and drank them."

"Why did you not insist she stick with the Greek wine?"

"She wished to save it for the evenings. For her treatment. It does seem to help her, Master," Kleia continued in a rush, forcing a smile. "Laksa puts in spices."

Fondly, Andros returned the smile and touched her cheek.

"I had noticed an improvement in her cough since you followed my recommendation. You look so *very* like your mother. You have inherited her exquisite...subservience."

Kleia was so stunned that by the time the kiss was over, she hadn't had the chance to pull away. She put both hands over her mouth, shaking her head. If *this* was what Ireni had meant—

"You feign shock," Andros said with undisguised irritation. "Did you not think that it would come to this, what with Ireni on her deathbed? I'm not made of stone, and you're nearly of age."

"You're my father," Kleia said, still dumbstruck.

Andros pulled her hands away from her mouth. "What?"

"You," she repeated, "are my *father*."

The slap sent Kleia down onto the sun-baked tiles.

Dazed, she struggled to her feet, clasping the elbow she'd landed on.

"My offspring you may be," said Andros, coldly, "but my daughter you are *not*. You're my slave, and I've let Ireni's fondness stay my hand long enough. You're mine to do with as I please."

"I've not yet begun to bleed," said Kleia, shakily. "Likely as not, I'd die if you tried. She'll be dead in less than a year." Her voice broke on the admission, the sheer knowledge of it.

Andros chewed on his lip again, considering her.

"You are right enough," he said. "For now."

And Kleia was alone then, shivering in the heat.

***

"Tell me he didn't," Laksa moaned, wringing her hands.

"I'm telling you, he did," said Kleia, showing off the bruise on her elbow. "I've bought myself a little time, probably, but—"

"But he's randy as a goat since Ireni's been unable."

Kleia nodded, already busy unwrapping the as-yet unfinished legs. The feet were her problem. She couldn't get them right.

"I did right in explaining the works to you early," said Laksa. "At least there'll be no shock when he comes to it."

"I'll not let it happen," Kleia said. She pinched off two pieces of loamy clay and set to shaping them. "Ireni won't die. She'll be well once I've finished and taken this to the temple – I'll burn the old wooden one so that those spirits don't hang about – and Master won't need to bed me."

"It's not so much a question of needing," Laksa sighed. "Ireni is beautiful, but your mother was Helen of Troy reborn."

"It won't happen," Kleia said, stamping her foot as she crushed the clay feet to nothingness.

They still weren't *right*.

***

93

Kleia woke to the sound of soft footfalls on the smooth flagstone and a single lamp light drifting slowly down towards her face. It was Zakarias. His eyes were red and swollen.

"Our good Lady Ireni," he said, "is dead."

Kleia's heart clenched and dropped into her empty stomach, heavy as a stone. "When?" she asked, unable to summon tears. She'd had shock upon shock, worse than any lashing. She wondered if the past week had been a dream, if she was only just waking.

"Sometime past sundown," Zakarias said, stroking Kleia's hair. "Laksa took in some hot spiced wine and found her cold."

Kleia closed her eyes and let the old man enfold her.

"May I go in?" she asked in a voice that sounded small and afraid. "Is Laksa still there? Is Andros—"

"They are both there," Zakarias said. "Master asked me to fetch you so that you may grieve with them."

Or so he can look at me, thought Kleia as they walked, a slow funeral march. *Look at me over my mother's dead body. Again.*

Kleia did not meet Andros's eyes when Zakarias shuffled her into the lamp-lit room. Instead, she flew to Laksa's side, huddling down upon her knees beside the old woman. Ireni looked peaceful, almost as if restful sleep had found her for the first time in months. Laksa had not quite managed to conceal the smear of blood on her pillow. A coughing fit had done her in.

"Mother," Kleia whispered, taking hold of Ireni's yielding hand.

Her unmarked wrist smelled of rosewater and unspoken regret.

***

Throughout the next day, visitors came to express their condolences to Andros. He did not have as many friends as Kleia had imagined, although their endless demands for wine and rosewater made it seem as though there were twice as many people flitting about the somber house then there actually were. Andros had hired a poet, a professional mourner with a harp, to sing. His song spoke of a house with a tree, a fountain, and a happy family gathered around it, and of how the tree withered and the fountain dried up when their mother died.

Except she hadn't so much family as that, Kleia thought angrily, handing a cup of Greek wine to the sour-looking old lady with ugly gold-dipped flowers protruding from her gray and upswept hair. *No brothers, no cousins. It was she who sat in the shade of the tree while I sat spinning and told her stories.* She stuck her tongue out at the poet and dashed back to the kitchen with her empty tray, humiliated. Laksa hugged her tight, face tearstained.

"Such a farce," she crooned. "They won't let me near her."

"Me either," Kleia said. "The flower lady smells funny."

"Stay with me for a while," Laksa said, handing Kleia the wooden stirring stick. "They'll get their feast the quicker!"

That evening while Andros dined inside with his guests, Kleia sat by the courtyard fountain with Laksa and Zakarias.

"They'll burn her at sundown," Zakarias said, taking a puff on his pipe. Where he'd got opium, Kleia didn't know. She breathed it in hungrily, drifting on the sweet burn in her throat.

"We mustn't go," Laksa said, placing her hands on Kleia's shoulders. "Zakarias must go alone and light the pyre."

"I'll stand watch till it's done," he said. "Till they've gone, every last one of 'em, the horrid snobs."

Kleia closed her eyes tightly. She'd failed. She hadn't gotten the feet done in time. If she had, just *maybe*...

"There now, don't think like that," Laksa murmured, rocking her. "I won't have it, love. You did all you could."

Not enough, not ever enough. "Bring me ashes," she croaked, fixing her blurred gaze on Zakarias. "So I can keep her near me."

"Child," he said, "I'd have done so even if you hadn't asked."

***

Kleia slept with Laksa in her small room off the kitchen that night, wrapped in a clean, but gravy-stained old robe. Her rest was fitful, filled with visions of gryphons bearing Andros's features.

Their talons tangled her hair and ripped at her bare flesh until she had no choice but to flee into the sandy underbrush ridden with stones and pomegranate saplings. She snatched a piece of the heavy fruit and found it ripe, bit deep. It bled bitter juice between her teeth.

Ireni spoke to her then.

Wash my feet in the fountain, she said, *and I shall be reborn.*

***

Kleia woke to the sound of voices and the smell of honeyed rosemary porridge, tangled in Laksa's robe and dingy bed linens.

"With all respect, sir, I'd leave her alone for a few days," Laksa said. "Ireni's the closest thing to a mother she's had. Not a real one, but a mother nonetheless. She's a hurt child."

"Hurt or not, she needs to learn discipline," said Andros between bites of something, presumably the porridge. "I mustn't be lenient any longer. The girl doesn't know her place."

My place is anywhere you aren't, Kleia thought, burrowing under the covers. *My place is in the sea, drowned with Ireni's ashes.*

"Grieving now, discipline later," said Laksa, in a tone that meant to any man no matter what his age, *Go away, little boy.*

Andros left without a word.

At noon, while Kleia and Laksa were busy mixing dough for bread, Zakarias entered the kitchen looking sooty, grumpy, and tired. He kissed Laksa on the cheek, set a small leather pouch on the table at Kleia's bruised elbow, and left again, yawning.

With trembling fingers, Kleia opened the pouch. Black, ash-fine grit peppered with grey. Bits of bone. Glints of melted gold.

Laksa drew the drawstring shut and folded Kleia's hands about the gruesome treasure.

"Keep her safe," she said.

Kleia blinked at the lump of bread dough till her vision cleared. Calm descended on her, as if last night's opium hadn't worn off.

"I'll do that," she said. "Andros will never find her."

***

Kleia worked late into the night by a single flame. She wouldn't have been able to sleep if she'd tried, and Laksa was so exhausted that there would be no chance of waking her.

The last of her unworked clay had nearly dried out, although she'd been diligent in keeping the effigy's legs covered with wet linen. She ground a small amount of the dried clay to powder, and then added water from the fountain.

With steady hands, she also added the contents of the pouch.

In the end, the mixture wasn't perfect. It was a bit too sticky, and the ash made it smell fearful and strange, nothing like earth or fungus. All the same,the sticky mixture held its shape when she broke it in two and then rolled each piece into an oblong.

At dawn, Laksa found Kleia fast asleep on the floor. On the table, she found an unshrouded figure made of clay. Its clear blue eyes caught the sunlight, prism-like.

They glittered as she noticed its shapely, slow-drying feet.

***

On the first night, Andros left her with two substantial bruises and a bloodied lip. In turn, Kleia left him with a chipped tooth and unsatisfied. She fled to the kitchen, where Laksa waited with pomegranate tea and an ample shoulder for her to cry on.

Her effigy was tucked safely away in a corner of the tiny bedroom.

On the second night, Andros left her with a third bruise and several of her braids shorn off roughly with a knife. In turn, Kleia kicked him hard in the ribs, snatched the knife when he dropped it, and sank it in his thigh.

Laksa locked her in the pantry and claimed to have seen her flee through the back door.

That night, surrounded by hanging herbs, cured meats, and baskets of fruit, Kleia dreamed that her feet were made of pale and perfect clay. She stared down at them in wonder.

And *walked.*

***

Kleia woke to the sound of Laksa's piercing wail.

Her first thought was that Andros had returned from his prowling of the city empty handed and considerably drunk. Kleia leapt to her feet, instantly aware in the fragrant darkness.

She heard footsteps drawing near the door, too light to be Laksa's.

When the key turned in the lock, she expected to see Andros standing there with bloodshot eyes, disheveled, bearing a knife. She squeezed her eyes shut against the piercing blade of light, praying to any god she could think of for her life to end quickly.

Instead, a pair of cool, smooth hands took her own.

"Daughter," said Ireni, whole again, and led Kleia into the kitchen. "Let me look at you."

She knelt and smoothed the sting of tears from the corners of Kleia's eyes. She touched the bruises on Kleia's arms, her expression cool and inscrutable.

She's perfect, Kleia thought. *Young again. Either she's a ghost, or I'm still dreaming.* She reached out with one trembling hand and touched Ireni's face. Her skin was warm, but her eyes were cold, so very cold as her lips formed a knowing smile.

"He's hurt you many times, hasn't he?"

Kleia swallowed.

"I tried to make you well, but you died."

"That's not what I asked," said Ireni.

"Yes," Kleia whispered, staring down at the pale, perfect fingers on her arm. No blood beneath the skin, no pulse in the wrist where it rested against Kleia's flesh. "But I didn't let him—"

Ireni pressed two fingers briefly to Kleia's lips, and then rose, taking Kleia's hand. She led her over to the battered old stool by the hearth and reached for what Laksa had left sitting there.

The knife was still streaked with Andros's blood.

"He'll be abed, no doubt, drunk out of his wits," said Ireni. She stuck the knife in her belt, which she must have borrowed from Laksa's quarters along with the tunic she wore. She bent and drew Kleia's hand up to her lips, eyes gleaming with mischief. "Shall we go to the market?"

Before, she would never have gone herself. Shopping was slaves' work.

"What for?" Kleia asked.

"You'll show me where you bought your clay," Ireni said. "We'll buy some with this," she added, fingering Kleia's gold neck plate. "You won't need it anymore."

Kleia's eyes filled again.

"Thank you, Mis—"

"*Mother*."

"Mother," Kleia whispered. "And then?"

Ireni smiled again and glanced down at the knife, scratching off a flake of Andros's blood. She ground it to a blackish powder between her thumb and forefinger, held it out for Kleia to see.

"We will work," she said. "But not to make him well."

Art by Eric Orchard

THE PAPER SWORD
ALEC AUSTIN

July 1864
Anhui, China

When Lin Jian Wu arrived at her cousin's outpost in Anhui, the sky to the northeast was on fire.

The word all along the Yangtze, from Wuhan to Anqing, had been that the Taiping capital was on its last legs. Jian hadn't believed it; Hong Xiu Quan (the self-proclaimed Brother of Jesus) and his followers had fought against the Qing Dynasty and its armies for almost as long as Jian had been alive. But now Nanjing had fallen, and as flames and smoke smeared the horizon a ruddy orange, Jian wondered if the collapse of the Taiping Heavenly Kingdom meant things would get any better for her family, or the other families she knew back in Hunan.

Somehow she doubted it.

The sentries outside the watermill her cousin Yang had occupied were only a few years older than Jian. They wore bamboo hats over their queues, clutched spear-like matchlocks, and wore Xiang army uniform shirts that were faded and stained with dirt. The smaller of the two was staring at the mist-shrouded terraces further up the valley, as if he expected a tiger to emerge from the fog.

"Who's there?" the larger sentry called as he noticed Jian approaching the mill.

"Sergeant Yang wrote home, asking for an exorcist," Jian replied, slinging her wooden sword case off her back. "So here I am."

At every step of Jian's journey, from Changsha to Wuhan to Anqing, people had frowned at her and asked if she wasn't too young to be an exorcist. Her father had cultivated a long, wispy beard and used the Taoist exemption from the tonsure decrees to grow his hair long and tie it in a topknot, but Jian had bound her hair in a queue and shaved the front of her head.

She could deal with people seeing her as young, so long as they saw her as a man.

The two sentries sagged with relief. "Thank heaven you've come," the bigger one said. "Sergeant Yang! Sergeant Yang! The exorcist is here!"

Yang Chao Sheng emerged from the watermill, already clasping his hands together in salutation. "Uncle Lin! How good of you—" He cut himself short, staring at Jian in perplexity.

"My father died before your letter reached us," Jian said. "So I came in his stead." As she spoke, she watched the confusion on her cousin's face turn to horror.

"Inside," Yang told her. "Now." Jian slung her sword over her shoulder and followed him in. Once they were inside far enough that the burble of the stream and the creaks of the millwheel would mask their words, Yang turned to Jian and demanded, in a low voice, "What are you *doing* here?"

"You said you needed an exorcist," Jian said. "I'm an exorcist."

"I asked for your father. I didn't ask my baby cousin to disguise herself as a man and trek across three war-torn provinces, carrying a sword that's useless against anything that's not already dead!"

"You don't think I can handle the job?"

Yang gave her a dead-eyed stare. "I don't think you could handle Taiping rebels, or bandits, or deserters."

"I know the Heaven and Earth Society passwords. The bandits I met on the way to Changsha gave me rice balls for the road."

Yang let out a hollow laugh. "That doesn't work on Taiping soldiers."

"And your guns and spears don't work on ghosts," Jian retorted. "At any rate, I'm here. Tell me about your problem."

Yang muttered something about Jian's Hakka mother, and how she'd birthed an impudent demon. Jian pretended not to hear. If Yang had unbent enough to beg her father for help, he wasn't about to refuse her assistance because her feet weren't bound.

"The village is full of hungry ghosts," Yang said at length. "Some of the villagers must have resisted a Taiping impressment party or something. Anyway, shortly after we got here, my men began hearing noises and seeing strange lights when they were on patrol. Little Chong saw an apparition with its mouth full of flames, and Big Zhang saw one with a neck like a needle and a belly large enough to hold a donkey. My men stopped going on patrol, and began making offerings of food when they thought I wasn't looking. Then Little Chong vanished."

"Vanished?"

"From his bed. The next morning, we found what was left of him spread across a terrace. The ghosts had stripped the flesh from his legs and arms, and feasted on his guts."

"That sounds more like a demon to me," Jian said.

Yang made a face. "Ghosts or demons, I need them gone. My men are jumping at shadows, and for all I know, there's a Taiping army corps camped above the village, ready to descend on us. Can you help?"

"I'll need payment," Jian said. "Compensation for my travel expenses. And an acknowledgement that we're the senior branch of the family."

Yang groaned. "That old argument?"

"It matters," Jian said. Precedence at family gatherings; not having Yang's sisters snub her in the street; even being able to charge more for exorcisms.

If Yang gave her branch of the family face, word would get around.

"Come on, Jian. Is that really necessary?"

Jian made a show of shifting her sword onto her back, and headed for the door.

"All right, all right," Yang said, intercepting her and bowing his head in supplication. "Whatever you want, you'll have. I swear it."

***

The first thing Jian wanted was rice wine, and lots of it.

"What are you going to do?" Yang grumbled as he gave her a pair of cups and two ceramic bottles he'd clearly been saving. "Invite the ghosts to a drinking party?"

"Not quite," Jian said. "I'll need also need a house where I can be alone. Unless you want to vacate the mill?"

"There's a storehouse a ways up the road," Yang said. "We were using it as a guard post, but now my men won't venture that far."

Jian smiled. "Perfect."

True to Yang's word, the escort he sent pointed out the storehouse, then scurried back to the watermill. Jian hummed a boatman's song under her breath as she trudged to the storehouse, took a bamboo mat out of her sword case, and spread it on the floor. Frowning with concentration, she arranged the wine bottles and the cups, and glanced outside. Was it late enough in the day? Probably not.

"Hei Sha, you old reprobate," she said to the air. "Come drink with me."

Nothing happened. Jian sighed, and settled in to wait. As the shadows lengthened and the sun slid behind the western mountains, she repeated herself, and poured two cups of wine.

When the wine reached the brim of the second cup, there was a swirl of shadows. They dispersed to reveal the minor deity Hei Sha, clad in the embroidered robes of a magistrate of the underworld, seated opposite Jian. His eyebrows were a thicket on his forehead, and an eerie purple light seemed to emanate from him, though that might just have been the ghostly flames bobbing by his shoulders.

True to form, he was already reaching for his wine cup.

"Your father," Hei Sha said, gulping down his rice wine, "never taunted me by inviting me to drink before nightfall." A thread of wine spilled from the corner of his mouth into his thick black beard, never to be seen again.

"My father is dead," Jian said. "As you are well aware."

Hei Sha waved a meaty hand in dismissal. "*Some* gods," he said, "might have hurried through their caseload and rushed off to get drunk at the moment of the invitation. But not I! Even when prompted by my best friend's daughter, my duty came first." He frowned at Jian, as if noticing her for the first time. "What on earth have you done with your hair?"

"I disguised myself for travel," Jian said. To forestall a lecture, she asked, "How goes your work?"

Hei Sha heaved a sigh. "Oh, it's awful. Nothing but trouble and complaints since Nanjing fell. All the newly dead feel they know better than the celestial bureaucracy, but the Taiping are the worst. Most of them complain that they were baptized and so they shouldn't be subject to the authority of King Yan Luo and the Ten Courts of Hell."

"So what do you do with them?"

"Oh, we process them and send them to the Eighteen Hells like everyone else. But you've never heard such wailing and moaning in all your days." Hei Sha paused to drain his cup, regarding Jian with a shrewd expression. "So. You need your uncle Hei Sha's help, do you?"

"No point in having connections if you don't use them."

"No doubt that boy hiding in the mill feels the same," Hei Sha said, scratching his armpit. "Oh, yes – I know all about his ghost troubles. I get reports, you know. Very meticulous reports, stamped by dozens of notaries and junior officials, telling me that so many ghosts are loose in the mortal world, and so many of them are misbehaving and likely to turn into demons. But can I do anything about it? Of course not. I just stamp the reports with my seal and send my recommendations up the chain, whereupon I get told that the Ten Courts are well over budget, and that we're just going to have to tighten our belts and go without until after the Hungry Ghost Festival." He snorted. "As if we don't all know the Qinguang King diverted the exorcism fund to pay for his new palace."

"I recall there was a time when you would go after misbehaving ghosts yourself," Jian said, filling Hei Sha's cup.

"Oh, certainly," Hei Sha said. "Why, the stories I could tell you about what your father and I got up to when he was young..."

Jian continued plying Hei Sha with wine, dutifully listening to the same stories about fox demons and hungry ghosts she'd been hearing since she got big enough to pour wine for her father and his patron god. She could have recited several of them word for word.

But of course, hearing new stories wasn't the point.

Once the first wine bottle was empty and Hei Sha was well into his cups, Jian directed the conversation to her father's sword. "Yes!" Hei Sha boomed. "The famous paper sword! Let us see it one more time!"

He leaned forward as Jian opened the sword case, revealing a weapon whose blade had been wrought by carefully pasting together hundreds of prayer strips. A wooden rod gave the layered strips of paper structural support, and in several places, characters painted on lower strips could be read through the intervening layers.

"These are your additions?" Hei Sha said, squinting at the most recent set of charms, which were written in a different hand than the layers beneath them.

"Yes, uncle."

Hei Sha grunted. It made him sound like the boatmen who'd ferried Jian to Anqing.

"Not bad," he said, lifting the sword from the case and inspecting it up close. "You'll need to shave down the edges soon. It's no good if you let your weapon get ratty."

"Perhaps you could show me how it should be used?" Jian suggested.

"Oh, no," Hei Sha demurred. "No. I just couldn't. There are rules about that sort of thing."

***

Half a bottle later, Hei Sha and Jian were headed for the center of the village, with Hei Sha brandishing the remaining bottle of rice wine like a weapon.

"Come, demons!" Hei Sha bellowed in a voice that echoed from the hills and mountains. "Face me, and answer to the judgment of Heaven!" He paused to burp.

"Aren't your judgments the judgments of Hell now, uncle?" Jian asked. "Ever since you became deputy sub-minister of the First Court, I mean."

"Semantics," Hei Sha said. "King Yan Luo was appointed by the Jade Emperor, so the judgments of Hell *are* the judgments of Heaven. Besides. 'The judgment of Heaven' sounds better."

"I think your yelling is scaring the ghosts away," Jian said as they approached a cluster of family compounds. Several compound walls had been battered down, and others were scorched and blackened.

"Never fear," Hei Sha said, slapping Jian on the shoulder. "One whiff of your tender flesh, and they'll come running."

"Is that supposed to reassure me?"

"Didn't you father tell you?" Hei Sha said, swaying slightly as he turned to face Jian. "You have to lure ghosts or demons out of hiding before you can banish them."

"So I'm demon bait?"

Hei Sha grinned at her, his teeth white as death amidst the thicket of his whiskers. "Exorcists always are."

Jian shuddered at the thought, and then again as the air grew cooler. A thin mist clung to the ground, and as a cloud covered the moon, threads of vapor began knitting themselves into distorted silhouettes.

One by one, the hungry ghosts stitched themselves into being — a burly farmer without hands or a lower jaw; a woman whose neck was as narrow as a bamboo reed, and whose distended belly could've held a wheelbarrow; a boy whose lips and cheeks had been burnt away and whose mouth was full of fire. Soon there were a dozen apparitions in a circle around Jian and Hei Sha, their bodies warped and marked with gaping wounds.

"These are just scavengers," Hei Sha declared as the ghosts wailed and moaned, the sounds seeming to come from the far side of an unimaginable gulf. "Seeking to steal a bite before the real predator arrives."

Drunken gods, Jian reflected as she brandished her father's sword, were not very good at calming your nerves.

The boy with the flaming mouth lunged at Jian, but a stroke from the paper sword bisected him. As he dissolved into mist, Jian formed a series of mudras with her free hand, making the other ghosts retreat.

The demon was a whisper on the breeze, a cormorant diving to pluck a fish from the water.

It might have been a tiger once, before it gorged itself on human flesh. It might have been a man. Now it was a ball of claws and fangs and bottomless hunger, and it hit Hei Sha like a thunderbolt, bowling the god over and pinning him to the ground.

Jian slashed the demon's back, parting its flesh and striping its fur with blood. The demon howled and turned on her, and Jian leapt aside, the demon's talons passing a hand-span from her nose.

Backpedaling desperately, Jian deflected the demon's attacks, forming mudras with her free hand and chanting incantations. She invoked the Emperors of the five directions, the Dragon Kings of the oceans and great rivers, and (without thinking about it) Hei Sha himself.

Her prayers had as much effect as prayers usually had on a tiger.

"Hei Sha!" Jian shouted. The drunken god had staggered to his feet, but was facing the wrong direction. "Over here, you lummox!"

Hei Sha turned, bellowed, and charged.

As Hei Sha smashed into the demon, Jian stumbled out of their way, inadvertently dispersing one of the hovering ghosts with her sword. There had to be something more she could do; some god she could invoke, some series of mudras she'd forgotten.

As Jian cast about for a way to banish the demon, she latched onto the wine bottle Hei Sha had dropped. By chance or divine intervention, it was intact, and she scooped it up, trying to think.

Demons and hungry ghosts were creatures of appetite. They *had* to eat and devour. It was their nature.

Hoping she was right, Jian hefted the bottle and flung it at the demon.

The demon, occupied with Hei Sha, failed to break off and seize the bottle in its jaws. Instead, Hei Sha snatched the bottle from the air and smashed it over the demon's head. As the demon recoiled, Hei Sha exhaled a gout of blue flame, setting the wine alight.

The demon smashed Hei Sha to the ground, and charged full-tilt into a compound wall. As it yowled and writhed, Jian limped over and laid into it. One stroke carved a gash in the demon's neck. A dozen more severed its head completely.

By then, the flames had spread to her sword, but Jian couldn't bring herself to care.

The rest of the hungry ghosts had made themselves scarce, so Jian dragged Hei Sha over to a wall and propped him upright. "That," the god wheezed, "was the least fun I have had in quite a long time."

"Oh?" Jian said, keeping an eye out for the other ghosts.

Hei Sha's laugh was low and pained. "Someday I'll tell you what actually happened when we fought that fox demon."

"That should be interesting," Jian said. "You weren't drunk then too, were you?"

"I try to be drunk whenever I hunt demons."

"Why am I not surprised?"

The two of them sat and watched the moon come out from behind the clouds. At length, Hei Sha said, "I once offered to replace your father's heart with one from the underworld. A scholar's heart, that would allow him to pass the most difficult of the Imperial Examinations. A hero's heart, to raise a rebellion or rise high in the service of the Qing. Or a poet's heart, that would make his verses and his name immortal."

"And he refused you?"

"He laughed. And we never spoke of it again."

"My father knew what the reed knows," Jian said. "Those who rise to great heights have farther to fall, and the strongest tree will break if it fights the storm."

"You sound like Zhuang Zi."

Jian gestured at the northeast, where Nanjing still burned. "No. I just have eyes."

"Fair enough," Hei Sha said. "What are you going to do about your sword?"

Jian glanced at the charred remains of the weapon her father had crafted. "Strip off the burnt prayer strips and layer on new ones. It's the ghost of a sword now; that should make it even stronger."

Hei Sha snorted. "Clearly I should have offered *you* the poet's heart."

"Clearly."

***

It took a few days of painstaking calligraphy for Jian to restore her sword, and another night to exorcise the remaining ghosts. They'd tasted human flesh, Jian reasoned, and so were well on the road to becoming demons themselves.

"So," Jian asked Yang the next day, as he entered the watermill after a patrol. "Did you find a Taiping army up in the hills?"

"Very funny," Yang said. "Don't you have somewhere to be?"

"I'll happily go as soon as you write me a promissory note," Jian said. "And any letters for your family, of course."

Yang grumbled, and muttered, and said nasty things about her ancestry, but come morning, Jian had three letters and a promissory note tucked away in her sword case.

"So," she said to Yang as they stood just outside the watermill. "I'm off to Hunan, and you're off to a glorious military career."

"Hardly," said Yang. "With the Taiping crushed, General Zeng will have to disband the Xiang army."

"You want him to disband it?"

"Better that than having the Qing see us as a threat."

"True," Jian said, glancing northeast. "We know what they do to threats."

Yang opened his mouth and shut it several times, as if struggling with himself. "When you first arrived," he said, "you said you knew the Heaven and Earth Society's passwords. That was a joke. Right?"

"Fan Qing Fu Ming," Jian said, smiling. It was the Heaven and Earth Society oath: Overthrow Qing, and restore the Ming. "Those rice balls were delicious. See you later, cousin."

Yang, stunned to silence, watched her go.

As Yang and the watermill vanished behind a stand of trees, it occurred to Jian that even now, her cousin might not have grasped that she had other letters concealed in her sword case.

Art by Kaley Bales

GENIUS JONES AND THE ROLLING RIFLE
MICHAEL EZELL

1862
Utah territory, USA

Sweat ran into Ramses' eyes, the blistering heat inside the machine threatening to melt his very damn bones. The cotton batting stuffed in his ears turned the roar of the steam engine and the thrashing iron clatter of the treaded locomotion belts into a bone-thrumming bass.

In his leather battle coat, skullcap, gloves, and goggles, Ramses looked like a demon from a metal Hell instead of a skinny kid of barely sixteen years.

Dressed in his own battle coat and goggles, Professor Merrill yanked on the steering levers, slewing the beast around to the left. Soot from the firebox dotted his long white beard.

Two hundred paces off the port side, the old covered wagon came into sight through the gunnery slit. Ramses cocked the reciprocating four-pounder. He figured for their forward speed and the slight uphill shot and yanked the firing lanyard.

Even the earplugs didn't quiet the flat *bang* of the cannon. The reciprocating mount Professor Merrill designed functioned perfectly, dampening the recoil and automatically opening the breech. The empty brass case *pinged* out– In the same instant, Ramses slammed a new shell home and locked the breech.

By the time the first shell split the old wagon and set it on fire, the second shell was on its way. Professor Merrill had trained Ramses in the fine art of downing birds with a shotgun, and that in turn made Ramses one hell of a gunner. The follow-up shot hit no more than a foot left of the first shot, turning the wagon into charred splinters.

Ramses gave out a shrill whistle, and their beast groaned to a stop. Professor Merrill shut it down and yanked open the locks on the portside door.

Both he and Ramses gasped when they stepped into the crisp Utah winter air. Neither said anything; they just ripped off their leather caps and stood there. Steam rose in wisps and tendrils from their overheated scalps and the open fronts of their battle coats. The Professor's housekeeper, Wilhelmina, made the coats herself from stout leather, with lamb's wool liners. They protected the men inside the machine from steam leaks and sparks, but they also made it hotter than the devil's asshole, as the Professor liked to say.

Ramses turned a mechanic's eye on the Merrill Land Yacht. (*Had to be a better name*, he thought.) She was a beauty. Shaped like the front portion of a steam train's engine, with Professor Merrill's treaded belts where a normal train would have wheels.

107

"Still too round," Professor Merrill said. His brows knit together in a tumble of white.

Ramses grinned at him. "You got four weeks, Professor. You still want to play with how it looks? It'll be the best machine there. We need to get this beast on a train to the Union."

"It's not how it *looks*, Ramses. We worry about the outer design for the same reason we design rapid-fire guns. We look to the future, and we see that our enemy isn't riding in covered wagons. He's got the same weapons, the same capabilities. How would we stop a machine like ours? How would we gain an advantage?"

Ramses' sharp eyes took in the burning wagon, then the land yacht. "You mean what if they could shoot back?"

"Your mind is quick, my friend. Look forward; see what they'd bring against us. What would you be afraid to face if you were in our land yacht fighting a battle?"

For a moment, Ramses' mind went away from the dusky red stone and sand of the Utah desert. On a future battlefield, he squinted along the four-pounder's sights, looking at something he'd be afraid to face...

"Slopes," Ramses said.

"Slopes?"

"If I had to shoot at someone in one of these contraptions, I'd be worried if their sides sloped up, worried my shells might skip off instead of punching through."

Professor Merrill's hoarse laugh echoed off the rocks around them, making Ramses feel warm inside. He loved it when the old man laughed. It took away some of the hard lines the years had scribed into his face.

"Genius. That's what you are, Ramses Jones." The Professor slung an arm around Ramses' shoulders and pulled him close, like a father proud of his son. "We should get started on those sloping sides tomorrow."

Ramses laughed and shook his head. "There's no time for that. It works. That has to be good enough for now. All the stories in the paper say those men back East can't get theirs to go through soft dirt because they're using wheels. All we have to do is show up, and that fat Union contract is yours."

Professor Merrill gave him a stern look. "Ours, Ramses. That contract is ours."

That struck Ramses silent. He had never given thought to ownership of anything. Not in this world. A world where certain folks fought for the notion that a human being could be bought and owned. As long as that person had Ramses' skin color, anyhow.

They stood there in the quiet, listening to the *tick-tick-tick* of cooling metal, interrupted only by the wind and the occasional birdsong.

One day, men would ride across places like this in machines spawned from the Land Yacht. Their leader would rule the world. Ramses only hoped the man led the Colonial Union and not the Confederate Alliance.

"I suppose we should head back, Ramses. Don't want to be late for supper again. Miss Wilhelmina will have our hides." The Professor led the way back inside the hot belly of the machine.

"You're the captain of the yacht; your hide might get skinned. Me? I'll get your share of the cornbread," Ramses said.

Professor Merrill laughed as he stoked the firebox and checked the pressure gauges. "If Mina's cornbread is at stake, we'd best stoke her up for top speed."

For the ride back, Ramses always got to drive. He engaged the gears and slung their nose around toward home. You couldn't have knocked the smile off his face with a hammer and chisel.

***

The beast growled its way inside the barn and tread belts chewed up the packed earth floor. Wilhelmina stood on the porch, keeping a safe distance until the machine shut down. Professor Merrill was very strict about safety regulations.

Ramses eased the roaring metal dragon alongside the small proof-of-concept version of the land yacht. Layered with the dust that eventually claims all forgotten things, the little machine was a toy compared to the Professor's latest creation.

After locking the barn, Ramses and the Professor trudged to the water pump to wash the grimy soot from their faces. Wilhelmina cast a critical eye over both of them. The stout German woman ran a clean house, no exceptions.

"More behind your right ear," she said.

Ramses hurried to wash off the offending dirt. Professor Merrill chuckled.

"I don't know vhat you are loffing about," Wilhelmina said. She took a small towel from the pocket of her apron and dusted black soot from the Professor's long white beard. Properly chastened, he stood next to Ramses for final inspection.

Wilhelmina sighed. "I supposed zat will do. Time to eat, ja?"

She turned away like a commanding general in a frilly calico uniform and they followed her inside. The Professor allowed her to keep his house as she would, which meant lots of lace and fine curtains, old leather furniture brought from Germany, and frosted glass covers for the gas lamps that provided the mellow glow in the house.

They all sat together for their meal. This made for a lot of talk among the people in town. The Utah Territory was neutral in the minor dispute between the Confederate Alliance and the Colonial Union. However, plenty of the locals still thought Ramses had no business in the same house as white folks, much less sitting at the table with a white woman.

But Professor Merrill saw Ramses only as a gifted apprentice, a talented kid who could do figures in his head and see imaginary gears and doodads that let him piece together his own small toys as a youngster. A *future engineer*, the Professor called him.

Ever the diligent Lutheran, Wilhelmina led them in a prayer of thanks. Then they tucked into the ham, beans, and cornbread Wilhelmina spent the day making. Ramses hadn't realized how hollow his stomach was until he took that first bite. Twice, he caught Wilhelmina's reproachful eye and had to slow his flying fork to a more respectable pace. At sixteen, he was already over six feet tall and his growing body seemed to have more control over his fork than his brain did.

He shoveled the last of the ham into his mouth and mumbled around it. "May I be excused?"

Wilhelmina gave him a good-natured swat with her napkin. "Not with food in your mouth, young man."

Professor Merrill looked at Ramses from under those bushy eyebrows. "Don't stay up all night tinkering with those rifles. We have important work tomorrow and you need your rest."

Ramses smiled on the way out. "You saved me the trouble of making that same speech to you."

Wilhelmina's laughter followed Ramses out the kitchen door and into the starry Utah night.

*** *

The steam cart bounced and jounced over the rutted road to town, rattling his entire skeleton. Despite the Professor's warning, Ramses stayed up most of the night tinkering at the workbench. He'd spent weeks working on a design for mounted repeating rifles so the land yacht's crew could repel troops on foot. The guns were the first official project Ramses designed and built himself, and the proud look on the Professor's face had been worth every sleepless night.

Ramses reached the edge of town and throttled down. He coasted to a stop in front of the General Store and shut down the cart. The Professor's machines were a common enough sight that everyone just went about their business. The townie men all wore sharp gray and black suits set off by felt hats of various types. The ladies reminded Ramses of colorful birds in their fancy dresses made from Chinese silk. Most were decent, hardworking folk, just trying to make their frontier town look like one of the sophisticated cities back East.

"Well, well, if it ain't Genius Jones."

On the other hand, some weren't decent at all.

Ramses ground his teeth. He knew the voice. Once a hired hand at Professor Merrill's place, Levi Robertson was two years older than Ramses. Levi overheard Professor Merrill call Ramses a genius, and ever since, Levi called him "Genius Jones" in the most sarcastic tone he could muster.

A bit too slow on the uptake and more than a little lazy, Levi had been fired after just one month. He'd come back to town and spread vile rumors that Wilhelmina entertained both Ramses and the Professor in the bedroom. Ramses often had violent visions of his own bloody knuckles and Levi with broken teeth and shredded lips.

Ramses stared at Levi and the two giggling teenage boys with him. Levi still wore that same dented bowler hat, along with a vest that had once been fancy, but now looked threadbare and sloppy. All three of them had drying mud on their pants up to their knees. Ramses figured they'd been mucking out stables to make some liquor money. Given the wobbling stances, they'd obviously spent their money well, and he wasn't anxious to have a confrontation with them.

He turned his back and climbed the two steps onto the porch of John McDonough's General Store.

An empty bottle smashed against the steps behind him. He maintained control and didn't turn to face the snickering idiots. He stepped into the store and found John McDonough waiting behind the counter. "Ramses, how the hell are ya?"

The wiry little man had a thick brogue and a red face to go with his hair. He prided himself on his ability to read, and had stacks and stacks of old books and newspapers lining the back wall of the store. McDonough held up the front page of one of those newspapers.

It featured a picture of a steam-powered contraption that looked to be about twice the size of Professor Merrill's. The thing had one giant cannon, and the gun crew stood in the open atop the metal beast.

The headline read: *Goodell Brothers Reveal Mobile Gunnery Platform.*

"Looks like the boys back East are turnin' up the heat on our old Professor," McDonough said.

Ramses scoffed at the picture. "That thing's way too big and heavy to drive through soft dirt or mud. The Professor's land yacht will put it to shame."

"Is he still callin' that contraption a land yacht? You fellas have got to come up with a better name."

"I know, I know. We're working on it."

Truth be told, only Ramses was working on it. The clunky name didn't seem to bother the Professor. He had bigger things on his mind. Landing a contract to build mobile gunnery platforms for the Colonial Union would mean a life of wealth and ease for the lucky winner.

"Did our supplies come in?" Ramses said.

"Oh, sure! Wait here a tic."

McDonough trotted into the back room, leaving Ramses to stare at the bright penny candies in countertop jars. The green stick candies were nice, but the brilliant red balls flavored with cinnamon were Ramses' favorite. Just one would last the whole ride back to the house, that glorious sweet fire burning his mouth and creeping into his nose, making his eyes water.

McDonough came back with a wheelbarrow containing two fifty-pound tins of gunpowder, and three long rods made of a unique metal the Professor ordered from the monstrous foundries of France. They would turn this hardened metal on the lathe to create special bullets for the rifles Ramses designed. If the cannon malfunctioned, the Professor figured bullets that penetrated metal would give the land yacht's crew a fighting chance against another machine.

"You fellas think you really have a shot at this contract?" McDonough said.

Ramses grinned. "Those men back East have never seen anything like what we're bringing. The Professor will get the contract for sure."

After loading the cart and saying his goodbyes, Ramses stoked the fire-box and turned the blatting steam wagon in a big circle to head home. He popped the candy he'd bought with his own penny into his mouth and enjoyed the cinnamon burn.

Just as he cleared the end of Main Street and the buildings became sparse, a dry horse turd hit him in the chest.

He heard the braying laugh before he spotted the stupid bowler hat. Levi Robertson and his two drunken companions giggled. They all started winging horse turds at Ramses and the steam cart. Ramses accelerated to get out of their throwing range. Which, given the alcohol, wasn't all that far.

"See ya 'round, Genius!" Levi called after him.

A left jab, a hard right uppercut. Levi's ignorant grin gone, replaced by bruises and a swollen eye. Ramses settled for the vision and drove on. Even if he did manage to take the three of them, the local sheriff would just lock him up, or worse, for assaulting white men.

So Ramses drove. Drove to something more important than three drunken assholes and his personal pride. He was going to help Professor Merrill change the world for the better.

***

The cloud of dust gave Ramses a certain gnawing cold in his gut. He didn't want to think it meant anything bad, but he somehow knew it did. A quarter-mile from the Professor's property, Ramses pulled off the road and parked the steam cart in the brush. He stood still and listened. The chilled evening air carried a familiar sound to him. Far off, from the direction of the house.

The land yacht's engine bellowed like an old bull.

Professor Merrill had planned to break her down completely for inspection before they put her on the train to the Union. By this time, he should have had most of the engine taken apart.

So why the hell was he spinning the machine around and around on its axis in the front yard? This gave birth to the dust cloud Ramses saw from the road.

Careful to keep his breath from sending up a white plume to mark his position, Ramses crept through a small cluster of pine trees. Some men stood by the house, watching the land yacht.

The machine suddenly stopped and a side hatched popped open. Professor Merrill stepped out, wearing his normal clothes. This made Ramses' heart sink. A stickler for safety protocols, the Professor never – *never* operated the land yacht without his leather battle coat and goggles in place.

A second man exited the hatch. A slight man, stoop-shouldered, with round glasses and a wide forehead covered in pale, waxy skin. He looked like he belonged in a sanitarium, instead of out here on the frontier.

Someone with a Southern drawl called out from the porch, "Well, Mister Wilkins, think you can handle that beast?"

The scant hope that this could be some impromptu demonstration fled when Ramses saw Trent LaTrelle. As always, LaTrelle wore a dandy's suit. Tall, broad-shouldered, with a smile that made even the most gentile ladies swoon, LaTrelle belonged on the cover of a dime novel.

At the moment, quite unlike a dime-novel hero, he held a pistol in Wilhelmina's ribs.

The stooped man named Wilkins gave LaTrelle the yellow smile of a heavy smoker. He had a high, reedy voice.

"I can handle it. The controls are simple enough, and the engine is basic. He has spare propulsion tracks in the barn, and I know how to change them out."

It was a small community out here on the Utah frontier. Everyone knew Professor Merrill built a machine to enter the contest sponsored by the Colonial Union.

LaTrelle could smell money the way a hound could smell a jackrabbit. He'd offered to finance Professor Merrill's venture and become a partner, but the Professor had refused.

The smile LaTrelle wore had nothing to do with charming the ladies. "Professor, I wish you had considered my generous offer of partnership. You have a gift, sir. A gift I wanted to help you share with the world. And it will be shared, you know."

"What's that supposed to mean?" Professor Merrill said.

"Oh, come now, Professor. You see things that others can't, in that big ol' brain of yours. Can't you see where this will go? The burning towns here in our land, burning villages back where Wilhelmina's people come from... Those contraptions of yours will roll right over the whole world."

"Not necessarily. The threat of them will be enough for most conflicts. Once people see them used," the Professor said.

That creepy little Wilkins inspected the land yacht's mounted four-pounders. "Speaking of using them, we'll need a hell of a gunner. There's a team from Connecticut that has a brace of eighteen-pounders mounted on their platform."

LaTrelle said, "Oh, I have that covered."

He snapped his fingers and a man stepped away from a group of armed thugs. Ramses recognized him right away. Billy Red Deer, a rabble-rouser and topnotch rifleman who worked as a mercenary for anyone who paid in gold.

Professor Merrill clenched his fists. He'd taught Ramses to box and Ramses had no doubt the Professor could trounce LaTrelle. Unfortunately, LaTrelle had guns to back him up.

"That Union contract is mine, LaTrelle. You won't be able to tell them how these things are built," the Professor said.

LaTrelle laughed at him. "That contract is pocket change, old man. We're going to win those trials with your ingenious machine. We'll take the Union's gold, then sell the design to the Confederates for twice as much. They'll have your machine's weaknesses in mind when they design their own."

"Why the hell would you do that?" Professor Merrill said.

"Money, you idiot. You know, Professor, for a genius, you can really be dense at times."

Wilhelmina turned to look LaTrelle in the eye, as if he didn't have a gun against her ribs.

"You are a foul man. You will one day pay for this evil."

"Is that right, missy? Well, it won't be today."

LaTrelle cocked his pistol–

Professor Merrill held up placating hands. "LaTrelle, please. You want to be partners? Fine. We'll split everything fifty-fifty. Just let her go."

The smile slipped from LaTrelle's face easy, like it was never meant to be there. "Too late, my friend. I'm afraid it'll have to be full ownership."

He swung the pistol away from Wilhelmina and shot Professor Merrill in the chest.

Rage exploded in Ramses' heart, and just as quickly the impotence of that rage settled in on him. There was nothing he could do against all those armed men. Except die. Which is what Wilhelmina chose.

She snatched a paring knife from her apron and went for LaTrelle. She had a clear shot at his neck–

But she fell at the *crack* of a pistol from the yard.

All eyes turned to Billy Red-Deer, his revolver still smoking in his hand. The other thugs burst out laughing and gave Billy a little cheer. Steam rose from both bodies in the cruel winter air.

Bitter tears coursed down Ramses' face as he cursed himself for a coward and crouched in the snow.

The reedy voice of Wilkins drifted on the wind. "What about the little colored boy?"

LaTrelle straightened his hat and stepped over Wilhelmina's body. "He doesn't matter. Nobody would listen to him, even if he knew who did this. He'll have to go find somebody who needs their cotton picked." The rabble he brought with him laughed at LaTrelle's joke, and he started issuing orders. His thugs loaded spare parts into two horse-drawn wagons and Wilkins fired up the land yacht. Before the bodies of the only two people Ramses had in this world were even cool, LaTrelle and his men were gone.

A burning sensation in his mouth made Ramses remember the cinnamon candy. He spit the red ball into the snow where it sat like a gob of congealed blood.

***

After he gave his folks (as he had come to think of them) a proper burial, Ramses sat on the front porch of Professor Merrill's house for a very long time, wrapped in three blankets against the bitter cold. The moon's muted silver light made the distant Wasatch Mountains look like the broken spine of some ancient beast that succumbed to the barren Utah desert.

Even Ramses' gifted brain couldn't come up with a way for a young black kid to keep this property, to keep the Professor's dreams alive. Townsfolk like John McDonough were good people, but they wouldn't go up against a private army. If LaTrelle claimed ownership of the land yacht, they'd silently go along.

And how could he even begin to avenge the Professor and Wilhelmina's deaths? LaTrelle had big guns and mercenaries, and Ramses had a .410 gauge shotgun he used for rabbits. Best to just pack up and move on, maybe try to make his way east to the Union. He might yet wind up working in a field out there, but at least it would be his choice and he'd get paid to do it.

He had pretty much made up his mind to leave, when just at dawn, a strange thing happened. A mule deer stepped out of the scrub on the east side of the house and stood there in the gray light, its breath steaming out of dark nostrils, wide ears twisting this way and that, alert for predators.

Suddenly, Ramses was nine years old again, shivering around a campfire with a group of runaway slaves.

Dark eyes shined in the firelight, always moving, always on guard. They shared out pieces of deer jerky one of the older men took from a smokehouse in the middle of the night.

Dogs barked in the inky darkness and they all scattered, leaving Ramses to run through the night alone. He ran and ran, until he fell in a ditch, exhausted.

He woke to see a white man with a bushy beard staring down at him. Ramses was captured!

But no, the man simply said, "My name is Professor Merrill and I'm headed west. You need a ride, son?"

A sob stirred Ramses from his memories. It took a moment to realize that it was his own lonely cry he heard. He leapt to his feet and shed the blankets like a chrysalis that had incubated his grief and rage, changing them into another beautiful, wonderful, deadly creature. Determination.

He ran to the barn, yanked open the big doors, and stalked inside to light the gas lamps.

The rough canvas tarps felt good in his hands as he pulled them away, revealing the small-scale model of the land yacht. Low-slung, it only accommodated one man lying prone on a forward-facing pilot's couch. It was tiny compared to the bigger machine, but it ran faster than a lizard on a hot rock.

Ramses had grown nearly a foot since he last piloted this thing; it would be a tight fit. And since it was only designed to prove the concept of the tread belts, it had no cannons.

He ran to the workbench and shoved aside papers, hoping LaTrelle's men missed them— Yes! The special rifles Ramses had designed for the land yacht. Ignored because they weren't cannons, or because they probably just looked like blocks of metal to those idiots. Still, even with the new bullets he designed, it would be a hell of a long row to hoe for this little machine to go up against the full-size land yacht.

What about the little colored boy? The reedy voice made Ramses' skin crawl even in memory. This was more than revenge for the Professor and Wilhelmina. If these men succeeded, the Confederate Alliance would have weapons to spread slavery to every corner of the country.

Ramses set about designing a mount for the twin repeating rifles that would arm his machine.

***

With just under an hour left before the midnight express pulled out, Ramses watched the Chinese men load his new machine into a boxcar. He'd waited until night because no one would be around to question his lies about Professor Merrill sending him ahead with the machine. Since Ramses never raised the alarm about the killings, as far as the stationmaster knew Professor Merrill was alive and kicking.

Paper money and a bit of silver eased any other misgivings. With a guilty heart, Ramses had taken the stash of money from the floorboards of the house. He knew Professor Merrill would have approved, but he still felt like a scavenger.

It had been a long week, building like a dervish, often waking up on the floor of the barn, a spanner or some other bit of oily metal in his hand, not knowing what time or even what day it was. It had all been worth it. He hadn't built a machine to win the trials; he had designed a machine with only one purpose. To kill the land yacht.

And then he'd deal with LaTrelle.

The engineer made it known that Ramses was free to ride in the boxcar with the machine, but not in the passenger car. That suited Ramses right down to his heels. He still had a lot of tinkering to do with the repeating rifles, and the four days of travel would be put to good use.

Once the machine was loaded in the boxcar, Ramses gave each of the Chinese men a silver coin, to their surprise. The engine huffed and chuffed, building pressure to pull out of town. With moments left, Ramses ran to his wagon to grab his food and water for the trip–

He saw Levi Robertson wobbling back and forth, trying his best to piss on the wagon, but managing to get more on his own boots than anything else. Bright light and rough laughter spilled out the back door of the nearby saloon, but Levi had come out alone.

Ramses strolled over, nice and calm. Levi snickered quietly, too drunk to realize he wasn't invisible.

"Howdy, Levi."

Levi spun around and Ramses had to dodge the stream. This made Levi giggle even more. "Hey, boy, don't go gettin' your dirty boots all over my piss."

This struck Levi funny. He gave out a yelping laugh and wiped tears from his eyes. Finally, he stopped and stared at Ramses in silence. Something about the way the younger kid looked at him seemed to sober Levi up just a bit. Not enough to grow any sense, though.

"Where's that ole massuh of yours, son? He givin' it to that fat-ass German whore?"

"I'm leaving town tonight, Levi."

"Well, good! Get yer sorry ass gone, then."

Bells rang, signaling the train's eminent departure. Up the line, the caboose man strode down the row of freight cars, slamming the heavy doors closed.

Ramses smiled and took a quick look around.

"What're you lookin' for, Genius?" Levi said.

"Witnesses."

"Huh?"

Professor Merrill had a passion for the "gentleman's sport" of boxing. He'd taught Ramses all about the kinetic chain that started with your feet rooted in the ground, drove up through legs and hips, torso, shoulder, elbow—fist.

The straight right hand caught Levi square on the jaw. Ramses may have been a middleweight, but he drove all six feet of his frame into that punch. Levi landed underneath the wagon, looking for all the world like one more drunk sleeping it off behind the saloon.

His hand would ache all the way to New York, but Ramses never paid a fairer price for anything in his life. He trotted to his boxcar and climbed in alongside his machine, anxious to pay off one more outstanding debt. After that, he didn't care what they did to him.

***

The President fidgeted in his seat on the observation dais. These darn folding chairs just weren't meant for his lanky frame. He stifled a yawn as a distant boom and crack signaled the demise of yet another target barge just offshore from Fort Hamilton. The proving grounds had been built specially for these trials, so the big guns could fire out to sea.

Red, white, and blue bunting tied to the rails blew in the breeze and obscured his view for a moment, but he had seen enough in the last hour. He wanted to close his eyes and take a nap, leaving the rest of this disappointing day to the two dozen military and civilian functionaries crowded onto the dais.

At the moment, four of the gigantic "mobile" gun platforms were having a gunnery contest with their eighteen and twenty-pounders. Steam and black smoke billowed furiously above the four combatants. Basically different variations of massive iron frames, they had all sunk to the axels immediately in the soft terrain testing area. Now they bellowed their fury at the poor barges moored one hundred yards offshore.

If this was the best the Colonial Union could do, then any silly notions of uniting this nation were doomed.

"President Lincoln, sir?"

Captain Lee, the young commander of the fort. The President liked him as much as the next military type.

"Captain Lee?"

"I think you'll want to see this, sir."

There was an oily character standing beside Lee, the squared-jawed, straight-toothed type who should be on the front of one of Mary's dime novels. He extended a hand.

"Travis LaTrelle, Mister President. Owner of what we call the 'LaTrelle Land Yacht.'"

The slick man waved his hat and a new machine roared onto the proving grounds. Looking like the front half of a steam engine with some kind of long flat belts where the others had wheels, it zipped over the soft ground like a water bug over a still pond.

It stopped and rotated on its axis, lining up a broadside with the target barges. The land yacht fire one, two, *three* shots in succession, splintering its target despite clearly having smaller guns on board. The crews on the large platforms could only stop and gawk.

The land yacht then executed a smart turn and roared into the obstacle course. It rolled over rows of logs, skidded around block walls put up as barriers, and used those strange flat belts to splash right through manmade bogs.

Smoke billowed out of its stack, and the deadly machine roared back along the course again. Several people in the observation stand began to applaud.

LaTrelle smiled at President Lincoln. "Sir, we would love to sell this machine to the Colonial Union. We'll even give you a discount."

President Lincoln shook the offered hand. If push came to shove, Union armies could roll right through Atlanta and down to the sea in machines like that.

Motion caught his eye–

At first, the President thought a black bull had somehow gotten loose on the proving grounds. Then he realized it was longer than a bull, but closer to the ground.

The sound of the engine reached him, and he saw smaller versions of the belted tracks from LaTrelle's land yacht.

A murmur ran through the crowd as the smaller machine roared straight at the larger land yacht. They all heard the *crack-crack* of what sounded like two large rifles. The *whang* of an impact on iron– two holes appeared in the side of the land yacht. The smaller machine roared past and ducked behind one of the block walls on the obstacle course.

"That little black bastard," LaTrelle muttered.

President Lincoln arched an eyebrow at the dapper salesman. "What do you know about this, Mister LaTrelle?"

***

Inside the small craft, Ramses felt like a roasted goose. A brisk New York winter day outside, in here it was a roaring iron oven with a slit window view of the world. He mentally kicked himself for wasting a prime opportunity. He let adrenaline get the best of him and fired too early on his first pass. He doubted Billy Red-Deer and that waxy little man Wilkins would give him another straight shot like that.

Ramses was right.

As he gunned his little craft ahead, clearing the obstacles for another firing pass, he heard the *boom* of the land yacht's four-pounder. A geyser of

118

earth and rocks erupted to the right. Shrapnel rattled against Ramses' hull like deadly hail, and he flinched out of reflex. This took him in a wide arc to his left, lining him up for a broadside from the land yacht–

Boom! Before he even heard the shot, Ramses had already yanked the hand brake. The shell buzzed past his nose like an angry four-pound hornet filled with gunpowder. It struck six feet beyond and exploded, peppering the smaller vehicle with stray metal again.

Quickly, a hard pull on the right control lined up the cross of metal serving as a gun-sight in the slit window–

Ramses slammed the throttle forward and roared straight at the land yacht, hoping that Billy Red-Deer hadn't practiced reloading enough to keep up with the rapidly changing range. As exploding shells sailed over his head, Ramses fired his own guns. The twin repeating rifles mounted atop his vehicle spat out .50 caliber bullets machined from the hardened French metal. *Alloy*, Professor Merrill had called it.

The bouncing slit window made it incredibly hard to do anything but keep the damn vehicle straight, but Ramses thought he saw ragged holes appear in the land yacht's flank, and the iron beast suddenly pitched right and skidded to a halt.

***

Inside the land yacht, chaos reigned. Steam jetted into the compartment from a damaged line, and the superheated moist air made it feel like being inside the womb of an iron dragon. Billy Red Deer tried to think over the sound of Wilkins screaming. That wound in the white man's thigh looked fatal.

Billy knew it was the kid in the other machine. That runaway slave who worked for the Professor. They should have stayed and killed him when he showed up, but LaTrelle had been in such a damn hurry to get this infernal machine out of there.

The smaller craft zipped past them, preventing a shot from the starboard side guns. Ignoring Wilkins' pathetic cries for help, Billy scrambled to the portside four-pounder. He had a clear shot at the quick little bastard's rear flank.

Billy hit the trigger and let out a war cry of victory.

***

Ramses hit top speed as he zipped past the wounded land yacht. He had aimed for their boiler tank, but since he didn't see an explosion or at least a big steam cloud, he figured he must have hit some vital control instead.

He was in the midst of formulating his next attack run when his world went topsy-turvy.

An explosion rocked his vehicle, and the whole thing tipped up onto the left treads. His adrenaline-charged brain stretched the next second into a panicked eternity as he roared forward on one tread, fate seemingly unsure of whether to roll the machine and crush him to death or—

And then he was back down, but spinning around and around to the right, ears ringing and blood running from his nose. The grinding of broken metal meant the right track was destroyed.

In a daze, he stopped his craft and peered out the front slit. His bouncing near-crash had taken him out of the firing angle of the portside guns on the land yacht. That didn't stop the four-pounders from bellowing Billy Red-Deer's rage. It was a near thing, with rounds hitting so close the concussion made it feel like Ramses' heart stopped with each explosion.

His hand clutched the control for the left tracks, and he nudged his little vehicle into line with the gunner's slit on the land yacht. He yanked the firing lever and his top-mounted guns fired two rounds each. Then stopped.

Ramses cursed himself for not keeping count of his bullets. Now the one glaring weakness of his weapon system came into play. He had to pop the top hatch and lean his upper body out to reload his guns.

***

Billy Red-Deer slapped a hot iron from the firebox over the wound in his shoulder, and howled in pain. The little bastard had shot him! Billy swore then and there to drag the kid's body out of that tin machine and drop his scalp into Lincoln's hat when this was over.

He staggered to the firing port and stared across the proving grounds. He couldn't believe it. The kid was half out of his machine, fiddling with his guns!

A quick check showed Billy what he already knew. Portside guns were out of ammo.

Billy yelled at Wilkins to move the machine so he had a clear shot with the starboard guns. When he got no answer, he turned to kick Wilkins – but the pasty little man had long since bled out.

To have the kid right there and not be able to do anything about it drove Billy into a frenzy. He kicked Wilkins' body out of the way and grabbed the controls. He shoved the control arms forward and breathed in Hell's own air as steam shot out of severed lines. But the iron beast moved, damn it, and that was all Billy needed.

***

Ramses heard the clattering of the land yacht's tracks as someone inside spurred it into action. He tried to concentrate on shoving the fat box magazines into his heavy repeaters, but his hands shook when the land yacht roared and came right at him. It looked like they meant to ram him while he was out in the open.

Something he had practiced dozens of times on the train ride out here suddenly became an alien concept to his panicked brain. Ramses slammed the metal magazine against the loading port of rifle number one and lost his grip. The magazine bounced down the armored side and fell into the dirt.

Steam billowed from the holes in her flanks now, but the land yacht bore down on Ramses nonetheless.

When the snarling, smoking beast was less than thirty feet away, Ramses finally slammed his last magazine home and charged rifle number two. He ducked back inside his vehicle with just enough time to pull the trigger and pray.

Bang-bang-bang-bang-bang! The big repeater fired hardened metal death into the front of the land yacht, punching through her armor, through Billy Red-Deer, and through the boiler tank in her rear.

The back end of the land yacht exploded in a brilliant mushroom of steam, rivets, and iron plate. With power lost, all that remained was momentum. The dying beast gouged double furrows in the ground, sliding right up, and just bumping the front of Ramses' little war machine.

A fearful silence fell over the proving grounds.

A crowd of soldiers sprinted across the dirt, forming a line between their President and this killer machine. When Ramses popped the hatch and came out, he found himself staring down forty rifle barrels.

No one seemed to know what to do from there. Finally, the crowd parted and Ramses snatched his leather skullcap off his head and tried to wipe some of the grime off his cheeks. Wilhelmina would have been sore if she found out he met the President with a dirty face.

President Lincoln stepped up to the steaming wreckage. He took off his tall hat and scratched his head, trying to work all this out. Finally, he turned to Ramses and stared at the mess of his little machine.

"What's the meaning of this, son?"

"Well, sir, Travis LaTrelle killed my friend Professor Merrill and stole his machine. That's the one you see there. LaTrelle wants the Union to buy these machines, and then he's going to sell the plans to the Confederate Alliance so they can build machines to beat them."

LaTrelle pushed to the front of the crowd alongside Captain Lee. His dime-novel hero confidence looked shaken.

"Th-that's a damn lie. This Negro boy is the thief. He stole one of my test machines so he could try to ruin me."

The President turned to Ramses and spoke quietly.

"Is this your machine, son?"

Ramses almost couldn't find his voice.

"It belonged to my friend Professor Merrill, sir. I just designed the gun system. But I can take them both apart and put them together again. I can tell any of your engineers what went into making these machines, step by step. He can't do that."

Ramses stuck his chin out toward LaTrelle defiantly. LaTrelle started forward, but several soldiers around the President stopped him.

"This is ridiculous. Why are you even listening to him? Where I come from, these damn people don't have any legal cause to speak on these matters. They can't even testify in court."

President Lincoln turned to face LaTrelle, and the handsome man gulped under the withering, hollow-eyed stare.

"Fortunately, we are not where you're from, Mister LaTrelle. And what this young man is describing is treason. And we shall look into it. Shan't we, Captain Lee?"

"With pleasure, sir," Captain Lee said. He motioned to the soldiers and they grabbed LaTrelle by the arms. The dashing salesman persona had all but disappeared, and LaTrelle lowered his head as he was led away.

President Lincoln walked around Ramses' little machine. He ran a hand over one of the rifles on top. "You beat one of those cannon-firing behemoths with what amounts to nothing more than a rolling rifle. That's a heck of a gun system you designed there, son. I daresay you're a genius."

Ramses smiled. "Some folks have said that, sir."

Several reporters pushed through the crowd and began shouting questions at Ramses. "How did you do it, kid? How did you stop that infernal monster?"

"Uh... well, I just tried to shoot for their pressure system. I knew if I hit the tank, that would stop it."

"The tank? Is that what you called those damned things?"

***

The stars didn't look the same over the bustling city of New York as they did over the wind-sculpted deserts of Utah. Then again, maybe it was his eyes that were different. Ramses stared down from his hotel room window at the people scurrying about below him. He had never seen a place so darned... *busy*. Even at night!

Ramses sat on his bed and read the front page of today's New York Evening Post for what had to be the fiftieth time. The headline screamed:

Genius Jones's Rolling Rifle Beats War Tank!

The fight with the land yacht yesterday seemed a lifetime ago. Plans were already in motion to build a factory in northern New York – *upstate* they called it, for some strange reason – that would turn out Ramses' newly designed slope-sided "tanks," as well as fast scout vehicles based on the Rolling Rifle.

Ramses was a bit embarrassed by the picture that accompanied the headline. He looked like a walleyed kid standing there next to the President and the broken machines.

Standing next to President Lincoln! He wondered what Professor Merrill and Wilhelmina would have thought of that. In a tiny corner of his brain, a place that wasn't dead, but purposely cut off from his conscious thought, he wondered if his real parents might someday see this picture.

Maybe, just maybe, if these new machines he and Professor Merrill had given the Colonial Union did what they believed they could, the day might come when Ramses would be able to look for his parents.

That day wouldn't be tomorrow. Tomorrow he had blueprints to draw up, war machines to design.

And tomorrow was already upon him, so Genius Jones put out the lights and lay down to get some sleep.

Art by Kim Miranda

THE GIRL, THE DEVIL
AND THE COAL MINE
WARREN BULL

1940
Kentucky, USA

My little brother Timmy's disappearance seven days ago created a chasm deeper than the coalmine Daddy worked in. I can stand on this side – now, and remember how good things had been before – then.

That night I said, "Can we sing and play tonight?" Daddy answered, "Not tonight, baby girl."

In my imagination I could hear Daddy playing the fiddle to accompany Mamma on her guitar while we sang about Barbara Allen or Little Moses. I'd play a few licks on the banjo, four-year-old Timmy would clap and we sounded like singers on the radio. When we sang gospel songs in parts, the three of us sounded like a full church choir. Mamma could really sing praise for the Lord. Just for fun we would swap the instruments around so I could learn how to play them all. The fiddle was the hardest to play but it could sound like anything from a banshee to an angel. It's not much fun without Timmy now.

I asked Mamma. "Can you cook cinnamon apples?" She answered, "I'm sorry, Ruby, but the smell makes me cry." It was Timmy's favorite food.

I could remember putting my cheek next to Daddy's, feeling his scratchy whiskers and giggling. Daddy didn't kneel down for a snuggle like he used to after what he called his, "shift in the shaft." Mamma no longer started each day with a song. Every day when I woke up Daddy and Mamma they looked older and sadder. They spent more time staring at nothing. Daddy seemed to be shrinking into his muscular frame. Mamma seemed to pay less and less attention to her appearance.

I remember that late summer day when Timmy vanished. I thought about it all the time. Wednesday, August First, didn't seem different from other days of the season. The black-eyed Susans and Queen Anne's lace were in bloom. Fat bees and fragile butterflies flew in slow circles around the morning glories. Like always, the steam whistle that signaled the beginning and end of three eight-hour shifts every Monday through Friday set the rhythm of life in the Black Mountain Coal Camp. Baseball games ruled on Saturdays and church services presided over Sundays. It didn't matter which shift men worked. In the mine it was always black as the mine owner's heart. It was wet, filthy, and full of rats.

125

On that day a new miner named Mr. Tanner came out the mine screaming. "I've seen the Devil!" He ran off still wearing his helmet with the carbide light still shining. He wasn't the first man to run away from the mine in fear. Mining was safer than it had been, but it was still a risky occupation. With the Depression so recent in people's memories, most were happy to have a steady job regardless of the danger.

If it had been Monday, Momma and every other woman in camp would have been washing in the constant battle against coal dust. If it had been Tuesday she would have been baking for the week. Since it was Wednesday, Mamma was weeding the garden, knitting, mending, minding children and cooking meals. We children worked quite a bit too. From the time we were old enough to walk we picked up coals that fell off the cars to burn at home. We weeded, cleaned and helped with whatever needed to be done. It didn't seem like work. Even the mine manager's children had chores. We were all poor except for the two families on "Bosses Row."

Since school was out, after cleaning, weeding, and running errands, I was able to spend time with my white friend, Luke, and my Polish friend, Anka. When school was in session, Luke attended a separate school and Anka was assigned to a different classroom.

When we went out to play that day was Mamma really more anxious? Did she ask me more insistently to keep an eye on my little brother Timmy or did I just remember it that way? She didn't try to keep him inside. He wouldn't have stayed, even if she'd hogtied him. Timmy followed me at first but he didn't stick around long. Everybody knows that four-year-olds are too impatient to listen to twelve-year-olds talk. They aren't interested in gossip about other families, sharing what we learned in schools and things like that. Timmy ran off as usual to play with other four-year-olds. Their games don't have a lot of rules but they involve a lot of chasing and hollering.

Luke limped up wearing the special shoe he had on account of his clubfoot. "My pa warned me that I won't be able to talk to ya'll much longer," said Luke. "He said white folks don't like to see a white boy like me taking to a colored girl and a foreigner. Ma told him the other boys won't play with me because I can't run or play baseball. She told him you two have been great friends to me but he just shook his head. He let me talk to ya'll today, but he won't allow it much longer."

"Why not?" asked Anka. "We're friends. Our fathers work together in the mine."

"Mamma said something like that to me too," I admitted. "I pretended I didn't hear her, but some folks are beginning to natter about us. I don't know how much longer we can keep on meeting. Most folks think coloreds, immigrants and whites should each keep to 'their own kind'."

"That doesn't make sense," said Anka. "You and Luke are the only ones who ask me about what I've learned. I teach you. You teach me. I want to be a schoolteacher when I'm older. Everybody else says, 'School is out'; they don't have to learn anything more until it starts again."

"It's the way people are," I said. "They wouldn't let me go to Luke's school. I'd get in big trouble if I tried. If a colored man looks at a white woman in a way a white man doesn't like, the white man might kill him."

Anka looked at me with wide-open eyes.

"It could happen," Luke said. "Lots of folks hereabout got a piece of the Devil in 'em. I remember when Bubba Kaywood accused a colored boy from up north of making eyes at a white woman at the company store. The boy nearly got hung until his granny pleaded that he was a half-wit and didn't know any better. They beat him half to death, but they didn't hang him. His granny shipped him back north before he got in more trouble agan."

"It sounds like his granny saved that boy's life," I said. "Was he really a half-wit?"

"No, but Bubba wasn't smart enough figure that out."

"They act like that in Poland too," said Anka. "The government is supposed to treat everyone fairly, but it never happens. Violence between groups of people who came from different countries was getting worse. That's why we came to America."

"Daddy says there could be another war because of that man, Hitler, the Chancellor of Germany," I said. "He says it's like we didn't learn anything from the Great War."

Wouldn't you know Timmy chose this moment to come running up.

"Play with me Ruby," he demanded.

"Play with your friends," I answered. "We're having us a serious talk here."

"What about?"

"Stuff you wouldn't understand," I said.

"Would too." Timmy said. My baby brother could be a burr under my saddle.

"You will understand when you get older," said Luke, not unkindly. "Not right now."

"Anthony can't come out 'cause he's sick and Ben's mad at me," said Timmy.

"Why's he mad?" I asked.

"I don't know, but it's his fault." Nothing was ever Timmy's fault, at least according to him.

"Find somebody else," I said. "We have important big kid stuff to discuss."

Timmy stuck out his lower lip. He looked so sad that I almost hugged him before I remembered what a pest he was.

"Play with me. Play with me. Play with me," he whined.

"You're worse than a coal mine rat," I said. I felt the anger in me flare up like when pine heartwood is tossed on a bonfire.

"Go away and leave us be," I said.

"Where can I go?"

"I don't care," I said. "Just go."

"I'm going to tell Mamma," he said. He stuck out his tongue and trotted off. I didn't think anything of it at the time.

Luke told Anka and me about what his teacher showed him through a telescope last night. He also explained eclipses. "See, I put down a rock for the sun, the earth and the moon. The earth what you call rotates around the sun." He drew a circle showing the path of the earth. "The moon, which is the pipsqueak of the three, moves around the earth. Now it happens from to time that the moon travels between the sun and the earth. It blots out some of the light from the sun." He moved the rocks to demonstrate. "At other times the earth passes between the sun and the moon." Luke rearranged the rocks to that position. "Then the earth's shadow falls on the moon darkening it. Enough light comes through the atmosphere that the moon can look red. Next month a solar eclipse will be visible in parts of Virginia and North Carolina. I wish I could talk my folks into going there."

"Do they happen over here in West Virginia?" I asked.

"My teacher says they will eventually, but not for a long time yet," said Luke.

"You'd make a good teacher," said Anka. Luke looked down. Pink showed on his face.

Anka said, "My aunt told me about prime numbers. A prime number is one that cannot be evenly divided by any number except the number one and the prime itself. The number has to be an odd number, but not all odd numbers qualify as prime. Twenty-one can be divided into equal parts by three or seven. Twenty-five can be divided into five fives without a remainder. But twenty-three located between those two divided by any number, except itself or one gives you a remainder." We figured out other prime numbers for fun.

I told my friends about sundials and how to tell time with them. I read all about them in a magazine Mamma brought home from town. We set one up and watched the shadow move slowly across the ground.

We talked until the whistle blew for the end of our fathers' shift. Then we skedaddled for home. I brought in lumps of coal from the shed with me.

"Thank you, Ruby," said Mamma. She opened the door to the stove and tossed in the coal. When the copper teakettle sang she poured boiling water into the big washtub on the floor. It was three quarters full.

"Where's your brother?"

I looked around. Timmy was nowhere to be seen.

"I don't know," I said. "He's usually home by now pestering us about when he can eat."

"Run find him," said Mamma.

I scooted out of the door, unhappy that I would not see Daddy sit down in the tub dressed in his work clothes. He'd come in looking black as two midnights in a pickle jar from the coal dust all over him and his clothes. As soon as he sat, the water would start to turn black. Then he'd shoo Mamma and me out of the kitchen so he could wash himself privately.

I thought he had more muscles than mighty John Henry in the song. Sometimes I imagined he had been carved out of one of the boulders on Black Mountain.

When I called on Anthony's family, I discovered the boy had been in bed all day with a hacking cough. His mother had not seen Timmy since early in the morning. I visited Ben's family next. His parents invited me to dinner, which was polite considering how hard they worked to keep the family fed.

Ben's Pa had trouble breathing, especially when the coal dust was heavy. Ben wasn't sure what time he seen Timmy last but you can't expect four-year olds to keep track of time.

Each family promised to keep an eye out for him. I wasn't sure what to do next. I knew dithering would not help so I headed off to the white section of town and went to Luke's house. It was no different than mine with two bedrooms and a large kitchen. Mrs. Cleveland kept the place tidy. She had dyed the curtains with coffee grounds and her hand-braided oval rugs covered most of the floors. She seemed pleased when I admired her work and concerned when I asked about Timmy. She promised to alert her neighbors.

Next, I headed over to the section of the camp some called, "Polack Place." My parents explained the word was an insult so I never used it with Anka. She lived in a one-bedroom house with her matka and tata. None of them had seen Timmy but, like the Cleveland family, they promised to ask their neighbors.

I returned home next because I didn't want my parents to think I was missing too.

"Where can he have gotten to?" asked Mamma.

"I can ask at the Tipple," I said.

"No." said Daddy. "You haven't eaten yet. I need to check on how many tons I loaded today and get my chits back anyway."

"I'm not hungry," I said.

"Neither am I," Mamma said.

So we all went. Mr. White looked up from his desk when we entered and raised his eyebrows.

"Something I can do for ya'll?" he asked.

"My boy, Timmy, didn't come home for supper," said Daddy.

"Haven't seen him," said Mr. White. "I have your chits so you can hang them on cars you fill tomorrow. I can show you your tonnage."

Mr. White tilted his chair back onto two legs. He looked at Mamma's worried face. Men always noticed her. He looked at Daddy maybe thinking that Daddy shoveled more coal than anyone else.

"I reckon I could run the bell and call for folks to help."

"Thank you," said Daddy. He was a proud man, not liking to ask for help. Many white men would not have offered to help a colored family.

Ringing the bell was no small thing. It rang only for emergencies so when they heard it women and children with men working in the mine that shift came with bandages and blankets, wondering whose husband among them had been killed or maimed. Other families, the priest, our colored preacher, the white preacher and the camp doctor would follow to offer whatever help and comfort they could.

Mr. White walked to the bell rope, spit on his hands and pulled. The clanging startled the whole camp and people came a-running. They were surprised to find no dead or injured men being carried out of the mine. Mr. White climbed on top of a table and spoke while people from the furthest end of camp were still arriving.

"No cave-ins. No methane. No explosions. Nobody's dead or injured.

Ya'll know Henry Cain's young'un, Timmy. He's four years old and about the color of coffee with a tablespoon of milk in it. We still got some hours of light left in the day. You men who hunt take your hounds to the Cain's house so they smell Timmy's clothing. Then divvy up the woods around and go hunt for his tracks. Each woman look around your house for anywhere a small child might hide. The rest of us will look in the churches, the schoolhouse and the company story. When somebody finds him send word back to me and I'll ring the bell three times. Tell all you meet still on the way here. Go on, then."

People scurried back the way they had come.

Mamma told me not to leave camp for any reason but to search out spots I knew Timmy liked. I thought if he was near he surely would have come out just to see what the ruckus was about. But it made sense to check everywhere close just to be sure. I tried every hidey-hole Timmy knew about and a few I'd used for hide and seek he didn't know. It was no help.

There was one place that was sort of in the camp and sort of out of it that fascinated Timmy. The coal company owned all the houses. When a man lost his life in the mines or got so injured he could no longer work, the company gave families one year to move out of their homes so a new worker could move in. Nobody who didn't have a family member working in the mine lived in the camp, with one exception. Mrs. Shaw's husband had died in the shaft while trying to burn away methane gas, a silent, odorless killer that could explode with no warning. It bubbled out of the coal itself. Even in gob shafts that are not being worked methane seeped out ready to explode. There's no telling how many men Mr. Shaw saved during his years in the mine. They used to call him "Canary" for his almost uncanny ability to detect the danger. Mrs. Shaw was respected for her willingness to help others and for her home remedies.

The Shaws lived in an old section of the camp. Shortly after Canary Shaw's death, the company hired men to knock down the old houses and put up new ones. When the workers the company hired came to Mrs. Shaw's place, she offered them cookies and lemonade. The workers left her house alone. Soon new houses rose around her old house. The Company managers acted like she didn't exist. Younger children liked to pretend she was a witch even though she attended church every Sunday. Older folks said she had "the sight." They said she knew ahead of time who would live and who would die in mining accidents although she couldn't prevent what was going to happen. As she grew older, her house became less like the others. I suppose it was no surprise that younger children told scary stories about her.

I was not scared of course. I just walked slowly because the dark was coming on and I didn't want to trip. Mrs. Shaw's house needed a coat of paint but it seemed solid. When I walked to the front door it opened before me.

"Welcome," said Mrs. Shaw. "Come on in. I got the kettle on and I baked cookies."

Two places were set at the kitchen table. Her blue eyes sparkled in her wrinkled face.

"Since you didn't get to eat your supper, you should at least eat a cookie."

The kettle whistled. It wasn't surprising that Mrs. Shaw knew just when I was going to arrive, although I had only just decided to visit. She knew I had gone without supper too. She always knew things like that.

"Let me pour you some tea."

The cookie was warm and moist. It was hard not to stuff it all in my mouth and grab another.

"I'm glad you thought to come to me, dear," said Mrs. Shaw, bringing two steaming white porcelain cups with rosebuds on their sides to the table. "I thought about seeking you out but it's better that you came here."

She smiled. "You eat another cookie while I make sure we are not disturbed." Mrs. Shaw picked up a box of salt and sprinkled white crystals making a line across the threshold of the front door.

She returned to the table and sipped her tea.

"I've been alive for a long time. I remember things others have forgotten, if they ever knew them. During the coal mine wars, on this date in 1921, Sid Hatfield and Ed Chambers were murdered on the courthouse steps in front of their wives. Their killers were known but never tried."

"I don't understand. Is Timmy...?"

"Dead? Oh, Good heavens, no. I didn't mean to scare you, although, really you should be scared. I only meant that on August first, Satan goes out of his way to bedevil honest miners and their families. It's a day to be very careful of what you say and do."

"You think it's my fault," I said. I stood up so fast that I knocked the cup Mrs. Shaw gave me to the floor. I gritted my teeth. My face flushed. I felt so much anger that I thought my hair might light on fire.

Mrs. Shaw regarded me patiently.

"You are not at fault," she said. "No matter how much you blame yourself."

My anger drained away like water when you pulled the plug out of the sink.

"I broke your beautiful cup," I said. "I'm so sorry."

"That's not important," Mrs. Shaw said. "It is important that you understand that today a hot-tempered girl might easily fly into a rage when she very much needs to remain calm no matter what someone does to egg her on. Just like an impulsive boy might be easily led to places where he is not supposed to go."

I bent down to pick up the pieces of the broken cup while I thought about what Mrs. Shaw said.

"The time will come when you will need to remember what I said to you tonight," said Mrs. Shaw. "Don't neglect your prayers. Think about your Sunday school lessons. Prepare yourself, young lady."

The search for Timmy was unsuccessful that night and every night after for a week. The hounds only ran around in circles and barked. It was like they were afraid. My parents got sadder and sadder every day. I prayed harder for Timmy and my parents than I ever had before. At the start of the new week Mamma gave me a brand new nightgown. Before she would have joked about me growing out of my clothes. Daddy would have made up a song. Timmy would have been happy for me. But time before was all used up. We were stuck in time after Timmy's disappearance.

I spied the first star of the night and wished that I could push the days backward until we got to the night Timmy vanished. I looked at the bed where he used to sleep near to my own. I dropped into a deep sleep. When I awoke it was black as the coal that came out of the mine. The night was quiet. That was odd. Ordinarily, the creatures of the night made as much as noise as their daytime relatives. A breeze tickled my ear. I heard a name, my name. "Ruby."

Who was calling me? It sounded like Timmy. I listened as hard as I could. "Ruby." It came a third time. "Ruby."

I jumped out of my bed and followed the voice. I didn't stop to dress or to tell anyone where I was headed. The voice led me through the camp and up into the hills. I was determined to follow it since this was the only trace of my little brother I had come across for a week. The farther I got away from the camp, the more the plant life changed, thistles and poison ivy crept closer and closer to the path I was on. It was like I was being herded. In the moonlight I could make out black willows and cancer drops. Snakeroot, ghost pipe and bloodroot popped up. Then rattlesnake hawkweed and deadly nightshade made their appearance. I knew who was calling me when devil's bit and devil's trumpet came to dominate the foliage I could see. In contrast to the plants, the farther I went along the path the wider and smoother it became under my bare feet. I remembered the preacher quoting Jesus, "Broad is the way that leads to destruction."

I shivered even though the night was only cool. I saw a light that became a fire. Seated, watching me approach was a figure resembling an old man. He might not have seen me at first. His legs looked like goat's legs that ended with cloven hooves. Then the legs changed and took on the appearance of human legs. Looking beyond him I could see Timmy asleep on a patch of green. He twitched and moved, as active asleep as he was awake.

"You know who I am?" asked the figure.

"Old Scratch," I said.

"Ain't you a smart one. You see I got what you want. He's mine, but I'll give you a chance to wager. Your soul agin his'n."

I thought to myself that Mrs. Shaw had given me good advice. I knew how to answer from what Daddy and Mamma told me and from sunday school.

"Oh, Father of Lies," I said. "That boy's soul is safe. He is a beloved child of God."

"Mebee so," said the Devil. "But that don't mean I got to give you his physical body 'less you better me in a game of wits."

The fire flared and shaped itself into a circle around Old Scratch and Timmy. It might have been just a show, but I could feel the heat from the flames. The fire crackled. Its color varied just like a fire would.

"I will not wager my soul," I said.

"Okay, but you have to give me something to make it interesting. I'll take thirty minutes of your time. You do what I want at a time and place of my choosing."

I wasn't sure what he wanted, but I'd seen folks barter because money was scarce. I knew better than to accept his first offer. I shook my head and sat down trying to look like I had settled in for a long time. He was not pleased by my actions. Sparks jumped from his fingertips. He emitted a whiff of brimstone.

"I will not allow you to force me into sin," I said.

"Wouldn't necessarily be sin on your part," said Satan. "I might agree to usin' you only to give a little push to someone straying toward the darkness. You wouldn't be harmed at all. I can see you're going to grow up to be a beauty like your Mamma. I have uses for beautiful women."

"That would be a sin," I said.

"Such a tender conscience. You are but a child. To survive in this world you will have to become more cynical. I will allow you easy access to your little brother in return for another opportunity later in your life to tempt you toward serving me. Assuming of course that you can beat the Devil in a test of wits."

I thought the offer up, down and all around. The preacher told us that Lucifer was always ready with temptations. I didn't see how what he asked gave him anything he did not already have. I noticed he'd dropped the phony country accent but I was not sure why.

"How does that help you?" I asked.

"Someone who bargains with me once is more likely to come to me again," he said.

"What sort of test of wits?"

"Questions, riddles. We alternate turns. At the end of three questions, the one who has the fewest mistakes wins."

"No," I said. "You are much older and more experienced than I am. You could ask questions that I would have no way of answering."

He smiled. "You can ask me anything. I will ask you only what a colored twelve-year-old girl in a West Virginia coal camp might know."

"I decide what a twelve-year-old girl might know," I said. "I can rule out any question you ask."

"Agreed."

I realized right then I had not prayed since I left my bed. I corrected my mistake immediately.

"I will ask my three questions first," said Satan. One, three, five, seven, nine, eleven and thirteen. Which number is not like the others?"

Of course after learning about prime numbers from Anka, I knew the answer. One answer, anyway. I wondered if there was another. Old Scratch sneered at me. Maybe he thought I was stumped.

"I'm going to say...nine."

"You guessed you—" The fallen angel stomped his feet. He howled. Then he started shouting at me in a language I didn't understand. He then switched to English, calling me a nappy-headed Pickaninny among other names. I didn't really get upset until he started in on my family. He saw me flinch when he said my father would make a fine Pine Tree Ornaments, which was a way of saying he could get lynched. I was about to tell him I was smarter than he thought and cuss back at him.

But then I remembered Mrs. Shaw's warning that I would need to keep my temper in check, even when provoked. That cooled me off. Then I thought about how foolish I had almost been to take on the devil in a cursing contest. That was so funny I had to chuckle. Satan stopped. The preacher always said the Devil had no sense of humor.

"Don't think you'll be so lucky again in your guesses, Missy. Tell me where you can stand in the moon's shadow."

Once again I knew an answer, maybe the right answer. I replayed in my head the conversation with Anka and Luke. I gave a quick thanks to God for the blessing of friends. "Next month in parts of North Carolina and Virginia or right where you are if you wait long enough."

If the Devil had been exasperated before, he was angry multiplied by ten now. The night seemed to shake from the violence of his words and actions. I let him carry on for a while. I needed to find questions for him. Was there anything he didn't know about?

Finally he calmed down enough to the point where he could talk without screaming.

"You are not the country hayseed I was taking you for." He narrowed his eyes. "Well done, little trickster. I will not underestimate you again. Tell me, when will the next big war start?"

"Entirely too soon," I answered without thinking.

The Devil's body started to shake. He wasn't able to keep up the false appearance he wore like a mask. I saw his furry legs and his cloven hooves. He put his hands over his face, which might have been more for his sake than for mine. At first I thought he was laughing, but then I figured out he was enraged.

"My answer was not wrong," I said. "It might not have been what you expected, but it is a correct answer. I have answered three out of three."

The circle of fire exploded upward. It blocked my sight of Satan and my brother. After a minute or so the flames lowered. Lucifer and Timmy became visible once more.

"After I answer your questions the second round will commence," he said. "We will see how you do then."

"My turn," I said. "First, tell me which of my many blessings helped me answer your questions."

His face twisted as he answered.

"Your blessings overlap. Family, friends, angels and The Almighty all helped you."

I pondered his answer. "I have to give you that one. Like my last answer, it wasn't what I expected but it isn't wrong."

"You're being fair to the Devil?" he asked. "How strange."

"I don't play by your rules. Here's something you might know. Tell me how many lives were lost and how many injuries occurred for every ton of coal taken from the Black Mountain Mine?"

The Devil grimaced.

"You don't know, do you?" I asked.

He shook his head. "What is the answer, Missy?"

"I don't know," I said. "I've wondered about it since we first came here. There was nothing in the rules you gave about the questioner having to know the answer."

Again the circle of fire shot upward. It expanded outward as well.

"I told you I'd give you easy access to your brother," said the Devil. "And I have. All you have to do is to cross the line of fire to him."

So the Devil had hidden a trick in the agreement and I had missed it. Well, I hadn't come so far just to turn around and leave. I spoke the words of the Lord's Prayer as I ran toward the flames. Even when I felt I was being roasted alive, I kept moving as fast as I could. I burst out of the flames and ran to Timmy. He sat up and spoke.

"I knew you'd come for me. Ruby. Don't be mad at me. I wanted to play with the puppy but every time I came close to him he'd run a few steps ahead. I got here and I was so sleepy. Is your nightgown on fire?"

It was smoldering. I slapped at places around my ankles where the fire hadn't gone completely out. My new nightgown was charred.

"I'm not mad at you, Timmy. I'm sorry I said I didn't care where you went. Let's get you out of here and go back home."

We held hands as we crossed the circle of what now were ashes. Tommy spotted Satan and pointed at him.

"I'm scared of him," said Timmy.

"He watched over you as you slept and kept you safe," I said. I almost felt sorry for him. I couldn't imagine how bad it would be to get kicked out of heaven.

The Devil vanished with a sound like thunder.

When we followed the path toward home, I noticed that the ground was rocky and uneven. Plants growing along side the path were just the ordinary varieties of the forest. From time to time the path became hard to detect. There were trailheads and other alternatives that didn't exist on the trail I had used to look for my little brother. The bugs and night critters sounded off like they did every night except last night. Less than halfway home, Timmy started to whine.

"Are we there yet? I'm sleepy. Will you carry me?"

Yes, things were definitely back to normal. Timmy was much too big for me to carry. He dragged his feet until our house came into view. Then he bolted ahead faster than a jack rabbit.I knew I couldn't catch him. He yelled as he burst into the house. The sun was just peeking over the horizon so my parents would have been up soon anyway. I followed quickly behind him.

Mamma and Daddy had Timmy it a three-way hug. They pulled me into it so it became a whole-family hug. Timmy rattled off about the puppy, the fire and the scary man with goat's feet. Over breakfast I told my parents what had happened.

"Do you mean to tell me that you went out in the night all alone without waking us?" asked Mamma.

"Yes Ma'am. I heard what sounded like Timmy's voice from far away. I figured I didn't have time to dress or wake you up and explain because if the voice died off I wouldn't be able to find him."

"Ruby, I am very proud of you," said Mamma. "You were brave and smart. You brought your brother back home. I am eternally grateful. And I want you to never, ever do anything like that again."

"Don't make Ruby promise something she might not be able to avoid," said Daddy. "Ruby, the next time you match wits with the Devil remember how he fooled you with that agreement. He is clever and dangerous."

"Yes sir. Daddy, is the Devil still around?"

"In the mines we say, 'Don't ask where the Devil is. He's here.' I don't want you to worry all the time. Just stay alert. And remember that you have a secret weapon against him that he doesn't know about. You were wrapped up in the love of God and the love of our family. The Devil doesn't understand love. It'll take him by surprise every time."

"I think we should keep the details of your adventure to ourselves," said Mamma. "We'll tell people that you found Timmy sleeping in the woods and brought him home. That's the truth. I wonder what we might do for Mrs. Shaw."

"Her house need painting," I said. "I can help with that. And how much does a teacup cost?"

Art by Paula Arwen Owen

HOW I SAVED ATHENS FROM THE STONE MONSTERS
ERIK JENSEN

415 BCE
Athens, Greece

Okay, so that thing with the statues? The smashed penises thing? That was my idea. But let me explain. I had a good reason for it.

Lampedo and I were in our spot by the south stoa. Well, my spot. I'd been here most every night for a year by then but it was Lampedo's first night outside the house. (Her name's not really Lampedo, but it's what we call her. Mine's not Mnestra, either, but I'm not telling you. It was my mother's and it's all I have left of her.)

There was a cold wind and we were sheltering behind the stoa wall with our flutes. I had my eye out for customers, but Lampedo was glaring across the street at a herma. You know what a herma is, right? Square stone post with a head carved on top and a penis halfway up poking out like an eager boy's? They're everywhere in Athens – in front of houses and shops, at cross-roads, in the markets. You can't turn your head without having a penis in your face.

"Mnestra," said Lampedo, "what is that thing?"

"Oh, come on," I sighed, "you see pins every night." (Yes, we call them pins, like hairpins, because they're always poking you in the wrong places when you can't see.)

Lampedo gave me her *You idiot* look. No one can do a *You idiot* look like Lampedo.

"The stone with the head on top," she said.

"It's just a herma," I said. "You know, protective spirits. Don't tell me you don't have hermas in Thrace."

"We have picture stones of Bendis hunting the dragon," she sniffed. "Much better. Your spirit is useless."

"Not my spirit," I said. "I told you, I'm an initiate of Isis."

I wished I was back in the house. There, men come to you and all you have to do is give them what they paid for. Out on the street you have to play the game. You blush. They wink. You tease a little with your veil. They clack a few drakhmas together. It takes more skill, but flute girls make more money.

I didn't want to be a flute girl at first, but Mema said I'd never make my keep in the house and I should learn. (She's not my grandmother, we just call her Mema. My parents were sandal-makers in Peiraias but they died in the plague. That's how I ended up in Mema's house. She takes good enough care of us, long as she gets her cut and you do what you're told. There's some older girls missing a finger or two. They don't say and we don't ask.) She said the same when Lampedo came. Too pale. Men don't want Thracian girls. Mema figured we'd work best as a set: she's pale, I'm dark, but we can play the flutes and dance together. There's some young twits think that's deep and philosophical and will pay good money to take us home and show all the other young twits how deep and philosophical they are.

So I got stuck with her. I mean, she can dance, arms like laurel branches, but we don't get along. She came to the house a couple years ago with hardly any Greek so Mema had me teach her. (I told her Egyptian and Thracian are nothing alike, but it's all just foreign talk to her.) At least in the house I could walk away when I got fed up with her, but she started her bleeding last month so Mema sent her out to work with me. If you're old enough to bleed you're old enough to breed, Mema says. (She has a lot of sayings. I guess she's deep and philosophical, too.)

"Let's go somewhere else," Lampedo suddenly said, pointing with her flute and starting off down the street.

"That's where they dump the fish that went to rot in the market!" I called after her. She came back with a glower.

"Look," I said, pointing up and down the street. "That's where the archers loiter all night. No one hires a girl while a Skythian archer is glaring at him. Over there is where Thersites's girls work. Don't go on their turf, they're eye-scratchers. Unless you want to go wander Kerameikos with the common two-obol girls, this is our spot."

She glanced at the herma.

"It's still looking at me," she said.

I rested my head against the wall. On a good night I could could get a customer, play and dance, all the rest, and even make a stop at the Isis house before getting back to Mema's with plenty of time to sleep before the next morning's wool-work started. This was not going to be a good night.

"Your Isis," Lampedo said, "tell me her story. She hunt dragons?"

"She heals and protects," I said, calling our hymns to mind. "She was a queen and her husband Osiris was king. Well, Osiris had a brother Set and he was a right little bastard. One day, he killed Osiris and chopped him into bits. You know what Isis did then?"

"Killed Set?" Lampedo guessed.

"No!" I snapped. "She went searching all over the land for the pieces and put him back together again. Except for his pin, which she never could find. Without a pin, he couldn't be truly alive again, but Isis' magic was so strong she made him live in death and he rules forever as king of the blessed lands out beyond where the world ends."

Lampedo looked at me as though waiting for more, then rolled her head.

"Your goddess is useless. Bendis would shoot Set with her bow."

I didn't feel like arguing. I just sighed and rubbed my forehead wishing *someone* would hire us.

Suddenly Lampedo cried out and grabbed my shoulder. I looked up to see her pointing at the herma.

"It moved!" she hissed. I looked at the herma. It was still sitting there looking dumb, like they always do. Lampedo saw my expression. "Not lying!" she insisted. "I saw it move!"

"Fine!" I exclaimed. I tried to remind myself she was new. It's hard not to be nervous your first night on the street. "We'll go somewhere else. Let's try the Peiraias road. We might get some business there, but it won't be as nice."

"Is it ever nice?" she grumbled.

"Sometimes," I said. "There are good ones." It wasn't a lie. Not really.

So we took our flutes to the Peiraias road. I found us a spot under a herma that had road signs sticking out near the head. It was a good place to stand. People look at signposts and we wanted to be looked at. I didn't pick it to spite Lampedo. That would be mean.

There were crowds on the road, mostly heading down to the harbor. Runners and porters were hurrying back and forth. Some street merchants were trying to sell off a batch of pickled tunny. Not our kind. Finally I spotted a gang of young twits swaggering down the road in line abreast. Their home-spun cloaks were pinned up soldier-fashion and their hair was tousled from the bath. They were laughing a little too loud and by their cheeks and their gait they'd all drunk a khous or two already. They weren't a good set for us, but it was near sundown already and we might not do any better. I nudged Lampedo.

"There's our catch," I said. "You play, I'll talk."

She put her flute to her lips and began to play a tune, moving her hips in time to the music. I caught the eye of the twit who seemed to be the leader and began to dance in slow circles. I teased with the veil, moved my shoulders and hips, all the usual things. The twits giggled and sauntered closer.

"Ho, ho!" called the lead twit. "Girls like you shouldn't be out like this! You'd better come along with us soldiers to protect you!"

"Four drakhmas and we'll go anywhere you like," I answered, not stopping my dance. They'd probably try to haggle. I'd settle for three, but no less. When men pay you like a flute girl they treat you like a flute girl. When they pay you like a graveyard whore they treat you like a graveyard whore.

"Four, ooh!" the twit cooed. His followers laughed.

"Who'd pay four for that?" one of them slurred, pointing at Lampedo. Her eyes narrowed but she kept playing.

"No, no, it's perfect," another one giggled. "Don't you see? That one's as white as an egg... And that one's as dark as an eggplant!"

"You'd know," one of them answered, "you've done it with an eggplant!" He added a bit of mime, just in case we didn't get the joke.

The lead twit gave the jokers a shove before turning back to us.

"Now then," he declaimed, waving one hand in the air like the talking-teachers, "it seems to me that four is rather a lot to ask. I think you should show us what we're going to get for it." When neither of us offered to lift our dresses, he added: "Come on, we ship out tomorrow. You can be nice to us for a night."

"For four drakmas," I said, "we can be very nice."

"Even in the market you get to sniff the fish before you buy," he complained.

He made a grab for me. I danced away but he caught my wrist. Lampedo stopped playing and drew back her flute to strike him. I saw the blow coming and tried to get in front of it. Better to take a few bruises and lose a customer than start a fight two-against-four. Like Mema says, dead girls don't get paid.

But before anything could happen, a man on horseback came riding up and waved the twits back.

"I say, is that any way for an Athenian to behave?" he rebuked them. "Tussling with girls in the street? Don't you know there's a war on?"

"Hands off!" the lead twit said, giving the rider an angry gesture. "We saw them first!"

The rider jumped down from his horse but I don't know what he meant to do next because as his feet hit the ground the herma next to us gave a snap and a groan. A crack ran down from the holes where the signs had been stuck in and half the stone post split off and crashed down on the ground. It would have crushed the twit like a ripe grape if he hadn't dropped my arm and jumped away. The carved head from the top of the herma rolled on the ground and came up leering at him.

"Well," the rider said smoothly, "Hermes has spoken, and I don't think he likes your attitude."

Now that I saw the newcomer face to face, even I knew who it was: Alkibiades, one of the richest men in Athens and general of the army that was readying to go abroad. (Or at least he used to be. Rumor was the ekklesia were replacing him with cautious old Nikias. Even in Mema's house the girls were talking about it.) The twits had been shaken sober enough by the falling herma to know when they were outranked. They slunk away down the street.

"When we get back from Sicily," one of them shouted over his shoulder, "we'll be rich and you'll still be whores!"

Alkibiades dismissed them with a wave of his hand, then gave us an appraising look. Even if I hadn't recognized him, I know a rich man when I see one.

"Thank you, sir," I said, with lowered eyes. "You're clearly a man of more culture than those rascals."

He smiled. I didn't like his smile, but opinions aren't bread. (Another of Mema's sayings. I told you she has a lot of them.)

"Hmm," he said, looking us over. "You're an interesting pair, aren't you? Come, I'm hosting a little gathering of friends tonight. I wouldn't normally hire in entertainment for such a modest affair, but I've never seen flute girls like you. Come, you'll amuse my friends."

He tossed me four drakhmas without even waiting for a reply. Men of his sort don't haggle.

A slave came puffing up on foot. Alkibiades galloped off and the slave guided us into one of the richer parts of town. It was a place I knew well. Not that I'd had that many customers hereabouts, but the Isis house was in the same district. Alkibiades' house had a large garden and a fancy gate flanked by a pair of hermas with particularly large pins. I figured it was just stress, but you know, I could have sworn that as we walked by, they both turned their heads to watch us.

The house was busy with arriving guests and we got shoved into a corner to wait. Once we were alone I looked Lampedo in the eyes.

"You don't want to leave a customer like this unhappy," I told her. "I don't care what they tell us to do in there. If they say stand on your hands and bark like a dog, you stand on your hands and bark, got it?"

She gave me the *You idiot* look again.

"I know what we do," she said.

We kept out of the way while the guests settled in and the first serving of wine went around. Once the party was bubbling along, the steward ushered us into the dining room. The walls were painted with frolicking satyrs and nymphs while couches with purple cushions were arranged around a table piled with steaming dishes of fish and pastry. On every couch lounged a man dressed in the best the markets could offer. A few of the guests had boys sharing their couches and Alkibiades had a girl not much older than Lampedo or me, but wearing the finest peach-colored linen and decked with gold. I kept my gaze away from her as we entered, but Lampedo spotted her and smiled.

Shit.

I had tried to teach Lampedo everything I knew, I really had, even when she didn't want to listen. Still, there's one thing every flute girl needs to know: don't smile at a courtesan.

See, we're flute girls, not graveyard girls or common two-obolers. You can't do to us the things you'd do to them, but men, they don't always respect the lines. They think they can treat us like that and we have to remind them that we're not. We're better. To a courtesan, that's what a flute girl is. A man sees us act like friends and he might get confused, think he can treat his courtesan like he treats a flute girl. And then she's stuck. 'Cause if she makes a fuss about it, she loses a customer, then he gives her a bad name with his friends, and soon she's got nothing left. But if she lets it go, then word goes 'round she's no better than a common flute girl, and nobody will treat her like a proper courtesan again. So if you smile at a courtesan, there's only one thing she can do: she's got to redraw the line.

Lampedo was in for it. I may not have liked her, but I still felt bad about it. I didn't say anything, though. No point setting her off about something she couldn't escape now.

Alkibiades coughed for attention and told the story of how he found us on the road and resolutely rescued us from some rude ruffians and rotten rubble. He went on to muse on how we made the perfect pair, one light and one dark, like the body and the soul. Philosophical. Deep. You know. I smiled through it all. Eventually, his guests shouted him down and demanded we start dancing. Alkibiades took a cup of wine and waved to us as he settled on his couch. We started playing and dancing while the slaves came in with another round of wine and water.

I danced my best. I did not want him regretting his purchase. After we'd done a few dances, Alkibiades decided he wanted to talk some more.

"Friends," Alkibiades began, "let us make this a festival of the mind, not only of the body." A couple of men near us snickered, but Alkibiades pretended not to notice. "Let me propose a subject for our discourse. What is the measure of a man's worth?"

"The length of his cock!" a drunken voice called out.

"The quality of his wine!" another added before the laughter had faded.

"His virtue," proposed an old white-head. A few other suggestions floated around the room. When the merriment had subsided a little, Alkibiades offered his own answer.

"I should say that the measure of a man's worth is the greatness of the challenges he has overcome. The greatest of all men I name Leonidas of Sparta who faced the Persians at Thermopylai. When the Persian king demanded that the Spartans lay down their arms, he answered: 'Come and take them.'"

"Then they all died and the Persians burned Athens," someone objected. Alkibiades was undeterred.

"What more can a man ask for than to face an unbeatable foe with unwavering courage?"

"Sending Nikias out to do it!" came an answer. Alkibiades's face went red and he sat down as the rest of the room exploded with laughter.

Then the courtesan stood up. She had taken something from Alkibiades's side of the couch and concealed it in a fold of her gown. Everyone hushed as she regarded the room with a wide smile.

"And what, my good philosophers," she asked, "is the measure of a woman? Is it not the man who desires her?" She stepped closer to us and looked Lampedo in the eye. Then she revealed what she was carrying. It was what we call a slider, a sort of fake pin made of stuffed leather. Some of the girls in the house have them to use with men who like it that way. I'd never seen one like this, though – perfectly shaped like a man's and without a seam or stitch on it.

"This one's about right for you, my dear," she sneered at Lampedo.

Alkibiades looked furious, but the rest of room burst out in hoots of laughter.

"Go on, girl!" the courtesan cried, pushing the thing towards Lampedo's face. "Your handsome bridegroom awaits. Give him a kiss!"

Lampedo's eyes flared and her shoulders tensed, but I touched her on the arm and leaned close.

"*Woof woof,*" I said under my breath. She got the point. She dipped her head and gave the slider a kiss while the party egged her on.

Then the courtesan turned to me. Of course. I wasn't the one who smiled at her, but I was there and the line had to be drawn. No way around it.

In my head I began planning out what I was going to say to Lampedo later (and how loudly), but I had to show the men in that room what the courtesan needed them to see: that she was one of them, not one of us. I knelt in front of her and lowered the slider to her hips. The hooting in the room grew louder as I leaned in to give it a deep kiss. It tasted strange, not like leather at all but like green barley after a spring rain.

The courtesan was satisfied. She gave me a flick on the head and went to lie back down with Alkibiades.

It was clear we had gotten past the deep philosophical parts of the evening. I glanced at Lampedo and she nodded, so we offered ourselves to the crowd. Soon I had a few more obols in my pouch. (Men are always surprised I carry a pouch, but I don't keep my coins in my cheeks – I'm no slave.)

I was just rubbing my sore hips after one who squeezed like he was trying to empty a wineskin when we started to hear people outside shouting and running. Then there was crash like a market stall falling down. The guests who weren't too drunk to move started peeking out the high windows and calling for the slaves to go see what the racket was. The squeezer was just starting to ask why the Skythian archers weren't doing something about that ruckus when a heavy thud made the walls shake.

One man who had climbed up to look out the windows exclaimed: "Zeus! They're coming this way!" Before he could say what was coming, another thud rang against the wall and knocked down plaster and tiles. A third blow knocked a hole right through the wall and a stony head came through.

It was a herma. A walking herma. It had torn itself up out of the ground and now stood as tall as a man on horseback. The bottom of the stone post had split into stout legs and its top had set out rough arms. It came pushing into the room with its stone pin jutting straight out and a deep moan echoing from its face. Another like it came after, then another and another. The moaning voice began to make words:

"BORN OF EARTH. LONG WE SLEPT. NOW WE RISE. FLESH WILL FALL."

Well, I think that's what they were saying. Everyone was screaming and the herma things were smashing up the room. I couldn't get my flute, just cinched up my pouch and ran for the door.

I was heading for the street, but as I came into the hall the two hermas from the front gate came smashing in through the door. I stopped and looked around. Everyone was running, guests and slaves tripping over each other. Houses like this always had side doors for deliveries and messengers. If I could find it maybe I could get away, but away where? How many of these monsters were there? I froze in place trying to remember the streets outside and plan my route.

"*Dele Bendis!*"

The shout shook me and I jumped back as Lampedo came tearing out of the dining room. She struck one of the hermas with her flute. The instrument went to splinters on the stone. The herma swung one rough hand at her. She tried to block with her arm, but the blow hurled her up against the wall and she dropped to the floor in a heap. I was sure the monster was going to crush her, but then one of the guests ran by screaming, slipped on his trailing cloak, and tumbled into a pile with a couple other men. The creatures both swung their heads around to follow the chaos as it rolled to the other side of the room.

I wanted to just run for it, but I knew if I got back to the house and Lampedo didn't, Mema would take it out on me. I scrambled to grab Lampedo and got her by her injured arm. She wailed as I pulled her with me.

145

The sound drew the hermas' attention and their heads started to turn back to us. I picked a door and dragged her towards it while she slurred Thracian curses at me.

The door took us into a narrow corridor. Good. It would be harder for them to follow us here, though they didn't seem to have trouble smashing down walls. I picked the smallest door and shoved Lampedo through it.

It was a storage room filled with wine jars and stacked dishes. Lampedo sank down between two big vats clutching her arm. I pulled the door shut and listened. There was crashing and screaming, but it didn't sound like it was coming our way. I sat down opposite Lampedo.

"*Isis' milk!*" I hissed at her. "What did you think you were doing, trying to fight those things?"

"A warrior always attacks," she answered, grabbing a wine jug. She pulled out the cork with her teeth and drank a big glug.

"We're not warriors!" I snapped. "We're flute girls. Don't you get that? We have to be smart."

"You say 'smart,'" she scoffed. "You mean weak."

"Have you ever seen an old flute girl?" I asked her. "No, there aren't any. Most of us end up as graveyard women spreading for scraps. You only get through if you have a plan."

"What's yours?" she asked. "Hide in a storeroom?"

I scowled at her.

"I'm going to have a sandal shop, just like my–" I stopped myself. *Don't talk about the past* is Mema's first rule. *No one here had a happy childhood and it's no use picking at wounds that won't heal.* I thought instead of the future. "I save a little money every night. It's not much, but in twenty years, maybe enough. That's my plan."

"Plan, plan!" said Lampedo. "Twenty years and you could be dead. What good is all plan and no do?"

I couldn't hold myself back any more.

"You don't understand!" I nearly screamed. "You're not from here! You didn't grow up trapped behind these walls with the plague! Figuring out where the safe water was that none of the sick had bathed in. Rationing out your bread crusts and trying to guess when the public ovens would be fired again. We survived because we thought ahead. Those who just *did*, died."

We were both silent. I tried to steady my breathing. It was no good going to pieces when those things were still out there.

Lampedo took another swig of wine.

"No," she whispered. "I'm not from here. I grew up on a farm. Plenty of food. Good water. No walls. Then raiders from Makedo came and killed the men. I took a knife from the table, but I was too scared. When they took the girls for the slave market, I didn't fight, just dropped the knife and went with them. They burned the village behind us. I swore an oath to Bendis: fear will never stop me again. I took my first chance, ran away, hid on the first ship I found. It took me here."

We looked at each other as if for the first time. I hadn't talked about the plague years to anyone since coming to Mema's house and I was pretty sure she hadn't told her story before either.

She shrugged and added: "Didn't expect stone monsters."

I let out a little laugh.

"No. That's new."

Lampedo touched her bruised arm and hissed something to herself in Thracian.

"Bendis doesn't heal," she said. "Maybe your Isis isn't so useless."

"I don't even really believe in her," I admitted. "I just joined up to have people to speak Egyptian with. If the gods were real, would they let things like this happen?" We both knew I wasn't just talking about the hermas.

"Gods don't do for us," Lampedo answered. "They teach us to do for ourselves. Bendis slew the dragon to show us how to fight. Your Isis made her man whole to show us how to heal."

"Almost whole," I reminded her. "Don't forget the pin."

"Why is it always pins?" she sighed.

"Men," I said with a shrug.

I held out my hand for the wine jug.

"Mine," she said, pulling it away. "Get your own."

I did. A mouthful of the pungent unmixed wine made my head spin but it also made me stop talking and listen. It was quiet outside. I thought I could still hear the moaning of the monsters' voices far away, but the crashing and screaming had stopped. I motioned to Lampedo. "Can you walk?"

She nodded and pulled herself up with her good arm.

"Where?" she asked. "Back to the house?"

"We can't risk it that far," I said, "but the Isis house is close. We can get there."

I eased open the door and peered out. The corridor was empty. I waved Lampedo behind me and we crept towards the entry hall.

The hermas had gone away, for whatever reason, but a pile of smashed debris blocked the door. A torch was still burning in the dining room, spilling its light out into the hall. The sound of a groan from the dining room made us stop. We edged up to the doorway and peeked into the room.

The couches had been tossed around and there was still a giant hole in the wall, but there were no hermas in sight. Alkibiades was kneeling in the midst of the wreck, fussing with something on the table. I realized it was the courtesan, tied down, with little bleeding cuts on her arm. She cried out again as Alkibiades squeezed her arm to make the cuts ooze. He smeared the blood over something in his hand: the slider she had made us kiss.

"Yes, yes, blood," he murmured. "Blood is best. They all answer me now."

I motioned Lampedo away into a corner of the hall with me.

"We should save her," I whispered. Lampedo stared at me.

"Why?"

"Because she might know something useful. Because he's clearly up to something and he wants her blood for it. Because having rich people in your debt is never a bad idea."

"Ah," Lampedo nodded. "*Plan.*"

"Yes, now time for *do*. I'll distract him. You sneak in and get her free, then we all get out through the hole."

She nodded. I tried to imagine I felt as brave as I sounded.

I stepped through the doorway and started circling to the left. The courtesan saw me and called out for help. Alkibiades looked up.

"What, are you still here?" he asked. "Good. I may have need of you when this one runs dry."

"What are you doing to her?" I demanded.

"It's life," he whispered. "I tried so many rituals, so many offerings, but what they wanted was *life*!"

"Help me," the courtesan murmured. "He's crazy."

"I noticed," I agreed. I moved along the wall and Alkibiades followed me.

"Not crazy!" he hollered. "But no one in this city understands a man like me. They thought they could sweep me aside and put doddering old Nikias in my place? Ha! When they find their city ravaged by creatures of stone in the morning, will Nikias save them? Will he prattle and make peace? No! Only I control them! Only I can stop them! They will have to give me the honor that I am due!"

Now that I had Alkibiades' attention, Lampedo slipped into the room and began circling the other way. I'd known men like this all my life. They liked nothing better than to tell you how clever they were. For once, it was what I needed.

"How did you do it?" I asked.

He held up the slider.

"Friends of mine bought it off an old miracle peddler in Egypt years ago. Thought it might give me a laugh. I thought nothing of it at the time, but I noticed that strange things happened to the hermas around me. One night I took it and sat before one until dawn. Such powerful spirits! So much anger! I wonder if our fathers truly knew what was in the stones they set up to guard their houses. The presence of the phallos stirred them in their slumber, but I did not know how to wake them, not until you showed me! All my rituals were nothing. They wanted the touch of life, a woman's life."

Lampedo began to silently work at the courtesan's bonds.

"What then?" I asked. "Your new pets smashed up your house. What can you do with such monsters?"

"Ah," he said, "What do I care for this house when I could have a palace on the akropolis? I didn't know how to control them at first, but now every one of them heeds my will. What can I do? I will rule Athens, and with my stone soldiers, why not all of Greece? Why not—"

We didn't find out what else he wanted because the courtesan kicked her feet free of the cords and upset a pile of shattered dishes. Alkibiades spun around at the noise and exclaimed in fury. Lampedo lunged for him with her good arm. I jumped up and started untying the courtesan's hands.

"Idiot," I cursed her, "you couldn't wait?"

"Get me out!" she shrieked.

As Alkibiades and Lampedo scuffled, slow footsteps thudded closer. A herma with road signs for arms loomed in the hole in the wall. Alkbiades braced himself and shoved Lampedo towards it.

"Crush her!" he yelled, brandishing the slider.

The herma caught Lampedo in its arms and began to squeeze. She struggled but couldn't get free.

Alkibiades turned on me. I saw the slider in his hands. The herma's ludicrous pin. Seriously. Why is it always about pins? Even Isis' magic couldn't make Osiris live if her didn't have one.

Couldn't live without it.

Maybe...

No, that was insane.

But so were walking hermas.

"LITTLE FLESH THING," the herma roared. "NOW YOU END."

Lampedo was going to die and me soon after if I didn't do anything. It was worth a try.

I made a leap at Alkibiades. He swung at me but I tumbled to the side, grabbing a bit of broken masonry as I rolled past. (All that dancing wasn't for nothing.) I came up between the herma's legs.

"*For Isis!*" I shouted, just because it felt good to shout something, then I smashed the herma's pin as hard as I could.

The stone pin shattered. The herma staggered back and the roar became a strangled hiss. Its legs stiffened back into a stone post. The road signs straightened out, dropping Lampedo to the ground. The head became fixed back in a rough grin and the whole thing keeled over to fall in broken pieces.

It *worked*.

"I have more!" Alkibiades shouted. "I have so many more! You cannot stop me!"

The courtesan shook herself free of the last bonds and jumped up, elbowing him in the throat. He staggered back and the slider slipped from his grasp. I snatched it from the floor.

"Give it back!" he shrieked, reaching out towards me. I waved the thing to taunt him.

"*Come and take it!*"

The three of us ran through the hole in the wall and across the garden towards the gate. The slider felt strange in my hands, warm and smooth. Holding it I could sense that there were hermas closing in.

"How does it work?" I asked the courtesan.

"How should I know?" she screamed. "Get away from me!" She shoved me down on the ground and bolted.

"Good plan," Lampedo grumbled, helping me up.

"We got out, didn't we?" I answered.

There was no time to try to figure out how to control the hermas. After seeing Alkibiades, I didn't think I wanted to. I tucked the slider under my belt.

"This way," I said. "It's not far, we just–"

"FLESH WILL FALL." The moan came from the shadows of the house and stopped me short. Footsteps were grinding towards us out of the darkness. "STONE WILL RULE. GIVE US LIFE." A signpost herma came lumbering into the moonlight. It was moving slowly but with such long strides it would be on us in no time.

We ran for the gate, but the two gatepost hermas stepped into the opening.

Two ahead of us and one behind. I grabbed a spade from the garden and Lampedo snatched up a stone.

"Go for the pins!" I told her.

We ran at the gate hermas together. The left one swung at me with its long arms and I ducked. It tried to kick me, but the creature was ungainly and wobbled on one foot. I grabbed my chance and whacked it in the pin. The pin came off and the herma crumbled to the ground.

I faced the other gate herma, now reaching out for me with both stone arms. I smacked its hands away, trying to get a shot at its crotch, but it was a little faster than its twin and smacked me back. I flew into a hedge and the spade fell from my hand.

The signpost herma was almost on top of us. Lampedo hurled herself at it with a yell. She ducked and dodged, trying to get between its legs, but the thing had four sign arms that kept swatting her away.

The second gate herma picked up the spade and broke it into bits. Then it snatched me up. I squeezed out of its grip and jumped off, catching myself on one of the arms of the signpost herma. The signpost herma staggered off balance and Lampedo got her chance to smash its pin. The signs came loose as it fell and I crashed to the ground still clutching one. The gate herma was reaching for us but I rolled between its legs and cracked it in the crotch with the sign. It went down.

Lampedo slumped next to me, cradling her arm and sucking in long breaths. As the panic of the fight ebbed away I found myself trembling all over and became aware of an awful pain in my ankle. I'm a dancer, I know my ankle pains, and this one was bad. I tried a little weight on it and nearly screamed from the agony. I felt the slider pulsing warmly at my side and somehow sensed that there were more hermas out there, many more, none close but all coming this way.

"I can't walk," I said. I took the slider from my belt and held it out to Lampedo. She shook her head.

"Can't," she breathed.

"I thought fear didn't stop you."

"Not fear," she answered. "Pain. Very different."

I lay back on the cool stones of the path and let the slider drop.

"This is it, then?" I said. "We end here, with monsters, in a garden?"

"Have to end somewhere," she said between deep breaths.

My head was trying to make a plan, somewhere to go or something to do, but my body just kept answering: *No. Hurt. Tired. No.* Lampedo was right. We all end somewhere. Everyone who lived through plague and war knew that all too well.

"Your sandal shop," Lampedo said. "Tell me."

"What for?" I sighed. "It's never going to happen now."

"I want to be somewhere else."

I told her. How I would pick just the right house down in Peiraias. How I would lay out the shop in the front room. How I would know all my customers by name, just like my mother.

"Can I work in your shop?" Lampedo asked.

I looked over at her.

"We're going to be dead by sunrise," I said. "And you don't like me anyway."

"No," she agreed, "you yell at me. Tell me what to do. But you tell me why, too. No one else tells me why, just yells."

"Sometimes I can't stand you," I sighed, "but you tell me the truth. We tell so many lies, to Mema, to men, to the other girls. At least I always know you mean what you say."

She reached out with her elbow. I nudged it with mine.

"Is this what we are?" I asked. "Are we friends?"

"Friends who don't like each other?"

"Good enough for me."

The moan of the hermas echoed in the air overhead. I touched the slider. There were so many and they were closing in.

My head finally kicked my body in the behind.

"I'm not dying here," I said. I threw myself over onto my good leg, grabbed the road sign, and levered myself up. It hurt like nothing I'd ever felt, but I did it. "I'm heading for the Isis house. Maybe I'll make it. At least I'll draw them away. If you can run, head for Mema's."

Lampedo watched me take a few steps using the sign like an old man's stick, then she rolled herself upright. She loosed her belt and used it to tie her bad arm up to her shoulder, groaning against the pain as she did.

"I run," she said, motioning me up on her back. "You fight."

I didn't bother asking if she was serious, just dragged myself up onto her back. She held me with her good arm.

"So light," she said. "You should eat more."

"Running now. Complaining later."

She took off at a lope and I directed her through alleys and narrow streets, staying away from plazas and wide avenues where the monsters could surround us. Hermas smashed through walls around us and their terrible moans echoed in the streets, but we kept on running.

A herma burst out of an alleyway on our right as we sprinted through one street. I leaned out and smacked at its pin with my sign. It shattered and the monster went down. Lampedo headed down another dark street and stumbled to a stop as we saw a dozen hermas lumbering towards us.

"Which way?" Lampedo gasped. I was dashing through my memory of the neighborhood, tracing where each alley led. Left: two streets, one small fountain square, down an alley. Right: winding alley, over a wall and across a street. Back the way we came... I realized I was getting stuck again, just like back in the hall when I couldn't run because I hadn't figured out all the steps ahead. All plan. No do.

"That way!" I shouted, pointing to the left. Lampedo went.

A few more turns and we'd be at the Isis house.

Lampedo yelled as a herma lurched at us from the left out of the shadow of a house. She staggered to the right out of its reach.

I tossed the sign from my right hand to my left and hit the thing in the crotch as we veered past.

"*Bendis!*" Lampedo cried.

"*Isis!*" I shouted.

As we came up the street I spotted Seneb at the door of the Isis house with a club in his hand looking terrified.

"Sister!" he called out to me in Egyptian. "What is this madness?"

"We have to get inside!" I answered him as I eased myself off Lampedo's back.

"Not her," Seneb said. "It is forbidden."

"We're both going in," I insisted, switching to Greek so Lampedo could understand.

"She is not initiated," said Seneb. "Isis will be displeased!"

"Let her in or *I* will be displeased!" I snapped. Lampedo may be master of the *You idiot* look, but I'll put my *You're a slave and I'm not* voice against anyone's. Seneb grumbled but stepped away from the door. I hated yelling at him, but I didn't have time to be nice.

Leaning on each other, Lampedo and I stumbled into the house and towards the sound of hymns ringing from the sanctuary. Meritamen was there with some of the other initiates. It's her house and she's our priestess. She's from Egypt, way up the Nile, and even darker than I am. She married a Greek merchant and followed him to Athens, then when he died in the plague she took over the business and made a fortune. The other initiates are mostly Athens-born Egyptians like me, but there's some sailors from Peiraias, a Persian goldsmith, and a Phoinician family. A few of the Egyptians and the Persian were there.

"Sister!" Meritamen called, sweeping across the room to us. I like it in the Isis house. It's the only place where no one calls me "whore" or "girl," just "sister." (Well, the Persian mutters something in his language whenever he sees me, but he does that to everyone, so I don't take it personally.)

Before she could say anything more or complain about me bringing an outsider into the house, I pulled the slider from my belt and thrust it towards her.

"This is what stirred the monsters," I said. "They want it. We have to get rid of it."

"Why bring it here?" said Meritamen. "This is a place of peace."

"But there has to be something we can do!" I insisted. "A spell or prayer. It's like the story of Osiris. There must be something!"

Meritamen tilted her head back.

"I know no prayer for this, sister. I will give you and your friend refuge tonight, but this mystery is beyond me."

I nudged Lampedo and she helped me into the middle of the sanctuary. I brandished the slider right at the image of Isis.

"What kind of a goddess are you who can't help your followers when we need you?" I shouted. "Take this thing! Take it far from here! I don't know the right prayers, but if you can hear me, do something!"

Then all was light. I blinked my eyes against a desert sun and glimpsed a ribbon of green land along the banks of a great river. A soothing breeze touched my back and behind me I felt a presence filled with love and sorrow. An unseen hand lifted the thing from my grasp. I felt, rather than heard, the words: "*We are whole and all will be well.*"

Then I was in the sanctuary again, empty-handed and blinking. The roar and thud of the hermas from outside was gone. Everything was still.

I sank down and Lampedo caught me. A cold sleep was claiming me and I didn't fight it. The last thing I heard was Seneb's voice calling: "They are fallen, all of them, smashed to bits!"

***

Lampedo found me sitting by the Peiraias docks. She shook her hand and I heard the jingle of silver.

"I found that courtesan," she said, setting next to me. "Gave me a handful of drakhmas for a promise she never sees us again."

It had been a month since that night. We'd both been tended in the Isis house until my ankle and her arm were healed. Lampedo had taken the first order of Isis, just out of respect. After the initiation feast, she had muttered to me: "*Bendis is still better.*"

Of course, no one said anything about stone monsters in the streets. When people had come out of their houses in the morning and there were no monsters to be seen, they all just told themselves it was rowdy young men smashing hermas for a laugh.

I took the coins from Lampedo's hand and added them to the ones from my pouch. (I'd claimed all my savings. Meritamen isn't just our priestess, she's our banker.) It wasn't a lot, but it was enough to make a new start.

"You're sure you want to leave?" Lampedo asked. "What about your sandal shop?"

"I've danced for sweaty drunks in too many of these houses," I answered. "I want to do something new. Some of the sailors are saying the Tyrrhenoi are hiring mercenaries and don't mind women. Are you up for it?"

"We are warriors," Lampedo said.

"No," I answered. "We have slain monsters—we are *heroes*."

"Like sun and moon," she agreed.

"Winter and summer."

"North wind and south wind."

"Eggplant and egg."

She poked me in the ribs and we both laughed.

"Come on," I said. "We've got a world to see."

Art by Lindsay Ishihiro

154

The Ostrich Egg Girl
JM Templet

1837
Liberia, Africa

The first cut was a shock. Lumusi felt the hot trickle of her own blood between her legs, heard the barking of the masked spirit above her as it chased away evil. Its face leaned towards her own, smelling of loamy earth and stripped tree branches. The orange of its skin seemed to extend to the very ground beneath it.

The second cut was worse. She knew it was coming. Her arms struggled to hold themselves down. This was right. This was ritual. Her mother had done it. Her father's first and third wives had done it. Her sisters after her would lie on the same ground Lumusi did, feeling the same dull blade cut into their flesh.

She would not cry. It was important not to cry.

The spirit pulled her up while she bled, dropping an egg on the floor. She picked it up, smearing dark red on its white surface. The egg was so large. She carried it in her arms like a babe as the other girls trailed behind her into the forest.

A day. A month. A year. However long it took, they would wait until their eggs hatched. Only then would they be recognized as full members of the tribe.

The spirit was a boy named Kovu, who ate ants like candy and pinched Lumusi's arms blue. Now he was Kankurang, their guide and watchman. The spirit stopped to chew on the bark of a nearby tree. Some of the girls were already gone, following their path. Lumusi and a few others straggled behind, listening.

One by one the other girls left. Until only Lumusi followed. If she could not find her path she would be led back to the village, forever a girl. Perhaps a fifth wife, if some rich man took pity on her. Or a servant, bent and broken.

The spirit stopped. Waiting.

He wanted her to fail. Not the spirit. Kovu.

Lumusi ran from him. His footsteps did not sound behind her but she knew he followed. She circled a tree, heading away from the middle of the forest. Branches slapped her face and arms. She burned inside and out. The egg felt so heavy in her arms. She wanted to drop it but she did not.

When she could run no longer she fell back against a tree, letting the dead leaves underneath cushion her fall. She could hear nothing but the quiet humming of the insects and animals. She closed her eyes.

There were voices. At least she thought so. Far away, near the water

155

maybe. Lumusi remembered watching a great boat dock a few weeks ago. People had come wearing strange clothes, speaking that strange liquid language. Their faces had been dark like real people but different. Distorted.

The elders called them copies or devils. The elders called for warriors to destroy the new settlements but no one knew what to do.

It had been strange watching the way the newcomers had moved like bees all buzz and feverish running. She'd imagined one of them might be a copy of herself. Imagined a whole life in which there was another version of herself living somewhere else. With some other name. Lumusi rolled her egg in her hands, wondering if that other her could scratch the smooth surface. Would the sound of her voice crack Lumusi's egg? Break it into so many pieces?

If her egg did not hatch she could never leave. If it broke or cracked she might as well stay and live among the monkeys and sharp beaked birds.

Lumusi would be a tale told just like her grandmother. One day, the old woman had taken to her bed. She neither spoke nor ate nor drank for three days. Lumusi and her mother pleaded with the old woman. Her father's first and third wives had helped with nursing and prayer but nothing lifted the old woman out of her spell.

Until one day she got up, dressed herself, and walked into the forest. She never came back out.

Months they searched. First, the whole tribe. Then, just the family.

No scrap of cloth. No shoe. No bones. Nothing was ever found.

Lumusi wanted to sleep. She wanted to crawl home into her hut and snuggle with her two sisters, Makini and Nua. She rubbed her face against the dark bark of the tree. She could almost hear their heartbeats. So small for such a big sound.

She wasn't sure what drove her to wake. The sun wasn't up and the night wasn't too chilly. She looked down at her arms and legs. They were not her legs and arms. They were colored red, not the light brown she was used to. The skin was moving.

She screamed. Ants. They crawled over her, swarming in her hair. Her nails. Her nose.

A few hundred had gathered under her egg and were carrying it away. She snatched it up as the ants held on, biting the tender flesh they were attached to. She followed the sound of water to the nearby river, jumping into it. She held on to that egg. Held on so tightly.

She pulled herself up out of the foggy river, mud soaked and choking, with the egg still in her arms. She fell asleep there with the salt of silt in her mouth.

When she woke it was dark. She used some of the mud from the bank of the river to soothe the worst of her bites. All around her the dark forest made sounds now. Birds called warnings as she trampled north. North was a good direction wasn't it?

Lumusi looked down at her skirt, remembering the last time she'd worn it.

Temit leaned back in the sun, her hair wrapped tightly. Her toes wiggled in the soft dirt. Bundura and Disa sat around her, their hands a blur as they wove colorful fibers together. Lumusi's weave looked clumsy next to theirs. Her hands felt like frozen claws.

"You'll never get a husband if you're not good at anything. You won't even be a third or fourth wife with that weave," Temit said.

Lumusi looked down. Temit's father was the richest in the village. She was assured of a good match. She wasn't good at anything either but Lumusi didn't say that. She didn't say anything.

Disa snorted, smoothing her soft skirt over her knees. She stretched her hands, one finger at a time. "At least Lumusi can hunt, which is something. All you can do is look pretty."

"A man wants a beautiful bride. Not one who can bring in game better than he," *Temit replied.*

Bundura hummed, continuing her weave. She'd been taken from one of the boats as a toddling babe. Elder Chidike raised her, promising to cast out all of the evil she carried. She did not speak or look at others when they spoke. She often bore purple bruises and had a ropey scar across her chest.

"You will end up with a man who has a belly as big as the moon," *Disa said.*

Temit grinned. "That just means he is so rich I will have to do nothing all day."

Disa shook her head. "I want a man fair of form. A fine man. I don't care what he owns. You cannot buy honor."

"No but you can pay it off," *Temit said. She picked the dirt from under her fingers.*

"What about old Golibe?"

Golibe had been the fairest girl in the tribe. Her father had given her to a man from another tribe for much wealth. After a week she had come home with a face out of nightmares. Her nose was not a nose. Her eyes were black slits. Her father sent her back. Again and again. Until she no longer came to the village for help.

When she was very old she had come, gnarled and scarred, to spit on her father's house. She showed the younger girls her back. The scars like tracks of a rough animal that lined her skin.

Golibe's father was dead by then so she was allowed to stay in his home. She stared out of the doorway with bird's eyes, pecking whatever came close.

She died in there. Elder Eseo found her dried up like an old piece of fruit, curled against the wall.

"Stupid woman. Men hit. It is their nature. Would you resent the cat for stalking the rabbit?"

Disa shook her head. "My father has never hit my mother."

"Your father is weak. I've heard my father say so," *Temit said.*

Disa lunged at the other girl, her hands going for the beads around Temit's throat.

"Don't talk about my father!"

Bundura started to rock and moan. She let out a screeching cry.

Lumusi put her hands on the trembling girl's shoulders. "It's okay," she said. "No one will hurt you."

She didn't know why she said it. It's what she would have wanted someone to say to her.

Temit had earned a scar on her chin from that fight. Her father demanded restitution from Disa's father, who couldn't afford the price. Instead, Disa had ten stripes across her back. She wore them proudly, never letting her head drop.

Lumusi straightened. She could be brave. She could be as brave as Disa.

She found an old tree and set her back against it. The bark was rough but comfortable. She would wait until dawn to hunt.

The tree moved behind her. Lumusi jumped. She'd missed the snake, lying still on the branch above her. It wrapped around her neck. She pulled but it only tightened.

"Stop that!" a voice yelled.

It sounded like her grandmother, Liseli. She'd had a face like the stump of an old tree, lines upon lines wreathed her smile. The snake hissed and let go.

"Foul animal. I told her not to nest here," the voice said.

Lumusi turned and saw the face of her grandmother in the trunk of the tree. There was no crop of white hair braided into curving lines. No long arms or sagging breasts. Yet Lumusi knew that face.

"Are you real?" Lumusi whispered.

Her grandmother's eyes opened. They were made of wood but shaped the same. Her grandmother's eyes looked at her.

"As real as you are, my granddaughter. As real as any dream."

"Why did you leave us? For this?"

Her grandmother's face cracked into a small smile. "For many things. The forest is my home, not my daughter's hut. I no longer bleed from cleaning. I no longer sigh from watching my daughter bow and scrape for affection. I nourish things here. Three generations of red throated birds have nested here. I am their grandmother too."

"It was not so bad at home."

Not so bad that her grandmother had to become a tree.

Though there was Uduak, her father who was not her father. Uduak, who kept reminding her mother how kind it was for him to take her and Lumusi in when they had no one. Uduak, whose hands were always grasping the soft parts of her body when they were alone.

Her grandmother's smile did not leave. "It is better here."

Lumusi did not believe that living as a tree was better than living as a girl. Her grandmother had no legs to jump. No arms to hold.

"You should go. Many dangerous things live here. And I am tired now. I want to sleep."

Her grandmother's wooden eyes closed. Her face disappeared. Lumusi touched the tree bark, searching for her grandmother. All she felt was bark.

She sighed, turning away. She would have to find something to eat.

***

Lumusi did not know how long she had been in the forest. More than a week. More than a month. No one stayed in the forest this long. The egg was supposed to hatch. She would go home and start life as an adult. Yet the egg stayed still. Silent.

Her clothes had long since devolved into tatters. She'd fashioned a sling to carry the egg from a part of her shirt. She'd sharpened several sticks to use for fishing and hunting. Her grandmother had taught her which insects and plants were safe to eat and where to look for them. She missed home. She missed her mother and her sisters. But she thought she'd done a fine job of not dying at least.

Amadi, a boy who'd undergone the ritual a year before, had only been in the forest three days before eating a poisonous plant and falling over. His father had found him bloated with hands reaching for a nearby stream of water.

She had looked for her grandmother again but hadn't found her. She talked to the egg instead, telling it her secrets. Her wishes. She wondered what she'd done wrong.

She was hunting one day when she heard a crack. At first she thought she'd stepped on something. The egg in her arms grew warmer. Lines of red formed on its surface. Red dust dissipated from the cracks as the egg shook. She almost dropped it but remembered she had to hold on. It was important to hold on.

Parts of the egg flew off, landing on the ground. In the middle was a round soft form with no features.

"You could be anything," Lumusi whispered. "Even a prince."

The form wavered, becoming so hot she had to drop it. It sprouted on the ground, growing legs, a torso, and arms. Finally a head appeared.

It was a man so handsome he must be a prince. He looked down at Lumusi.

"Shall I rescue you then?"

She looked down at her feet, the man put his hand under her chin, raising her gaze up. She imagined living with him. Lying in the sun doing nothing but enjoying the day. Kissing those lips under that perfect nose.

Beyond him, the forest loomed. Full of dark secrets and hidden places. She had been born there, as much as the egg.

"No thank you," she said finally.

"Are you sure?" he asked.

She nodded. "But there is a girl who needs you. Her name is Disa. She is very kind and very sad. Go to my village and find her. Take her with you."

The man started to walk away then paused. "I could make you happy. This place is not safe."

Lumusi remembered the ants. The snake wrapped around her neck. The rough skin of the bark of her grandmother tree.

"It's safe enough for me," she said.

She watched the prince walk away, knowing Disa would leave with him. She held her pike tightly in her hands, already missing the warmth of the egg. She turned, heading deeper into the forest. She wasn't going to turn into a tree. At least not yet. There were many places she wanted to go. Grandmother would wait.

Art by Jay Bendt

NORTH
IMANI JOSEY

1919
Detroit, MI, USA

Between the day's work in her uncle's restaurant, and the alien greeting of the seasons in Detroit, Viola was perfectly distracted from the letter on the countertop. Though Mrs. Walker, the near blind but ever faithful waitress, had dropped it amongst Viola's belongings that morning, she hadn't opened it. Instead, the two danced intricate choreography, almost crossing paths without actually doing so.

October is the ugliest month, she thought, hands tight on the broom handle and eyes cast to the floor. October was once a relief, the mark of autumn when children returned to school between planting seasons. But here it was slick pavement and silver breath, cold as rotten as it was awful. Viola pushed a small pile of dust into the center of the floor. She'd already swept the restaurant twice, and there wasn't much left to heap.

The whispers would mount like her piles. *There goes that niece of Richard Lowe again, tall as a boy and working like a mule.* Like her general reticence, Viola's work ethic was oft the subject of commentary, especially from her uncle who liked the place neat, but didn't care about spotlessness. He was a businessman like all of the Lowe men, and protective to the point of ridiculousness. *Young ladies don't walk home in the dark*, he'd say. Viola reminded him that it wasn't dark at all; the city lights brightened the streets better than any road in Huntsville.

Her broom hit the tile, and she didn't pick it up. Instead her eyes flickered to the clock above the entrance, its hands ticking near *9:30.* She'd have to leave soon. Time moved fast in Detroit. It slunk lazily at home, thick in the heat, swelling about her limbs. The sun went up, and like the broom crashed down. But with each day she was closer to a train north, one she'd board in the dead of night and a county over, in someone else's clothing, and an axe tucked inside her traveling bag. She switched off the lights and darkness shrouded her, accompanied only by the glow from the streetlamps.

She sauntered over to the counter where the letter sat and picked it up, noting its lightness. Her mother must not have had much to say. She took a seat before tearing it open. As her fingers tugged the paper inside, the door creaked open. Vi stifled a groan and dropped the letter where it had been. "We're closed," she said, words stretching longer than intended. She hadn't mastered the clipped, sharp speech of the city yet. The chatter outside the Black Bottom restaurant buzzed through the entryway.

The door soon shut, but she wasn't relieved. The stranger hadn't gone.

Instead, he shifted his weight as a stark image of Vi's axe came to mind. She wished she'd kept it with her instead of at her bedside. She straightened her back, mustering all the authority she could. "We're closed," she said. "We'll be open tomorrow morning."

"Vi," the stranger said. The tightness in her back unraveled at her name, and the voice who called her. She swung around. She had a new, more consuming fear now, one shooting white-hot electricity through her limbs. A man, eye level with Vi on a good day, stood near the glass door. The evening shadows veiled his features, and she couldn't rightly identify the mirage before her as the man she'd known, as Albert.

She pushed onto unsteady legs, and they buckled. Before she hit the floor, the strange visitor was at her side. His hand slid across her back and held her, near enough to faintly smell walnuts on his breath. Walnut trees grew all over the Lowe grounds, and Albert was known to climb them a time or two. "Breathe, Lowe," he said. His sparkling eyes found hers, a mosaic of slate and gray. There was no disbelief now.

He helped her to her feet as a rusty sound escaped her mouth. "How?" she managed.

"How what?"

"How are you here?"

His eyes narrowed as if she'd asked an absurd question, before he countered, "How are *you* here?"

"*Albert.*"

He pointed to the entrance. "You ain't lock your door." She sat again as he walked over and latched it. She watched patiently, though her head was light and her thoughts crashed against each other. He took a seat beside her upon return allowing his scent, walnuts and handmade soap and maybe the Alabama sun on his skin, to fill her nose. His presence drummed up so many questions, but the familiarity of this smell washed them in and out like the tide.

Despite this, she forced the rust off her windpipes. "Your mother got the letter," she stammered before dropping her voice an octave. "I *saw* the letter." She searched his face for understanding, but he just smiled again. Not a smirk, but the wide smile she hadn't seen in so long. It reached his eyes, and something inside her broke, reassembling better than before.

"Seems like you got yourself a lot of letters," he said, plucking the note on the counter behind her.

"Put that down."

"Make me," he said wickedly. He inspected the letter, recognizing the return address. "Mrs. Patsy is fast."

Vi rolled her eyes. "Mrs. Patsy is a lot of things."

"Be nice," he said, smoothing his coat down the sleeves. "She's your mama." He wore a dark, wool overcoat with a large brim hat. She hadn't noticed his attire until then, but it had to be standard issue with the doughboys, something they gave him in Paris. He looked distinguished and older. But digging muddy trenches to the tune of men's bellows would age someone. He began to open the letter as Vi's fingers fell atop his. He stopped moving, and dragged his eyes up to hers.

"Albert," she said, voice thin. "But that *other* letter—"

His eyes danced over her face, her neck, before he spoke. "Sometimes they're wrong, Viola," he said. His gaze left her, suddenly taking in the restaurant. "You like it here?" he asked. "I knew your uncle was going to open something nice, but nothing like this." Vi's uncle hadn't returned to Huntsville since the war broke in Europe. He and the first wave of southern émigrés left at the call of labor agents. Often disguised as insurance men, they snuck through the colored sector of town, whispering, *See me to go to Detroit*. With the steady stream of European laborers drying up, the North needed men and women. Most landed in Black Bottom, or areas like it, and her uncle followed with plans for a restaurant to serve them.

"I do like it," Vi said. "But it's cold."

"It is cold," he said with a nod and trained his eyes on her again. "Why you take yourself up north?"

"My uncle needed someone to work here he could trust. And—" His smile faded as she continued. "You weren't coming back." He leaned forward and wrapped his arms around her, an embrace to warm the October air.

"But I'm here now."

"Albert," she said with a shiver. He didn't get a chance to respond. The latch on the door clicked open and they sprang apart. She was darker than Albert, but knew her face was flushed. Her eyes shot to the entrance as her Uncle Dick fumbled his way through. He held a few parcels, and she rushed to help him. "Oh, thank you, Vi," he said, handing her one of the smaller packages.

She waited, ready for her beloved uncle to start cursing, to see her alone with a young man, the guilty hue of her cheeks. At home if Albert was interested in a courtship, he would get fifteen minutes with her in the front room after church, either Patsy or her father Lewis accompanying her. If Lewis liked him, he'd later get thirty minutes and neither he nor Patsy would chaperone. But Uncle Dick looked down at her admiringly as always. "You not feeling well? You red in the face."

Vi knotted her brows. "You ain't mad?" she asked.

"Why would I be mad?"

"Because," she said, glancing over her shoulder to Albert.

Her uncle followed her gaze. "Because you left that broom on the floor over there?" He laughed as he set the remaining packages on the counter and marched to the back. "Rather leave these here. Didn't want to fool with them in the morning," he announced of his load.

Viola didn't answer. She couldn't. Where Albert had been was nothing, just the broom on the floor and the letter on the counter. She inspected Albert's seat, touching the warm cushion. "Viola," her uncle called, emerging from the back room. She snapped out of her trance long enough to walk with him to the door. He swung it wide, but stopped himself. "Go on home," he said, patting her on the shoulder. "You're working too hard again."

Vi nodded. Perhaps she was.

***

July 1917

Chuck adjusted in the seat before her. He was stalling, racking his mind for new topics as they'd exhausted the polite ones: the weather, the church revival, the upcoming harvest. He picked at a button on his dark vest. He wore the high-falluting style, fitted and smart across his chest, with slacks like the military issue. As if he'd even consider going off, Vi thought. Charles Hawthorne had a few minutes before her father would ask him to be on his way and she was counting every one of them. He had called on her twice already, this being his first unchaperoned visit. Her parents liked him. If only Vi did also.

After her sixteenth birthday, they'd come calling: two young men her parents weren't fond of, and Chuck Hawthorne, who they adored. He was like a peacock, all fluffed and plumed, with a straight back and nose stuck in the air, and shiny leather shoes that caught the light when his foot twitched. There was only one colored family in the area with money to match the Lowe's. They were the Hawthorne's, a clan who supplied goods to local businesses with large, noisy trucks.

Vi should have been happy to have a man like Chuck calling on her. Every girl in town drooled over him as he paraded his truck and ignored them. His only fault was that he stirred Vi as much as the furniture or the clock on the wall. But as her mother reminded her, affection wasn't the deciding factor in courtship. "Best be getting on," Chuck said, breaking Vi's thoughts.

"Oh, you sure?" Vi asked. He stood with a nod, taking his traveling cap from the table beside him. "I'll walk you out."

At the door, he tipped his hat to her. "Miss Vi," he said in the way that made her feel oily all over.

"Mr. Hawthorne," she said in parting as he started down the front steps. He'd almost reached the landing when he abruptly stopped.

Vi inched back in the doorway. "You alright?" she asked. He turned back to her without an answer. Before she'd realized, he was at her side again and took her hand with an awkward jerk. "Chuck?" she asked as his eyes raked her. He brought her hand to his mouth and kissed it, lips hot and wet and slobbery against her skin. He was the richest colored boy she knew. Most things did belong to him. But his smug, satisfied grin made her want to be the last woman on earth he made claim to.

Something cut through the air and connected with Chuck's brow in a violent flash. He staggered, yelping as his cap slipped off. He rose again, nursing a brown welt on his forehead as if the Great War had made its way to Vi's porch. "What was that?" he wondered aloud.

Vi could barely contain her laughter as she scooped up the sign from God – a walnut – rolling near her feet. "We have a lot of nut trees," she offered Chuck's grimace. He muttered and turned away, her muffled chuckles escorting his retreat. Vi watched dirt churn behind his truck until he disap-

peared.

With supper approaching, she needed to head inside. She didn't, however, make it far. "Thank you would be nice," a voice called out to her. She turned to see Albert Brown in her yard, a soiled linen shirt and trousers clinging to him, and a mixture of sunlight and sweat dripping down his neck.

Vi stepped toward him and folded her arms in amusement. Al Brown's family worked for hers. She'd known him as long as she could remember and despite the weekend, he must have been in the fields for extra wages. "Why would I thank you?" she asked.

He motioned to the walnut in her hand. "Thought I'd help you out."

"I was fine," she said. "Chuck was just—"

"Calling on you," he finished. "Everybody knows he's calling on you. Well, if you won't thank me, I'll do it for you. 'Thank you, Mr. Brown, for saving me the shame of old Chuck pawing me down my daddy's porch.'"

"Albert," she growled as he marched off. She flew down the stairs after him, throwing the walnut between his shoulder blades. He winced as it bounced off, but didn't slow down. "See how you like it," she said, struggling to catch up with him.

"You grateful and you know it." He slowed his pace. "I've been working the last few Sunday's, and every time he comes, you look like you about to meet your maker."

Viola shrugged. "Mama and Daddy like him. That's all that matters." He grunted but didn't counter. A gentle breeze passed them, and Viola hummed in appreciation. Albert was often working, so the stroll was a rarity not to be wasted on Chuck Hawthorne. "Why you working Sunday's?"

"Money," he answered quickly. The road forked through a patch of shrubs, bouquets of blue cornflower and spiked rattlesnake master reaching for the sun. A creek wound near their path. A bed of speckled rocks lay beneath the calm waters, and men fished there on Sunday's after church. Albert's family lived on the other side.

"Well thanks for what you did. I don't get to throw things at Chuck much."

"Plenty of time for that when you married," Albert said. It was her turn to grimace. "So what exactly are you doing?"

"What do you mean?"

"Why you still walking with me, Lowe? Nothing to report from the fields," he said, cool eyes twinkling at her. Her words jumbled in her mouth, but before she could arrange them, he spoke again. "It's fine, though. I wanted to ask you about something."

"Alright."

He waited a beat before words tumbled from his mouth. "What the hell were you doing last week?"

"Oh that," she said, her face flushing. Albert didn't have much going in his favor that day. It was still early in the season; most of the bolls wouldn't open until August. Men could pick more than their weight when the harvest got good. The Browns were no exception – a family of talented pickers. But the trait had somehow skipped Albert. He hadn't neared even a woman's magic number of one hundred pounds. In fact, he'd been out from sun to sun cursing, spitting, and kicking up dirt. Vi's bedroom overlooked much of the field and the commotion rang through her window. She poked her head over the pane, wanting to scream at him for the noise, but even from her room she could see his light bag and tight brow.

She left the house so as to not disturb her parents, and wove through the rows of white buds as the sun took to the horizon. She found Albert toward the middle of the field hunched over, nursing a swollen wrist. Her shadow caught his attention, and he straightened his back. She wore a dress with black lace trim and pearl buttons from the white side of town, a stark contrast to his tattered work clothes. He protested her help, which gave her enough time to snatch his bag and shoot him a murderous look. He gave up the fight with a long sigh as she draped the bag over her shoulder. They crouched to pick in silence.

The motion was mind numbing and repetitive, straining Vi's head as much as her hands. At first, she delicately plucked the bolls from the pointed cocklebur that held them. In turn the barbed plants nipped at her fingertips, puncturing and bruising them. By twilight, she snapped the plant off without much technique. When the bag gorged, she set it down and pushed it over to Albert, batting an unruly strand of hair. Some of her hairpins had come undone during the work, and her pressed locks mixed with sweat, puffing up at the root.

She looked like death, but Albert didn't mind. With the hum of dusk around them, he kicked the bag to the side and extended his hand. She eyed him but soon placed hers in his. He gently turned her palm up, letting his thumb trace budding calluses on her fingertips. He was a sharecropper. His hands were a minefield of bumps and bruises, of scratches and tough skin. A girl like Viola didn't need tough skin. She didn't need to pick cotton, and she didn't need to dirty her fine dress. But she willingly did. She drew a breath, preparing to say something, anything, but he let her hand fall. In an instant, he'd picked up the bag and breezed by her.

It was a week beforehand, but neither knew what to make of it. "Don't worry about it," she finally said.

Albert's voice was low, dark. "Viola," he said.

The tone stopped her midstride. "What's wrong?"

He paced. "I have to tell you something." Her wary eyes watched him still. "I'm leaving soon."

"Leaving? North?" she whispered.

He shook his head. "Tennessee and then Paris," he said. "I entered the draft."

He might as well have said the moon. "That's why you doing all this Sunday work?" she asked as he nodded slowly. "Albert, you could die."

"And I can't here?" he asked. Vi diverted her eyes, wrapping her arms about her though she wasn't cold. They lived in a volcano always simmering, always ready to blow. Written and social laws in Huntsville, like anywhere below the Mason Dixon, were harsh for colored men and women. In-

fraction could be as arbitrary as a misplaced look or an uppity turn of phrase, with justice carried out in the backwoods with ropes and kerosene. "It's a good wage. Show Huntsville I'm a patriot."

"They'd string any colored patriot up to a tree," she said.

He took a measured step toward her. "Not trying to upset you." Her eyes narrowed stormily. "Don't be like that," he said as he closed the distance between them. His hands ran up along her shoulders, drawing circles on her skin. She shook, maybe from the news, maybe from his proximity.

"Be how I want," she snapped. He laughed, trailing his fingers alongside her face. It didn't help her trembles.

"I didn't just bump into you and Chuck," he admitted. "I was waiting for him to go, so I could tell you about the draft. I timed it so I wouldn't see him, but I was off." He shook his head.

"And you took a cheap shot?"

"Real cheap shot," he said. "But it just wasn't fair."

"What wasn't fair?"

"In a fair world I wouldn't have to worry, not here or overseas." There was no space between them now. Every nerve in her body, every bit of her blood sang. "In a fair world, I'd get to call on you."

***

October 1919

A train screeched to a halt near Viola's window. She winced and rolled over. She'd barely shut an eye between the evening screech of the freight trains by her building, and the howls of the bulldog next door. She lay in bed tossing and turning, praying to nod off. But even under the best circumstances, she wouldn't have. She'd seen Albert, and her mind and heart were reeling.

A rustle in a shrouded corner of the room caught her attention. It wasn't uncommon that vermin found shelter in the neighborhood crannies as the air turned colder. The drafty room she rented a floor up from her uncle was nothing in comparison to her spacious bedroom overlooking the fields, and the mice had already taken to the walls. This odd, heavy rustle didn't, however, belong to a mouse. When her floorboard creaked, she shot up in her bed. The creak, the bend of the wooden planks under leather shoes, caused the hairs on the back of her neck to rise. He was there. She could feel him.

Albert emerged from the shadows near her bedroom corner, still in the overcoat and hat, and Viola threw her covers off in a rush to him. The pair collided with a hard thud. As he found his balance, her fingers danced across his shoulders, inspecting his skin and clothes. "Vi," he said, squirming when she poked his abdomen. "Vi, stop." He took her hands and held her still.

"Alright," she relented. He smiled and let her go, attention falling to the braids framing her face. Vi's soft hair was in many ways like the cotton the Lowes grew, fluffy despite its tangles with the hot comb, rich strands of auburn in a sea of brown. He played at loosening one as she curved into him.

"Albert, tell me how."

"You asked," he replied.

"Asked what?"

"You asked," he repeated, "for me." He smiled and shook his head as she attempted more questions. "You need to open the letter first."

"What letter?" she asked, lowering her tone before speaking again. "I saw the letter to your mama."

"No, the one in the restaurant."

She recoiled. "I don't want to read that. Mama just wants to complain about me going north." He shook his head and scooped her up in his arms, holding her so tight she couldn't breathe and didn't want to. He nuzzled the crook of her neck and inhaled her scent, perhaps committing it to memory as if he may never see her again. "Read it for me," he said. Viola closed her eyes as a wash of air danced around them. When she opened them again, he was gone.

***

August 1919

The stretch between the planting and harvest seasons was brief, the only time the watchdogs were less vested in guarding the train platforms. Their duty was to keep field hands in the area, but without fields in need of tending, they had other priorities. Vi had never really worked the fields, but she was colored, and enough had left already. If she was going to meet her uncle in Detroit, it was the best time to do it.

Vi prepared all week swelling her lone traveling bag, borrowing clothing, and arranging a wagon ride over to the next county. Her mother Patsy watched the exhausting work without comment until it was time for Vi to leave. Patsy then became the unmoving boulder, and made no effort to say goodbye. "Well, you don't look like yourself," her mother announced.

Vi stood in a tough, cotton dress, muddied at the hem and fit for a field hand. She belonged to the only colored family in Huntsville to operate as planters, and Patsy loved for her children to dress reflecting their station. She'd never wanted Vi in the fields, and she never wanted her to look like she worked them. "I ain't disappearing forever," Vi said after a long silence, as it was known to happen. Whole families disappeared when they could, heading up to one of the manufacturing cities like Chicago, Detroit, or Milwaukee. They left on the winds, without a word of warning or a murmur of farewell.

"It's far for a woman," Patsy said, eyes like rocks. Vi took after her father and was a head taller than her mother. But Patsy could instill the fear of God in her daughter with a pointed word or look.

"For your daughter," Vi corrected. "I know this ain't what you saw for me. That if I was going north, I could at least been married."

"To that boy?"

"Albert is a good man."

"He's a Brown. Browns work for us."

"Lowes worked this land before that planter left it to Granddaddy. If not, we'd be just like them. All our families came over at once." Her mother's mouth set into a firm line. She didn't like reminders of how the colored families in Huntsville arrived a century beforehand. Patsy came into the world during the great Reconstruction, when white soldiers in northern blue forced the planters to play fairly. And they did, at least until those men in blue packed up and left.

Patsy saw the signs sprout up soon after, one weed at a time. Colored Only. White Only. The railcars separated. Voting was barred. Every little liberty her parents and grandparents fought for in the Civil War was stripped. A new generation sprang up, her contemporaries and Viola's, in many ways more hostile to out- of -caste men and women than their slaver forefathers. Patsy grunted. "Got advanced schooling for a woman. You'll marry Chuck Hawthorne, be a teacher."

"I don't want to marry Chuck," she said. "And I may be a teacher, but I haven't decided." Vi crossed her arms. They'd had this conversation before. The only difference was that now Vi's bag was packed and the train to Detroit left in the morning. "I'm just going to work with Uncle Dick for a while. See what it's like up north, with the good wages."

"You're going because you saw that damn letter." It wasn't actually a letter. It was a telegram, and Albert's mother called for Viola as soon as she received it, a few months before the war ended. It started off like all telegrams of the sort, remorseful, and quickly relayed that no one in Albert's regiment would ever come home again. Mrs. Brown couldn't read, so Vi choked out every word. From then on her world was a dream, a nightmare without end.

"She let me read the letter as a kindness, so I wouldn't be... waiting."

"Her son was no match for you, rest his soul."

"He loved me."

"Trying eating that," Patsy snapped. When Viola said nothing, Patsy sighed and flicked her hand. "Go on to Detroit. Get this out your system. Then come back and marry." Silence wedged between them. Vi slowly walked over to her bag as Patsy raised her hand in the air. Vi stilled. "Before you go, I need you to do something."

"And what's that?"

Patsy undid the top button of her collar, and pulled out a link chain with an amber pendant. No matter the day, no matter the weather or occasion, Vi had seen it on her mother's throat. She was surprised when her mother unsnapped it, and motioned for Vi. "Take this to your grandmother," Patsy said quietly and extended a necklace. "She wants to see you before you leave."

"Why?"

Patsy sat back, lacing her fingers over her stomach. "Just does."

Oak trees lined the dirt path, their long branches stretching further than Vi could see. Squirrels hopped from the plant limbs overhead, rustling the leaves and dropping fruit and nuts in their wake. Vi thanked heaven that *her grandmother's was en route to her meeting point with the wagoneer, but tried to remember why her grandmother lived so far. She could have spent her twilight years in the spacious Lowe home or anywhere else she wanted. But her grandmother, Mother Ann, chose to live in the backwoods.*

The waking sun cast a glow along Viola's path toward the single-story home. Once at the front, she ascended the steps, batting away insects that dared stir around her in the muggy air. She set her bag on the porch as her eyes traveled up to moss draping the roof. Her heart pounded.

Moments passed after she knocked without any sign of her grandmother. She had to be inside; there was nowhere else for her to be. Viola knocked again. This time the door popped off the hinge ever so slightly, but when Vi poked her head inward, she found no one on the other side. "Mother?" she called out.

Nothing.

Vi knotted her brow. The elder woman usually loved welcoming her guests. Vi crossed the threshold with her bag and closed the door behind her. She brushed her feet on the mat, and maneuvered to the sitting room. The interior was plain as she remembered. Only a few pieces of carved, wooden furniture decorated it, unlike her mother's sitting room with its plush tapestries and European-style finish. Mother Ann had only lit one lamp, which sat on a table in the middle of the floor. Its shadows mixed with the soft sunlight, and played tricks on Viola's eyes.

A voice, gravel on concrete, called out. "Gal," Mother Ann's alto carried from the kitchen, and Vi wondered how something so low could fill the whole room. Mother Ann had many grandchildren and great-grandchildren, all of whom she called boy or gal. "Set your bag down," Mother Ann said.

Vi placed her bag next to a chair and took a seat. Her grandmother appeared, carrying a tray with a pitcher of water and a small basket of biscuits. Mother Ann was petite like Patsy with dark skin not nearly as weathered as it should be for her age. A salted plait hung to the nape of her neck as her hands curled oddly around the tray. She set it on the table between them before sitting. "Patsy told you to come by?"

Vi nodded. "She said you wanted to see me."

"I do," Mother Ann said.

Vi waited for comments, concerns, or commands from her grandmother that never came. Instead, Mother Ann gingerly sipped her drink. Vi tried to encourage her grandmother with her eyes to speak. No such luck. "Mam," she finally said. "What would you like me to do for you?"

"Nothing," she said. "I want to tell you your future." Mother Ann smiled, and though her eyes weren't particularly sharp, Vi could feel the heat of their gaze.

"Mama's got my future planned," Vi muttered. "After I get it out of my system."

"You talking about that boy?"

"Mama told you?"

"No." Mother Ann shot her a conspiratorial wink. "It would about kill

Patsy to admit her daughter's carrying on with anybody." She took another sip before continuing. "Your Mama has her mind on one of those Hawthorne's for you anyway." Vi crossed her arms. "But Patsy done an awful thing."

"What do you mean?"

"She trying to tell your future when she know she can't."

Vi tried to drain the amusement from her tone. "Right, because you will."

"Exactly."

Vi narrowed her eyes. "And why is that?"

"Patsy sent you with something for me?"

"Oh," Vi said, digging in her pocket. She soon produced the necklace, and handed it to her. "Mam," Vi asked. She didn't know what about the necklace made her mother and grandmother behave so strangely. "Mam, what's going on?"

Her grandmother ignored her, busy admiring the chain. "I haven't seen it up close in so long." Mother flipped it over and tugged at the chain, inspecting it. Something warm passed behind her grandmother's eyes, a sweet memory, a particular dream. Whatever it was, Mother composed herself and continued. "Of course when I had it, it wasn't polished up so pretty. Looked more like an ugly, little rock."

"You gave it to Mama?"

"No."

Vi sighed. "I'm confused."

"My mother gave it to her, just like I'll give it to you."

Viola liked gifts, but the strange way Mother stared at the necklace made her push back in her seat. "Mama and Daddy gave me enough fine things."

"Neither can give you this," Mother said with a chuckle. She stopped fiddling with it long enough to tangle her fingers in the chain and place it in her lap.

"What is it?"

"A wish. A prayer. I always saw it as a choice. It was my choice. Then it was your mama's choice. And it'll be yours. I'll give it to you, just like my mother gave it to Patsy, and you'll give to your eldest granddaughter."

"You can't know if I'll have girls, let alone granddaughters."

"You will," she said so certain that Viola shivered.

"I still don't understand," Vi whispered.

"In you and your mother, in all of us is a kind of," she chose her words carefully, "blood. Goes back to the first families that came over from Virginia to Huntsville, to our ancestors. Before the first harvest season, a young woman bathed in the woods near her quarter when she caught sight of a child bathing near her. The child was alone, so she kept an eye on her, but the peculiar girl was calm and quiet. When the woman began to leave, she heard little arms thrashing in the waves. She looked again and the child wasn't bathing, but drowning.

In a rush, she yanked her up onto the bank. The child didn't breathe, so she pressed on her, breathed air into her until finally she coughed water out. The woman said she'd take the little one back with her, but before she could, the child took her hand and held it firm like a man. It startled the woman, especially as the child took on a shine like heaven and her voice became rolling thunder."

Vi drew a breath. "Like an angel?"

"Wish I knew. Can't say I've run into any," she said with a shrug. "But for her kindness, our ancestor received this." She held up the necklace. "It was just a rock then, but the token is for first daughters in our family. It creates a choice in this world, a choice given from grandmother to granddaughter when like the harvest, the time was right."

Vi narrowed her eyes. Her grandmother wasn't one to exaggerate, but it was too fantastic a story to go without scrutiny. "So why didn't our ancestor wish to the trade and all servitude?"

"Your wish can't fix the whole world. Just yours. When my mother gave it to my eldest daughter, Patsy chose the first thing that tumbled foolishly out her mouth."

"Mother, you can really believe—"

Mother Ann raised her hand in the air, quieting her. "Means." Vi's thoughts ran over her home, her clothes and privilege in life as she knew it.

"You aren't saying..." Vi asked, eyes wide.

"I wouldn't lie to you," Mother Ann continued. "But there's more to life than means, especially when you can choose any life you want."

"The only life I want I can never have."

Mother's gaze was steely. "You haven't chosen," she said. "I'll know when you do."

**

October 1919

The door flung open as Vi rushed into the restaurant. It was early enough to see stars in the blushing sky, the one'd normally stop to admire. Jealous streetlamps didn't let anything else shine through in darker hours. Today she didn't. Instead, she shrugged her coat off and hurriedly searched the counter for a letter that was no longer there. The irony was not lost on her as her eyes darted each way. The day before she wanted nothing to do with the letter, but when it was all she wanted, it was nowhere to be found.

"What're you doing there, girl?" Her uncle's booming voice startled her as he emerged from the backroom. The restaurant wouldn't open for an hour, and Richard Lowe, never the early riser, usually dropped in closer to that time.

"Did you see a letter for me?" she asked in a single breath. "It was sitting right on the counter."

He thought for a moment. "S'pose I did," he said and pulled a crumpled envelope out of his pocket. Before he could properly hold it out, she'd snatched it. Surprise peppered his laugh. "Good news?" he asked. Vi didn't answer, instead folding herself in a booth away from his watchful eyes. His words drowned out as she focused on the ink, the words on the page. To her surprise, the letter was dated before she'd even left Alabama.

Dear,

You've left us to go about our days as if they're easy, though you've taken something from us. You took the piece of our hearts that will always be yours. But we can't fault you. A piece of yours left some time ago. By now you've visited with Mother. I wish I could have been there with you, or be there with you now, to help you set your mind. Since I can't, I'll tell you what I did, and hope it is a light.

My grandmother called me at the end of a harvest. The season was good, but the planter gave us nothing for it. He said we broke even, and that my daddy didn't owe. I hadn't eaten good but once that week. When she called me to choose, I made up my mind on the spot. I never wanted my children to know a belly that swelled from hunger pains. I wanted means. She gave me this strange, little rock and said it would be.

I thought I'd leave that night with a full stomach and fine clothes, but I didn't. Nothing about my life differed until Lewis Lowe showed up at our porch after service the next Sunday. Of all the colored boys, Lewis would be the wealthiest. His family managed land after Emancipation, and he was the only colored boy I knew that never had to pick cotton. He called on me in grand style, with horses and driving his own wagon. I'd never seen a Lowe look twice at someone like me — someone who didn't have shoes let alone leather ones — until he was there, the answer to my wish.

But everyone knew Lewis was promised to the daughter of a minister the county over. When he came to see me, it was the first thing I said to my parents. But they didn't remember the girl. I thought they were just being some type of way until I asked around about it. Everyone just shook their heads. When I finally asked Lewis, he didn't know what I could mean. It was like the memories of them together had vanished from everyone's minds.

I was promised to Lewis soon after, and was happier than I'd ever been despite how he came to me. Before our wedding, I rode over to the next county with him. Of course I caught sight of that girl. No one had spoken of her and Lewis in months, but when she saw me mounted on Lewis's wagon, she shattered. She sobbed right into the dirt because of my wish. It tore a piece of me right out. Only two people in the world remembered how it was supposed to be: the pair of us.

Even happiness has a price. It must be worth the cost.

Always,
Mama

Vi's uncle and Mrs. Walker, caught in morning chatter, stole her attention from the dancing words. Vi pressed the letter to her chest and took a long breath, unable to quiet her thrumming heart. She was vaguely aware that Mrs. Walker had stopped speaking with Richard, but she couldn't focus on anything other than the letter's spilled secrets. She pulled herself out of the booth, tucking the note in her pocket.

"Viola," her uncle called out. She stopped, having all but forgotten he was there, and met him at the counter.

"What's wrong?" she asked, taking in his heavy eyes and taut face.

"I didn't want to say nothing, but your mama told me about what happened before you left."

"Oh," she said, surprised her mother had told anyone about Albert. His mention brought a mixture of warmth and fear. Wishing for him carried an unknown price, one she or Albert would have to pay.

"If you still ain't feeling well," her uncle said softly, "we can send for your mama or get you a ticket home."

The words tumbled out gracelessly. "I don't want to go home."

"Viola, you ain't eating. You thin as a rail."

"Don't send me home," she pleaded.

"It's not what I want." Richard placed his hand on her shoulder. "Just tell me how to help you."

"Let me stay." She searched his eyes. He patted her head as if she was six-years-old. "It'll get better."

"The New Year, alright, Viola?" he asked after a beat.

"Alright," Vi said. He turned to go about his day and though Richard didn't protest her state further, she knew he didn't believe she was fine. She couldn't let it bother her, though, and forced the day to pass in a blur of hungry guests and pasted smiles. After Richard and Mrs. Walker left, she lingered to see if Albert would appear again. He didn't, leaving her to return in defeat with the letter still crumpled in her pocket. Normally a sanctuary, her bedroom closed in as she stared at the walls, her breath short under mounting thoughts.

When the time pushed after one o'clock, she changed into a night dress and folded herself into bed. She couldn't, however, will herself to sleep. Her thoughts – the fields and tall grass near the creak, her tea dress, those eyes like gray quartz – crashed against each other. "I need air," she announced, sitting up and throwing her legs over the bedside. She stretched her fingers and toes as a collection of her mattress springs creaked under the weight of another.

Her eyes shot to the young man lounging at the end of her bed as if on a park bench. Albert smiled when their gaze met, his plain trousers and blue shirt making his eyes shining pools. "Hello, Viola," he said as she collected as much air as she could. "You're tired," he assessed.

"Didn't sleep last night."

"I suppose you had reason." He leaned forward. "You read the letter?"

"Yes," she said. He began to speak, but she took his hands, stopping him. A question burned in her chest, the one she'd had since seeing him in the restaurant. She needed an answer, even if she didn't want it, so she blurted it in a short breath. "Albert, did you... are you...alive?"

Time slowed as she waited for his reaction. With his face unchanged, she considered repeating herself until he started laughing, the sound like the thrash of a hammer against the quiet. "Don't I look alive?" he asked.

"Yes, but you just *appear*," she flustered. "And a letter came to your house saying your regimen–"

His eyes grew heavy and the laugh cut short. "I know," he said. "The truth is you saved me."

"Saved you?!" she almost shrieked.

"You asked for me in your pillow at night, when you swept and mopped your uncle's floor, when you look at me now like your world flipped over. Your wish gives me a second chance."

"My wish," she whispered, wondering how her heart could soar when her stomach dropped. "The wish ain't safe," she said. "It has a price, and I don't know who for. You might not remember me or I might not remember you."

"Listen to me," he said, shaking his head. "I already know the cost," he said. He looked over her, the fine night dress she'd brought from home. "Not at first, but soon there will be nothing to go around in the country, for anyone." He took her hands. "If you go home, be with your parents and wait it out, you won't suffer."

"And marry *Chuck*?"

He ignored her. "But if you choose me, we won't have anything when it comes, no big house or fine clothes," he said. "Nothing you're used to." He looked in her eyes. "I can't ask you to do that for me." He expected her protest, not her silence. "Viola?" he asked, searching her face.

She outstretched her hand, palm up and coaxed his hand over hers. His fingers began to trace her skin as if it was that twilight in the fields. "Only world I want is the one with you in it," she whispered. A faint snap beckoned her eyes downward where Patsy's necklace now rested at her throat. She'd chosen, and it was hers now. Viola had a mind to touch it, but Albert had already stood and pulled her to her feet. His arms wrapped tight around her. He'd already dusted a kiss on her mouth light enough to be cotton in the air, a single piece dancing on the winds.

He was gone before the morning sun touched the window pane. She thought the entire world would be new when she woke, but pink and scarlet stained the morning as before and her bread and jam tasted as it always had. Albert never appeared from any corner of her room, no matter how many times she called out. For the exceptional happiness that coursed through her, she had nothing to show for it. She left for work with solid doubts, their only contradiction being the chain around her neck.

She cut through the city streets alert enough to dodge the trolleys, but too distracted to notice she'd passed the restaurant and had to circle back. "You need a better coat," her uncle said when she finally arrived, kicking sodden leaves off her boots. He sat at the counter, reading the morning paper.

"Why?" she asked, shrugging her coat off and placing it on a hook.

He turned the page in his newspaper before looking up at her. "Your face is red again. It's too cold up here for those light coats."

"Oh," Vi said, touching her cheek. "I'll write to Mama for another." The clock had barely struck *8:00*, but the restaurant thrummed with hungry workers. Mrs. Walker balanced plates on her forearms as she served a few tables, and buzzed around Viola for help.

"Vi," she strained, "grab table nine."

Glumly, Vi nodded. She took an apron off the nearby rack and tied it around her waist. A nasty crack ran through table nine's window allowing wintry air to gush through. If she had to work in the vicinity, any layer of clothing would help warm her. She dragged her feet until she reached the table and its guest. "How can I help you this morning?" she said to a hunched man whose large brim hat cast a shadow over much of his eyes and nose.

"Coffee," he said without bothering to take off his hat or even look at her.

She wrinkled her nose. "Alright," she said, eager to leave. The sooner she served him the sooner she'd be done with him.

He spoke again.

"Vi," he said as her blood iced and electrified. "Too cold up here for this broke window." She whipped around as Albert removed his hat. She launched herself into the booth, her squeals tangling with his laughs, his limbs enfolding her own. She was sure Uncle Richard's mouth was agape, like everyone else's in the room, but she was too swept up in the song of walnut trees and cotton fields, of harvests and magic, to care.

He'd say he kept himself alive in war's grip for her. He'd say he returned from Paris, and Tennessee, and Huntsville to the concrete city for the girl he couldn't let Chuck Hawthorne marry. He'd never mention the other night, or even remember it. He'd never know that Viola saved him in the only way that mattered, a memory she'd never ask him to recall.

Art by Kaley Bales

ACCLIMATING FEVER
PETER MEDEIROS

1827
Liberia

Borforh sat on the docks, dreaming of a day when he might sail a ship instead of unloading one. He and a dozen other boys watched a pair of dinghies heading slowly out to a French schooner; it would come back with more cargo for hauling into one of Monrovia's waterfront warehouses. They would come with Parisian furniture, wardrobes and chaises and settees in the plush European style. Furniture so soft Borforh didn't see how they lasted more than a week.

Borforh wondered if a deya witch could cast a spell to make him strong. But the part of him that believed in witchcraft wasn't the same part of him that had to finish the moving.

Nearby, a group of Americoes watched him, chatting and laughing with Borforh's boss. Despite the heat, they wore stovepipe hats and high collars despite the heat. They were all older, taller, and lighter than Borforh – who was cable-strong from work, but at fourteen had yet to finish growing – and the unloading would have gone smoother if they helped. But precisely because they were perhaps a shade lighter, and born in across the sea, and lived in fine houses of imported lumber here in Monrovia – for all these reasons, they would not stoop to help a native-born Kru boy like Borforh.

"How many more?" one of the other porters asked. He was even younger than Borforh, maybe twelve, a Grebo.

"We'll get done when we get done," Borforh said, meaninglessly. The younger boy didn't understand how much of life was spent waiting.

They weren't working long before some disturbance drew everyone's attention.

Zachary Matthews pushed his way through the Americoes and ran towards Borforh. He was a tall man of forty, dressed in a black jacket and trousers with a gray stripe down the side. He was dark as Borforh, but he was a proud Americo settler from one of the "honorable families" – he had come over with one of the first ships from Philadelphia, and he never let anyone forget it.

Mr. Matthews was also the adopted father of Borforh's friend Gordon. Gordon had left with an expedition to the interior some days before, and now Borforh felt a sharp, sudden fear for what could have befallen him in the jungle.

Borforh set down the ottoman he's been carring and ran to learn what happened to his friend.

"Borforh," Mr. Matthews panted, "Gordon's expedition has returned. They were looking to seek out the Watkins River head–"

"Were they attacked, sir?" He wasn't sure why he said it. He was a Kru himself, and he knew that local headmen had no interest in another skirmish with the Americo settlers.

"No, nothing like that. They're *sick*, Borforh. Sick to a man. They all fell sick with acclimating fever."

Borforh had heard how acclimating fever had killed hundreds of Americo settlers when they arrived six years ago. "All of them were sick? How could they *all* be sick?" It was troubling; Borforh was curious.

Mr. Matthews only said, "Gordon's in the hospital now. He's asking after you. I've spoken with your boss. If you could come–"

"Of course I'll come with you, Mr. Matthews."

"Good lad, good lad." Mr. Matthews stomped away, leaving Borforh behind.

Before he could catch up, Borforh felt his boss's hand around his arm. Like most bosses in Monrovia, he was an Americo mulatto, and very vocal about it. He always wore short-sleeves to show off the light coppery hue of his brown skin. Some Kru (not Borforh) called men like the boss *white black men* – though always in Grebo, never in English.

"You want to be a sailor?" the boss said.

"Yes, sir," said Borforh. "Some day."

"I could see it in you, how you study on the ships like they're women. Well, then, you'll need to learn how to take orders, boy. How to take care with a man's things, do the work properly. Without having your fancy friends come to distract you."

Borforh shook his arm free. He said nothing. He wondered if anyone would still call him *boy* when he was fully-grown, climbing the rigging of some beautiful frigate out on the wide blue sea. When he was finally *going* somewhere.

But he knew the answer: if the captain was an Americo, and knew he was Borforh, then they'd always call him *boy*.

***

When they arrived at the hospital, Mr. Matthews said that Borforh could go inside himself; in his delirium, Gordon had asked for him. Borforh saw that the man expected his adopted son to die; he was offering the boys a chance to say goodbye.

Borforh entered the squat hospital. Saw-blade coughs came from every open door. The building smelt like sweat, feces, and dirty rain.

He found Gordon in a narrow cot at the end of a long central hallway. His friend had the same lanky frame and true-black skin as him, clear signs he was not born of an honorable settler family. He had changed his name from Gonlekpei, but no one would mistake him for an Americo.

"Oh, Gordon," Borforh breathed. "Can you hear me?"

Gordon coughed. "I'm dying, I'm not *deaf*."

182

Borforh could see that Gordon was not exaggerating — he *was* dying. Gordon was bare to the waist and his muscles were visibly twitching; and though it was wet and hot out, the end of the dry season, he shivered.

"Your father came to get me," Borforh explained. "He wants to know what happened." It sounded cruel out loud. *What happened?* was very different than *How are you?*

"Stop looking at me like that," Gordon said. "You might as well get used to getting by without—" More coughs, a sound like a boat splintering apart, over and over.

Borforh disagreed. He would not have to get used to getting by without Gordon. If his friend died here, there was nothing to keep him in Monrovia. He would go to the French schooner while it was anchored off Cape Mesurado, away from the capital. Either they would take him aboard as a deck boy, or they'd throw him in the sea.

But Gordon wasn't dead yet.

"This isn't acclimating fever," Borforh observed, "whatever they're saying."

"No." Gordon sounded disapproving, like Borforh had rudely called attention to some social taboo. "The men with the expedition, they think the sickness comes from 'miasma.' From the air here. My father disagrees, but he still thinks it's a disease. But we all fell sick at once, Borforh." He tried to snap his fingers to illustrate the point, but there was no strength in his hand.

Borforh stated the obvious: "It's a curse. Or an angry *ku* spirit in the river."

Gordon looked at the ceiling. "I would've argued yesterday. Everything I said about you hanging onto to superstition—" He trailed off.

Mr. Matthews had studied to be a preacher when he was younger, and part of Gordon's education revolved around the civilizing effects of Christianity. Borforh still prayed, sometimes, to Nyesoa and his half-remembered family spirits; and the boys quarreled about it often.

"But what we saw out there?" Gordon continued. "It wasn't 'miasma,' it was like a...*dark light*. The trees were sick too, like the water was poisoned. They were turning brown and wilting, like they'd been poisoned. There's nothing they can do for me. I'm going to die here."

"That's shit," Borforh said. "You wouldn't have asked for me if you didn't know there's a way to fix this."

Gordon sat up on his elbows. "Borforh, that's not what I wanted! Do not go talk to any of those people!"

"What people?"

"Some native *deya* witch! If this is the work of a *ku*, who do you think sent it upon us? Who do you think—?" Again he was interrupted by a fit of coughing. He brought his long hands in front of his mouth, like he could catch his breath and return it to his lungs.

"Jayplo will know what to do if it is an evil spirit making you sick."

"How can you trust her?" Gordon snapped. "She lives out in a strange hut—"

"We used to live in 'strange huts,' even if you don't remember it."

The words cut. Borforh saw the wounds in his friend, and they were old wounds, scarred and healed many times over.

They had both lived with a small tribe until he was eight, under a headman the Monrovians called King Anslem – and it seemed King Anslem had taken on the name they'd given him. Then, after the Americoes arrived and made deals with Dey tribes for the land – as if the Dey spoke for everybody living near Cape Mesurado – Borforh and Gordon were both traded to Americo families as wards. Along with plenty of other children.

Traded. Borforh wished he could think of a kinder word. But King Anslem had told him in no uncertain terms that he was to learn the Americoes' *kwi* ways, to learn their letters and their religion. But his adopted parents – short Americoes, warm but distracted, and permanently tired – died of some stomach-sickness after a single year. Borforh shuffled between dilapidated vagrancy houses for some months after that, then began working as a porter and sometimes-translator for Americo meetings with Grebo and Kru. Now he lived in a "Kroomen tenement house" on Marine Street.

Gordon, meanwhile, had been a good trade. He lived with Mr. Matthews, who owned one of the finest houses in all of Monrovia; he had bought it a fortune he earned overnight, from trading palm oil with the French. He was an educated man who had travelled the world and studied its peoples. Borforh got lessons from an overworked schoolmistress at a beneficent house, who was never sure if she wanted to talk about arithmetic or the Lord Jesus, while Gordon had a private tutor. Borforh hauled boxes between anchored ships and a mildew-y warehouse, retracing the same rotten wood, while Gordon was trusted to help guide a Monrovian expedition to find the head of the Watkins River...

Borforh stifled these selfish thoughts. If Gordon caught acclimating fever, as the Americoes called it, he could be dead in hours.

"There are plenty of preacher-men here, but they get mad if you even *mention* spirits," Borforh said. "We need help from someone who understands curses. It doesn't matter what you think of her. I am going to speak with Jayplo."

Gordon relented. "Don't tell my father where you're going. Or your boss man."

"Wouldn't dare," Borforh said.

He called to mind images of Gordon when he was playing, jumping between shafts of sunlight, to drive away the memory of his deathly face and the meaningless arguments that interrupted their friendship.

***

Leaving Monrovia, it struck Borforh how needlessly wide the streets were. The boss told him once they had to be that big so that ox carts could turn around; but Borforh had never seen an ox in Monrovia, or any draft animal.

It took Borforh four hours hard travel to reach the old village where he used to live. He came back several times a year, since he could translate for

Monrovian merchants who did not speak Grebo. Still, the sight of his child-hood home gave him a dizzy, uneasy feeling. No, not even a feeling, but the outline of a feeling; not homesickness, but the knowledge that he had no home to be sick *for*. He could walk there in four hours, but it had been stolen from him all the same.

Do not have a bitter heart, he told himself. You are here for Gordon.

He passed thatched huts and long low houses. A woman in a white wrap and ropy bracelets cooked over an open fire, but when Borforh hailed her she only glanced at him incuriously. He tripped over a pair of children who seemed to be chasing each other. Somewhere men laughed, real belly laugh-ter, over unheard silliness. Borforh only ever laughed like that with Gordon.

He skirted the center of the village to avoid speaking with the headman, King Anslem. He did not have the patience today.

He found Jayplo crouched over a very different sort of fire from the cooking woman: there were rocks beneath the kindling, each marked with intricate white lines. Jayplo herself was likewise painted, with white markings across her cheeks and forehead. She wore an orange dress that fell down to her bare feet.

"Tell me," she said in Grebo, "you did not bring any more of those white black men. They were out one of their 'expeditions,' and I was praying they'd be satisfied with whatever they found and go home."

"Just me," Borforh said. "But I *am* here to talk about the expedition. They all got sick. Not from fever, but a curse."

Jayplo rolled her eyes. "Oh, a real *shame*."

"It is more than a shame. Gordon is dying."

Jayplo stood up and paced close to him, unblinking. He could smell her, smoke and pepper and acid. She was older than Borforh, but still young for a *deya* woman. They had played together as children, before Borforh was given to the Americoes as a ward. At some point she had decided he was a white black man, like the settlers, and they had not been friendly since. He waited for her to send him away, already disappointed.

"Tell me why you think it's a curse, then," she said.

They set down around the fire, balanced on their heels. Jayplo seemed perfectly comfortable, but Borforh wobbled and had to catch himself; eventu-ally he settled back on his rump and stayed that way.

He repeated what Gordon had told him, about the trees. How the Americoes got sick all of a sudden. Jayplo agreed that it sounded like a spirit sickness, but there was nothing she could do without finding the *ku* or the sorcerer who was working it. That could take a long time.

"How long?" said Borforh.

"Why you want to help those people, anyway? Those people who took you away. Who talk so much and mean none of it? They tell you about Mano men taking slaves and how horrible it is, and how they came here for–" She puckered her lips like she'd tasted bad fruit.

"Liberty?" Borforh suggested.

"Yes! And freedom and all that, and how *awful* the white men treat them across the sea. But then they come and tell us where we can and cannot go, like *we* are *all* slaves."

Borforh did not disagree. "Maybe you think I'm a fool working for the *kwi*. I don't know if that's right, but I know that Gordon will die, if we don't help him. And he said it was killing all the trees around the river. The people fish and bathe there, Jayplo. A confused *ku* won't care who it kills."

When he was done talking, Borforh looked at his hands. It was hard for him to ask a direct favor of anybody. Asking for things got you hurt when you were a Kru living in Monrovia.

Jayplo stood up, rolling her shoulders. She had legs like a porter's, like his own, thick from work. Borforh had grown unused to seeing a woman's bare skin – Americo girls wore bonnets, shawls, and dresses with short puffed sleeves. He wanted to tell her they had something in common, that his legs looked like that too, that they ached in the mornings at the thought of the day's labors, but did not know how.

"Well, let's find out who is working this sickness," Jayplo said.

Borforh had to stop himself from thanking her profusely; she would say it was more empty words, more Americo-talk. "How?"

"If it is a *ku* spirit, I will ask who summoned him." Then, as if Borforh had protested, she added, "I will make him tell me true."

***

It was evening before Borforh and Jayplo reached the expedition's abandoned campsite. It wasn't hard to find. Gordon and the Americoes had left deep footprints in the mud along the river, which led straight to an unnatural clearing. "They take brooms to the jungle," Jayplo observed, "and treat it like one of their mansions."

"You cut trees for your homes. You clear brush too." Borforh shut up quick when he realized what he had said. *You*. Not *we*.

"Yes, we clear for our homes. This is not their home." She stopped walking. "Look."

There were long gray scars running up the trees. It was as if the bark was turning to ash from the inside, rotting from some unseen disease. Like Gordon.

It was every single tree. Borforh realized they had been walking through a sick jungle for a while. This was not Americoes's work.

Jayplo gave orders and Borforh followed. She had a sack across her front filled with unlit torches, which they split between them. They planted them at intervals around the dying trees. Borforh lit them with a packet of matchsticks he always carried in his trousers' left pocket. The flame from each match seemed to leap towards the torches, like eager dancers moved by the beat of a drum, and soon Borforh stood in a ring of fire. Smoke poured from the torches faster than from any natural flame.

The torches, Jayplo said, were fashioned of gleaming blackwood, the ends wrapped around with some gauzy cloth Borforh did not recognize. And tucked in the cloth? Dried insects, snake teeth, wide leaves thick with orange veins, and a gummy blood-colored paste Jayplo had produced from a small wooden bowl. "Tree toad," she had explained. "For confusion."

"Confusion?" Borforh replied. "For us or the spirit?" Jayplo only laughed.

He planted the torches at intervals in the soft earth, then set about lighting them.

"Is it working?" he asked.

"Don't you trust me?"

The smoke turned from black to brown to a vivid green. Long streaks of blue appeared in the growing cloud, leaping and splintering and disappearing an instant before Borforh could see what shape they were forming. Next to him, Jayplo closed her eyes and began speaking quickly in a language he did not know.

A wind rose, and as it grew Borforh heard a sound like the groaning of a ship as it is rocked by the waves.

Now the smoke roiled. It solidified. It turned an oceanic blue. Borforh could not put a name to what he saw moving in the smoke, because it seemed to have many shapes, many possible names. It had something of the tiger, something of the shark, something of a prisoner who sees his chance to escape. Teeth and desperation.

If he had been alone, Borforh would have run. But Jayplo was beside him, studiously unafraid, or else masking her fear.

The *ku* spoke, and its words shook Borforh's jawbones: "How did you know I was here?"

"I knew it was sorcery," Borforh whispered to Jayplo. "I told you."

"So," the *ku* purred, "is it only you two little children? You have come all alone? Very *brave* children, then."

Jayplo gave Borforh a withering look, then turned to the demon. "You cannot hurt us in this smoke, foolish spirit."

"Ah, but what if the skies opened up and the rain came down and washed your smoke-tricks away, spirit-woman?"

"Suppose the ground opened up and swallowed you whole," Jayplo said.

"I would like nothing better." The thing in the smoke pulsed, flickered, disappeared, and finally returned, longer and less luminous. "I was brought here, children. I was *taken*. You think I *want* to be here, so far from my home?"

Borforh was surprised to find himself stepping forward. Something about the spirit's protest made him angry. "What do you mean, you don't *want* to be here? Why did you attack my friend?"

The jungle seemed to grow darker. The *ku* was looking at him. "I'm from the place between places, and I *liked* it there. I'm not one of your little water-spirits that dwell in these shallow spaces, living off your prayers. Things get lost in the between spaces, and that's what I feed upon. If your people's spirits are so weak they cannot pass through me without falling sick, that is no fault of mine." It flashed deep purple, the color of a shrug. "As I said, I was brought here against my will. I was taken from my home."

"Right," Borforh said. "That's what we need to know, then. Who brought you here?"

"Who brought *you* into the world, child? Who wanted you here? Who wants you anywhere?" It laughed, a sound like crackling bark.

Borforh looked back to Jayplo, helpless. "I thought you said it had to tell us truth."

"You need to hold it," she said, "and ask it directly. Then it has to answer you."

"Can't you do it?"

She looked at him flatly. "I brought you this far, Borforh. If you care so much about the Americoes, you can handle this yourself."

"I'm here for Gonlekpei." Borforh shook his head. It had been years since he'd used the name Gordon was born with. "I mean Gordon." He swallowed. "Fine, then!"

Borforh walked into the smoke. It stung his eyes and scratched at his throat. The *ku* slipped out of view, and when it reappeared it was not in one place but everywhere, tendrils of blue moving through the air like tree branches with teeth.

"Who brought you here?" Borforh asked the spirit again, though he hadn't caught it yet.

"Wh-wh–" The *ku* was laughing so hard it seemed like it could hardly speak. "Who wants you here at all, little boy? I can see well enough that you're not where you belong, either."

"They don't know me," Borforh said, "and neither do you." He reached out, groping. His hand closed around nothing but air, air so hot it could burn.

The spirit slipped across the back of his neck. By the time Borforh spun on his heel, it had skittered away. "I don't know you, no. But who does? You have searching eyes, little boy. You want away from here even worse than I do!"

Borforh knew it was no use arguing with the spirit. "I want to leave," he said, "someday. I want to see the world. I don't want people to get hurt."

"Oh, that's it?" the spirit teased. "You want to travel, and to keep people *safe*? Noble ambitious! I'm curious, did you take that from a book?"

"Yes, as matter of fact!" said Borforh.

"Borforh, this was a mistake," said Jayplo. "I'm sorry I made you do it. This *ku* is very strong."

Borforh ignored her. "I did get my ideas from books. The Americoes' confidence, everything about them, it comes from how they use their past, which they set down in books. I've read about the bad things that happened here. I've read about the fighting with the Malinké, when the Americoes first came. All the people who died. It's important to remember."

"Oh! And you think it could have been stopped if you were there?" said the spirit.

"I don't know."

"What do your books say about what happened to you people? Was it *terrible*?" The spitit was very close now.

The smoke had snaked its way deep into Borforh's nose. His eyes might have been scooped out of his skull. His skin felt crisped and loose, like he could peel it off with his bare hands. "It was," he said with certainty, though of course he was too young to remember.

Still blind, he turned and shot out his hand. It caught something wet and slippery and hot, made of damp earth full of nails. The *ku* fought, writhing, outraged. Borforh felt a knife flicker across his face. Blood leapt into the air. Jayplo was yelling in Grebo, but he held on tight. He held on until it felt like his hands were stripped of their flesh, skeleton hands, and finally the spirit went still.

Borforh was crying, and he had to fight to speak. "Tell me," he demanded. "Tell me who brought you here."

The spirit was crying too.

***

Borforh put both hands on Gordon's shoulders before he told him what the spirit said, in case Gordon tried to leap from the hospital bed and rush into the street. "It told me it was your father, Gordon. It said his name, very clear."

Silence settled around the room, hanging down like thick vines between all of them. It began to make Borforh nervous. It didn't help that Jayplo and Gordon glanced at each other like wary wild animals, ready to pounce.

Finally Gordon said, "Mr. Matthews has been strange, and for a time now. All he talks about is clearing the land and planting more dura trees, for the oil. So maybe it was him. But maybe he thought it would only kill the bushy trees along the river. Maybe he didn't know it would make us all sick." He glared at Jayplo. "Then again, maybe it wasn't him at all."

"Maybe you've got dung in your head," Jayplo muttered.

"Gordon, look," said Borforh. "Jayplo couldn't be *bothered* to use a sneaky trick like that. And she wouldn't come into Monrovia unless there was real trouble. She hates it here."

"It's true," she said, glancing around the hospital room with distaste. "This whole place smells like death."

Borforh saw his friend wrestle with the truth and lose. "All right. So what can you do about it?"

"Jayplo said your father would need all sorts of...things. To bring the spirit, I mean."

"He probably has an altar," Jayplo explained. "Or a magic bush plant. Or something. If we find what he used to bring the *ku* here and get rid of it, the spirit is gone. Maybe it takes the sickness with it."

"So we all go traipsing about my father's house?" Gordon protested.

"For God's sake!" Borforh's frustration gave him a strange clarity, and he rushed on, sure this was his one chance to convince Gordon: "You're half-dead, Gordon! And if you don't care about that, then you should care about the *ku*! If it stays out there, there will be more people getting sick. The Americoes can't go deeper in, and if that happens they'll rely more and more on us Kru. Not just the Kru, the Mano too. Lots of others. How do you think that will end? You think we'll all get along?"

Gordon stared up at his hospital room's narrow window like he could fly away. "He gave me an education," he said. "He has been good to me. But he did not like me to touch him. And he would not stay, when he saw how sick I was. That was when I asked for you, Borforh." He put his face in his hands and pretended to wipe away a sneeze. "We can look for this altar, but I am coming with you."

Borforh and Jayplo helped Gordon out of the bed. His white cotton shirt was stained gray with sweat and he breathed through his mouth like an old man, but he hobbled out of the hospital without a glance from the nurses.

Borforh figured they had their hands full.

***

Mr. Matthews lived in Monrovia proper, far from the Krutown tenement where Borforh shared his room with other young workingmen, Bassas and Grebos and Kru all waking early and coming home late. Where Krutown seemed alive with breath and whispered song, Mr. Matthews's neighborhood was quiet and still. Unnaturally quiet. The only sound was a tinkling piano scale, poorly played. The streets smelt like warm hay and wood smoke.

Gordon led them to a two-story house, glaringly white above the dusty brown street, with four ornate columns outside. He had told Borforh that it was done in the style of houses in the southern United States, which were themselves modeled after Greek temples.

Borforh was intimidated, envious...and yet, somehow, glad that the world could be so wasteful. The people who built houses like these thought so much of themselves, and where they came from. Such pride was like a well-made bow – beautiful by itself, but too often used to hurt.

"Do they all live in homes like this one?" Jayplo asked. Even she was quiet in the shadow of the big house.

"No," said Gordon. "My father is a very successful man. He works hard." He paused. "He sent me out of the house a long time ago, working for the expedition. I have not been here in a long time. We have not spoken."

Gordon unlocked the front door with a key from his trousers pocket, but it was Borforh who led the way inside.

The house felt empty. There was a dining room with fine silver, a parlor with green sofas and four tastefully crammed bookshelves and a flowery wall pocket above the fireplace, three bedrooms upstairs, cramped and abandoned servants' quarters, and a refreshingly cool basement divided by oak wine racks.

They searched the entire house and found nothing. Borforh grew exasperated. Part of him had looked forward to incriminating Mr. Matthews, the smug devil. Now he was merely unsettled. "We are missing something," he said. "Where are the servants?"

"Mr. Matthews let them go," said Gordon. "He did not want any distractions. Preparing for the expedition, like I said."

Borforh had the strange sensation that if he clenched his fist, something solid would appear in his grip. He could not say what. "Is there a way he could hide something in here?"

Jayplo took one of her magic torches from the bag across her chest and gave it a jaunty shake.

Gordon was worried that they would burn the house down, but Borforh ignored him. He lit one of Jayplo's torches and carried it down to the cellar. He waved the flame to the right and left.

One of the walls began to shimmer and hum. All three of them edged closer together, but there was no spirit, no attacker. Only midnight blue door, where before there had been slate gray stones. Borforh felt a breeze on his face, smelt hot tin, heard a sound like birds' wings beating in his skull.

"There's not going to be a good explanation for this," said Gordon, "is there?"

Borforh shook his head. "I'm sorry, I think your father's a sorcerer. Jayplo, what is this thing?"

It was Mr. Matthew who answered. "Gordon. Why did you let these monkeys in my home?"

He emerged out of the portal. First his face, then the rest of him, dressed as ever in a waistcoat, trousers – and now with a cheery yellow cravat. He smiled, his hands out by his sides, unthreatening. But then there were lots of things that looked unthreatening before they killed you; when Borforh was young, he heard King Anslem say that some Kru thought cannons were stone ovens, when they first saw them.

"Monkeys?" Jayplo snapped. "Who let you on our damn beaches?"

Gordon only pointed at the blue door behind Mr. Matthews. "What about you? Who let–" He doubled over and clutched his chest and spat thick yellow mucus on the floor. Mr. Matthews looked at it with distaste. "You've worked some sorcery! I'm sick! You've *killed* me! But you said you would always–"

"I never meant for you to fall ill, Gordon," said Mr. Matthews. "I learned to open these portals between places during my studies in France, a long time ago. The gnostic masters' apocryphal texts never mentioned this sort of soul-disease. I never meant–"

Jayplo let out a short, hard laugh. "What *did* you mean to do, summoning a spirit like that?"

"You will address me with respect, you impudent–" Mr. Matthews saw Gordon looking back at him and stopped himself. "The ancient gnostics could force angels and devils to do their bidding. I only meant for it to drain the life from the trees. To clear the way, Gordon! It's taking so long for us to explore the interior, to begin planting further inland. The natives oppose us at every turn–"

"You noticed!" Jayplo said.

Mr. Matthews turned on her, suddenly furious. "You won't interrupt me again!" He showed his teeth and snarled. His pupils disappeared. His hand snaked around to the belt inside his waistcoat and came back with a flintlock pistol, iron and gilt brass gleaming in the torchlight. Borforh could see down its regular, eight-sided bore. "Nothing will interrupt us."

Until now, Borforh had been paralyzed. They had confirmed what the *ku* told them: it was Mr. Matthews behind the strange spirit sickness. Now that

191

they knew, what could they do about it? He had kept silent while Mr. Matthews talked; he had grown used to being silent, as he'd grown used to his boss calling him "boy."

But when he saw the pistol, the silence in him broke. Jayplo was a powerful *deya*, but she couldn't stop a bullet.

Borforh screamed and charged. His voice filled the basement, knocking around the stone and clattering among the glass bottles. He did not recognize himself.

Mr. Matthews fired, and for an instant its thunder drowned out Borforh's desperate cry. But he kept going, wrapped his arms around Mr. Matthew's waist, and carried them both through the open door, out of Liberia.

***

The space between worlds was surprisingly crowded.

Borforh came down hard. Pebbles bit into his palms. There was sand in his eyes. He heard the surf. A heavy brine scent filled his nostrils.

He scrambled to his feet and found himself on a grassy beach. Wrecked ships were all around, run aground. Two-mast brigs, three-mast schooners, and massive creaking frigates, all with their ropes and sails tattered and drifting in a light wind. The wrecks formed a maze, and Borforh could not see further than a two hundred yards in any direction. Only the towering masts and distant crow's nests told him that the coast went on.

Mr. Matthews lay flat out on his back, holding his stomach and wheezing. The pistol was gone.

Borforh watched him struggle to his feet. "Mr. Matthews," he said, "can you get us back?"

"Y-you stupid little boy," Mr. Matthews said. "It takes time and preparation to move between worlds. I was careful when I captured that spirit to clear the land, but now–"

"You're saying you can't go home." It figured.

"No, you miserable little bootlip!"

Borforh blinked. "I have never been to America, Mr. Matthews, but I've heard that word usually means the both of us." He turned to walk away.

"Where are you going, boy? You can't just leave me here! Come back, dammit, I *demand it*!"

Some distant part of Borforh had a hard time ignoring this command; in Monrovia, it was dangerous to ignore an angry Americo. But this wasn't Monrovia.

Borforh decided to climb the nearest ship, to get a look of his surroundings.

But before he could begin his climb, a great howl went up all around him.

The wind whipped at his cotton shirt and ran warm fingers through his hair. Somewhere beyond his vision, hooves or paws or great iron shoes beat the sand.

"Oh, God," Mr. Matthews muttered. He picked up a piece of smooth driftwood and held it up. It made him look particularly foolish.

A pack of animals tore the nearest ship. They were the same purple-blue as the spirit in the jungle, but more defined, sharper around the edges even as they shifted and ran together. At first they seemed like hyenas, four-legged and brutal; in the next moment they swam through the air like serpents, took long two-legged strides like unhurried men, skittered sideways on strong thin legs like ghost crabs. They poured over and into one another until Borforh and Mr. Matthews were surrounded by a ring of hazy blue.

One of them detached itself from the roiling cloud. A lioness, with great searching eyes and a burnt yellow coat with only a hint of blue playing around her flanks. The spirit addressed Mr. Matthews, her voice high and feminine and hard to hold, distended like a dream: "You took one of us from here, man-thing. We have been mourning our brother, singing our grief-songs from the between places where your lost things go, so we did not forget."

To his credit, Mr. Matthews did not break and run. "You're mistaken. I merely *invited* your fellow into a better place, where he has plenty to feed upon. Believe me, he wanted to come with me."

"Lies," hissed the spirit.

"It's true," Mr. Matthew insisted. He turned to Borforh. "Isn't that right, boy?"

If Mr. Matthews had called him anything else, Borforh might have lied for him. If he had not said *boy*, and everything else that said about him.

"He's lying," Borforh told the lioness. "He took your friend away from his home, through some kind of trick. He is in great pain, and he wants to come home."

Borforh would remember what happened next for the rest of his life. He knew, even as it happened, that this moment would bury itself within him, the way men at the docks said certain women burned themselves into their minds, so when they closed their eyes at night it was like stepping out of their homes and into the beating sun of perfect memory, moments better forgotten.

The lioness screamed, leapt, tumbled over and around Gordon's father. The other spirits followed.

They took him apart. Then they took the parts away.

When they were done, only the lioness remained. She prowled around Borforh. "And what about you, little one? We are not held to debts like you, we owe you nothing. But I would give you a gift. Not as repayment, you see. Only a gift." Borforh nodded, but he did not see the distinction. "Would you like to stay here with us?"

"This doesn't seem like a place for people," Borforh replied, uncertainly.

"That is not an answer. And from what I know of your home, there is *no* place for a child with a heavy heart and a wandering soul."

Borforh considered this. "We are trying to make a place, I think, like that. And I want to be there to help. For a while."

The lioness laughed at him. The laugh turned into something deeper, lower, fulsome. She padded up to Borforh until he could not look away from her blue-black eyes. She took a deep breath, and when it exhaled Borforh smelt berries and chocolate, like the coffee Americoes drank on their porches in Monrovia.

"You are brave, to want what you want," the lioness said. "I will send you home, then."

Borforh was thrown backwards, whipped out over the waves.

***

Borforh fell back into Mr. Matthew's basement. He knocked his head against the ground. Gordon was at his side with a face full of worry. Jayplo examined him with mild distaste, as though he had fallen down from too much drink.

Before Borforh could recover to tell them what happened, they heard the doors of the house slamming, blown inwards. A blue cloud tore down the basement steps. It whipped through the door in the wall, the door to the between place. The door shook, shrunk, and collapsed to a single point – then disappeared.

"What the hell happened?" Gordon asked.

Jayplo answered for him: "Whoever bound the spirit is dead, or else Borforh broke the spell, so the *ku* could go home."

Gordon looked at her. "Well, which is it? It makes a difference!"

"I'm sorry," Borforh said. "Gordon, I'm sorry." He searched his friends face. "But your fever is gone. Isn't it?"

Gordon clapped his hands to his forehead. "He raised me. For a time. He taught me to read."

***

Borforh went to work the next day, unloading ships like nothing had changed. While he worked, the men talked about the expedition, their miraculous recovery, and Mr. Matthew's disappearance.

Nobody ever got over acclimating fever so quickly, they said. They seemed to have forgotten that nobody ever caught it so quickly either.

***

In the weeks that followed, Borforh saved as much of his money as he could. He kept it in a small purse under his shirt, so what he saved would not be stolen. He studied the ships in the harbor.

One day, Gordon came to see him after his shift. They took off their shoes and sat on the docks. Borforh remembered how they used to play their feet in the water.

"He left me the house," Gordon said. "In his will. He never told me."

"That was kind of him," Borforh said. He meant it. It *was* kind, and unexpected.

Gordon shook his head, looking even more vulnerable than he had laid up in bed. "The house is spooky, you know. It's too big for one person. I don't think the neighbors trust me, a Kru boy living there by himself. You should come stay with me."

"I'm still saving up to leave," said Borforh, "but I would be glad to live with you. For a time, anyway."

"I'd like that," said Gordon, quietly. "It feels like there could still be bad spirits in there."

Borforh noticed that their hands were very close together on the dock. An uncertain quiet enveloped the boys, and he thought about pushing Gordon into the water for laughs.

"You know," Borforh said, "I know someone who could help with the bad spirits."

When they went to see Jayplo, she seemed to be expecting them. This time, Borforh did not need to convince her to help. "I'm curious about the door," she said, grinning like a shark. "It could still be open. It could be bad for you Americoes."

But Borforh thought she felt bad too, about what happened.

So they lit torches and carried the flames through Gordon's new home.

They didn't find any spirits.

When the sun was low and the fires burned out, they picked a bottle of wine from the cellar and sat on the front porch, drinking out of clay mugs because they could not find Mr. Matthew's fine crystal.

Borforh watched the sky turn shades of rose and violent, with Gordon on his left and Jayplo on his right. After a time they gathered up the glasses and the empty bottle and went inside. They walked through the big white house together, bolting all the doors and windows for the night.

Art by Kathryn Weaver

AN BAILE NA MBAN
THOM DUNN

1920s
Ireland

35 Days Before Termination

Caoimhe had been raised amongst the Irish Travellers, who despite their nomadic nature did instill in her a deep piety. This is why she would not skip on the debts she owed the Church for taking her in when she was with child. This also meant living after Christ Himself, providing for the meek and leprous – or at least, that's how she justified stealing from the stock house underneath the Bon Secours Home and selling the supplies out on the streets. Sure she wasn't taking straight from the Lord Himself, like.

Caoimhe waited for the cover of darkness before she made her way down the crooked cellar stairs that led beneath the Home. The dim light of the moon shone through the barred windows, and illuminated the room just enough for her to see a large gate standing locked and chained between her and the healthy stock of canned food and pills that stood upon the shelves. Strange, she thought, for Sister Maire Cahan had never locked the supplies before. The space between the slats was too narrow for her to fit through, so she tried to stretch her arm out as far as she could towards the quinine on the shelf. Her fingertips just barely grazed the bottle.

In the two years that she'd run her black market deals, the nuns had never let on their suspicions. Caoimhe couldn't understand why they would start now. Had the pig-faced girl gone and squealed after catching her in the stable with the club-footed man? Caoimhe didn't think the Proddy had it in her – not that the nuns would have believed her if she did. That girl was sure a pity case if there had ever been one.

Then Caoimhe heard the sound of creaking wood behind her. She turned and saw Sister Maire Cahan descending the stairs with a belt in her hand and a stern look on her face. "Looking for a bite?" she said as she stepped out from the shadows. "Take as you'd like, but I'll be adding to your credit."

"Of course, Sister." Caoimhe stepped away from the gate with her head bowed and hands clasped before her. She turned to the nun and spoke in reverence. "Forgive me. I did have some pain in me gut. Thought perhaps some quinine would help." Sister Maire Cahan remained standing at the base of the stairs, her stone grey eyes staring into Caoimhe like a falcon about to strike. "It was just a dram," Caoimhe muttered. "Seems it's settled anyhow. Best be heading back to sleep then."

She made as if to leave, but Sister Maire Cahan blocked the way. And though her nausea was a tale, the dank and musty stench of the cellar was indeed making Caoimhe ill. She caught a fetid waft coming from behind the door past the supplies, where the stillbirths and cot deaths all were stowed, hidden from their mothers and the townsfolk alike and left to rot away in isolation.

"A dram would be fine, had you asked permission." Sister Maire Cahan stretched the belt between her coarse brown hands, testing it for strength and tension. "It's hard enough with the Tans blocking our supply routes. It seems we have a thief now as well."

The auld nun frowned. She took a long, slow breath and said, "Lift your shirt, Caoimhe. And don't you be tinkering about me things again or I'll have you right back on the streets where you belong."

Caoimhe steeled herself with thoughts of freedom, of returning to the Travelling community with her beautiful baby girl. Not that she'd seen the child in the two years since her birth, but the thought of it was nice, until the lashings came and ripped her from her dreams.

53 Days After Conception

Aisling was hardly eight weeks along and still looked near to burst. The thing that grew within her was flailing and kicking and burning up her insides, and she wished nothing more than to tear it from her womb. But she had no means of termination – and even if she did, such a thing would be a sin. When she asked Sister Maire Cahan for help, the wicked nun just laughed. "Are you bleeding?" she asked, and Aisling told her no. "Right, so. Supper's held at six. Meantime, you can fetch your water from the pump like the rest." But the water from the well flowed in shades of yellow-brown, and it was a good day when there wasn't something slimy swimming in it. On worse days, the same things got stuck between your teeth. Such was hospitality at the Bon Secours Mother and Baby Home.

And so it was that Aisling made her way through the desolate hallways, past the rows of beds like funeral plots to the stable out back for a taste of brisk winter air. Despite the mulch and rotting wood – and the fact that the outer gates were locked to keep the women from escaping – Aisling knew that the stable offered better ventilation than inside the Home, where the stale air was tainted by the filthy functions of its residents.

But she did not expect to find the wooden stable door ajar when she approached, open just enough for a sixteen-year-old girl to slip through if she weren't with child – at least, not the way that Aisling herself had grown these past two months. She pressed her hand to the door to push it the rest of the way, but stopped herself when she heard a man speaking on the other side. He was joined shortly thereafter by the voice of a young girl whom she recognized as the Traveller girl, Caoimhe, a working resident at the Home who had pegged Aisling as her enemy from the first day she arrived.

Aisling's father had always warned her to stay away from the Travellers. The Catholics were savages, sure, but at least they could be tempered – unlike them wild knackers. They'd stab you in the back and steal your wallet while they sweet-talked your mammy, he'd say.

Of course, that was before he was killed by Catholic rebels. He hadn't much advice to give since then, sure as Aisling could use it.

Aisling stayed still and listened to the conversation. Perhaps she could gain favor with the nuns if she had some dirt on the Traveller girl. After all, the Bon Secours had strict rules about men coming up to the Home, and even the townsfolk of Tuam knew better than to risk the wrath of Sister Maire Cahan.

Try as she might, Aisling couldn't parse what it was that was being said. Parts of it resembled the Irish, though Aisling knew it wasn't. She recognized a few words of English as well; she didn't have the language herself, though she did know the sound of it. But most of what she heard then was garbled nonsense.

"Thú gloree a'me? Grespan do loorkoag, there's a slaask on the djigger, nokh? I ukh a shorik! The lub sturth the sloofa is byianniyan and I ain't grawbaltha fit. The shaykar did catch me when I's sramaling, and lowber til I had to kuldrum with me graydan ashirth for odd grakhton," Caoimhe said.

But this time when the man responded, he was speaking directly in Irish: "Are you going to stand there dropping eaves, like?" There was a brief pause before he spoke again. "That's right, yourself by the door. Something I can help with?"

Aisling could have fled right then, but found herself compelled by both her fear and curiosity. She pushed her way past the groaning door and entered the stable, where she immediately recognized Caoimhe by the curly auburn hair flowing down behind her like waves of blood, her gypsy flesh looking filthier than usual. The girl stood beside a smallish beggar man dressed in tattered rags that fell loosely off his hunched and bony shoulders. His snake-like eyes were a sickly shade of yellow, and his skin was swathed in fuzzy black film by the shadows cast from his frayed hood. Aisling made him out to be a sídhe, one of the Good People – which meant the knacker girl was up to something far worse than whoring.

"I didn't mean to bother. I came out for a breathe of air when I heard voices," Aisling said as she placed a hand upon her swollen middle. "The little one was throwing quite a fit."

"Aye, sure it was, so," said the sídhe, and Aisling caught the jaundiced glimmer of a smile creep across his face.

"Both yourselves are Travellers then, is it?" she asked.

The man in the rags stood upright like a panicked rabbit. "Traveller? Sure, I travel about. But not the way you're thinking." As he hobbled toward her, Aisling noticed that his left foot was twisted up and curled around like the head of a club. He reached a slender, hirsute arm towards her stomach. "And yourself, ma vourneen? You must be, what: five, six months along now?"

As soon as his hand touched Aisling's blouse, the thing inside her erupted in a frenzy, like it was under attack and hoping to kick its way out through her flesh. But the sídhe kept his hand pressed against her, like he was tempting the beast for a fight. His slitted eyes grew wide, though Aisling couldn't tell if it was from excitement or fright.

"Perhaps you should be going," Caoimhe said to the man. She pulled his hand away from Aisling, then moved herself between them. It was the first time the Traveller girl had shown her any sympathy.

A flutter of rags passed by in a blur and the sídhe was gone before Aisling had a chance to know what happened. The thing inside her quickly settled down.

"I'm sorry that you did hear us going on as such. It's not polite to use the cant 'round themselves who don't have it. But it's the way that we do speak amongst our own," Caoimhe said to Aisling. "This used to be a vagrant's home, before the Bon Secours began to bring the women here. Some of them still wander by from time to time, looking out for scraps and like. They don't mean a bit of harm."

Aisling knew it weren't a vagrant with them glowing eyes, or could make himself disappear like that, but she was afraid to say as such. "There's rules about the menfolk coming up here to the Home. I'll be having a word with Sister Maire Cahan about this. She'll put you right out on the streets," she said.

"Not while I still owe her debt, she won't," said Caoimhe with a sigh. Then she walked back through the stable door and went inside.

4 Days Before Termination

It was after services and near a month from their last council when Caoimhe came again upon the club-footed man. "Your Holy Man has a way with words, he does, going on about the Tans like that in sermon," said the man standing as he was near the bushes at the backside of the church, his brown rags blending in with the dry brush underfoot. He brought a cigarette to his lips and sucked in air to light the tip of flame at the end of the roll. His voice gave Caoimhe quite a start and shook her from her brisk, determined steps back towards the Home. It was a Sunday, and though it was the one day she was allowed to walk to town unescorted, she still had food and linens to prepare for the resident mothers-to-be.

Caoimhe collected herself. She straightened out her skirts then stood upright and said, "Father Connell is an honorable man. He spake on the Lord's behalf, and so I'm right inclined to take him at his word." She glanced hesitantly at the man's clubbed foot, all gnarled, grey, and calloused like a swine's. The tattered flaps of broken shoe that fell around it did nothing to protect his sole from weathering. The sight of it alone made her stomach wretch.

The club-footed man exhaled, and the smoke did sting as it blew in Caoimhe's eyes. When he spoke, he switched to Gammon, the cant of the Irish Travellers. Caoimhe found comfort in hearing that familiar language of her people, even if the man's accent did seem a bit off. "You missed our last two meetings. I waited hours for yourself in the usual spot, but you never did show."

"I'm sorry," Caoimhe said. She reached behind herself, gingerly stroking the scars left behind by the nun's lashing. She hadn't slept on her back in a month. "It's as I told yourself: Sister Maire Cahan was onto us, and she built a gate to keep me from the food and medicine. I can get your money back if you–"

"Keep the cash, lackeen; you'll be needing it yourself more than I." The man took several hobbling steps towards Caoimhe then stroked her cheek with his rough hand and said, "I'm here to offer you a different bargain. A simple favor, like. And when it's done, you won't hear from me again unless you will it."

The club-footed man let his shoulders drop, and pulled back the moth-eaten hood that hid his face in shadow. While Caoimhe had recognized the strangeness of his eyes before, she was still surprised to find how the rest of him did match. His face was covered all in fur with a small button nose, and his jagged teeth had more in common with a fox than a man.

For all those years he hid his face, and only now did Caoimhe recognize him as a púca, one of the Daoine Maithe, and she felt all the more foolish for it. On top of all her sins, she'd been conspiring with faeriefolk. She had truly carved out her own spot in Hell, but hadn't realized til then how deep it went. But there was no coming back from it, so she thought it best to comply and extend her mortal life while she still could.

Caoimhe clenched her fists at her side to fight back from the trembling that swelled within her core. "What is it you need?"

The púca dropped the fag to the ground and stomped out the flame with his bare clubbed foot, and if the fire burned his skin, then he never let on as such. "The Protestant girl with the straw-colored hair – Aisling, was it?"

"What about her?" Caoimhe said, though she was like to ask why he'd remarked upon her hair and not her upturned nose or cherub face. Perhaps Aisling had something in common with the púca's bad foot; they did look similar enough.

The púca reached into his rags and after some shuffling removed a small glass bottle containing a translucent yellow liquid. He was leaned in close enough to her that Caoimhe could see the spiderwebs of brown tobacco spit that spread across the gaps in his crooked teeth when he smiled. "There's something special about the gawthrin grows inside your wan," he said. "Its well-being is of interest to some. I'd like for yourself to give her this – St. Anthony's Fire – and be sure she drinks it all it all. Do you understand what I be asking of you?"

Caoimhe nodded. She'd been around the Home for long enough to know about St. Anthony's Fire. A small amount could help to stop a mother's bleeding after birth. What the púca had given her was at least four times as much, and Caoimhe couldn't know what such an overdose would do.

But the púca made his offer before she could inquire any further: "When that's done you have me word. I will help you leave the Home forever, and show you where to find your little girl."

And so of course she took the deal.

<u>31 Days After Conception</u>

Sister Maire Cahan tossed the dented tin bowl onto the table. It landed with a solid clang, and Aisling watched its curved edges warble in oblong rings until it found some sense of balance on the askew surface of the unfinished wood. The tawny slop inside of it remained motionless.

"Eat," she said, her thin black lips moving just enough to accentuate the shadows in her wrinkled face.

"Not particularly hungry," Aisling said. They were in the nun's office, a square and windowless room that stank of mildew and poitín. She glanced down at the food before her, and couldn't stop herself from scowling at the sight of the brownish carrots sticking out of the mashed potato sludge like petrified trees in a swamp. "If I were, I'd have lost whatever appetite I had."

The nun let slip a smile like the crack in a rotted stump. She adjusted herself, standing upright to fix her posture, then folded her hands in front of the off-white apron she wore about her waist. Aisling wondered if the nun did ever clean the thing. "It's for the good of yourself, and the child as well," she said, the crackle of her voice sounding suddenly sweet.

"I never asked for any child," Aisling said. "Particularly not a thing like this."

"The same could be said for Mary, could it not?" The nun draped her lithe fingers on the table, letting their tips trace the rough woodgrain. She began to circle around Aisling with precise, controlled steps that clicked in ominous rhythms upon the concrete floor. "There is something special about the wan inside yourself. I made a solemn oath before the eyes of God Himself and on behalf of the Republic that I would let no harm befall the two of yous so as long as you remained in my care."

Aisling was startled by the sharp snap of the woman's shoes right behind her. The cloth habit that fell upon the nun's head grazed the back of Aisling's hair as she leaned in close and whispered: "I will let nothing harm you. But I will hurt you if I must, to protect both yourselves."

Then Sister Maire Cahan took her bony hand like the edge of an axe and chopped it against Aisling's throat, cutting off the airflow to her windpipe. Instincts took over and Aisling's mouth shot open, gasping desperately for oxygen. The nun used her other hand to bring the bowl up to Aisling's face, shoveling the rancid meal into her mouth until the slop filled her throat, bringing Aisling near to choking. Then the nun cast the bowl aside and used her two free hands to clamp shut Aisling's mouth. The bowl hit the floor with a clatter that echoed in the tiny room.

Aisling couldn't stop herself from swallowing, desperate as she was for air. But she couldn't get it all down in one gulp, and Sister Marie Cahan still forced her jaw hinge shut. Aisling took in deep breaths through her nose and let her cheeks swell with the excess meal, its rotten taste teasing at the vomit in her gut.

"Not until it's done," said Sister Maire Cahan with her hands still clamped on Aisling's mouth. Though it took her some time, she swallowed down the rest of it. And even then, the nun still waited, like she was calling

Aisling's bluff. Between the spinning of her suffocated head and the adrenaline pumping angrily through her veins, Aisling couldn't tell how long she waited for the nun to free her face. "The child that you carry is of utmost importance to the cause," said the nun. "I would be most pleased if both of yous came out of this unharmed. But if you force my hand, I will make these eight months miserable to ensure the child's safety. I promise I will never let you die – but if you push me, I will make you wish you could."

With that, the nun released her hands from Aisling's face and walked out of the room, calm as a Sunday morning after mass.

1 Day Before Termination

Caoimhe lay awake on the cold, hard cot, the lone Traveller amongst a sea of expectant Irish mothers, each one writhing and groaning in her own time, and reminding her of the child that she had long since given up. But it wasn't just the pain in her back from the nun's lashings that kept her up that night; Caoimhe's thoughts had been running wild since last she'd seen the púca. She wondered how the creature did know about her child, and was he acting on behalf of the Tans or the Rebels – or if it all were a trick of the Divil himself.

Not that Caoimhe had much stake in the war herself. She'd been raised to stay out of the affairs of Settled People, excepting for cash, work, and supplies as needed. She only became aware of the conflict when she first met Diarmid, who himself did then go off to fight, leaving her with their unborn child in the care of the Bon Secours. She reached a hand into her skirt pocket and rolled the bottle of St. Anthony's Fire in her hands as she called a silent prayer out to the Lord.

But her communion ended swiftly when her eyes caught a motion through the darkness. It was not so uncommon, an expectant mother getting up to piss in the middle of the night. Caoimhe vaguely recalled doing so herself. But the high moon outside was casting out its rays through the barred windows at the top of the eastern wall, and when the girl passed through one of the broken beams of light, it was enough to illuminate her straw-colored hair and her squat nose.

Aisling. And she wasn't making her way towards the toilets. Sure enough, Aisling opened the door to the cellar, being careful not to wake the other women by the creaking of its joints – although Caoimhe could hear her groaning as she strained to move the heavy wood. Was it the púca himself that was calling her down there? Had Caoimhe waited too long to act, and he'd taken it upon himself?

Caoimhe cast aside her sleeplessness and followed Aisling down the cellar, moving as swiftly as she could by the tips of her toes. When she came to the top of the stairs, she stopped for a moment and watched the pig-faced girl as she flailed her stubby arms between the holes in the gate that kept her out of the supply room and whatever she was looking for.

"It's locked for a reason," Caoimhe said as she came down the stairs, and she could see Aisling freeze at the sound of her voice. "Is there something you're looking for, or should I tell the nuns that it's yourself who's been stealing from the Home?" She glanced down at Aisling's swollen gut, which seemed near twice the size it was last week, and wondered how the girl was expecting to sneak in anywhere at the size she was.

The pig-faced girl snorted when she looked at Caoimhe. "For a place that's meant for taking care of us, your kind don't spare much by way of comfort," she said, with a flippant laugh. "Do you hear this? I'm after something to settle my stomach, and you threaten retribution. You Catholics have a twisted way of working in the name of the Lord."

Aisling's jab made Caoimhe even less inclined to help her. But the little bottle of ergot was still there weighing in her pocket, and this seemed like the best chance to rid herself of its burden.

"Everything's locked up tight until the morning, and Sister Maire Cahan's the only one who has a key. Lucky you, I keep a few things in me apron for emergencies," Caoimhe said. She reached into her front pocket, pulled the bottle out, and handed it to Aisling, who drank it down to the very last drop and made her way back up the stairs without a word of thanks.

17 Days After Conception

The kinder of the soldiers who had captured her – Diarmid, so he called himself – was charged with bringing Aisling to the Home. On the day's ride from the camp at Lough Corrib, he had made clear his concern for her comfort, asking after how she sat or was she hungry or did she need a rest and such. She'd found herself so taken by his charm that her mind kept letting slip what he had done. He was just three years her elder, with a boyish face hid beneath his unkempt blonde hair and wild patches of fuzz that grew along the hard line of his jaw. She did always have a weakness for rebellious types, much to the chagrin of her father.

And so were her affections for him shattered, when her thoughts came back around and she thought of what Diarmid had done to her father, for no crime but worshipping Christ in what he and his kind had deemed a contrary way that made them sympathetic to the crown. But even that he did explain away sweetly:

"It's an honor what you're carrying inside yourself. Though I do regret the way it all did come about. A gift for all of Ireland, you'll see. The promise of freedom, resting in the womb."

When they arrived in Tuam, they were greeted by a grizzled old nun whose scars were only hid by the fleshy folds of wrinkles on her black face. But Aisling had made the mistake of letting Diarmid know that she didn't have any English, in the same breath as she tried explaining that her family had no British sympathies. As such, the boyish soldier was careful to only speak to the nun in English, save for a few choice words – something about the women's league of the Republican Army and what they called the war of independence, though neither came as a particular surprise.

"Sister Maire Cahan will be taking care of you, she will," Diarmid said to Aisling before he left. Then he removed the flatcap from his head, his nervous hands wringing it between them, and turned to the nun to address her directly. "Before I go, will you tell me – how is Caoimhe?"

"She's well," the nun answered. "But you won't be seeing her, not until you boys put an end to your fighting. I will help you in your aims as best I can, but I have promised these girls to keep them safe. That means keeping them out of your war."

"It's not 'our' war. It belongs to all of us who've—"

"Oh, cop on," said Sister Maire Cahan with a fierceness on her tongue. "Zealotry is not so becoming on a boy your age, and these ears have heard it all. I will support the Sinn Féin until me death, and accept that there are evils must be done, but I wish no part or knowledge of them. That's no world for a woman or a child."

Diarmid placed his flatcap back upon his head and tipped the brim as he replied, "Aye, sure, but it's still a better world than what the Tans have left behind. Pearse himself did say that an Ireland unfree shall never be at peace."

With that, the soldier boy was off, and Sister Maire Cahan escorted Aisling through the cold and sterile corridors of the Home. "Our residents receive the best care we can provide, whether they be Catholic or the Church of Ireland alike," she explained as they walked. "You're allowed ten minutes of outdoor time each afternoon, to keep the air inside you fresh. We serve three squares a day, and keep a healthy stock of medicines to ease a woman's pain." Though Aisling doubted they could find relief for what she had endured.

They came into a large hall with vaulted ceilings and barred windows high up on the walls. The room was lined with neat rows of off-white cots that reminded Aisling more of cemetery plots, and she followed the nun to a bed in the far back corner where a homely girl with olive skin and auburn hair was tending to the linens. Aisling could still make out the yellowed indentation of a pregnant woman's body pressed into the sheets, and she wondered if they at least cleaned for the Catholic girls.

"This is Caoimhe," said the nun. "She's been with us three years now. Any questions you have, she can answer."

"Cheers," said the girl.

But there was something strange about the girl's accent. When Aisling finally placed it, she turned to the nun and asked, "She one of them knackers? Aren't they all thiefs, like? And you're expecting me to trust her?" In truth, she had never met a Traveller before, though she'd certainly heard stories of their kind, full of magic and deception and wandering ways. Time was she was more afraid of them than she had ever been the IRA.

Sister Maire Cahan peered down at Aisling, her upper lip curling into a snarl. "You mean, is she a Traveller? You can ask her that yourself, you can." The nun then excused herself with swift, stern silence, leaving Aisling alone with the Traveller girl who, by the frown on her face, had already marked Aisling as an enemy.

Termination

A terrible howl ripped through the Home, tearing Caoimhe from her slumber. She was quick to find that she was not the only one whose ears were pushed to bursting by the sound, as the other girls were likewise rousted from their beds, setting each of them in a dour mood.

But it weren't the bean sídhe's wail that'd come calling for a mother's child – it was Aisling herself that did be shrieking so.

Sister Maire Cahan was already knelt attending to the girl, so Caoimhe bolted out of bed and rushed into action beside her, weaving her way through the narrow rows of cots and the pregnant women huddled in horror at the sight of such a wreck. This was hardly the first time she had seen a miscarriage.

But Aisling's pig-like squealing made it clear that this was different. And by the time Caoimhe reached Aisling's cot on the opposite end of the hall, it was already too late. The girl was gone, the ecru sheets beneath her soaked through to a wet and rusty red.

Sister Maire Cahan ran her hand across the girl's face to close her eyelids. Caoimhe always did admire the nun's attempts to calm her girls, no matter the tragedy. For all the pain that she'd put Caoimhe through over the years, there was an uncanny softness about her when it came to birthing traumas, like the only time her maternal instincts did appear was when a girl was after suffering through labor pains. Did she know firsthand the ills of forcing out a child through the space between your legs? Or did she merely accept that the tortures she inflicted were nothing compared to the all-consuming ache of creating life inside yourself, and the glorious absolution that overcame when your wan did make it out into the world?

The nun then pushed herself up from the floor with calm deliberation, her auld bones creaking as she went. She crossed herself in the name of Christ, then folded her hands in prayer and dismissed the other girls, begging privacy for the passing of their dear departed sister.

Caoimhe waited until the crowd of shaken women had dispersed before she stepped up to offer her assistance. It was then that she did see the inhuman monstrosity that Aisling had expelled from out her womb, sprawled amongst the sanguine sheets. It was near a half-meter in length – hardly a premature size – with drab green skin that had flushed to grayish-blue from loss of oxygen, and an elongated muzzle for a face with lips that did not move. Its unformed limbs looked more like flippers and hooves, and Caoimhe felt ashamed for thinking how it did resemble its own late mother.

Then Caoimhe heard a mechanical click and felt the cold tip of a pistol pressed against her head.

Sister Maire Cahan leaned in close to her, and spoke softly. "Did you think I wouldn't recognize the signs of Traveller magicks? It was your poison killed the mother and her child. The girl herself did tell me so," she said. "You knacker scum are nothing more than savages and sinners, and I was wrong to think that you could live among the civilized people without your Pagan ways raining Hell upon our lives."

Caoimhe swallowed. "I mean no disrespect, Sister, but you do be speaking madness. I have served the church for all these years, still owing a debt for–"

Sister Maire Cahan jabbed the barrel of her pistol into Caoime's temple, which sent a shock of dizzy pain spinning through her head. "The Church forgives your debt, child, but it will not forgive your sins," said the nun. "The Republican Army will not share my mercy. They'll be after you for what you've wrought this day, and they do not take kindly to traitors."

This last part left Caoimhe baffled, even moreso than the freakish stillborn on the cot before her. But Sister Maire Cahan held the gun as such that Caoimhe dare not turn her head, or inquire any further after the role that the rebels did play in it.

"I will give you five minutes to leave this place," the nun said. "And if you ever once look back I will not hesitate to kill you, with the Lord here as my witness."

Caoimhe took off running, barefoot and all, as soon as Sister Maire Cahan eased the pressure on her skull.

Conception

The rebels pulled a bag over Aisling's head, their rough hands clamped tightly around her arms to keep her from wriggling away. It didn't matter that she'd already let herself fall limp; they handled her body with the delicate touch reserved for stacking wood, and she was tossed in the back of the covered cart with the same disregard. Even in the darkness she could still smell the flames that were tearing through her home, felt the heat lick at her flesh and then get washed away by drops of sweat as her body worked overtime to find its calm. Any hope she had that her father might have lived was lost when the cart started moving and she overheard the soldiers speaking in the Irish:

"Did you hear that bastard crying?"

"Aye! 'Please, I'm only doing as the Tans had asked of me!' Well that was your problem, wasn't it?"

"Them Proddies think they're innocents, just because they ain' directly killing off their own, like. But their hands are bloody just the same."

"We gave him a chance, you know? If he'd stood beside us like an Irishman, he could have done some right."

"That's the problem, Diarmid. They don't think of themselves as Irish."

"Neither do I. That's why I put a bullet in him."

The two men talked for the rest of the ride, but Aisling couldn't bring herself to listen. She closed her eyes – not that she could see out the bag anyway – and tried to rest, to let her mind slip away to somewhere else, but the bumps in the road kept tearing her away from her slumber. Even so, it was easy for her to lose track of time, as she had no way of knowing where they were taking her.

When the cart did come to a stop, and the bag was pulled off Aisling's head and tied around her mouth to keep her quiet, she found herself at a Republican camp near the Lough Corrib. It was nearing dawn, and they dragged her to a hollow by the water's shore where a handsome, muscled man named Murchadh did be waiting. His long black hair was damp and there was seaweed braided through it. He spoke with the soldiers while Aisling stood by, still bound and gagged and unable to hear them.

The soldiers finished up their conversation, and left her there with the dark-haired man. Aisling watched in horror as he changed before her eyes, fleshy webs spreading between his fingers and his face stretching out like the snout of a horse. His tangled hair transformed itself into a singular mane of kelp that travelled along his back like a plume, and his flesh took on a tone of greenish-bronze like the Ech-Ushkya water sprites in the stories that her father used to tell, that he would never tell again.

Murchadh stepped towards her, his muscles moving with the grace of a stallion. Aisling found herself entranced by his beastly beauty in spite of herself and the trauma she had seen that day. She couldn't help it. Even when he freed her from the bonds that held her hands and mouth, she still was unable to move or speak, hypnotized as she was by the sight of him. It was something in his eyes that took control and left her passive as he forced himself inside of her, ripping apart her innocence like an animal and leaving her alone there on the shore when he was done until the soldiers returned to collect her broken form.

<u>After</u>

"They weren't kidding when they called you Travellers. Took me near a month to track yourself. But then I'm not so well for walking, like."

Caoimhe awoke to the púca's voice from her slumber in the shade of an uprooted fearnóg tree, its web of roots stuck thick with dirt to protect her from the rain. For a fortnight she had followed the path of the rail from Claremorris up to Sligo, hoping to find some form of sanctuary in Donegal Bay, where she had last seen her family caravan. It should have come as no surprise that they were gone these years later, and that all she would be left with was the púca that had gotten her into the mess.

Caoimhe pushed herself up from the dirt. She kept her right hand hid behind her, and groped blindly for the hefty stone that she had kept near her for protection. "Are you here to kill me?" she asked in the Gammons, its now-unfamiliar rhythms strangely soothing on her tongue.

The púca let out a jovial laugh, so much so that his clubbed foot slipped on the wet, dead leaves, causing him to stumble backwards in the forest thick. When he'd caught his balance, he said, "You're a sweet thing, so you are. But you haven't a clue what you're dealing with. Mind if I take a rest then? Me feet are aching something awful, like." He plopped himself in the dirt beside her with all the grace of a pig, without so much as waiting for her answer.

"You tricked me," she said. "I asked your help, so you went and killed a woman and her child."

"To be fair, she was a Protestant. Figured it wasn't much a loss for you and yours. Not that I've a stake in either side but – well, that's the whole thing, innit?" said the púca as he massaged his gnarled foot. "Besides, if we're being technical, it was yourself who killed them two. Alls I did was give the means to do it. You see, Caoimhe, there's three sides to every conflict: them who disagree, and the rest caught between. It's that third group tends to suffer most."

"Women and children. Right." Caoimhe understood what he meant by this, but not quite how it mattered. She tightened her grip on the stone beside her, careful not to let the creature know what she was hiding.

"And oftentimes the Good People, like meself. When you're after living for as long as I have, you tend to see the foolishness in human squabbles. Sure, this one's been on for years, but it's not so different from the ones that came before it, or the ones are yet to come. I'm more concerned for Ireland herself than who it is that claims her."

"So you killed a mother and a child for the sake of Ireland? You're full of it. I should have known to never trust your kind," Caoimhe said, remembering when Aisling rightly said the same of her.

"Here's the thing, child: for all the wrong the Brits have set upon the land, there's little the Republicans could do that would be worse than what's been done to them and theirs. But there's sins that get forgiven, and there's deals with the Divil that you don't be coming back from. Do you understand?"

Caoimhe did not.

"The wan that grew inside your friend? It wasn't human. Not entirely. The Irish have been desperate for to gain the upper hand – and for that, I cannot fault them. But I draw the line when it comes to half-breed demonspawn made as weapons for the war. For down that path lies a darker world that none of yous are prepared for. So I made a choice."

"Sure but it wasn't your choice to be making!" Caoimhe spat.

The púca just shrugged. "When you've lived as long as I have, you don't much worry on the details."

But Caoimhe had seen firsthand just how the war could ruin lives. Her choice to get involved with Diarmid in the first place had led her to that very moment, and all the loss that she had suffered could be traced back to that decision. Now she herself had been turned into a soldier, too. The púca had used her, just as the rebels had made their use of Aisling.

Still seated, gripping the stone in her hand, Caoimhe scooted herself nearer to the weary púca, whose attentions were focused on easing the pain from his clubbed foot. "You still owe me your end of the bargain," she said.

The púca looked up with a forced frown, until a small lilt of laughter slipped out of himself. "I helped you leave the Home, did I not? By my count you've been free near a month now."

Caoimhe's stomach turned. She'd been played for a fool in more ways than she'd known. She had lived a life of cons and double deals, and should have known better than to trust a púca.

The arm that held the rock was primed to swing, but Caoimhe took a breath and regained control of herself. "And me little girl?" she asked. "You promised you would bring me to my daughter." Caoimhe only ever had a glimpse of her child before Sister Maire Cahan whisked her away, but she had longed for that day when they two would reunite, and felt certain she would recognize her kin even after all these years.

But the hope inside her slipped away as she watched the púca's shoulders slump. He was no longer laughing; indeed, she could see the pity in his serpentine eyes. "I said I'd show you where to find her, not that I would bring you to her," he said.

Caoimhe knew what to expect before he finished his thought, but still could feel her heart sink as the words fell from his mouth: "She's buried in the cellar of the Bon Secours Home, with all the other cot deaths."

Blackness swallowed Caoimhe's mind. By the time that she came out of it, she could already see the jagged bone sticking out from what before had been the púca's one good leg, his hot blood splattered on the stone still in her hand and all caking underneath her fingernails. She wondered if the Good People truly were immortal, or did they just outlast their natural deaths. She raised her hand to bring the stone to his skull and find out for herself, and in her rage she was deaf to the whimpers of the creature sprawled beneath her.

Caoimhe let the stone fall from her hand. It hit the ground with a soft thud, gathering dirt and leaves that stuck to the púca's drying blood as the stone rolled off into the brush. "You robbed me of a choice," she said. "Made me into a killer against me will. But now I choose to let you keep your life, though it's not 'cause you deserve it."

She could hear the púca's pleas behind her as she walked away, for he had no means to move from where he laid. She paid him no mind. Despite her sins, Caoimhe had sworn to live as Christ Himself, which meant having mercy on the souls of the damned – including herself. And as she travelled north towards Donegal Bay, a calmness overcame her, lulled by the rhythm and the motion of her steps like a newborn in its rocking cradle. Sure as she was travelling alone, but it felt more home than the Home had ever felt.

Art by Anna D'Amico

IN HIS OWN IMAGE
E.C. MYERS

1907
Seoul, Korea

Jun-min crowed softly when his fingers encountered the carcass of a rice steamer in the commitment bin. The brass pot was dented and it smelled of moldy porridge, but he bet there was nothing else wrong with it; the wealthy families in Insadong often discarded useful things merely for aesthetics. If it was really broken, he would fix it.

He eased the treasure into his cloth sack so it wouldn't clank against the other items he'd found to repair and sell. He yawned and then reached into the bin again with both hands. As he carefully rummaged, feeling around sharp edges, he heard distant ticking behind him. The sound grew louder, coming closer. Quickly.

Bauble bumped hard against his ankle.

"Ow. What?" Jun-min whispered.

Bauble clicked and released a warning puff of steam.

"Shhh," Jun-min said.

The alley echoed with lark song – dawn was close. The neighborhood would wake soon, and Jun-min wouldn't want the residents to catch him going through their garbage.

He used to love mornings: the fresh, dewy air; the seeping gray that gradually revealed a world hidden by darkness. The sudden flare of the sun as it crested the horizon and flooded the streets with yellow-orange light. He closed his eyes, the distant memory too bright and too painful.

Jun-min heard the collector rumbling three blocks away. He still had a little time before it reached this street. He kept searching in earnest.

The streets of Seoul's Jongno District had been sparse lately, but this single commitment bin had turned up more than he had found in a week of evenings. His most promising discoveries were an adding machine with a cracked lid, a typewriter with three missing keys, and a sewing machine with a bent bobbin.

Bauble plucked at Jun-min's trouser leg with a retractable pincer.

Jun-min ignored him, too excited by the long brass pipe he had found. It was slimy and crusted, but whole. He already knew exactly where it would fit.

Bauble shrieked, a high-pitched whistle that he knew Jun-min hated. Jun-min snapped back to the moment. Too late.

Footsteps.

"Looks like we found our thief," said a man, standing three meters away. How had he gotten so close? A soft humph of agreement next to him. Two people. Jun-min smelled tobacco, sulfur, lotus flowers, and... machine oil?

"I can't believe your plan worked. I thought this was a waste of time," the man said.

"Turn around, thief." A woman's voice, sharp as a sickle.

Jun-min turned slowly toward the pair, clutching the brass pipe like a club. The woman stifled a gasp. He pulled his hood low over his forehead.

"Drop your weapon," the man said.

Jun-min lowered the pipe to the ground and placed it gently at his feet.

"He's blind," she muttered.

"Stealing is still a crime. Boy, you know that, don't you?"

Boy. The Army of the Enlightenment considered 18-year-olds suitable for military service, but Jun-min's injury had denied him that dubious honor. "Even if the sky is falling, there will be a hole in it," his father used to say.

Jun-min's throat went dry with fear. "Is it a crime to pick up trash?" He hoped they didn't hear the quiver in his voice as clearly as he did.

"Speak up!" the man said.

"Is it a crime to pick up trash?" Jun-min repeated. To him, it seemed like he was shouting, but he was so soft-spoken others always strained to hear him. Not that he had anything but machines to talk to.

"That's a commitment bin you're stealing from." The man raised his voice and spoke slowly, to help the blind kid understand him better. "This 'trash' is spoken for. You trying to lose us this war?" the man said.

As if a brass pipe or a banged-up rice pot would win the Great Han Empire victory against Nippon.

"Did you know that, boy?" the woman asked.

She didn't even sound much older than him. He despised her pity, but her unexpected weakness was his best way out.

"No. My mistake." Jun-min bowed. "I'm so sorry."

"He's out after curfew," the man said.

"Just don't let us find you here again," she said.

She was letting him go?

"I'm not doing another of these stakeouts," the man grumbled. "I'm a soldier, not a damn collector."

"We all must do our part for king and empire." She recited the familiar slogan with a hint of sarcasm.

Who was she? She seemed to be in charge, so she must have vital skills to be a high ranking woman in the military. But then why did she care enough about missing metal to set such a trap?

Jun-min smiled. He picked up his bag and slung it over his shoulder.

The man laughed. "Oh no. Leave that here. The Enlightened need all the metal we can get."

Jun-min hefted the bag with regret then rested it on the ground. He hated the thought of these precious, beautiful, useful devices being melted down to make more gigans to fight a pointless war. All the Han war machines could do was kill. Only they weren't particularly good at it.

The Empire was losing. The Enlightened armies were holding Nippon at Kaesong, but they were no match for the enemy's advanced technology. The curfew, marshal law, rations, and the commitment bins that were robbing Jun-min of his livelihood were all desperate attempts to turn the tide.

"Thank you," Jun-min bowed low and then shuffled away, kicking his feet in the dirt. Bauble rolled ahead, ticking and huffing to tell him where to go.

"We need *all* the metal," the man called. "Including that shiny football."

Jun-min froze. *No.*

"I need him," Jun-min said. "It."

"The Empire needs it more."

"*Kyu-won*," the woman said.

"Leave it here," the man, Kyu-won, said.

Jun-min had never heard a gun cocked before, but there was no mistaking that cold, deadly sound.

"Please." Jun-min swallowed. "I'll donate more scrap metal."

"You've been withholding?" Kyu-won said.

"No!" He sobbed. "Please. I beg you, anything but this."

"We're just doing our jobs."

Jun-min slowly crouched. He lowered his hands to the ground and cupped them together like he was scooping water. Tears splashed onto his palms. Bauble rolled into the cradle and thrummed.

Jun-min fingered the dents he'd been meaning to hammer out, savored the warmth of his only friend's brass surface. He pressed his forehead against Bauble, smelled the oil and steam and listened to the ticking that had been his constant companion for eleven years.

Bauble whirred and clicked.

"I'm sorry." Jun-min wiped his tears from Bauble's glass optic port. "Thank you."

He put Bauble down. "Go." He hoped Bauble would pick up on his tone and zoom off in the opposite direction, to safety.

Bauble rolled toward the soldiers. Paused. Rolled back to Jun-min.

"*Go.*" Jun-min stood and pushed him with a toe.

Bauble's ticking moved away.

"What is this anyway?" Kyu-won asked.

"He serves as my eyes," Jun-min said. *My friend.* "Please. Let me keep him."

"Give it back, Kyu-won," the woman said.

Give it back! His middle school classmates had taunted Jun-min when he returned after the accident, scarred and blind. They hid his toys, pencils, and books.

Bullies had never stopped tormenting him.

"My father made him for me," Jun-min said.

"Your *father*?" the woman asked. "What's your name?"

"Shim Jun-min," he said.

"Shim," she said.

"This is advanced, Yo-reum. This is *tech*," Kyu-won said.

"We must bring it to base and study it. Maybe—" The woman was cut off by a horrible crash and crack.

215

"Oops," Kyu-won said.

Bauble screamed. He engaged his mechanical legs and they skittered against the ground.

"Bauble!" Jun-min said. "Run!"

Bauble chuffed wildly.

"Cute. It's a mini-gigan. A toy," Kyu-won said. "Time to grow up, boy."

A shot rang out. Bauble clicked, clicked, whirred. Fell silent. The acrid smell of gunpowder and burnt metal lingered in the air.

Jun-min had not heard this in a long time: the absence of ticking. The shock of it stilled him. He couldn't breath. He couldn't think. He couldn't move.

"Dammit, Kyu-won! Why did you do that? Such a waste," Yo-reum said.

"Such a waste," Kyu-won agreed. "Get out of here, boy."

Jun-min turned and stumbled away without knowing or caring where he was going.

***

He got home somehow, after wandering for hours in a haze.

Before Bauble, Jun-min had memorized the streets of Hanseong. He had practiced walking with a cane and finding his way using the sun's warmth on his face, the aroma of cooking food wafting from stalls and homes, the unique hustle and bustle of people in each neighborhood. But he rarely left the workshop, preferring to listen to his father build and repair. Listening to gears turning, tocking, ticking.

The mechanical guide, what Father had called a Seeing Eye, had given him his life back. No, a new life. Bauble took away Jun-min's anger and fear and replaced them with confidence and curiosity. He had freed him from darkness of spirit.

Then Jun-min's father was killed, so his twin sister reluctantly took in Jun-min. When the war came, Aunt Eun-hye left him too; Hanseong was a high-risk target, so she decided to move them to the country. But 14-year-old Jun-min refused to abandon the family workshop, and she had never much liked children, especially boys. Especially Jun-min, who reminded her painfully of her dead brother.

Aunt's train was destroyed two minutes after it departed Hanseong for Jemulpo, at 10:18 a.m. on November 17, 1905. No survivors.

The surprise attack by a Nippon kamikaze mecha, Kappa-Class, had decimated Dongjak District and the Han River Bridge. Two years later and that portion of the fledgling railroad still hadn't been rebuilt.

Jun-min pushed his way into the shop and closed the door. He slumped to the floor and wept into his trembling arms.

Ticking filled the room and he lifted his head. This was a harder sound than Bauble's. Hollower. Hydraulic servos juddered and leaden footsteps clomped toward him.

"Hey, Pop." Jun-min sighed.

Pop placed a heavy hand on Jun-min's shoulder and patted it clumsily.

Jun-min winced at the rough contact.

What's wrong, Jun-ee-oo?

"They took him, Pop. Bauble. He's... gone." Probably melted down by now.

I'm sorry.

Pop straightened. He lurched over to the old mobile dangling above the tool bench and cranked it. It played a discordant rendition of "Arirang" and tin birds tinkled against each other as the baby toy spun.

"Thanks," Jun-min said. "That fixes everything."

He had always hated Father's automaton. It embodied everything that was wrong with him – with them. Father had wanted to keep working while raising baby Jun-min, so he built a machine to wind up the mobile, instead of simply making a longer-lasting mobile. As Jun-min got older, Father had added more entertainment functions to the automaton.

If Jun-min fell and skinned a knee, it was Pop that comforted and bandaged him. Pop played with Jun-min, with infinite, pre-programmed patience. Pop drew pictures with him and played football and walked him to the park.

Once, when Pop was bouncing him, something inside the automaton broke and spurted steam. Jun-min's left thumb was scalded raw, but it could have been worse. Jun-min ran that thumb over the scar tissue ridging his eyes.

After that, Father had installed a spring mechanism in the automaton.

Pop sputtered and spat. Its gears ground down and black oil spattered onto the floor. A steady drip, like rainfall. Or tears. *Plop. Plop. Plop.*

Jun-min sighed. He got up and retrieved the brass crank from the bench. He started winding Pop up.

Now it was Jun-min who cared for the automaton. He kept its many intricate parts clean and running smoothly, replacing them with spare components he found on his nightly rounds of the neighborhood garbage heaps.

He kept it functioning, but he couldn't reprogram it. It kept performing its three dozen tasks in eerie response to Jun-min's needs, almost intelligently it sometimes seemed. It had been designed with a purpose, and it would carry it out until it wore down beyond his ability to repair it.

What would he make it do if he could change its programming? Could it become his new guide? Its sensors were more rudimentary than Bauble, but better than Jun-min's useless eyes.

Even if he managed that, people tended to get upset when they saw a 180-centimeter tall mechanical man lumbering through the streets.

When Pop whirred back to life, it bowed to Jun-min, bumping into his chest, and then puttered off to the small kitchen in the corner. A silver kettle rattled in the sink.

Tea?

"Sure." Jun-min wandered through the shop, running his hand along the broken bits and pieces of other machines. He plucked everything he thought he would need and arranged them on the workbench. Then he rearranged them. He had never succeeded in building a machine from scratch, but he needed a new Bauble.

He brushed away his tears and got to work.

Four hours later, he gave up. He swept the gears and brass plates and springs to the floor.

"Damn," he said. That was stupid. He couldn't afford to damage the scarce parts.

Pop sprang to life and began picking up the scattered pieces.

Jun-min was drinking cold barley tea when he heard a knock at the door. Pop dropped an armful of brass fittings with a clatter and clomped toward the door.

"No, I'll get it, Pop." Last week, Pop had badly frightened the yogurt delivery woman.

Jun-min opened the door. "Yes?"

He smelled machine oil and lotus flowers. It was *her*.

Jun-min stiffened. "You. The woman from last night."

"Hello, Jun-min. I'm Pak Yo-reum. May I come in? Don't worry, I'm alone."

"Do I have a choice?"

"Yes, of course. I just wanted to return this."

She waited a moment and then Jun-min felt something solid, round, heavy, and familiar nudge his breastbone. He wrapped his arms around it.

"Bauble?" His throat tightened and he skipped a breath.

"I'm very sorry about what happened. I'll go now," she said.

"Wait. Come in. Have some tea."

Jun-min turned and walked back into the workshop. The kettle was already whistling; how did Pop do that?

He prodded Bauble all over, assessing the damage. The guide's retractable mechanical legs had been pushed back into their compartments. He had a new, large ding in the side and a number of scratches. Jun-min shook Bauble and a small metal piece rattled sickeningly inside.

And there was the hole. Only one, so the bullet was still lodged inside. A terrific shot dead center in his glass eye, so it had probably pierced Bauble's heart. Jun-min felt the wound's rough edges and the hairline cracks radiating from it.

"Can you fix it?" Yo-reum asked.

"Yes," Jun-min said automatically. But he wasn't sure.

He settled Bauble on his table and got to work, quickly removing the machine's outer shell.

"That's amazing." She sipped tea, standing at his elbow. Jun-min felt to his right and there it was, a fresh cup of tea, still hot.

"How do you fix things you can't see?" she asked.

"How do you kill Nipponese? This is what I'm meant for."

She was quiet.

"Sorry. That was too much." He shook his head.

"I apologize for being insensitive. I've just never seen anything like this."

"Me neither." Jun-min smiled. "To answer your question: this is easier than most of my projects because I know Bauble better than I know myself."

He deftly removed the upper hemisphere and set it next to the lower half. He felt inside, disturbed by how cold and lifeless the machine was.

"Your father was Shim Sung-min, wasn't he? I recognize his work. He built that remarkable mechanical man, too?"

"Yes."

"He was a genius."

"If that was true, he would still be alive," Jun-min said.

"He died for his country, in the line of duty. It was a terrible accident, just like..."

"Yours," she was going to say.

Jun-min closed his eyes and kept working. Soon he found the source of the critical damage. He removed the broken fragments of the deadly bullet from the remains of Bauble's spherical power core.

He pulled out the wrecked component and placed it on the table.

"You said your father made this... Bauble. For you?" Yo-reum asked.

"It was an apology. He blamed himself for the accident that blinded me."

"What happened?"

"I was five. I was here one day, as I was on most days, standing right where you are." Jun-min turned his head toward her. "Watching him work. He didn't notice me, he hardly ever did, but if he had he would have told me to stand back. He was experimenting with a new power core for the gigans." A larger version of the broken component in front of Jun-min.

"The casing cracked under the pressure and steam blasted into my face. My eyes. I screamed and screamed. That's what I remember most: the screaming. And unbearable pain. And then darkness."

The last thing Jun-min had seen was white. The hot steam had cooked his eyes and scarred his face like a raccoon dog's mask.

Jun-min also remembered his father's panicked, anguished cries. Strong, callused hands holding him close as he carried Jun-min to a doctor. Cool cloth pressed against the hot, fragile, stinging skin. The painful throbbing behind his closed eyelids. For weeks, his father had finally paid attention only to Jun-min, crying himself to sleep at his bedside.

Yo-reum put a hand on Jun-min's shoulder. Her slight but firm hand was nothing like the cold, metal touch of the automaton. Jun-min shivered and shrugged her off.

He swept Bauble's useless core away from him. It rolled along the table, but it didn't hit the floor. Yo-reum handed it back to him.

"It's junk," he said.

"You can fix anything. That's what your sign says out front."

"That's my father's sign. But even he couldn't fix a broken heart." Jun-min tossed the ruined core across the room. "I need more parts for Bauble."

"Just don't scavenge the commitment boxes again." He could hear her smiling. "I'll bring you what I can."

"In exchange for...?"

"Can you fix some things for me?"

"Yes."

***

219

Jun-min pressed his forehead against the machine Yo-reum had brought for him to repair today.

"It's a longcase clock," she said.

"I know. Shh."

These were rare in the Great Han Empire. He had only ever seen one of them before in his life – another of Father's mechanical follies.

Jun-min listened and felt the subtle vibrations of the components inside. Everything had its own unique signature and if he listened, he heard them talking to each other, working together. They told him how they were supposed to function and what was wrong.

The clock's ticking synchronized eerily with Pop's, like they belonged together. Tick. Tick. Tick. Tock. Tick... There was a catch in the pendulum mechanism.

Jun-min opened the front of the case and winced at its creaky hinges. That would have an easy remedy at least.

"It's beautifully made. Where did you get it?" he asked.

"It's from the military base at Yongsan. They use it to coordinate missions, so it's vital that it keeps accurate time."

"Who made it?" To his knowledge, there were no clockmakers with this skill in the Empire. It must have been imported.

"Don't you know?" she asked.

Jun-min felt along the inside of the metal door, down toward the bottom. He found the three Chinese characters inscribed there.

Submerge. Succeed. Cleverness.

"Father?" This was the same clock he had watched his father build years ago. Whereas most Western clocks were built of wood, Sung-min had fashioned his from copper – easier to get in quantity at the time.

"He created a lot of things for the military," Yo-reum said. "This one was special though – a symbol of the change the Independence Party wants to see in the country: An age of technology and open trade, allowing Western influence to advance our own society."

Jun-min scowled. That was the kind of thinking that had inspired the Enlightenment and led them down the dark path to war.

"You didn't approve of his politics? You would rather we remain 'the Hermit Kingdom'?" she asked.

"I was a little boy. I didn't know anything about that. I just liked watching him put things together. I loved this clock."

He closed the case, with more force than he'd intended.

"You don't know what's wrong with it?" she asked.

"I know exactly what's wrong with it. But I don't have what I need to fix it." He instantly regretted his accusatory tone.

It wasn't her fault that metal was increasingly scarce in the Empire. If he could even get his hands on a roll of tin, he could cut new parts. Maybe he could get Bauble working again in some fashion.

He wondered why they hadn't melted down this clock yet. What was more important? Victory or sentiment?

"That's a shame," Yo-reum said. "Can we leave it–?"

"Wait. There might be something..." Jun-min pressed his lips together. He shouldn't have said anything.

"What?"

Jun-min walked over to Pop.

Want to go for a walk, son?

"Not right now, Pop. I want to check something first."

Yo-reum had followed him, closer than his shadow.

"You talk to it?" she asked.

"Sometimes." Jun-min blushed. "It helps me think." He didn't tell her that he imagined he heard the automaton speak in his father's voice, repeating things he'd often said to Jun-min.

"This automaton is a masterpiece. You can see how he incorporated its basic design elements into the gigans, on a much larger scale." Yo-reum's voice was filled with awe.

"You thought *I* was a thief? Father stole from his customers. They would bring things for him to fix, and he would slip out a gear here, a spring there. He could jury rig the devices so they would keep working for a while longer, but they always came back."

"He needed the business?"

"He didn't care about that. He needed *parts*. That's how he built this automaton. And that clock. Want a look inside?" Jun-min used the flat edge of the automaton's key to pry open the access plate in its back. He stuck his hand in and pressed the switch that turned off the machine. He didn't want to lose a finger.

Yes, there it was. A small gear, in exactly the size he needed. It made sense that machines from his father's workshop would have interchangeable parts.

Jun-min traced the rubber belt over to a portion of the automaton's shoulder assembly. If he slipped it free... Pop wouldn't be pouring tea anymore. A small sacrifice.

It would work in the short term, just until he had more materials. He could have the clock fixed and send Yo-reum on her way. Another satisfied customer.

He pried the gear out and unfastened the gear belt.

"Doesn't it need those?" Yo-reum said.

"It's extra," Jun-min lied. He flipped the switch to turn the machine back on and waited anxiously to make sure Pop didn't suddenly fly apart at the seams. It was shaky but stable. Jun-min closed it up.

The gear fit perfectly inside the clock, like it was made for it. Jun-min slid the damaged gear, teeth worn smooth, into the pouch always by his side. Nothing should be wasted.

"What time is it?" Jun-min asked.

"10:04."

He set the clock's pendulum swinging and reset its hands.

Jun-min felt its confident ticking like a strong, rapid heartbeat under his fingers. Tick. Tick. Tick. Tick. It was out of harmony with Pop now.

Yo-reum clapped. "You're as talented as your father."

"Nowhere close. I can't make things like him. I can only keep them operational," Jun-min admitted.

But now that he'd had a chance to probe the clockworks, he had glimpsed his Father's creativity – the organized chaos that set his machines in motion and lent them the appearance of life.

***

Yo-reum entered while Jun-min was finishing his repairs on a pneumatic cleaner.

"Oh no! What happened to Pop? Vandals?" she said.

"Huh? Oh." He patted the remains of Pop's arm on the workbench. "No. I needed a few parts to fix customers' machines."

Jun-min thought of it as returning what Father had stolen to the people they belonged to.

"But you've ruined it," Yo-reum said. She sounded distraught.

"It's okay. Look."

Pop feebly raised his right arm, still mostly intact. Jun-min grasped his hand. A sudden memory overwhelmed him: squeezing his father's limp hand after the accident that had killed him. He dropped the metal proxy and it thudded to the worktable. Jun-min's own hands were shaking.

"Jun-min?" Yo-reum said.

He breathed in and out. "H-how are you, Pop?"

Tick. Tick. Whir.

He didn't hear Father's voice anymore. Pop's eyes clicked. Jun-min reached up and found its eyelids closed.

"I'll put him back together later, after the war when there will be plenty of parts," Jun-min said.

After the war. People said that as if certain they would defeat Nippon. It could easily go the other way, in which case "after the war" would be no improvement.

"I may be able to requisition additional automatons, if you could build them." Yo-reum said. "You and I could work together—"

"No." Jun-min spoke firmly. "Even if I could replicate it, I wouldn't. No more weapons."

No more ghosts.

"It could end the war sooner. Save lives," she said.

"How?"

"I think this automaton was a prototype for a new kind of gigan that doesn't require human pilots. Dozens of the toys and trinkets in this workshop and your father's lab at Yongsan Garrison are small-scale versions of devices he built for the Enlightened. Even Bauble."

"Bauble?"

"He's more than a Seeing Eye. So much more. He's an artificial brain, Jun-min."

Jun-min gripped the round power core inside Pop's chest, almost pulsing with life energy.

"Jun-min?"

The metal sphere was warm, getting hotter the longer his skin touched it. He held it more tightly, pulled. It uncoupled easily, far too easily for something so important. And Pop died on the table.

"What have you done?" Yo-reum asked.

Which was more important? Victory or sentiment?

"I should have done this before." Jun-min groped for Bauble, still in two halves like a sliced pear apple. He had overhauled everything else, pounded out the dents, polished the scrapes. He was good as new. All he needed was a heart.

He slid the core home and connected the pipes, belts, and wires. Would it be compatible?

Jun-min rejoined the two parts and rotated them until they clicked solidly into place.

Bauble hummed to life.

***

The spring hit the wall above Jun-min's workbench with a twang and bounced to the floor. Bauble rolled over, scooped it up, and carried it back to Yo-reum. She laughed and threw it again toward a different corner. Jun-min shook his head and continued to examine the device she had delivered today: a broken phonograph.

Instead of playing recorded music or speech, it stored what she called machine code on a metal platter. Jun-min pointedly did not ask what programming it contained, and Yo-reum pointedly did not offer this information. They had come to an understanding; Jun-min would not repair anything that had an application for war.

"But anything can be used to advance our cause," she said again. "Imagine what a Bauble the size of Deoksugung Palace could do."

Jun-min grimaced. "He could lead blind giants?" he suggested. "Hey, do you want me to fix this phonograph or not?"

"Please! I'll take you for barbeque after."

"Deal."

Jun-min tinkered with the phonograph until he thought it was working.

"I can't be sure unless I know what it does," he said.

"It's working. You can fix any—"

The room shook and the ground rumbled. A warning siren sounded in the distance. Bauble echoed it with a low, irritating whine.

"What?" Jun-min asked.

The spring dropped to the floor and Yo-reum raced to the door. It slammed against the wall as she ran outside.

Jun-min grabbed Bauble's harness, connected it, and then made his way to the threshold. "Yo-reum?"

He heard her a moment later, trying to catch her breath. "Another attack. A dirigible just dropped a mech in Jeong-dong. It's a big one, at least nine meters tall. Kitsune-Class."

"The fox? How many tails?" Jun-min asked.

"Three."

He drew in a breath. Those would do a lot of damage.

"Go down to the basement. Stay there. You'll be safe," Yo-reum said.

"What about you?"

"I have to do something! Take care."

"Yo-reum? What are you going to do?"

She was gone.

Jun-min cursed and started running. He didn't know where she had gone, but he bet it was toward the screams and thunder.

"Bauble!" he yelled. Bauble rocketed past.

Since Jun-min had repaired the machine, he had been more distractible, like with Yo-reum and the game with the spring. Bauble wasn't always where Jun-min expected him. Before, he always had been attentive to Jun-min's needs, but now it seemed like Bauble had developed other desires of his own. It figured that Jun-min hadn't been able to fix him as good as Father would have. And yet, Bauble didn't seem *broken* – just different.

Jun-min went as quickly as he could on the uneven ground. Bauble's modulated ticking and huffs of steam told him about the terrain ahead, and he followed the sounds about three clicks behind the guide.

Suddenly Bauble stopped and steamed a warning.

"Jun-min! Help! Here!" Yo-reum called.

"Are you injured?" Jun-min made his way toward her voice. He coughed, breathing in scorched air. His nostrils filled with the smoke from a wood fire, and burning rubber.

"Not me," she said.

Intense heat warmed Jun-min's face. The ground vibrated. There was a machine ahead, a large and powerful one. The sharp hiss told him it was steam-driven clockwork, so it wasn't the enemy mech.

"A gigan?" he asked.

"It's not moving. There's something wrong with it. And the pilot. She's injured. Bad."

"What can I do for her?"

"I have to bandage her. You take care of the machine."

"Yo-reum..."

"Not now, Jun-min. Stuff your morals. People are dying. Our city is in danger. If Hanseong falls..."

Jun-min hesitated. There had to be more gigan on the way. This was the capital, after all, and home of the military headquarters. But the war effort was spread pretty thin, and he couldn't remember how badly the city's gigan sentinels had been damaged in their last battle. This could be all the help they would have.

Jun-min needed to be useful, and there was only one thing he was good at.

He pressed his cheek against the trembling leg of the fallen gigan. This was a mid-sized unit, about six meters tall so it only required one pilot. He pressed his fingers against the machine.

It was screaming silently in anguish, the brass and copper and steel torquing with stress. It was shaking like it was about to fall apart.

Jun-min listened.

He envisioned all the pieces of the gigan, the cogs and switches and sprockets inside it and how they fit together, *seeing* them as clearly as if he was looking at schematics. He saw what was broken and how it could be fixed – and how the machine could be improved. He saw his father's spirit in the machine.

Jun-min gasped.

"Report!" Yo-reum spoke sharply, the way she had when they first met, when she was just a soldier to him.

"It's... The power core."

"Is it functional?"

"Yes. It's functioning too well, in fact. It's overheating, the pressure is building much too quickly."

"That means more power?"

"For now. Until it explodes. I've felt this before."

Jun-min reached up and slapped his palm as high as he could against the metal beast. "The core will tear itself apart unless there's a controlled release of steam. It's like the blast that killed my father. He was testing the limits, pushing the heart to do more, and the metal could only take so much."

"It's going to blow up?"

"Yes. Soon."

"Stay with the pilot." Yo-reum grabbed Jun-min's hand. He held on.

"What about you?" he asked.

"I'm going to drive this thing. I've always wanted to."

"You haven't before? Aren't you a soldier?"

"Not in combat. I was only conscripted two years ago, fresh out of Hansung High, as assistant engineer. A desk job."

"Then you can't go out there."

"You volunteering?" She squeezed his hand. "Bauble, take care of him. Jun-min, take care of the pilot."

She kissed him on the cheek and then let go of his hand. Heavy boots clanged on the metal rungs of the ladder leading up into the cockpit of the gigan.

Jun-min knelt beside the pilot, listening for how Yo-reum was progressing in the gigan. Pistons pumped, the core thrummed. Steam hissed. Understanding how the machine worked didn't mean she could operate it herself.

Their first steps were uncertain and catastrophic. Bricks and broken glass tumbled down from the building across the street.

"My leg," the pilot whispered. "I can't feel it."

Jun-min felt below the woman's right knee and met metal.

"A prosthesis." A simple, unyielding one.

Jun-min sketched out plans in his mind for a better model, a miniaturized version of the fully articulated mechanical leg in the gigan currently lurching its way toward the center of the city. Toward the sound of gunfire and sirens.

"No, the other one," the woman said.

Jun-min groped for her left leg and found a wet bandage at the knee. Everything below it was gone. His fingers were warm and sticky with blood-soaked dirt.

Bauble whistled. He rolled up and dropped something next to Jun-min with a sickening thump like a hunk of raw meat. It was shredded and bloody, already cold. Unsalvageable. Human parts were so much less durable than machine parts.

Jun-min hurled it away from him. Bauble rolled after it. "Leave it, Bauble!" he said harshly.

"What's your name?" he asked the woman.

"Gim." She gasped painfully. "Min-jae."

Jun-min bowed his head. "I'm sorry, Min-jae. It's bad news."

I wish I could fix you, he thought. *I want to make this better.*

A deafening explosion rocked the neighborhood. Jun-min lifted his head and shielded his eyes reflexively. He *saw* the flash of a gigan's power core detonating. Was it just an echo in his mind's eye?

The hairs on the back of his neck rose and he smelled ozone. Even through the dull ringing in his ears, he heard the screech of a dying mecha – a hideous, soul-rending sound. It collided with earth. Metal fragments rained down. Jun-min crouched over Min-jae and gritted his teeth as tiny metal fragments buried themselves into his flesh, shredded his back and arms and hands.

Yo-reum?

***

Bauble zoomed down the hospital corridor, not even waiting for Jun-min to catch up.

"Useless speeding eye," Jun-min muttered.

He squeezed the pine box against his side with his left elbow, and tapped his way forward with his cane until he heard Bauble's frantic clicking inside a room at the end of the hall.

Jun-min knocked.

"What are you doing here?" Yo-reum asked. "I don't want anyone to see me like this." She didn't sound like herself. Her voice was worn thin, faint, like less of it was there.

"You don't have to worry about that with me. I only came to hear you." He smiled.

Yo-reum grunted.

Bauble bumped against a chair beside the bed to get his attention, but Jun-min remained standing. He breathed in the subtle fragrance of the hibiscus plants surrounding her bed – a demonstration of the gratitude of Hanseong's citizens.

After a long silence, he heard Yo-reum whisper, low enough that anyone but Jun-min would have missed it:

"What am I going to do?" she asked.

"What you're shockingly good at. You'll keep on living," he said.

It was a miracle that she had survived an explosion of that magnitude. The reinforced cockpit of the gigan had absorbed most of the blast.

"I'm an engineer with no hands," she said.

"You saved the city. Two hundred thousand people," he said.

"I won a battle, but I'm out of the war. How can I do anything to help the Empire now?"

"They offered me your job," Jun-min said.

She didn't say anything.

"I turned it down, of course," he said.

"Why? You should take it. I recommended you as my assistant, before. We can use you."

"I'm not interested in fighting. Or building better weapons."

"Yes. You're a fixer."

Jun-min held the box out to Yo-reum.

"Are you kidding?" she said.

Jun-min's jaw dropped. "I'm so sorry." He bowed.

She laughed. "It's okay. But maybe you could open that for me."

Blushing, Jun-min slid the lid from the box.

"Jun-min. Are these Pop's?" she said.

"They're yours now." He placed the box on the bedspread and lifted out one of the metal hands. "I made some modifications to update them to the specifications of the gigans and fit them with controls you can work with your arm muscles. If I had resources, I could make them smaller and lighter."

"I'm honored," she said.

He didn't need Pop anymore. He had already taken too many years to say good-bye.

"Help me put them on," she said.

Jun-min unfastened the leather buckles. "Are your wounds healed?"

"They won't ever *heal*. But I suppose they won't hurt as much one day."

"No. They won't hurt," Jun-min said.

Jun-min fitted Yo-reum with her new mechanical hands and adjusted the fit. He had to close his heart to her muffled cries and gasps as the metal bit into the still-raw tissue over the stumps at her wrists.

"There." Jun-min stepped back. "I brought gloves too."

"Feh. I want everyone to see them."

The hand clicked and rasped as she flexed and tested each point of articulation. The effort left her sounding tired and in pain.

"It will take practice," Jun-min said.

Her cold metal fingers slid into his hand.

"Thank you," she said.

"Thank *you*," he said. "You were teaching me, bringing me Father's machines so I could learn by working with them."

"I thought it was worth a shot. I also hoped you would see that his life and his inventions meant something. Even if he couldn't be there for you."

"Hmm."

"So you think you can make more of these?" She squeezed his hand, with surprising delicacy considering they could crush it just as easily.

"I want to," he said.

Yo-reum's sacrifice – triggering the power core to burst prematurely, close to the enemy mecha – had saved the capital, but she wasn't the only person injured that day. Gwangjewon Hospital was full of victims of the the attack and the explosion, people who were crushed by falling debris, trapped under buildings.

"What do you need?" she asked.

"Parts to craft mechanical limbs for the patients here, and the many more to come before this war is over."

"I'll make a strong argument to my superior. Anything else?"

Jun-min hesitated.

"What?" she asked.

"I want to study the Nipponese mecha."

Though crippled, its pilot dead, no mecha had ever been captured so intact. Its advanced technology could accelerate the Empire's own tech. Components of the machine were actually electric! The need to learn its secrets was like an itch Jun-min couldn't reach.

"It's probably classified. If I can get you access, you'll have to share your discoveries with the military."

"I want to share them with everyone!" Jun-min said.

"That's something your father would have said."

Jun-min knelt beside the bed and lowered a hand. Bauble rolled over and nuzzled his palm.

"Not so surprising. He did create me," Jun-min said.

Art by Ivonne K. Moran

NELLY
KATE McCANE

1909
Edmonton, Canada

Lizbeth woke at sunrise, as usual. Her mother was away for the school term; a teacher before she had married, she had decided to go back to work, even though it wasn't allowed. ('Ridiculous,' she scoffed, 'as if being married has endangered my ability to teach! And besides, we need the money.') It wasn't allowed of course. Lizbeth giggled a little as she imagined the scandal it would cause; a married teacher! That's why Mama had to travel to Red Deer and pretend to be a spinster. Her ring sat hidden in the chimney of the cast iron stove, waiting for her to return. It must be lonely, thought Lizbeth, in that boarding house room, in that tiny little town, having to pretend that Lizbeth, Nelly, and Papa didn't even exist. They did need the money though.

Papa was off right now too – seeking railway building work. A big, gruff man, he'd tousled Lizbeth's hair before he left, and swung Nelly clean around the kitchen. "No money these days in a bit of honest magicking," he'd said, winking at them both. So now the household chores fell to Lizbeth. She sighed as she stoked up the fire, adding an extra log, then perked up a bit at the thought that it was Wednesday – bread breaking day. This was an excuse to have the stove at full blast all day, a bit of warmth in the drafty little kitchen. After all, the bread had to rise.

Of course, there was no need to be careful with the wood they'd stored for this winter. Lizbeth could keep a roaring fire burning on a single log for most of the year, with just a little effort. She wasn't really strong, not like Mama, Papa, or Nelly, but she got along well with fire. Mama forbade it though.

"No need to call attention to ourselves. Besides, chopping wood keeps young girls like you out of trouble."

Lizbeth snorted at the memory. She was 15, hardly a young girl anymore. Why, some of her contemporaries were already working outside the home; some of them were even married. Not Lizbeth. She didn't intend to marry, at least not just yet. She couldn't go to school anymore, on account of having to look after Nelly, but Mama tutored her in the summer holidays. There was talk that Premier Rutherford was going to pass a bill for a coeducational university in Edmonton, and Lizbeth had every intention of attending.

Poor Nelly was never going to go to school. It made Lizbeth sad sometimes, to think of it, although Nelly didn't seem to mind. She shivered as she thought about her trip to the grocery yesterday, the disapproving stares of the neighborhood wives and the taunts of the children. She couldn't just leave

Nelly inside all day. She had to take her out sometimes. But she heard and understood the mutters:

"A scandal. That girl ought to be in an institution."

"What they are thinking, I'm sure I don't know."

Yesterday, the children had been so brazen that even Nelly had noticed.

"Bebet," she had asked, peeking shyly out from under the new hat mother had made just before going away. It was a bonnet, and Nelly was really too old for it, but she couldn't seem to get the hang of hat pins.

"Yes Nelly?"

"What's a modgolod?"

Mongoloid. Lizbeth hated the word. Nelly was Nelly. She might look a little different, and her brain might not work quite right, but she was kind and graceful and strong and stubborn and just... Nelly.

"Never mind them," she said, just as she had heard her mother say a thousand times, "they're just small minded."

Nelly nodded thoughtfully.

"They don't like us," she said. Lizbeth sighed. Nelly was slow, but she wasn't stupid.

Lizbeth hugged her.

"Come on," she said, unsure what to say, what to do. "We've got to get more flour for tomorrow." At that moment, she had missed her mother more than ever.

***

As if summoned by her thoughts, Nelly appeared at the top of the stairs.

"Bebet," she said, looking very solemn, "my buttons went wrong." Then she grinned, what Papa liked to call her cherub grin. Nelly could button her dresses just fine, and often did. But sometimes, she woke up and just didn't want to. So she pretended she had forgotten how. Lizbeth shook her head. Slow, but not stupid. And on some days, just plain lazy.

"Come over here then," she called, dusting the flour off on her apron. "I'll button them up." It was an old ritual. Lizbeth thought of it as The Buttoning of The Dress. Nelly would squirm, and shake, and refuse to sit still. She would grin that cherub grin of hers, and poke her tongue out. And then, just when Lizbeth was ready to give up and let her run around all day in an unbuttoned dress, she would stop and hold perfectly still. Just barely long enough for Lizbeth to do the buttons. Then she would slip out of Lizbeth's reach, grinning that cherub grin all the while.

Sometimes, as a kind of reward, Nelly would give Lizbeth a flower after the ritual. Nelly loved flowers. It had been a real problem when she was younger, because she had a talent for them. Papa had to dig up the rose bush in the garden one December, because Nelly decided she wanted roses.

"Roses don't grow in the winter, my darling girl," Mama had said. "Be patient, and wait until spring. Now we have evergreens and mistletoe and hellebore, aren't they lovely?"

But Nelly was going through a stubborn phase. So she made the rose bush flower. Those roses were beautiful. Every single one of them was perfect. Nelly really did have a talent for flowers. And Papa had to dig up the rosebush. It was no use doing anything else. The family was in a precarious enough position without calling attention to their gifts. Nelly was older now, and Mama had finally convinced her to confine out of season flowers to her room.

That had been a difficult year. Nelly was 10 years old and coming into her full power – and she was powerful. But no matter what they tried, some things just didn't want to stick in her head. She'd seen one of the neighbors drowning a bag of kittens, and rescued them, scolding him all the while. It might have been funny, if he hadn't fallen over one of those kittens and broken both legs the next day. Old Hester Delaney, whose lungs had never been good but who was prone to giving Nelly sweets, started breathing easy for the first time in decades. And finally, the icing on the cake, the rose bush. The whole neighborhood had seen it.

It was no good. They had to move. That was when they'd come to Edmonton. They'd had money for the train then, and the journey had been pleasant. They'd spent the first year in a tent, because the housing boom made it difficult to find a place to live. Then they bought the house, and fortune seemed to turn on them.

"She does that, sometimes," Mama had sighed. Papa had lost his job at the bank. Mama's customers stopped asking for home remedies and simple charms. Even Nelly's flower arrangements, made only on special occasions and put in front of the house on a table, hadn't sold as well. That was August. Now, it was November, and although Mama and Papa were sending money, Lizbeth knew it was going to be a tough winter. Besides, she didn't like being here alone. Her talent only ran to things like keeping the stove warm, and Nelly... You could rely on Nelly to do something powerful, something big. But you never knew what it was going to be. Goddess touched, Mama said. More interested in balance than anything else.

Lizbeth's hands pounded the dough furiously as Nelly flitted around the kitchen, 'helping'. As usual, this meant making a mess, and asking annoying questions.

"Bebet, can we make apple cake?" (No Nelly, we don't have apples.) "Bebet, Mama says I can use the stove." (No Nelly, Mama says it's hot and you should keep away.) "Bebet, will you sew me a new dress?" (No Nelly, the only fabric we have is fit for curtains and nothing more.) "Bebet, Papa needs us."

Lizbeth stopped kneading and turned to look at Nelly. She had stopped flitting. She was standing stock still in the middle of the kitchen, moon-shaped face turned to the ceiling. Her voice wasn't changed, exactly, but Lizbeth understood that this was Nelly's power speaking. Her face was still and serious. Goddess Touched. It was rare, but it could happen. Lizbeth had just enough talent to recognize it when it did. Her heart jumped to her throat – Papa must really be in trouble.

"Bebet," Nelly said, and now her voice was normal again, scared and small sounding "Papa needs us. Papa. Papa needs us. Now Bebet, now now

now."

Later, Lizbeth was never sure how she did it. Somehow, with Nelly, whimpering and practically throwing a tantrum, she managed to find extra winter cloaks for them both, pack some bread, turnips, carrots and some cheese in a basket, get Nelly dressed for the snow, find the outdoor blanket they sometimes used for picnics, tuck the envelope Mama had sent last week with some money into her petticoat pockets for safety, and leave the house.

Nelly perked up immediately. "This way!" she called, marching gaily and briskly through the snow as if they were going to tea at a friend's house. "Over here Bebet." Lizbeth struggled to keep up. Her boots were old, and they kept slipping in the snow. Nelly marched onwards through the streets of Edmonton, not even stopping to look at her usual distractions – dogs, smaller children, bunting – none of it caught her eye. The usual calls and taunts got worse as they moved out of their own neighborhood and into areas that weren't used to seeing Nelly out and about, but Nelly ignored them, so Lizbeth did too.

"Are you sure this is the right way, Nelly?" she asked finally, filled with doubt. The stares were starting to get to her. She was worried someone was going to call the police. Or worse, a doctor. They'd tried to take Nelly once before. And Nelly did get strange ideas sometimes, and she was incredibly good at play acting when she wanted to be. Maybe this was all some sort of prank?

"Papa said he was going south, to Calgary, but right now we're going west."

Nelly stuck out her tongue and rolled her eyes upwards, clearly thinking hard.

"South," she confirmed, still walking quickly towards the west. "Papa is south. No time Lizbeth." She stopped for a moment, and turned to face her sister. "No time for walking. Short cut."

Lizbeth's breath practically stopped in her throat. Nelly never used her full name. And there was only one thing 'short cut' could mean.

"But Nelly–"

"Now Lizbeth!" And she said it in such a commanding tone, that it was clear to Lizbeth that even if this was a prank, Nelly was committed. Lizbeth had better go along to take care of her. But a short cut... Lizbeth shivered.

"You use those paths sparingly," Mama had said. "The likes of us don't belong there. We just borrow them sometimes. And mind you don't eat or drink anything!"

Almost a full hour later, they were out of the city. The only thing around for miles was snow and the occasional farmstead. Nelly's gait had slowed, and she moved her head back and forth, scanning the landscape. Lizbeth's heart was still pounding, or she might have laughed at how silly Nelly looked.

"There," Nelly announced proudly, pointing at a tree. Lizbeth stared, disappointed. Somehow, she had been expecting more. But it was just a poplar, branches stark and snowy, pointing towards the sky. Nelly grabbed Lizbeth's hand, and started circling the tree. Once, twice. Nothing happened. Then Nelly started to dance, a strange shuffling step that left threads of power glowing in her footsteps. Then, she started to sing.

> "Ring a ring a rosy
> a pocket full and posy
> tissue way tissue way
> we all fall down."

For once, Nelly's voice was perfectly clear, ringing in true harmony. So different from the way she usually sounded. It was so mesmerizing that Lizbeth took a moment to register the change in scenery. Suddenly, they were in the mountains. The sun shone bright and clear. The air smelt warm. The poplar was gone, replaced by a tree the likes of which Lizbeth had never seen before. You would need at least one hundred Nellys all holding hands to make a ring around it.

"Come on Bebet," Nelly said, letting go of Lizbeth's hand. "Don't forget what Mama said."

Mama said it was dangerous, and we shouldn't come here, thought Lizbeth. Mama said we would be all right, that she was only away for the winter. And Mama had also said, late one night when Nelly was fast asleep and Papa was off working, "You watch out for your sister, Beth my girl. You make sure she's taken care of. But you remember that she's Goddess touched. She doesn't think like you or me. She'll happily make a man sick, or cause a storm, just as easily as she'll rescue kittens or cause a rose bush to flower. The Goddess doesn't mind about what we think of as right and wrong. The Goddess serves the Balance. And Nelly serves the Goddess. You just keep that in mind, and I'll come back to both my girls, safe and sound, you hear?"

"How long do we have to be here, Nelly?" Lizbeth asked quietly.

Nelly shrugged, and plucked a small pink bud from a bush beside the tree. "Geranium," she sighed happily, and placed it carefully into the ribbon on her bonnet. Then she circled the tree again, as if making sure, and set out down the mountainside.

It was soon far too hot for their cloaks, so Lizbeth bundled them up and carried them on the basket. That made walking difficult, and her boots weren't getting any more comfortable. But Nelly forged ahead, following a path through the trees that only she could see.

An hour passed, and then another. There was no bird song here, and Lizbeth was sure the wind was trying to whisper unpleasant secrets into her ear. The trees were huge, the flowers brightly colored in an unpleasant sort of way. Branches clung to their clothes as they walked.

She was desperately thirsty. She hadn't thought to pack water, because she had been planning on melting snow to drink. But they couldn't do that here. Nelly was starting to feel the strain too. She was singing quietly under her breath, some sort of made up nonsense. No more clarity. She was back to being as off-key and random as ever.

Suddenly, as if out of nowhere, they came to a cave. Nelly stopped singing. Lizbeth drew in a deep breath. A figure appeared at the mouth of the cave. Small and wiry, his black hair and blue eyes made for a startling contrast. His skin was smooth and tanned. He was beautiful, but there was something mean about the corners of his mouth. Lizbeth disliked him instantly.

"My my my, what have we here?" His voice was snide. "You two don't belong here, oh my, but you don't."

Nelly was silent. The man looked quizzically at them both. "You know," he said quietly to Lizbeth, as if confiding in her, "there's something not quite right about your sister. Funny in the brain, she is. And it's very wrong for two young women such as yourselves to go unaccompanied. Why, something might happen to you both."

"Move!" Nelly made a shooing motion at him. He grinned at her, and reached over to steal the flower from her bonnet.

"Sensible families in your line get rid of the imbeciles like you," he said, his tone getting even nastier. "It's no good, you know," he said, addressing Lizbeth once again. "She's a cripple. Your mother should have left her in the snow to die. What are you going to do, hey, when she gets even more powerful? How will you keep her under control?"

"The Goddess—" Lizbeth started.

"Silly slip of a girl. The Goddess doesn't care about you or your sister. Or your Mama, or your oh-so-precious Papa. They're mobbing him right now, you know. Somebody watched him light a fire last night without the use of matches. Silly old man. Almost as silly as this one here." He glanced pointedly at Nelly, who had gone silent again, staring at him sullenly.

Lizbeth tried not to let anything show on her face, but he must have caught her surprise.

"Oh don't look so shocked, little one," he sneered. "The likes of us, we keeps an eye on the likes of you. We do. Just in case you come running into our world, all in a panic over your darling family, or maybe on a mission from your Goddess bright." He spat in disgust. "And when you do, well, it's people like Pereted who catch you, oh yes. All that bright power. And a chance to rob your Goddess" – he spat again – "of not one, but two of her servants. And now it's your turn, coming here and running into little old me. I don't think you should be allowed to leave. You or the Mongoloid."

There it was. That word again. Lizbeth could feel the rage building up inside of her. It wasn't just this stranger, this rude little man with his snide remarks and his threats. It wasn't even his insinuation that he was an enemy of the Goddess, someone Lizbeth knew, deep down inside, could really hurt them both, which was why Mama told them to avoid the paths in the first place. It was like the entire 12 years of Nelly's existence, the whole litany of rude remarks, pointed whispers, uncomfortable silences, evil looks, all of it, years of wanting to defend Nelly and keep her safe, knowing that there was nothing she could do to change the people who pointed, and whispered, and laughed; all of it, all of that rage, that frustration, all the times that Mother had laughed it off, telling her, telling Nelly 'they're just small minded', all the times Lizbeth had turned her back despite the pain in her mother's eyes, left it alone even though Nelly had walked home crying, not caused a fuss although she herself wanted desperately to punch and pull hair, all of it came bubbling up and boiling over. She could feel her power gathering in her, suddenly fueled by years of hatred, all of it summed up in the picture of this one, slimy man, standing at the entrance to the cave, blocking their way. She couldn't think of anything clever to say, didn't really realize she was going to say anything, until the rage couldn't contain itself in silence any longer and as her hands burst into glowing blue flames, shooting up almost to the top of the cave roof she yelled, loud and clear and angry:

"GO AWAY."

"Oh now," said the little man, staring at her hands nervously, slowly backing away from the cave mouth, "now that isn't fair. Nobody said there would be fire, oh no. Nobody said Pereted would have to deal with fire. I was told you could barely even spark. Well then. That changes things." He smiled smarmily, and gestured towards the entrance. "Off you go then ladies. Pleasant journeys. Just," he glanced once more at Lizbeth's hands, "just put those out, will you?"

Lizbeth was not inclined to comply.

"They'll be more, you know," he yelled as they walked into the cave. "Don't think that Pereted is the only one. Oh no. Not everyone is afraid of fire!" He shouted the last word, so that it echoed through the cave as they walked away... ire, ire, ire...

They increased their pace. The knot in her stomach told her that Mama was right. This place was too dangerous for the likes of them. It had been a mistake, coming here. Next time, maybe she wouldn't be able to keep Nelly safe. But they had to keep going.

Lizbeth kept a small flame in the palm of her hand to light the way. The cave was huge, the ceiling distant. Their shadows danced around them in the flame, sometimes in front, sometimes behind. Ominous, threatening. Lizbeth resisted the urge to shrink away from the walls. Nelly stayed silent. Occasionally, a tear rolled down her cheek. A little slow, but not stupid. Nelly knew exactly what that little man had said. But there was no time for comfort. They had to keep going. Lizbeth broke off a piece of carrot for them both to suck, to help with the thirst. It was better than nothing.

Nelly stopped. They had reached a magnificent rock, sprouting like a small mountain from the floor of the cave. It was beautiful, with whirls of iridescent inlay curling and weaving across it, shifting and sparkling to and fro. Nelly pointed at it, silently.

"Go on then," Lizbeth said encouragingly. "You know what to do."

Nelly shook her head, and pointed at Lizbeth. Lizbeth started.

"But Nelly my darling sister, I can't transport us back and forth. I don't have the power. You know it as well as I do. It has to be you."

Nelly pouted. "Can't," she said, refusing to look at Lizbeth. "Too stupid." Lizbeth let the flame die out.

"Come on Nelly," she cooed, taking her sister into her arms. "You know that isn't true."

"Everyone says," Nelly retorted, tears flowing freely now that it was dark. "Everyone knows."

Lizbeth's heart broke a little.

"They don't matter," she whispered in her sister's ear. "They're just small minded. Mama knows, and Papa knows, and *I* know that you're brilliant. You're our Nelly. You make the flowers grow for us. You help me with my cooking. You always know how to cheer Mama up when she's having a bad day, and you help Papa when he has a headache. We love you, Nelly-bug, through and through. And look. You're better at Magicking than I ever will be. I can't open the portal, love, I don't know how. But you do. You know how to get us to Papa, to make him safe. Come on. You can do it."

Nelly shook her head, sobbing. And then, they heard the footsteps. Loud. Coming towards them. The whole cave shook. Lizbeth's breath caught again. Nelly still had her face buried on Lizbeth's shoulder.

"Come on Nelly," Lizbeth said, serious now "You've had your cry. We need to get out of here. I don't have time to treat you like a little girl. You're 12 years old. That's old enough to serve the Goddess, and it's old enough to get us out of here! No more dillydallying. Go!"

Nelly took a step back, and wiped the tears from her eyes. Cave dust was starting to fall from the ceiling. The walls boomed with the sound of steel on rock. A voice, loud enough to hurt Lizbeth's ears, yelled: "Where are the tasty little morsels, trespassing on our paths? Where is the glowing power of the Day-Bitch, ready and steaming for me to eat. I'll have you both I will, worming and wriggling and screaming. WHERE ARE YOU?"

Lizbeth looked at Nelly, who had clapped both hands over her ears.

"Now honey. It has to be now!"

Nelly grabbed Lizbeth's hand, and circled the rock, once, twice. The third time, she started dancing again, that same shuffling pattern, and singing in that remarkably clear voice:

"Fee fi fo fum
I smell the way back home we come
be he alive or be he dead
no grinded bones to make our bread"

Lizbeth had one terrifying glimpse of a giant of a man, face red with anger, bellowing in rage as they disappeared.

It was freezing. Lizbeth hurriedly took the cloaks out of the basket and wrapped first Nelly, then herself. Greedily, both of them stuffed cold snow in their mouths to still their thirst. It made their teeth ache, but it felt so good. Lizbeth handed Nelly a piece of bread and cheese, hoping that a bit of food would cheer her up slightly. Her face was still red and puffy from crying.

By the looks of things, they'd lost very little time on their 'short cut'. The sun was more or less in the same position. The landscape, however, was completely different. There were mountains off to the North; that must be the Rockies, thought Lizbeth. She'd never seen this part of them before. And in the distance, maybe about a half-hours walk, she could see a small camp.

"Is that where Papa is?" she asked Nelly. Nelly nodded dolefully, her mouth full of bread and cheese.

"Have to wait," she said.

"But you were in such a hurry!"

Nelly shook her head. "Too early." She refused to say anything more, simply sticking out her tongue and rolling her eyes when Lizbeth pressed. Lizbeth made herself some bread with cheese, and warmed up some more snow for them to drink. She could hear birds calling, and there was no wind. The landscape was filled with trees, most of them dead and barren at this time of year. The sun barely seemed to move across the sky. Every once in a while, Nelly would turn and squint at it, then nod carefully to herself as if confirming some sort of scientific measurement.

Finally, after what seemed like hours, she stood up. "Now, Bebet," she said, eyes still full of sadness. "This way."

They walked towards the camp. They were almost there when the shouting broke out. Lizbeth started to run, boots scrabbling madly for purchase in the snow. Nelly was ahead of her, faster and surer somehow, running like lighting.

"I seen it," the voice rang out clear across the camp "Last night. Jacob here seen it too. No matches, he's got, no flint and steel, we all know the wood's been wet for days. And he up and lights the fire as if it weren't no big problem. Not even touching it, he was. It's not normal."

Nelly was fast at first, but she kept getting her feet tangled together, and Lizbeth caught up just as she raced into a clearing outside the camp. There he was, their father, looking much the worse for wear, sweaty and pressed, with ten or so other workers facing him across the clearing, all of them pointing guns. He saw them a second before everyone else did.

"Nelly no!" he yelled, as she came barreling across the clearing towards him. Lizbeth followed.

Nelly stood in front of her father defiantly.

"Bad men!" she said, pointing her finger at the group of workers.

"What on earth—" one of the men started. But Lizbeth had stopped paying attention. Nelly was... glowing. Bright, and powerful. Some things they just couldn't get to stick. Nelly cared more about balance, said Mama, than she did about good and bad. Goddess Touched. But it wasn't the Goddess shining through Nelly's face, directing that power. It was pure Nelly, in a rage because these men were going to hurt her father. Lizbeth's mind raced. The Goddess punished those who used their power for ill. And Nelly in a rage could do terrible things. It wasn't her fault, not really. She got so frustrated that she couldn't think anymore. But Lizbeth shuddered to think what she might do to these men, these men who wanted to hurt her beloved Papa. She had to do something.

They were still speaking, and Nelly was starting to dance.

"And now this! We're a good half-days walk from the nearest homestead. It ain't natural, him lighting the fire like that, and it sure as hell ain't natural for these ladies to be out here in the middle of nowhere, one of them retarded and all."

Lizbeth had had enough. She strode out into the clearing, putting herself carefully between Nelly and the workers, and grabbed Nelly's hands. "No," she said firmly, in the voice she used to keep Nelly from touching the stove. "No Nelly. You did your part. It's my turn now."

Nelly screwed up her face, and looked at Lizbeth. "But—"

"No, Nelly. We got here in time. Papa is fine. Nobody needs to get hurt. Ok. Nobody." The last word she directed upwards, at the Goddess. Maybe She even heard it. The look of pure fury left Nelly's face, and she sighed, and stopped dancing. Her eyes closed, and the power left her. She grabbed hold of Papa's hand, and sank down to sit in the snow.

"Get out of the way, little girl." Lizbeth had almost forgotten the workers facing them. "This is men's business."

It had been a long and tiring day, and after the wiry man and the giant, and the thought of Nelly really hurting someone, a lumber worker with a shotgun just didn't seem all that threatening. She stepped up, in front of both her father and Nelly.

"I'll thank you to leave my sister alone," she said, in her coolest tone of voice. "Especially considering she appears to be more civilized than you will ever be."

"Now look here—" he began.

"No" she said firmly, using the same voice she had used on Nelly just a moment before. "That's enough. Here you are, all ten of you, pointing guns at my poor, unarmed father."

"But he—"

"Yes, I heard. Lit a fire without using matches. Understandable, that you would want to shoot him for that. After all, nobody has ever mistaken what they've seen at the end of a long day of work. It's never ever been the case that someone, tired and perhaps a little worse for the drink" – she caught the guilty gleam in his eye – "thought they saw something strange, has it? Certainly it seems reasonable enough to shoot a man over."

"But you—"

"I," said Lizbeth calmly, shaking inside, "am here with important news for my father. My sister is too young to be left alone, I had to bring her with me. We caught a wagon, if you must know, but the driver wouldn't take us further than the last homestead, and so we've walked. I'm afraid there was no money for a messenger, and the message is quite urgent."

Lizbeth could see that she was taking the wind out of the other men's sails. But the ringleader was almost as stubborn as Nelly.

"I know what I saw. And besides, if you've no money for a messenger, how did you pay for a wagon?"

Lizbeth gave him a withering look. "I didn't. A farmer was kind enough to take us, which is why we simply could not press when he didn't want to go any further. Any more questions, or can my sister and I have some time with our father now?"

"Come on Pete," one of the men tugged at his shoulder "we can't do anything with them here anyway. Wouldn't be right. Leave it alone."

Pete stared down the barrel of the gun for a second longer, eyeing the girls and their father. Then he spat, violently, and shot straight down into the ground at his feet.

"Fine" he said, looking at them all in anger. "But I don't want you anywhere near my work crew ever again, Nathaniel Waters, you hear me?"

"Fine by me," Lizbeth's Papa said in his strong, deep voice. "Fine by me."

It took them much longer to get home than it did for the initial journey. Papa didn't want to use Nelly's short cut. Truth be told, neither did Lizbeth. They camped rough for a few days getting to Calgary, Papa hunting for game and Lizbeth using her talent to keep them all warm. Papa scolded them both something fierce, but his eyes turned serious when he thanked them for saving him, and she knew they had done the right thing.

"My girls," he said lovingly. "A talent for magick and a talent for words, both of you. I couldn't be prouder."

That night by the fire, with Nelly fast asleep beside her, Lizbeth told him the whole story. He was quiet through the lot of it, listening in that careful way he had. When she had finished, he looked at her with a funny gleam in his eye.

"You're a good girl, Lizbeth Waters," he said, reaching out to take her hand. "I think the Goddess knew just what She was doing, when she sent you along with Nelly. Balance is important to Her, after all."

***

Something they had done on the journey must have pleased fortune. Papa found a job at another bank. Mama returned home to keep house. Lizbeth went back to school, studying hard. And Nelly... well, Nelly was always going to be Nelly. But something had changed on their journey. Lizbeth didn't notice it at first. But the Goddess touched Nelly more often, after that winter, and less violently. She was stronger, somehow, surer. People stopped whispering on street corners and muttering snide remarks. Nobody talked about institutions. Nelly became an accepted part of the neighborhood.

Lizbeth asked her about it once a full year afterwards, late at night, when their parents were asleep.

"What happened, Nelly? What did you do to change them?"

"Nothing changed with them, silly Bebet silly," Nelly replied. "With me. You said I was strong, and smart. Papa is proud of us. Mama is happy again. Now I know. Nobody can hurt me now." Then she smiled, stuck her tongue out, and went to sleep.

Art by Charis Loke

PURPLE WINGS
NITRA WISDOM

1934
Georgia, USA

I can hear em talkin bout me. They think I'm sleep, but I can't sleep til I hear Daddy snorin. When he all deep in his sleep like that I know everything's okay and me and Mama gon make it through the night. But tonight him and Mama up late. So I'ma be up late too.

Mama cryin cause Daddy say he can't afford to feed all of us, now that his labor been cut out on the field and Mama lost her job. She used to clean houses for rich white folks. But after that man touched her and she slapped him, his wife yelled and screamed at Mama and told her she would never work another house in this town again. She called Mama a funny name I never heard before, and when I asked her what it meant her eyes got to waterin' up. I can't stand when Mama cry; it breaks me up inside. I held her hand real tight and we walked home not sayin nothin. When Daddy found out, he got mad and almost went to that rich white man's house. Mama cried and begged him not to go cause he would get hisself kilt and she couldn't make it in this world without him. Daddy fussed and cussed for a little while, but Mama has a gift and she can always make him calm down. She like magic, yanno?

Anyhow, Mama don't work no more. I guess that mean ol' rich lady was right. Mama never cleaned another house, 'cept our own. Some of the ladies on our street tried to help us out for a little while, but Mama say folks got worries of they own. Miss Brenda was my favorite. She would bring casseroles. It had chicken and cheese and rice and broccoli. I love broccoli. They look like little trees and I feel like a giant when I eat em. I loved Miss Brenda's broccoli casseroles and coulda ate em every day. But after the night ghost men killed her husband, she stopped bringin 'em. I heard em talkin at the funeral bout how they put Mr. Thompson up a tree cause he aint know his place, to be workin while white folks was outta jobs. But Daddy say they always callin us lazy, so I don't know why they was mad if he was workin and not bein lazy? I asked Mama, and she say some white folk just aint right in the heart, and that's why they did what they did to Mr. Thompson. Cause they souls is missin. I told her maybe they should use they time lookin for they own souls instead of takin ours, and then everybody would be happy and left alone.

I ain't like seein Miss Brenda lookin all sad and missin her husband. I think maybe when them men took Mr. Thompson, they took part of Miss Brenda's soul too. She don't come out her house no mo'. Sometimes I sneak out my window at night, walk up the road to her house and put my ear to her back door and I hear her talkin to nobody. I told Mama, and she said Miss Brenda prolly talkin to her husband. I asked her how can she talk to a dead person, and Mama said that just cause a person body is gone don't mean they spirit ain't around, and sometimes talkin to the spirit of the people you love is the only thing to keep you out the nuthouse or the county jail. I like Miss Brenda so I don't want her to go to the nuthouse or the county jail. The folks that go to them places don't never come back. So now when I go listen at her door I think about what her husband might be sayin from the spirit side. Not even the night ghost men could get all of his soul. I wish he would tell Miss Brenda to bring us some more of them casseroles. But maybe dead folks forget that livin people need to eat.

But Daddy boss know, cause he aint dead. But he aint bringin us no food and I'm so mad at that Mr. Baker cause he cut my Daddy's worktime and now he can't feed me and I gotta go somewhere away from my Mama. I know that Daddy loves Mama more than me, and that's why I gotta go and she gets to stay. But it's okay. I love Mama more than anything in this whole world, and if I had to keep one of 'em, I would hug Daddy real tight around the neck and tell him he gotta go cause I gotta take care of my Mama. I love her more than anything, even her cookin. I just wish I wasn't so hungry for it all the time. Mama say it's cause I'm a growing girl and I have to build up my strength for when it's time for me to grow up and save the world. Sometimes I pretend I'm already big and I save all the kids round here from bein hungry all the time. I open my arms and they turn into big ol' purple wings and I carry all them kids up to the Black Mountain, way, way down the road past the Old Witch's house. We sit up at that mountain for all time and we get to eat every day, instead of havin to skip days like we do. We fill our bellies with oranges and catfish and rice and breads. And Miss Brenda's casseroles, cause they so good. I wish I could fly up there right now and eat til I'm full, so I won't have to leave Daddy and Mama.

I wonder where I'ma have to go.

Guess I'm gon' have to learn to sleep without Daddy's snorin anyhow.

***

I can't believe Mama would do this to me. She must don't love me like she always say she do. That ol' witch gon' eat me and Mama just gon' let it happen! Mama say I'm tellin tales, that she takes good care of the kids that go live with her. I don't believe her; I ain't never seen the kids that go in there come back out. A long time ago I seen some girls walk down that way with they Mamas, but they Mamas came back up the road and I aint never see them girls again.

Cause she ate 'em. I know she did. When Mama told me I was goin there, I ran out the house and climbed to the top of my tree. I told Mama I wasn't never comin down, that I was gonna live up in this here tree and eat the leaves since her and Daddy don't care 'bout me no more.

I gotta learn to mind my mouth. Soon as I said it, I knew I hurt her feelins. I can't stand for Mama to be hurtin'; it's a hundred times worse when

I'm the one who did it. So I climbed down and told Mama I was sorry for sayin her and Daddy don't care about me, but I don't know why they would send me to the lady who eats kids and what if I try really really hard not to be hungry no more and they ain't gotta worry 'bout feedin me. Mama sat down under the tree and held me in her lap, shushin me and rockin me back and forth like I was a little baby again, til I fell asleep in her arms.

I talked to my friend Tessa, cause she know everythang. Her daddy got a white daddy so they got money and she go to a real schoolhouse. She say she don't like it though, cause them girls too uppity. Anyhow, her mama from here, and her mama and my mama grew up close so me and Tessa cousins. Mama say sometimes the way life work out, you get to pick your family members to make up for some of the ones you was born with.

So I asked Tessa what she know bout witches. She say witches come from Africa, where all our ancestors come from. I asked her what's a ancestor, and she say they our family from a long, long time ago when me and her and even our Big Mamas was stars in the sky. She say some of our ancestors were special – real smart ladies who knew how to heal theyselves and other people too – witches. They was good for the village. But sometimes folks get other ideas in they head and they don't wanna heal. They wanna hurt. So some witches is bad and some good, just like regular people. I asked Tessa what kinda witch she think the Old Witch down the way is, and she didn't say nothin. She just turned her head and started diggin at the dirt with her foot, like she always do when she don't wanna tell me no bad news.

But the witch can't be all bad, right? Mama say ain't nobody all bad and everybody got some good in em. It's like a candle light. Sometimes it lights up they whole soul and you could see it on they face, how they shine from the inside. And some folks only got a teeny, tiny spark, and they soul so dark, you can see that on they face too. I asked her what kinda light I got and she jumped back and covered her eyes like the sun had bust in the door! I laughed so hard – Mama the funniest person I know. Then I asked her what kinda light she think the Old Witch got.

"Titi, Umi is not a witch."

I wanted to ask her what's a Umi, but Daddy say don't never interrupt when somebody is talkin. Even if they talkin slow. Some folks need more time than others to say what's in they heads, so you can't be jumpin in and cuttin off they thoughts. You gotta listen so yall can talk for real.

"Umi is a healer," Mama said, "and she gon heal this family. She gon' teach you some thangs too."

"Is she gon teach me to be a witch? Or she gon eat me? Cause I seen kids go in there and they don't never come back, Mama. Don't you want me to come back? I know I gotta go away for a lil bit Mama, but how come I can't go up to Baltimore on the train like Ruby Dalton and her family did? Oh Mama, maybe I can go live with Ruby and her Mama and Daddy. They could keep me, you know? We always got on fine at church. What you think bout that Mama?

"Mama?"

She ain't say nothin. She opened the kitchen window then turned around and looked at me. I set my spoon on the table, sat up in my chair and stared back at her. It felt like we sat there and looked at each other for all time. But I can't never say no to Mama, cause I love her too much. I think sometimes maybe she use that to get what she want.

I walked over to the wash tub where she was standin, leant over and stuck my hand out the window.

"Close your eyes, Titi. And I want you to feel in your heart how much I love you."

I closed my eyes real tight and soon as I did, the wind started blowin. It came quiet and soft, then it rushed all around the house, kickin up the dust and knockin over the stick barn I had made on the porch. I forgot to show it to Daddy this mornin before he left for the fields. The wind came up from under the house, and blew hot on my hand, shovin it up to the sky, and I could hear all the leaves in my tree shakin and dancin. They sounded happy. I wished I could feel what they was feelin.

The wind stopped whippin around and the leaves fell back quiet. I kept my eyes shut tight, and could feel Mama breathin behind me, could hear her heart beatin. I thought about how much I love her and I don't wanna leave her and I wish we could go up to the mountain together. I started cryin and that's when I heard em, growlin low with the wind. I opened my eyes and saw 'em sittin there under the window, the red one and the little gray one, with their big ol tent lookin ears, and little black eyes, starin up inside me. They don't never do nothin when they come, cept stand there and look at me. Sometimes I think they tryna tell me somethin, but soon as I move at em, they disappear. They don't walk away or run, they just don't be there no more. Mama calls em my soul foxes. I'on know what that mean or how she even see 'em cause Daddy can't. Mama say it's cause they come from her bloodline.

I put my hand down and me and Mama stood at the window lookin at the foxes, and them lookin at me.

"Mama and Daddy love you so much, Titi," Mama said behind me. "And we would never put you in the way of trouble. We sendin you to Umi cause it's time, and it's the right thing to do."

I didn't say nothin else about it. I know my Mama love me. My Daddy too. And if they sendin me there, they must know somethin bout the Old Witch – Umi – that I don't. But maybe Mama will think about what I said to goin up to Baltimore with Ruby. I think Daddy would rather visit me there anyhow.

***

Well, I been here two whole Sundays and I aint been ate up – yet. Mama was bein true – Umi aint really that bad. She don't say a whole lot, and she don't rock me or play with me like Mama do, but she aint mean or nothin. We aint really did nothin, cept dig around in her big garden out back. She got a whole little farm with chickens and goats and even a cow. She grow all her own food, vegetables and everything, by herself. I asked if she can show me how she do it, so I can go back home. She say when she done with me, I'll know how to feed a whole town with my bare hands. But she ain't taught me nothin yet. We go out there every day and dig around. She say she want me to get comfortable first, cause it's the only way I can "cultivate my gifts," whatever that mean. I done snuck around this whole house at night and I aint seen no presents — aint seen none of them other kids neither.

When me, Mama and Daddy was walkin down the road to come here, I tried real hard to be strong. Only two tears came out and I wiped em fast so Mama and Daddy couldn't see em. I wanted them to know I was mad, so I ain't say nothin the whole way there. I don't think they minded too much though; it was too hot to be talkin and carryin on. Most days like that, all of us go down to the creek and splash on each other til it get cool again. Thinkin bout how much I'ma miss Tessa and splashin in the water made me even madder. I looked up at the birds that was followin us, flyin along and singin like it was a regular ole happy day. I mostly like when the birds sing. I sing back, and pretend that I'm flyin right up there with em. But I wasn't in the mood for no bird songs. I wished they would shet up. Mama kept lookin up at the sky like the map to Umi's house was in the clouds or somethin. I squeezed her hand real tight and tried to tell her with my mind that we could run off somewhere, the two of us. I think Daddy would understand. She didn't hear me though. She just lifted my hand up, kissed it and looked back up into the sky. The birds seemed to like that. They started sangin louder and faster. I wanted to shoot 'em with Daddy's gun.

After walkin down that road forever, we saw Umi's house. It was a blue house standin all by itself at the end of the road, with a yellow door that made me think of the sunflower field I used to lay in, behind Mr. Tucker's house. Umi musta felt us close cause she came out the door, and soon as I saw her I couldn't hear the birds no more and a twister started up in my belly. I was scared, and ... oh, she was so pretty. I ain't know witches could look like that. She looked more like a queen or somethin. She seen me starin at her. She looked at me like she knew every thought and feelin I ever had in my whole life, even the bad stuff. Even the bad stuff about her.

Oh.

She smiled at me, and I think I started shakin. I thought about what Tessa said, how she said nothin when I asked her what kind of witch she thought Umi was. The twister in my belly got bigger and stronger, started movin my insides all around. When we walked through the gate I knew I was gon vomit.

Umi looked to Mama and said, "Don't worry Georgia Mae; your baby will be fine. She'll be home as soon as you're both ready."

Mama thanked her, then gave her a hug. "I know Umi. I know we doin the right thing. But this is my only baby, and—"

I wanted her to say *"and I don't want you cookin her up in your pot,"* but she just bent down, pulled me in her arms and talked real quiet in my ear. "This gon be so good for you, Titi. You wait and see. I aint never done you wrong, have I?"

Not ever.

"I love you more than my own life, baby. And I need you to have faith."

I ain't wanna have faith. I wanted to go home. I wished I had them purple wings right now so I could fly right up to the mountain and be away from em all! I don't know what Mama and Daddy thinkin. Even if she is the prettiest thing I ever seen, all I know is them kids that was here ain't never came back home. Soon as I got ready to run, Umi took my hand and looked down at me.

"Your mother is right Tituba." Nobody call me that, cept my Mama when she mad with me. It didn't sound mad comin outta Umi's mouth though. It sounded ... different. I looked at my Daddy, and he looked at Umi, then down at me. He winked at me like he do when we have a surprise for Mama and she keep guessin wrong. I aint know how to feel. I breathed real deep then looked down at my double-crossin feet.

Umi looked at Daddy and said "Okay," then he smiled at her, picked me up and gave me a big ol hug and kiss. I hugged him tight and I aint wanna let go, but I stepped back, then turned around and walked in the house. I ain't turn back to look at Mama and Daddy. I wanted them to see me brave. And I wanted to see it too.

She showed me to my room, all the way in the back of the house. Umi shut my door and let me unpack in private, which was fine by me, cause I ain't wanna be around nobody, 'specially not her. Not even Mama. I missed her already. So much it made my chest hurt. But I was mad at her too, and I aint wanna think about her. I stared at the window out at the garden, the barn and the mountain right past it. It cut the sky right across the middle. It was bigger than I ever thought it could be, and bein up to it that close, I could almost feel my wings. I started thinkin bout all the kids that came here before me. If maybe they was already up on the mountain, if they was always hungry, and if they Mamas was sorry for sendin 'em away.

I dunno when I fell asleep, I guess it was all that cryin – or maybe Umi put me under a sleepin spell. I know witches do that sometimes. Tessa say witches is always puttin spells on people – 'specially kids. When I woke up, I could smell Miss Brenda's broccoli casserole. I thought maybe I was still dreamin or somethin, so i laid in the bed with my eyes closed, smellin the air. Then I felt the empty in my stomach. I could tell that the cheese was almost done turnin brown at the top. I tried to lay in that bed as long as I could...

***

I asked Umi was she a witch. We was sittin at her little wood table in the kitchen, eatin broccoli casserole like we do every Sunday since I got here. She know how to make it just like Miss Brenda used to, and she let me help sometimes. She was nice, but I ain't forget nothin Tessa said. Plus I was tired of guessin and sneakin around the house at night tryna find clues. If she had anything to tell on her bein a witch, she hid em real good. Prolly with a disappearin spell. So I asked her.

"Umi ... is you a– is you a witch?"

She took a bite of her casserole then sat back in her seat, and looked at me with them eyes that make me feel all twisted up inside. They make me wanna run, far, far away...and right into her arms, at the same time.

"Yes. I am."

I just knew my eyes was gon' pop out my head.

"And it's not a disappearing spell. It's a concealment spell. Sounds the same, but they are vastly different, with different consequences. So you can stop sneaking around. You'll see what you need to see in time."

My whole body was shakin, but I tried my hardest not to look scared. I breathed from deep in my belly, closed my eyes and asked her my second question. The question I ain't wanna ask, cause I was hopin she was gon say no to the first one.

"You gon' eat me?"

She laughed this little bitty laugh, like I never heard from her before. It had a kind of light in it, and for a quick second it made me think maybe she was more like a magical fairy kinda witch.

"No, child. I'm not going to eat you." She said it like I was silly to even think it, and I wanted to believe her...

"They left, Tituba. On their own accord."

"Huh? I mean, Ma'am?"

"The other children. I didn't eat them. They left. After they received their lessons, they left. And when your time comes, you will leave as well."

"Well, if they ain't here no more, how come I never seen them kids back round by the creek or even in church or nothin? Where they at? What kind of lessons you teach em? Witch lessons? Was they witches? Oh! Am I a witch? How long it's gon' take me to learn? You been nice and I like you teachin me how to cook and thangs but, I was thinkin now that I know how to do that, I can go home, Umi, and—"

"It's true, they haven't yet returned. But they will. You have a lot to learn, Tituba. And like them, you will remain here until it's time for you to move on to your next lesson. How long it takes depends on you. Everything comes back around, and you will see them all again. You'll have been so changed you may not recognize them. But the work will pull you together. Work that connects each of you, including the ones who should have come, and didn't. Your bond will be immediate, undeniable, and everlasting. You'll see each other, yourself and the world differently, more clearly. And this will change everything.

"And then I can go home."

"Home? What you mean Umi? Ain't this your home? Ain't you always lived here? Mama say you been here since before her own Mama was a chile."

Umi got up and walked outside to the porch. It was rainin real hard, and the sky was so gray it was almost black. I was scared and I wanted to ask Umi if maybe we should go into the storm cellar, but she didn't move, so I ain't say nothin. She stood out there on the porch, sippin her tea and lookin out at the rain. I went out on the porch behind her, and stared at her real close and for a long time. I wanted to ask her a whole bunch more questions, like where her real home was at, why she been gone from it so long, and how old she was.

Daddy say you not supposed to ask a woman that cause it ain't polite.

But if they ask you to guess how old they look – cause some of 'em like to do that – Daddy say you always tell a woman she look younger than you really think she is. Mama say you ain't gotta do that with colored folk, cause we always look younger than we really is. Even the ones of us that's had a hard life. Mama say it's a gift, God's way of makin up for all the hardship we gotta go through in this world. Umi look like Pauline's big sister, Billie, and she 18. I know Umi ain't 18, cause she been here forever and she don't talk like a 18 year old. She talk like a grandma. Like she done seen and heard everythang. Like she seen the whole world – everywhere, even Africa.

Tessa say if they don't get found out, some witches know how to live for a real long time. Like 200 years, and some of em can even live forever and never die, til they ready and tired of livin in this world. Umi seem like one a those. It's somethin in her eyes. But sometimes Tessa just be talkin cause she know she smart and talk real pretty. So I ain't ask or say nothin to Umi. Instead I just stood on the porch behind her, lookin at her and the rain.

***

Umi say it's time for me to start my lessons. I thought we was doin that already. We been doin a lotta talkin and she make me read a lot. I love readin, all the time, and she always got more books for me. Sometimes I forget to eat, cause I been in my room all day with my "nose in the book," like Umi say. I think I prolly know more than Tessa now. And plus I been helpin out more in the kitchen. Sometimes I cook a whole meal by myself. She let me do it all. I even know how to get the eggs from the chickens without wakin em. I don't think it's good as Mama's cookin, but it seem to taste a little more like hers each time I try. Mama and Daddy done even come over a few times to sit with me and Umi. I cook for all of us, then we sit out on the porch and listen to music and dance. Mama and Umi say they favorite is them Blues women. I don't care neither way. I'd listen to anything that'll make Mama and Daddy stay all night. They never can. They always gotta get home before the sun go down. Mama say it's the way life is right now. Umi say my gift gon change all that. So today we goin out back in the garden.

I don't know how today's gon' be no different cause I play out here all the time. I love bein out here; it make me not miss my magnolia tree so much. It's so quiet, it feel like the world still asleep. The goats ain't even up, and it seem like they don't never sleep. Umi usually let me sleep in on Sundays, but she say today we gotta get out here before the sun heats up the dirt.

She tell me to put my hands deep into the dirt. I done that before, so I don't see how it's part of my gift. I put em in there anyway. I look up and she shakin her head.

"Deeper. Move the soil, dig."

I move the dirt and push my hands down some more. The deeper I go, the harder I gotta work to get the dirt to move. I start to wiggle my hands from under the ground and push the dirt back and forth with my fingers. It's cold and wet and pushin up under my fingernails. I feel a feelin inside me, same as the day me and Umi stood on the porch watchin the rain. It's like a tiny, happy bubble floatin around inside me. A worm down past where I can see touches my marriage finger and it tickles. When I can't go no further, I look up at Umi.

"Close your eyes," she say. "Take a deep breath, and I want you to envision your favorite thing to eat."

"Envision?"

"To make a picture in your mind."

I start to laugh, but when I see she serious, I blink my eyes shut, then squeeze em real tight. "Oh. It's broccoli. Like in Miss Brenda's – our casseroles."

"Then broccoli it is."

It's maybe because I never listen to Umi with my eyes closed, but she sound so different today. Her voice is all soft, and kinda croaky, like Daddy's snorin. And even though I know she right here kneelin beside me in the dirt, it sound like she speakin from inside my body. That make me feel funny – I'm not sure if I like it.

Umi puts her hand on my shoulder and says, "Focus, Tituba. And relax your eyes."

I do what she say, sayin "Broccoli," real low, over and over. I ain't feelin nothin. Nothin different anyhow, cept the dirt and the bugs and the heat from the sun startin to wake up. Maybe I don't know what I'm supposed to be feelin. I don't know why we gotta be doin this anyway. It prolly ain't the right time and I need to read more or somethin. Or practice cookin. I was gettin real good in the kitchen too. Daddy say my skillet corn taste same as his now.

This don't make no sense. I'm hungry and still sleepy and wanna get back in the bed. I open my eyes and look down at the ground. Aint nothin there different, only some ants crawlin by and takin little pieces of dirt from the piles I made. I look at Umi and I can tell she ain't bout to let me move.

"Stop thinking about it," she say. "I said envision. See it in your mind. See the seeds opening deep inside the ground, setting roots, and spreading out through the dirt."

I close my eyes again and think of that picture of broccoli seeds in that heavy plant book from her big trunk of books. I see the little red seed in the ground sittin quiet while the bugs and worms and stuff move around it, throwin dirt on it, pushin it more down into the ground. My fingers is startin to tingle and i think i feel the ground move a little bit. Like a shake, almost. I jump up, and look all around the ground, but I don't see nothin. Nothin but dirt. But I know I felt somethin ...

"I ... I'on know bout this, Umi. I ... maybe I should go back in the house. I don't know why I need to be out here no way. You done showed me how to milk the cow and tend to the goats and everythang and even plant seeds. And now I know how to cook too. I can do all that back home. I can help out now. Ain't that why you got me here? Well, I know how to do all that now. I wanna go home. Back to Mama and Daddy. I know they been missin me cause they been over here a lot. Plus, I ain't no witch like you, Umi. I'm just a regular ol' girl. Please, can I go home?"

She looks up at me with those eyes, black and strong like the mountain.

Mama and Umi just the same in that I can't never say no to 'em. I can't never win. I get back down in the dirt, stuff my hands inside and try to close my eyes real tight without squeezin, makin em heavy and hard to open from the inside, like when I'm sleepin. I take another breath and I push Mama and Daddy, Tessa, and even Umi out my head. Everything is black like when there ain't no stars out at night. I think about my hands in the dirt. I move em around til I can feel that little quiet bubble come up in my belly again. I try to look inside the dark, like when I try to look up through to the other side of the sky. A star at night turns into the seed in the ground. It starts wakin up, movin around inside the dirt, and the roots come out, all skinny and wavy, stretchin out through the dirt and reachin down to where it's real dark and soft. My hands start tinglin again, but I don't move. I sit still as I can, and see into and underneath the ground, where the roots stretch out far as they can go. I keep my eyes shut and see a little green stem start growin, pushin up through the dirt, and the tiny bubbles inside me that start to fizz up.

"Hold on to what you see, Titi. Feel it. Send it all of your energy." Umi sound like she talkin from inside me again, and this time I'm sure I do like it. She make me feel strong. My heart feel like it's gon come out my chest, and all the hairs on my neck is standin way up to the sky. I got a ball of dirt, way down in the ground between my hands, and I hold it and try to take the growin broccoli out my head and in the dirt. The ground starts movin again, I'm sure of it. I get scared and I want to jump up and run, but I don't. I stay still and try to make my whole self quiet. When I get all the way still and breathin smooth, the ground stops shaking. I open my eyes and look down, and see the little stem pokin out the ground with a green leaf sittin on the top of it. This little bit of green in a sea of chocolate. Same as I saw it in my head. I jump up and look at my hands, shakin and covered with dirt. A shining black beetle flies off the back of my hand and the little worm done wrapped itself all the way around my marriage finger. I look over at Umi, sittin on the ground with her legs crossed, smilin up at me real big.

How did I–? What did you do?!"

"It wasn't me. You did that Titi. Your hands and your vision. You've always known how to do this. And you can do so much more. Oh honey, you have so many gifts. This is such a small example. Your mother knew this – your Grandmother too. You come from a long line of healers, Tituba, and your spirit has been here far longer than your 9 years on this earth. Stay with me a little longer, and I will help you remember."

I can't speak. Can't move. All I can do is stand here, lookin down at the ground, at my hands, then at the ground again. I think about Mama and Daddy, and how maybe I can take Miss Brenda some of my own broccoli casserole to show her what she done taught me. I know it won't bring Mr. Thompson back, but it might make her smile, and then maybe she might start comin back out the house and sittin in the kitchen with Mama and Auntie Shannon again. I feel all them little quiet happy bubbles pop inside me and I start cryin. I can't stop. I fall down on my knees and let my tears hit the dirt, and on the little plant that I made. That I made with my own hands.

The ground shakes again, real low and heavy and I open my eyes and look up. The sky is dark purple and the sun peeks through the big ol' grey cotton clouds comin our way from the mountain. I ain't never seen a sky like this. It don't make me feel good or strong. I stand up slow and look over at Umi, who laughs real loud, like someone told her the funniest thing she ever heard. I don't know what's funny, but her laugh is almost the most beautiful thing that happened today. She stands up and takes my hand.

"Come on baby. It's time for Mother to work. Let's go inside and put on some music ... Today feels like a Kitty Waters day, no?"

As we start back to the front of the house, I can feel them. The foxes. I can't see 'em but I know they're close. Maybe this time they'll stay.

Art by Jay Bendt

THE PROMIJED LAND
J.J. HAWTHORNE

1836
Scotland

My people are known by many names. In Ireland, we're known as the fair folk, and in Wales they call us the mothers' blessing. In my native Scotland, they call us the daoine sith, the mound people. According to my mother, we came from the Sea. When we first arrived, we were powerful people, bursting with magic. She said that we stood twelve feet tall, terrible of mien and strength. She told me that we shrank the longer we stayed with mortals. Not just in height, though that's true enough, but we became less all over. We lost the magic. We joined with the mortal folk, and forgot our heritage. We, who had once included the wise ghillie dubh and the life-devouring baobhan, but we had lost our magic. We had become mortal.

She told me that some power remained in our blood, though. She said the magic was tied to the moon, so women could still sometimes wield it. In men, it was passive, though it produced many great warriors, like the Hound of Ulster and Pendragon's son.

There are legends about us. There are tales of fishermen catching a seal-skin and winning a faery bride. My mother never spoke to me about when she and my father met, but after she passed, my father would tell me almost every night about the time he found a sealskin on the far shore of the firth, and fell in love with the beautiful silkie to whom it belonged. Whenever he told the story, he had the same faraway look in his eyes.

She never transformed for him, he told me, and he was never totally sure it wasn't a story she had made up to avoid questions about her family, but I knew the truth. When I was very small, my mother found me trying on one of her dresses. She took me down to the ocean and showed me how she could change.

"You must keep this a secret forever, mo chridhe," she told me, once she had turned back into human form. "Even from your own father. You have fae blood and you must know what that means, but the mortal folk don't understand. They can't. So, keep it aye quiet."

She said she saw the moon in my eyes, no matter what I was born as. She said that there had always been those born under the wrong light, as she put it. Our people had, in times long past, recognized these folk and let them live as their rightful self.

In the mortal lands, that changed. My mother apologized for it. She told me that she wished things had been different, and that I could choose my path, instead of traveling down the road set out for me. I didn't really understand until a year after she passed, when my father took me hunting with several of the farmers that lived nearby. Never before had I felt so painfully out of place. I had nothing in common with these men and their sons. I wanted nothing so much as to escape, to return home, to spend time with Archer, my horse. I dutifully remained with my father, however.

We spoke about it later, once we were home. It was hard to put into words what I had felt, and it was evident that he did not understand what I was going through. He told me, though, that my mother had tried to explain to him that this day was coming, and to make him understand.

"I don't," he confessed, "but I trusted your mother. You're my son, though, and even when I don't understand, I'll stand by you."

***

For the next three years, he did. We didn't talk about it often, and when I told him how awkward I felt in my own body, he did his best to comfort me. And he bought me my most prized possession: a gorgeous cotton dress all in pale pink. It was a few years out of date, but that hardly mattered to me – what mattered was that it was mine, sized nearly perfectly, and that I looked like any fashionable Scottish girl when I wore it. My father forbade me from wearing it out of the house, and grew anxious when he saw me in it, so out of respect for him, I put it on only rarely, and only when not in his presence.

Everything changed for me shortly thereafter. It was a little more than four years after my mother had passed, just before my thirteenth birthday. I had a rare spot of free time, and had slipped away to the attic of our tiny home to try on my dress. The attic was my own private area. I had a little mirror, my dress, a small wooden box of toys and mementos, and, most recently, a flyer advertising for emigrants to help settle the new colony of South Australia. My father had brought it back from a trip to London a few weeks prior and presented it to me with an excited grin. It promised free passage for settlers looking to colonize.

"It's the promised land," he told me. "A land of freedom for everyone. Where folk can get a brand new start." I had tacked up the flyer in my attic. The idea fascinated me, and it was a handsome bill. I liked to admire it from time to time.

I had been up there quite a while, I am embarrassed to say, admiring myself in my little mirror. In normal dress – especially in my formal kilt which, thankfully, I only wore infrequently – I do not look much like a girl. I was certainly somewhat effeminate, but in a kilt or trousers, I looked like a mildly underfed, underexercised boy. I did rather wish my father would let me grow out my hair, at least, but on that point he was adamant. My hair remained much shorter than I would have liked.

In my dress, however, I no longer looked like a girlish boy, but rather a tomboyish girl. That was one of the things I loved about it so much. Even my short hair didn't bother me so much. Certainly I had seen the occasional farm girl who had hair not much longer, when my father took me to the village. There was even a Black family – I thought they were the now-grown children of former slaves who had settled instead of returned to their home when Parliament had outlawed the trade – and the mother kept hers even shorter than mine, though normally she covered her head with a scarf. They had a son about my age, but of course my father did not allow me any contact with him.

It was a simple pleasure just to admire myself, even if it were vanity. It made me happy in a way that few other things ever did. My hair had grown out a bit, and it was only a matter of time before my father sat me down to chop it short once again, so I was taking the time to enjoy it whilst it lasted.

My father knew, I think, what I did in the attic and did not bother me, but I still preferred not to spend too much time hidden away. It wasn't fair to him when there were chores to do. But every now and then, I would lose track of the time. I didn't realize how long I had been there until, as I was again admiring the flyer, I caught a scent on the wind, something strange and foreign and frightening. I had always had a good nose, but this was a scent of unique intensity, and I decided to investigate. I stuffed the flyer into my sleeve, then crept towards the hatch in the floor and climbed back down into the house proper. I could hear raised voices, my father's among them. I snuck to the window and peeked out. The sun was low in the sky, the shadows creeping.

My father was standing next to Archer on the little path that ran from our house to the old road that lead into town. A few yards away stood three men, all mounted. I immediately recognized the one in the middle as John Outerbridge. He styled himself laird of this land, though in truth he had married into the family. He wasn't even Scottish, but an English trader. He had made a great deal of money in the fur trade in its heyday, before returning to England as an importer. The old laird's family had been heavily invested in the slave trade; when that was outlawed, the family had lost nearly everything. An uprising in Jamaica took the life of the laird's only son and the last of the family wealth. Marrying off the eldest daughter to this Englishman had saved them.

Outerbridge was frighteningly handsome. I don't mean to say that I found him attractive, though he was, by any measure. He had a narrow face, with high cheekbones and a strong jaw, and achingly blue eyes. His hair was brown and straight, and looked casually tossed. His skin was so pale it seemed to glow. He wore elegant clothes, but they were distinctly English, not proper Highland garb. He had tossed a seal skin tossed over his shoulder like a cape. It was the exact same color as my mother's hair.

He was tall and muscular, and on another person I suppose that I would have called him comely. There was an expression on his face, however, that was not handsome. It was cold and cruel, and it transformed his looks from angelic to devilish. He looked like a beautiful monster.

"You can't do this," my father shouted, pulling me out of my examination of the laird.

"I assure you, I can," Outerbridge said in a deep, resonant voice. "All this land is needed."

"I have a child, please. What will I do? We need the farm!" my father said. His voice shook; he sounded on the edge of tears.

"You can join the croft," Outerbridge said with a careless gesture. He considered my father for a moment. "We'll take the horse, too. I don't see as you'll have much need for it."

That was too much for me. I burst through the door and as I shouted "No!" I threw myself between Outerbridge and Archer, as though I, a thirteen year old kid, could prevent three adults from taking my horse.

Outerbridge raised his eyebrows. "A girl, then?" he asked my father. "I was under the impression that your spawn was a boy." Despite myself, I felt a sudden rush of pleasure at being properly recognized. Outerbridge went on, "I suppose I can understand your decision to hide her." He caressed the seal skin as he leered at me, and a shudder ran up my spine.

My father flushed. I had never seen him angry before. His hands clenched into fists. "Keep away from my child," he sputtered.

The two men on either side of Outerbridge chuckled darkly. Their voices were not nearly so pleasant as the laird's. "He can do what he wants," the one on the left said. He had a Borders accent, and was scrawny and narrow, and a pinched face like a rat's. His hair was dirty black, his eyes a jaundiced grey. He looked like a dearganach, a redcoat.

"We'll take good care of her for you," the other man said, in a distinct Yorkshire accent. He was big, with a mane of blond hair and deep brown eyes. With his fur-lined coat, he reminded me of a picture of the god Hercules I had once seen.

My father dropped Archer's reins as he leapt forward. He yanked Hercules off his horse by the coat. They collapsed to the ground with a nasty snapping noise and a blur of shouts and fists. Hercules's horse reared and whinnied in alarm, dancing away from the fight at its hooves. I grabbed Archer's reins, but my Clydesdale didn't move, except to turn and nudge at my shoulder. I suppose it should not have been any surprise that he was better trained than some prancing gelding. Probably the English thug had bought the horse for his looks.

Outerbridge produced a pistol – bright and shiny and alien looking. I had seen handguns before, of course. Several of the local farmers, especially those who had fought against Napoleon, had pistols. Outerbridge's gun, however, was wholly unlike any weapon I'd ever seen before. It was boxy, and seemed almost entirely of metal, and had a bizarre, spinning bulb just above the trigger. Outerbridge fired once into the air. Archer flinched for the first time, nearly pulling me off my feet. The gun had only a single barrel, but Outerbridge thumbed back the hammer and fired again, straight up. I could not fathom how it could fire multiple bullets like that, nor what strange science made Outerbridge so confident that he could afford to waste two bullets.

The sound seemed to work, though, and my father straightened, with Hercules trapped in some sort of chokehold. Hercules wheezed as his face turned slowly redder.

Archer continued his back step, and I was pulled away from the fight. No one seemed to be paying much attention to us.

"I have three more bullets," Outerbridge said as he leveled the gun at my father. "I suggest you let my man go."

"So you can shoot me clean?" my father retorted. "Get off my land."

"I had you for a halfway intelligent man," Outerbridge said, "but I see you have all the wits of any other Gael. This is my land. It's all my land, and you are being formally evicted." Archer and I had nearly reached the side of the house. He wasn't saddled – I didn't even know why he was reined – and I wasn't really dressed for riding, but I clambered onto his back as best as I could. I had never sat sidesaddle before, and my precarious position was unnerving. Archer was a very large horse, not designed for riding, and without a saddle I felt like I might fall off any moment. Still, I could hardly run away from two men on horses when I was on foot and in a dress, and this, at least, evened the field a tiny bit. I readied myself to ride out and grab my father once he let go of Hercules.

"Over my dead body," my father spat. He tightened his grip around Hercules, cutting off the wheezing entirely.

"One less Highlander to muck about, then," Dearganach said, his lips peeled back in a sneer. Outerbridge's face was an emotionless mask as he thumbed back the hammer on his strange gun. I saw a small lever swing down from the barrel. It took me a moment to recognize it as the trigger.

My father stiffened, but he didn't flinch, nor did he release Hercules, whose eyes had rolled back. I tried to call out to my father, but my voice caught in my throat, and the quiet squeak I may have made was drowned out by the explosion of the bullet.

I froze, but Archer, brilliant horse that he was, took off. There was a second shot behind us, and I nearly fell off Archer's back, but I caught myself in time. I let go of his reins and leaned forward to cling to his broad neck, bouncing uncomfortably along as he galloped across our field, heading for the forest's edge. There was a third shot, and I felt something cold brush my arm.

I heard shouting behind, coupled with curses that no good Christian soul would ever repeat, and the sound of chasing hooves. I chanced a look over my shoulder, and saw Outerbridge and Dearganach trampling down the wheat – so close to harvest, too – as they gave chase. Archer was not fast, but he was more sure-footed than their horses, and could navigate the rocky scree at the far edge of the wheat field. Dearganach's horse, apparently as well trained as Hercules's, stopped dead rather than gallop into the uneven terrain, almost tossing her rider into a tree. Outerbridge's horse slowed more gracefully, but he had to kick it viciously to move at faster than a walk, and it stumbled and slid as Archer carried me into the dark woods and out of sight.

**

I was starting to feel lightheaded as we emerged from the far edge of the forest, on the shore of either the loch or Beauly Firth. My mother, many years ago, had told me that the loch was home to faerie horses – kelpies. The sight of the water gave me the idea that they could help. I slid off of Archer and hit the ground hard, much harder than I had intended, and doubled over into the sand.

Everything had happened so fast that I hadn't had much time to think.

Curled up on that beach, I realized I had lost my home and most probably my only family. I would like to say that I was a brave Highlander lass and did my parents proud, but I am trying to be as honest I can, and, in honesty, I cried. I curled into a little ball and cried harder than I ever had before.

I don't know how long I lay there, my poor dress steadily getting sandier and a dull pain radiating through my left arm. I thought I might stay there forever.

My self-pity was broken by the sound of splashing. I straightened up and wiped my face with the back of my sleeve, which did little to aid to my composure, but it did give me a moment of stability.

There was a rock, about the size of my fist, nearby, and I grabbed it. If the sound was Outerbridge or his men, I intended to put up at least as much fight as my father.

But it was not Outerbridge. It was the Black boy, walking the edge of the loch.

He was wearing a kilt in the old laird's tartan and a simple cotton shirt, but his hose and shoes were tied off and draped over his neck. He had a small net filled with fish in one hand, and a simple fishing pole in the other. I had never really seen him up close before, but he seemed no different than any other boy of our age, albeit with dark brown skin and short, curly black hair, mostly hidden underneath a tam-o-shanter hat. His eyes were a very bright shade of green.

"Are you alright?" he asked as soon as he saw me. To my very great surprise, he had a burr as thick as any Scotsman.

"Fine," I said, somewhat haughtily. My voice sounded thick and snuffly.

"You're bleeding," he said, pointing at my arm. I looked down and found that he was right. My left sleeve was ripped open, and a deep gash ran along my bicep. It was crusted with sand and half-dried blood, but still oozing steadily. The sleeve was completely ruined.

"Here," he said, kneeling down in the sand next to me. He started to rummage in his sporran, pulling out a roll of cloth and a small pair of scissors. "How'd you injure yourself?" he asked as he cut away the sleeve.

"I was shot," I said, watching him. "Why are you all dressed up?"

"My family was supposed to meet the laird today. The other crofters keep pushing us off the best parts of the land. He wasn't in, so I got sent out to catch some fish." He cut a length of cloth and got up to wet it.

"He was busy shooting me," I said, unable to keep the bitterness out of my voice. He looked shocked, and I explained what had happened, though not why a dress might be unusual on me. I became aware I was crying again, and looked down at my feet so he wouldn't see.

"One of the other farmers nearby had the same thing happen," he said. His voice was carefully neutral. "There's a new English tenant, raising sheep there now, and the old farmer's a crofter now. He's not the first, either. Hold your arm up." He washed away the sand and blood, and then wrapped my arm tight in the remainder of the cloth. "I'm Yusuf," he said, offering his hand.

We shook hands. It seemed polite, after all, and it was hard to reconcile his gentlemanly manner with the stories of African savagery that the other farmers' children had told whenever he or his family had come to town.

"I'm Bridget," I told him. That was not, of course, my name, and I did feel a little bad about the lie, but giving him my real name would require me to explain more about what was between my legs than I cared to.

He sat down on the sand a polite distance away. "Do you have a piece of paper?" he asked as he pulled an old pen from his sporran. I handed him the flyer.

"What are you doing?" I asked.

"Asking God for help," he responded. "My uncle taught me how to do this. Only," he looked up, his eyes creased with worry, "don't tell anyone? I'm not really supposed to be doing this."

I frowned a bit. I had never heard that phrase coupled with any action that had turned out well, but all he seemed to be doing was writing. It seemed harmless, so I didn't protest when he ripped off the bit he had written on and showed it to me.

"What's this?" I asked.

"Arabic. Tuck it into your bandage." He frowned suddenly, then his voice turned stern. "But don't bleed on it. That's disrespectful."

"How am I supposed to stop myself bleeding?" I asked, irritated, but I did as I was told, tucking the scrap of paper into the bandage. I was careful to keep a roll of cloth between the paper and my wound, though.

A sudden thought struck me as I tucked the bandage back around the slip of paper.

"What?" Yusuf asked.

"I know what to do now." I pointed at the flyer still in his hands. He frowned, then turned the paper over and read it.

"Oh, yeah, my uncle told me about that. He said they're calling it a free colony. He even says they said they won't take the land of the people who are there; the law says that the natives get to keep any land they already own." He shrugged, unimpressed.

"That's where I'll go then," I said.

He eyed me. "That's crazy."

"You just said that it's supposed to be free."

"There's no such thing," he said. He stood up and brushed off his kilt. "People are always going to be people. Maybe it'll start as a free land, but it won't end up that way. It never does. What good will it do to run away from your problems?"

"What's there for me here? I don't have a home, or parents. All I have is Archer."

"Because this is your home," he swept his hand out to indicate the forest and the loch. "If you don't stay to make it better, then it won't get better. You're giving up."

"I'm not giving up," I said, jumping to my feet. "What's the point is staying and getting myself killed?"

"That's naïve. Whoever said that Australia will be safer than Scotland? Or that Australia won't become like Scotland?" He kicked a rock into the water. "You're just running away."

I scowled at him. I walked up the shore to get away, then knelt down at the water's edge. I knew there were kelpie in there, but I wasn't entirely sure how to call them out. They could carry me out around the coast, maybe even as far as Portsmouth, and then I could take the next transport to Australia. 'Free of Cost.' It was perfect.

"What are you doing?" Yusuf asked. He had followed me, and that just made me scowl more.

"Looking for help," I told him. "Now leave me alone."

He crossed his arms and raised his eyebrows, making it clear that he intended to go nowhere. I turned back to the water and tried to put him out of my mind.

In my mother's stories, the kelpie were meat eaters, and loved the taste of humans, especially the young. I was still pretty young, so I guessed my best chance would be to offer a bit of myself to lure them out. She had described kelpie as like horses, perhaps green or blue, with curly manes and sharp teeth. They were known for promising mortals rides, then diving down, where the mortal would drown and the kelpie could feast.

I undid the bandage around my arm. The piece of paper fluttered out, and Yusuf caught it. He showed me the back, where he had written his prayer. To my amazement, it was blank. Even more amazing, my wound had already scabbed over. It looked disgusting, but it didn't hurt at all, except when I poked it.

I had been planning to bleed into the water directly, but I didn't want to reopen the wound to do it. So I tossed the blood stained bandage into the water instead, and hoped that would work. I watched the cotton float lazily away from me for a moment, then knelt down right at the shore's edge and whispered a plea for help into the water itself. The water smelled fresh, clearly this was the loch, after all.

"What are you doing?" Yusuf asked again, his voice sharp. I caught a scent I'd never smelled before. I glanced back at Yusuf. He was anxiously watching the bandage drift out.

"Asking for help," I repeated, in what I thought was a cool tone of voice. I sat back in the sand and turned back to the water.

"From what?" he said. "There are things in the water here."

I started to respond, but swallowed the retort when the bloody scrap of cloth suddenly sunk beneath the waves. I wanted to retreat, but I thought that might make a poor impression, so I remained where I was, trying to control my breathing.

The first thing I saw were two glowing points of golden light in the dark water. They were eyes, and my breath caught in my throat when they fixed on me. The surface of the water rose in a solid, tumor-like bulb, before the water broke with an indescribable sound, revealing the kelpie. It stood on top of the waves, staring at me. It didn't look anything like my mother had described. It was seaweed green, though I couldn't tell if had hair, like a horse, or mossy skin. It had a long, tangled mane that was curly, for lack of a better word, like a mess of burned kelp. Its head resembled a horse's in only the vaguest way:

it had a long, narrow muzzle, but its mouth stretched at least back to its neck, like pictures I'd seen of crocodiles, and was filled with several rows of razor-like teeth, all clearly visible in its lipless mouth. It smelled like posies and rotting meat.

I heard Yusuf hastily step back and trip, falling into the sand.

"You called, Daughter of the Moon?" the kelpie asked without moving its mouth. Its voice sounded like rancid honey, sweet and smooth and dangerous.

It took me a moment to get my mouth to work again. "Yes, I did. I need help. Will you help me?" I asked. My voice came out in a rush.

"You can't be serious," Yusuf hissed at me, scooting over. "That's a monster!"

The kelpie opened its mouth and hissed wetly. I think it was supposed to be a laugh. Behind it, two more rose from beneath the water, one with red eyes, and one with purple. I shivered.

"Is this an offering, Daughter?" the first kelpie asked, gliding forward as its gaze turned to fix on Yusuf. "A gift for our help?"

"No!" I said, standing up and putting myself between them and Yusuf. "He's my friend, not an offering." Which wasn't entirely true, but I didn't want him to be eaten, no matter how nosy he was.

The kelpie came ashore. Its legs ended in skeletal talons, like a hawk's. I couldn't help but imagine how easy it must be to capture someone in them. To pull flesh from a skeleton. "What help do you require?"

"Can you carry me away from here?" I asked.

It nodded, tossing its mane. The other two came ashore, spreading out, and I became horribly aware that they were surrounding us. "Of course, Daughter," the kelpie said, walking towards us. It didn't walk like a horse, and I felt a little nauseous at the unnatural movement of its legs. "Climb on my back."

"No," Yusuf whispered, grabbing my shoulder. "That's how they capture prey. It'll drag you down to its lair to eat you."

I looked up at the kelpie. It was massive, dwarfing even Archer. It lowered its head down to stare me in the eye, only a few feet away from me. "Come with me, Daughter. And your friend. Let us carry you away."

"No!" Yusuf repeated, louder. He began to pull me backwards, away from the kelpie. I closed my eyes and shook my head to clear it.

"Wait," I said, and pulled myself free of Yusuf's grasp. "You recognize me?" I asked the kelpie.

It hissed its laugh and nodded.

"If I ask you to do something, do you promise to be bound to do that thing?" I could hear Yusuf muttering behind me. I had no idea what I was doing, really, but they hadn't pounced yet. I thought the key might be to get them to promise things in advance. That's how it had worked in mother's stories, though, admittedly, none of the ones about kelpies.

"We require payment, Daughter," the kelpie said. "Food. Flesh." The purple-eyed kelpie slipped behind us and said something not in English. It wasn't quite Gaelic, either, but something older.

The first kelpie looked at Yusuf again. "This one smells of the kirk and the iron," it said. "Of new ways."

"He is under my protection," I told the kelpie sternly. "We need you to carry us to the far end of the loch. The southern end," I added. I felt sweat beading on my forehead. They wanted to eat us, that was clear from the hungry looks in their alien eyes. I wondered what made them listen to me, instead of just pounce, and if it had something to do with the sith blood in my veins. It was the blood that had called them from the deep, after all. "Alive and unharmed." I switched to Gaelic. In the old stories my mother had told me, the characters had always spoken Gaelic. "Take us, unharmed, to the southern end of the loch, and you can have the fish."

"Those are mine," Yusuf said, in Gaelic. Really good Gaelic.

"How do you speak Gaelic?" I asked him, momentarily distracted.

"How? Better than you, apparently," he said smugly. I ground my teeth.

The kelpies had stopped laughing. Gold-eyes stared at me, then looked up at Archer. "What about that?"

I hesitated. If I let Archer go, he would run back to the farm, where he'd almost definitely be captured by Outerbridge. He couldn't come with us, and I certainly couldn't let them eat him. There was really no choice.

I stepped out from the circle of kelpies – Yusuf kept close to me – and removed Archer's bridle before giving him a smack on the hindquarters. He snorted and trotted off into the woods. "Don't worry about my horse," I told the kelpie, forcing myself to stare straight into its strange eyes.

It looked disappointed, but nodded. "Let's go."

***

"You're crazy, you know that?" Yusuf told me as we sat around a fire at the southern end of the loch. We were across from Fort Augustus, and its dim lights were visible in the looming twilight.

Yusuf had spent the rest of the day replenishing his fish and not talking to me. It was really an improvement. He was so nosy that I preferred the silence to trying to have a conversation with him. He hadn't returned until I had built a fire, after the sun had set. I suppose I couldn't blame him. I had somewhat inadvertently carried him twenty miles or more from his home. I hoped his parents weren't too worried.

"I got us away, didn't I?" I told him.

"You nearly got us eaten."

I shrugged. The kelpies hadn't been comfortable to ride, but they had been swift, crossing the loch in minutes. In any event, I was too busy planning out my route to worry about what he thought of me. I would have to walk, and I reckoned it would take me days, if not weeks, to reach Portsmouth, without food or money. I couldn't hunt, but I could find wild plants easily enough. I thought I could forage enough to keep myself alive.

I told Yusuf my plan.

"And what about Portsmouth?" he asked. "You could be waiting for weeks. You can't forage inside the city."

"I can find a job," I told him.

He snorted at me.

"Yes, well," I said angrily. "I can worry about it after I get there."

He stared at me, then sighed. "After we get there, at least. I can't let you wander off by yourself, you're liable to be eaten by something you called up."

I started to argue — who was he to tell me whether I could take care of myself, honestly — but stopped short.

"What?" Yusuf asked.

"I heard something," I told him. It was a snap, like a twig breaking. I shushed him, even though he wasn't talking, and stood up to investigate.

It was Archer. The big horse trotted out from the shadows, right up to me. He nearly knocked me over as he pushed his head into my chest. I patted his neck as I looked over to Yusuf. I was utterly bewildered.

"What's that?" Yusuf asked, pointing at Archer's flank. I pushed the horse's head away so I could take a closer look. It was a wound, oozing blood around a sharpened stick, inscribed with strange markings. They were just simple lines going up and down, sometimes perpendicular to the edge, sometimes at a slight angle, but they made my skin crawl. I threw the stick into the fire. It burned green.

Yusuf was already cleaning Archer's cut, using another scrap of paper from the flyer. I didn't pay him any attention. Instead, I had faced outwards, towards the forest.

Something felt wrong. It took me a moment to realize that I could smell the wrongness. I had picked up some scent that was blowing towards us from the forest. It was sharp and rank, and smelled of danger. I sniffed, like a dog, short, quick breaths. Yusuf scowled at me. He probably thought I was being unladylike. I felt my nose begin to run, but that just intensified the smell.

I don't know how to describe what it's like to really smell something, if you've never done it before. It's a little like when you first open your eyes in the morning. It takes a moment to focus on whatever is before you, but as you focus, it becomes clear, and you can begin to pick out details.

The wind brought more information. There were three people. One smelled of power and danger, the other two of subservience. I could pick up metal and gunpowder, horse, sheep, and a multitude of other tiny scents that made up the bigger smell, like little details on a painting. It hardly mattered, though. I knew it was Outerbridge. Somehow he'd enchanted that stick, and then sent Archer to find me.

"What is it?" Yusuf asked, as I wiped my nose on my sleeve, trying to get Outerbridge's scent out. I told him, tersely. He looked dubious, but tore the last bit of the flyer in half and began to scribble on it.

I checked Archer's cut. It had already stopped bleeding. I climbed onto his back and maneuvered him around to point at the forest. The smell was getting stronger.

"You head back," I told Yusuf. "I don't think they know you're here. I'll lead them away."

He finished whatever he was writing and looked up at me. "I can't do that," he said. "You're just a..." He trailed off, looking embarrassed, but it was clear what he was going to say.

"I'm a Highlander," I told him, scowling. "I can take care of myself."

"Yeah, alright." He shrugged. "But still."

The smell was getting stronger, and I didn't want to waste time arguing. "Get on, then," I said, holding Archer steady. As soon as Yusuf had climbed up behind me, I urged Archer into a trot, trying to put as much distance between Outerbridge and us as I could.

"Go across that river," Yusuf told me, once we had reached the tree line. It was barely a wee burn, let alone a river, but I guided Archer across it. Yusuf let the slip of paper fall into the water as we passed. I felt a rush of wind, like huge wings beating the air around me, as soon as the paper touched the water.

"You can't follow me all the way to Portsmouth," I told Yusuf as Archer carried us south. I was feeling pretty sure of myself. Outerbridge would find the remains of the fire, but then have no idea where we'd gone.

"Why can't I?" Yusuf said. "Can I have your horse when you get on your boat?"

"If it crosses the ocean, it's a ship," I snapped. "And no, you can't have my horse."

"They won't let you bring him on the boat," he pointed out. I hated that he was right.

A sharp crack ended our argument, and I tucked my head down instinctively. I glanced over my shoulder and saw Dearganach atop a wiry nag of a horse, hastily reloading a pistol. Yusuf said something that I assumed was both Arabic and not for polite company, then wrapped his arms around my middle and kicked Archer hard. My horse snorted in disgust but took off at a canter. I would have fallen off if Yusuf hadn't hunkered down over me.

There was another crack, and I looked up to see Hercules, without a horse, out of breath in front of us. His shot seemed to have veered off into the forest somewhere.

"Good thing they've terrible aim," I said, as I reined Archer to the left, away from Hercules.

"Alhamdulillah," Yusuf said. I began to suspect the nature of the rushing wind. However, before I could say anything, Outerbridge popped up almost directly in front of us, brandishing his bizarre pistol. He fired thrice in short succession, but each bullet whizzed harmlessly into the foliage.

Archer pulled short, and I tumbled forward, falling to the ground. I heard Yusuf yell, but another shot from Outerbridge's pistol sent him and Archer running into the forest. Outerbridge grabbed my hair and hauled me back to my feet. I struggled, but that just caused some of my hair to part company with my scalp.

He paid me about as much mind as a butcher pays a pig as he tucked his pistol into a pocket and then pulled out a knife. It looked like it was made of stone, with a wrap of oily cloth for the handle. The blade was covered in dark brown stains. I stopped struggling.

"M'lord," Hercules had come up behind us. I did not like the grin on his face. "What about the Colored boy?" His voice sounded raw.

"Of no importance," Outerbridge said. He pulled my hair back, exposing my throat. "Do you think the dress is salvageable? It might be worth a few pounds, if we can repair it."

Hercules grabbed my arm to examine the missing sleeve. "Perhaps, M'lord." He sounded dubious, but began to carefully strip my dress away. I tried to pull away again, heedless of the pain, until Outerbridge pressed the stone dirk into my throat. I could feel it move when I swallowed.

A crashing noise off to my left preceded Dearganach tromping into view, his horse lost. He had one hand clamped on Yusuf's shoulder, the other pulling Archer's reins. "Oh, good, you caught her," he said. "I got this one."

"Let me go," Yusuf was struggling just as hard as I was. One of his hands was clamped on Dearganach's wrist, but the other was behind his back. When Dearganach pulled Yusuf forward, I could see the last scrap of the flyer clutched in his fist, covered in that strange script.

"M'lord," Hercules spoke up. "I've a ship bound for Saint Helena, leaving in a few days. I could sell him to merchants I know bound for Texas."

Outerbridge shrugged. "Whatever." Yusuf began to struggle harder, even after Hercules struck him across the face. I thought I saw a tooth go flying. Outerbridge glanced at me, then nodded at Dearganach. "Best strip off the underthings, too. No sense getting blood on them." He helped Dearganach strip me naked, even lifting me off the ground at one point as I tried to break free. I did everything I could, kicking and scratching and even attempting to bite Outerbridge. I screamed as loud as I could, but that just made the men laugh. They didn't bother trying to remove my coarse chemise; Outerbridge just sliced it off with his stone knife, leaving me naked.

They stopped laughing. All of them, even Yusuf, went still and stared at me.

"You're a boy," Yusuf said.

"I'm not a boy," I shouted.

Dearganach looked to Outerbridge.

"Might as well try," Outerbridge said, shrugging as he shoved me onto my stomach. "In the worst case, at least there'll be one less Gaelic brat running around."

He knelt down on my wrists, while Dearganach held down my legs. I cried into the muddy forest loam and tried to pull any one of my limbs free, but I was no match for two grown men. One of my wrists creaked and pain shot all the way up my arm.

Outerbridge leaned over me, and I felt the cold stone blade run up the back of my leg, separating the skin. I screamed again, and Outerbridge shoved my face down into the dirt, muffling me. I could feel blood start to run over my thigh.

"The hell is that?" Dearganach said.

"That means it's working," Outerbridge said. He shifted slightly, inadvertently lifting up his knee just enough. I yanked my arm free and swung upwards as hard as I could.

Perhaps it was unsporting of me to punch him there, but in my defense, it seemed my best chance at survival.

He collapsed sideways with a groan, clutching at himself. I twisted to see Dearganach still pinning down my legs, looking stunned.

"Bridget!" Yusuf called. I turned to see him toss the scrap of paper.

It should have fluttered to the ground a few feet from him. Instead, a breeze caught it and carried it almost directly to me. I snatched it out of the air and felt a jolt through my whole body. Dearganach yelped and jumped back. I scrambled to my feet and charged Hercules.

I felt powerful, even though blood was still streaming down my leg. I remember the way I had felt when my mother showed me how she changed, and I seized that feeling. I shuddered, and then my arms stretched out in front of me, coarse grey hair spreading outwards from my palms until it covered my whole body. My spine lengthened, my hips tilted, my nose and mouth stretched forward into a muzzle. My vision turned grey but my sense of smell increased a thousand fold.

I was a wolf.

My forelegs left the ground as I pounced on Hercules. My fangs clamped down on his throat and he screamed as I prepared to rip it out.

I felt a hand on my shoulder and glanced up to see Yusuf shaking his head. I growled. We couldn't let Outerbridge and his men get away. Yusuf shook his head again.

"We can't kill them," he told me. "God wants us to show mercy. I will stop you, if I have to."

As if he could. I released Hercules and stepped off the big man, snorting. I supposed it mattered very little to me – I was still going to leave, and I doubted that Outerbridge would follow me all the way to Australia. But I couldn't leave him to get away with it. I turned away from Yusuf in time to see Dearganach flee into the forest.

I flitted over to Outerbridge, just now regaining his breath, and broke his wrist with a sharp bite. While he howled in agony, I grabbed the stone knife and carried it over to the scrap of paper that had saved my life. I laid the knife on the paper, then looked to Yusuf.

He took my meaning, and carefully wrapped the evil blade in the prayer. The Arabic burned with a white light, etching its way through the stone. It smelled horrible, like burning sewage. In an instant, the blade had crumbled away to dust, leaving just the handle. The edge was neatly cut in the shape of the writing.

Hercules must have run away, too, though I didn't see him go. As we watched the knife break, Outerbridge pulled out his pistol. We turned when we heard the hammer click back.

"I still have you," he breathed, aiming down the gun at my head. I snarled at him. "I can't skin you, but I can still kill you."

I tensed, ready to pounce, but Yusuf stepped in front of me.

"Don't be stupid, boy," Outerbridge said, still holding the pistol steady. "I have at least two bullets left."

"You can't kill me with that," Yusuf said. The force of his conviction made me shiver.

Outerbridge's hand was shaking. I could smell him, too, full of fury and adrenaline and just the first blossoms of flowering fear. He shouted and pulled the trigger, but his bullets went wide, whizzing into the trees and the ground, leaving us unharmed.

I slipped past Yusuf and broke Outerbridge's other wrist. For good measure, I savaged the pistol, leaving it a mess of wood and metal, and I ripped my mother's skin from his shoulder. Then I left him to curse me and my family.

***

Yusuf accompanied me another day's journey south. Transforming, once I had felt the first change, turned out to be as easy as breathing. We didn't talk about what had happened in the forest, and though I know he wanted to ask me about what lay in my chemise, he thankfully did not. We parted, not as friends, but at least friendly to each other, and he promised to write me, and I him, and we did for many years after. I did let him keep Archer.

As a wolf, it took me only a few days to reach Portsmouth, and I managed to book passage to the new colony within a few days after that, without having to resort to anything more unpleasant than hunting wild game. The passage was uneventful, if sometimes long and tedious.

As for Australia, well, that is a story for another time.

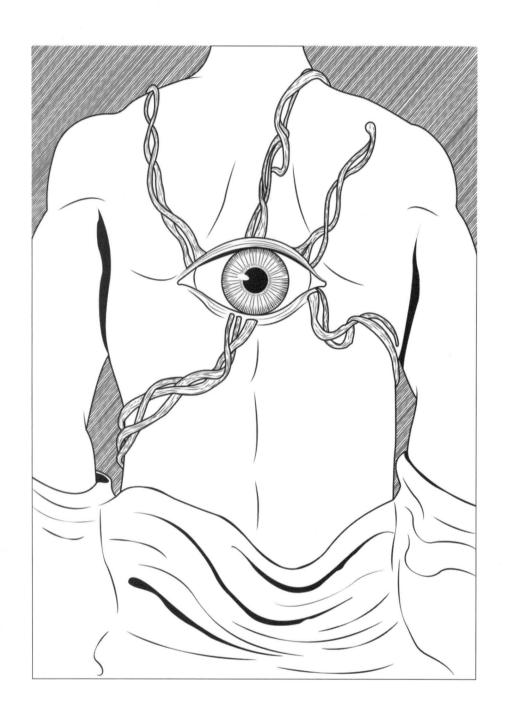

Art by Patrick Thicklin

THE MOUSER OF PETER THE GREAT
P. DJÈLÍ CLARK

1704
Tsardom of Muscovy

Ibrahim watched as Tsar Pyotr of the Russians was seated into a wooden chair in front of a fireplace. It was made for a very big man, with a high back and curved arms carved like lions. And the Tsar was certainly big, taller than any of the other men in the room. Taller perhaps than any man Ibrahim had ever seen, and he wondered if these Russians were all ruled by giants.

The Tsar settled into a long red coat trimmed in gold, drawing it tighter as if seeking warmth. He leaned forward, inspecting the two boys that stood before him. His appearance – those black eyes, and even blacker hair, all on a face that could have been cut from stone – should have been terrifying. And it might have been, had the man also not looked so very tired.

At a nudge from Bilal, Ibrahim lifted his gaze to meet the Tsar. This Pytor of the Russians didn't sit in his great wooden chair so much as he sagged in it – as if doing all he could just to hold himself up. The whites of his eyes were tinged with red, and the skin around them swollen. His face looked drained, so that cheekbones showed just beneath the flesh. And he was so very pale.

Well, Ibrahim mused, that wasn't so uncommon here. Not like at the Sultan's palace, where there were pale people, sand brown people, bronze people and every type of people you could imagine. Some had even been like him, with black skin and hair that curled and coiled. Here, everyone was pale, or red, like they'd been pinching each other's faces. But this Pytor of the Russians was even paler than that – pale as milk. When he spoke, the tiredness that showed on his body filled his voice.

Ibrahim listened, and understood nothing. He and Bilal had only just arrived in this Tsardom of Muscovy, this place with no sun and only clouds, where it rained cold white ashes that covered everything in ice. At the Sultan's court they had been instructed in Turkish, which he now knew well. This was definitely not Turkish.

"His Majesty is speaking to you," someone said.

Ibrahim turned to look upon a silver-haired man in a long green coat with bright yellow stripes, reminding him of a bird in the Sultan's palace that bore the same color of feathers. He and Bilal had met the odd man when they arrived. He told them to call him Spafarius. But they had already named him No-Nose – on account that he had no nose. There were just two holes where a nose should have been, and Ibrahim wondered if perhaps some people here didn't have noses. Or maybe in all that pinching of cheeks, it had been pinched off. The nose-less man did, however, speak Turkish.

"The Tsar asks if you know how old you are?" Spafarius No-Nose translated. He gave Ibrahim an expectant look, knuckling at long silver whiskers that drooped on his nose-less face. "Come on boy. Vasil'ev said you were the bright one."

Ibrahim blinked. He opened his mouth then stopped. How did you say numbers in this language? Deciding on another course, he held up one hand to show five fingers and a second to add three more.

The Tsar smiled, a slight spark touching his dreary face. He spoke again.

"Clever," Spafarius No-Nose remarked. "His Majesty asks if you know your name?"

"Ibra—" Ibrahim began, then changed to, "Abram." That was what they called him here. *A proper Christian name,* the man Vasil'ev had said, the one who brought he and Bilal to this place. To Ibrahim it didn't matter much, because in truth neither of those were really his name.

"And were you and your brother treated well in your travels, Abram?" No-Nose translated once again.

Ibrahim looked to Bilal who just shrugged. Bilal seemed to shrug at everything these days, and Ibrahim thought perhaps his brother blamed him for having to leave the Sultan's palace. Well it hadn't been his fault. At least, he hadn't meant for it to happen. He thought some more on the Tsar's question. Treated well? They hadn't been beaten on their long trip with Vasil'ev. They had been fed. And dressed in thick furs when it turned cold. But they were still slaves, as they had been before. Of that he was certain.

"Da," he answered finally. Then gave a bow, like he'd seen some men here do, and added, "Tsar Pyotr."

The Tsar's eyes rounded at this and he laughed aloud, shrugging off some of his tiredness. Ibrahim met Bilal's surprised look with a satisfied smile. He'd picked up a few things. The Tsar lifted a long finger to point at him and spoke.

"His Majesty is impressed," Spafarius No-Nose winked. "He would have you in his personal service, Abram."

Ibrahim bowed again. He'd become accustomed to the ways of powerful men at the Sultan's palace, and knew this was not a request.

There were a few more questions and then an exchange of words between the Tsar and the other men in the room. After a while, some of them helped him to his feet. He grumbled but leaned his tall frame on them, letting the men guide him. It was as he turned to go, that Ibrahim first saw the eye.

It was an ugly eye. A big pale grey thing, with long fleshy roots that clutched to the Tsar like a weed. It sat there riding his back, twisting this way and that, glaring out upon the room. When it caught sight of Ibrahim it squinted thick eyelids on its stalk, looking him up and down.

Then it shrieked.

Ibrahim cupped hands to his ears, clenching his teeth at the sound. No one else did. No one even paid the ugly eye any attention. Not Bilal, not Spafarius No-Nose, or even the Tsar. Because he knew, none of them could see it or hear its angry screams. And that bad feeling that came from it didn't prick their skin like needles and make them shiver either. He could see it, hear it, and feel it, because that was who he was – who he'd always been.

The shrieking didn't stop until the Tsar was gone. And when Ibrahim took his hands from his hears he found Spafarius No-Nose eyeing him. There was a curious look on his face.

"Your brother will come with me," the man declared. "You however, Abram, will stay here. The Tsar is not well. His sleep is troubled and he eats little. He is here secretly at the home of his friend, the Count, while the Count and his family are away. There are only a few servants in the house to care for him – and now, you. He needs your very special help I think."

Ibrahim looked up at the man, trying not to stare at his no-nose. Bilal had said that was rude. "Me? What can I do?"

The man knelt, so that he was nose-less to nose with Ibrahim. His breath smelled of onions and things both sweet and bitter. "I want you to hunt mice Abram. As you did for the Sultan. You know how to hunt mice, yes?"

Ibrahim thought of the eye, and knew right away that Spafarius No-Nose wasn't really talking about mice.

The next day Ibrahim found himself alone in the big house. Spafarius No-Nose had taken Bilal away and now there was no one to talk to. The servants bathed and dressed him. They gave him new clothes – a blue coat with tight sleeves, white puffy pants and brown house slippers. It was more clothes than he'd ever worn. But he was cold all the time here, and so didn't complain.

He hadn't seen the Tsar all morning. He'd dreamt about that shrieking eye though. And that bad feeling still hovered in the air. Spafarius No-Nose wanted him to do something about it, like he'd done for the Sultan. But how was he supposed to do that?

The sharp sound of echoing laughter suddenly caught Ibrahim's attention. Curious, he followed it through several rooms of the big house. The tingling scent of unfamiliar spices and cooking meat told him he was in a kitchen. There, an old woman was trying to roll out a bit of dough. But each time she did so it folded back up, sticking together.

Ibrahim could see the problem. It was a little man, no taller than himself. He was covered in long black hair like a shaggy dog, with an even longer grey beard. He tugged at the dough between hairy fingers, pulling it and pushing it even as the old woman tried to smooth it out. Each time she grunted her frustration he giggled and did it again.

"Why are you doing that?" Ibrahim asked.

The old woman looked up over a bulbous nose then clucked her tongue, saying something he couldn't understand and waving him away. But he wasn't talking to her and the hairy little man answered.

"Because it's fun," he remarked.

"It's not very nice."

The little man seemed set to dismiss him then stopped, looking up with round shining eyes. "You can see me?"

Ibrahim nodded. In a blur the hairy little man was in front of him. He looked Ibrahim up and down. "But she can't see me, or hear me. How can you?"

"I just can," Ibrahim answered truthfully. He always could. The old woman looked to him again and frowned. Not that she understood spirit-talk, which he knew sounded like nonsense to everyone else. Still, he'd learned at the Sultan's palace that speaking to things others couldn't see frightened people. He didn't want that here.

"Let's go somewhere else," he suggested.

The little man nodded eagerly, trailing along behind. They found an empty room and the two sat down across from each other in big wooden chairs.

"Are you a witch?" he asked.

"No," Ibrahim answered. At least he didn't think so.

"Where do you come from?"

"Far away," he answered. "I wanted to ask—"

"Can everyone there see? Like you can see?"

Ibrahim shook his head. "No. Just me. Have you seen—?"

"And your skin," the little man cut in. "It's so...black!"

"It is. But do you—?"

"Does it come off? Your skin I mean?"

Ibrahim frowned. What a silly question. "Of course not. Does yours?"

The little man pursed his lips and thought hard. "I don't think so."

Ibrahim sighed. "I just want to know—"

"Your hair is so curly! May I touch it?"

"No!" Ibrahim snapped. "Touch your own hair!" He had hoped to ask the little man something about the eye, but this was becoming annoying.

"Does everyone have hair like you where you come from? And skin? How far away is it? Do you have a Tsar? Are you *sure* it doesn't come off...?"

Ibrahim sat listening to the endless questions, and grew increasingly frustrated. Mostly he was frustrated because the little man wouldn't stop talking. And because he was, after all, only eight, what he did next was entirely understandable.

Ibrahim reached into the air and pulled out a sword. It was a big sword, with a broad curving golden blade. One of the guards in the Sultan's palace had owned such a sword, and Ibrahim had wanted one like it. So he made one up, the way he was able to always make such things up. It was almost as tall as he was, and should have been much too heavy for a boy of eight. But as he was the one who conjured it, the sword weighed whatever he wanted it to weigh. He lifted the large blade above his head and glared at the talkative little man.

"Be quiet! Or I'll chop you up like a radish!"

The little man let out a single shriek and vanished in a puff of hair.

Ibrahim felt his temper die down and he put away his sword with a sigh. That had probably not been a good idea.

It took all morning to find the hairy little man again, hiding under a set of stairs. It took still another hour to coax him out. When it was all done the two sat by a window, looking out at the cold ash coming down from the grey sky. The hairy little man called it snow.

"I'm sorry I said I would chop you up," Ibrahim apologized. He really was sorry. "I'll answer your questions if you answer mine." He paused. "But you still can't touch my hair."

The little man blinked, as if he'd forgotten about that entirely. "I'm Domovoi," he said, "a house spirit."

"Domovoi," Ibrahim repeated. "Is that your name?"

The house spirit shrugged. "All Domovoi are named Domovoi. We help take care of homes."

Ibrahim raised an eyebrow. "You didn't look like you were helping this morning."

"Not my home," Domovoi explained. "My house was here long ago. I cared for an old man and woman. I would spin straw for them and mend broken things. Then someone sent them away. Or they died. I can't remember which. This bigger house is built where their house once was. And so I remain."

"My name's Ibrahim. That's the name the Sultan gave me. Now I'm Abram."

"What was your name before that?" Domovoi asked.

"I don't know," Ibrahim admitted. "I don't know my name."

"Where did you come from then? Before the Sultan?"

"I don't know that either."

Domovoi cocked a hairy head. "Don't you remember?"

Ibrahim shook his head. He didn't. Neither did Bilal. All the two of them remembered was that they came from somewhere else, where there was always sun, and people had faces like them. He told Domovoi as much.

"We were taken by men. It happened at night. I think they wanted me, for what I could do, what I could see. But I was with Bilal, so they took him too. Then they worked some kind of magic and made us forget."

"Where did they take you?" the little man asked.

"Far away from our home, to the Sultan's court. That's where we learned Turkish. Then one day the Sultan's mother called for me. She told me I had to help the Sultan. There was a bad spirit in the palace she said. It haunted the Sultan in his dreams. She knew what I could do, and I was put in his room at night to find it."

"Why was this bad spirit angry with her son?" Domovoi asked.

"The Sultan got his throne by taking it from another Sultan – his brother," Ibrahim explained. "The spirit haunted the new Sultan for doing this bad thing."

"Oh!" the little man exclaimed.

"One night I awoke to find the spirit there. It was a great big ogre with a fiery eye. It frightened the Sultan. He was so scared, he couldn't even call for his guards."

"What did you do?" Domovoi whispered, his bright eyes round as plates.

"I pulled my sword," Ibrahim said. "And I fought the ogre."

Domovoi inhaled. "You fought an ogre?"

Ibrahim nodded. "For a long time. We fought and fought, all around the room as the Sultan watched. And then I chopped off his head." He made a cutting motion with his arm and Domovoi gasped. "The Sultan cried when it was over. He laid his head on my lap and just cried and cried. The next day, his mother sent Bilal and I away."

"But why? You helped him. You chopped off the ogre's head!"

"I think because I saw him cry. I don't think Sultans are supposed to cry."

Domovoi made a face. "That's silly. Everyone cries."

It was Ibrahim's turn to shrug. He didn't understand it either. "A man named Vasil'ev took us. We traveled on a river, then over land and then on a ship across a lot of water. Someone called it a sea. The man brought us here where Spafarius No-Nose took us to see the Tsar."

"That is quite a story!"

Ibrahim supposed it was. "Are there others here?" he asked. "Like you?"

"I am the only Domovoi in this house," the little man said proudly. "But yes – there are many others! A Kikimora lives in the kitchens behind the stove and steals food, but she's stingy and won't share any. There's an absent-minded Lesovik nearby that likes to scare cattle. He tends to forget where he lives and spends a lot of time wandering about. There's a Bagiennik or two sleeping under the ice in the lake. We don't want to wake them up however – big eyes and teeth and very bad tempers. Almost as bad as those Rusalki nymphs..."

Ibrahim listened as Domovoi listed more spirits than he could possibly remember. The little man would probably go on forever if he didn't jump in.

"What about the eye?" he asked. "You've seen it? "

Domovoi's mouth clamped shut. He made a face and nodded. "I only saw it for the first time when *he* arrived."

Ibrahim guessed *he* was the Tsar.

"It's an omen," Domovoi went on. "That's what the others say – of something bad to come. That's why so many of them are leaving..."

"Leaving?" Ibrahim asked sitting up. "You mean the spirits?"

Domovoi nodded. "There are barely any in the house any longer. When *he* arrived with that thing on his back – most of them left. Something's coming, and no one wants to be here when it arrives."

Ibrahim frowned, thinking of the bad feeling. It hadn't gone away. If anything, it was stronger now. "Why aren't you leaving?" he asked.

Domovoi grinned, showing blocks of white teeth. "Because I like it here!" In a blur he was gone. From the distance came the sound of something crashing. Someone shouted and that familiar laugh echoed through the house.

Ibrahim let the mischievous spirit have his fun and sat back, thinking on what he'd learned. Only then did he notice the girl. She sat in a corner of the room, looking at him with watery blue eyes beneath long brown hair. He wondered how long she had been there? Had she seen him talking to Domovoi? Well no, he'd look like he was just talking to himself. That was hardly better.

As if waiting to be noticed, she got up and walked over to him, sitting nearby. She looked near his age, and was just as tall. When she smiled he smiled back, fumbling through his head for something to say. But nothing came to mind. So they just sat there, staring at each other until finally the girl giggled. He giggled too, uncertain what else to do, and soon the two were speaking the one language it seemed everyone understood.

Their laughter was interrupted when the old woman from the kitchens walked in. She looked flustered – Domovoi's doing no doubt – but called the girl over, handing her a pastry. The two walked away and into another room leaving Ibrahim alone again. Disappointed, he settled back down and was surprised when the girl quickly reappeared. She ran up to him with her pastry, grinning as she broke it in half and gave him a piece.

"Vatrushka," she said before leaving.

Ibrahim watched her go and wondered if that was her name or the pastry? He decided at the moment he didn't much care which – only that maybe he'd made a friend. Two, if he counted Domovoi. Then he ate the pastry happily.

The next day Ibrahim woke up to find the bad feeling had gotten worse. It seemed outside the sky was filled with more clouds. Even the flames in the fireplace looked dim, as if struggling to stay alight. He was staring at them when Domovoi found him. The hairy little man sat down right in front of the fireplace, wriggling his long toes at the heat.

"You were talking to old Varvara's granddaughter yesterday," he remarked.

The girl, Ibrahim remembered. "We didn't really speak."

"She gave you a pastry," Domovoi sulked. "She never gives me pastries."

"She can't see you Domovoi," Ibrahim reminded.

The little man's bright eyes flared. "Oh! That's right!"

Ibrahim stifled a laugh. "What's her name?"

"Eva," Domovoi pronounced. "She and old Varvara belong to the house."

Ibrahim frowned. Belonged? How could people belong to a thing?

"They're slaves? Like me?"

Domovoi shook a hairy head. "Not like you. They belong to the house. You belong to the Tsar. A Tsar is more important than a house. So you must be more important. That's good, yes?"

"I don't want to belong to anyone," Ibrahim replied.

Domovoi shrugged, as if there was nothing more to say. Then he blinked and sat up. "I almost forgot! I found someone you can talk to – about the omen!"

"Who? Someone...like you?"

Domovoi nodded. "He keeps to himself. The others don't like him much. But he knows a lot of things. Or he thinks he does."

"Take me to him," Ibrahim begged. "Please!"

Domovoi jumped up and motioned for him to follow. They walked through halls and up stairs, to another part of the house. A few times Ibrahim had to run to keep up, yelling at the hairy little man to slow his blurring pace. Fortunately this part of the house was empty so no one else could see him. They finally stopped at a set of doors and Ibrahim pushed them open.

It was another large room. There were books everywhere, some on shelves and more heaped in piles on the floor. Ibrahim followed the house spirit past what looked like small wooden ships, some of them half-built and on their sides. There were other things here that he couldn't name: round glasses filled with colorful liquids, contraptions of wood and metal that somehow fit together.

In the middle of it all was a small man – as tall as Domovoi, but not hairy at all. He wore a long blue coat with gold buttons and tight short pants that fell to the knees with white stockings. Stacks of books rose up around him like miniature hills, and he muttered beneath his breath as he read and scribbled on a piece of paper with a feather quill. He seemed to exclaim at every other word, wriggling his pointed pink ears through a curly white wig. Ibrahim walked up and introduced himself.

"And is that supposed to mean something to me?" the small man asked, never bothering to look up. He scratched at the end of a long nose, leaving a smudge of ink.

"I was looking for help," Ibrahim said.

"Help?" The small man smacked his lips together, showing two large front teeth that jutted down like a rabbit's "I have no time to help. Can't you see I'm busy?"

Ibrahim eyed the stack of books. "Doing what?"

The small man pulled a hand from his quill, which continued writing all the same. He looked up at Ibrahim with black eyes over wire-rimmed spectacles. "Doing what?" he repeated. "Why plotting the future! The future is coming! We must plan for it! We are so behind! All of you are lucky I'm here!"

"And who are you?" Ibrahim asked.

The small man sputtered, looking offended. "Why I am the spirit of progress you silly boy! The spirit of invention and proper government! Do you know of the salons in Paris? The Royal Society of natural philosophers and experiments in London? Where's our Descartes? Who has written our Leviathan? How shall we compete? We must strive to move forward boy! Always forward!"

Ibrahim watched as the excitable little man went back to his writing, muttering the whole time. He looked to Domovoi.

"I told you no one liked him," the house spirit remarked.

Ibrahim could see why. "Where does he come from?"

"I came back with his Majesty's Grand Embassy," the small man answered before Domovoi could speak, sparing the house spirit a glare. "His Majesty has placed his hopes in us. We work to make our land more modern, like those of the West!"

Domovoi laughed. "The Tsar cut off their beards!"

"What?" Ibrahim asked, now completely confused.

"His Majesty ordered that all men of the nobility shave their beards," the haughty spirit proclaimed. "These are the ways of the men of the West that we must adapt."

"He made them dress different too," Domovoi added. "And if they wouldn't do as he said, they had to pay money. They didn't like that."

"All part of the struggle to make a backwards people modern," the other spirit huffed. "But some are stubborn. They don't want us to move forward. And now they hobble His Majesty with their superstitions!"

Ibrahim perked up. "You mean the eye? You know about it?"

The spirit looked back up over his wire spectacles, grimacing. "A Likho," he spat. "A curse."

Ibrahim had heard of curses, in stories at the Sultan's palace. You could put them on another person to do bad things. That's what the eye was. The Tsar had been cursed!

"How do we make it go away?" Ibrahim asked.

The spirit shook his head. "The Likho is vile. Try to cut it away and it will make His Majesty cut off his own hand. Try to drown it and it will let His Majesty drown before floating away. It eats at his life and infects all about him with misfortune. But it is only a part of the curse. The Likho draws something else here. It calls it. Something more terrible." The small man's long ears fell and his eyes fixed on Ibrahim. "Can't you feel it?"

The next day Ibrahim could feel it. And it seemed, so now could everyone in the house. The servants went about their tasks stooped and bent, barely even whispering. The Tsar wailed through the night in his dreams so that no one slept. A gloom settled over everything, as completely as the snow outside.

That day, Spafarius No-Nose arrived back at the house. He went up to see the Tsar and came down again looking tired. He sat in front of a fire and sipped from a cup, hugging himself as if he couldn't get warm.

"Two bits of advice for you Abram," he slurred. "One, never intrigue against a vengeful prince with a sharp knife." His finger tapped the space where his nose should have been. "Second, never drink cheap bread wine made by peasants. It has the taste of feet." He grimaced into his cup, but took another sip anyway. "Your brother has a gift with his voice. I am thinking he may do well in music, once we give him a proper Christian name. How goes your hunt for mice?"

"I haven't caught any yet," Ibrahim admitted.

Spafarius No-Nose sighed. "No? Well I hope you do soon. His Majesty is so tired he cannot rise from bed. I do not know how much longer we can go on like this. We have kept the Count's servants quiet of the Tsar's presence. But now the girl is sick, and they will talk."

"Who's sick?" Ibrahim asked puzzled.

Spafarius No-Nose took another grimacing sip before answering. "The old cook's granddaughter."

Ibrahim inhaled. "Eva!"

Spafarius No-Nose raised an eyebrow. "You have met then. She has taken with a terrible fever. It burns her up, and nothing can be done for it. The servants fear it is something to do with His Majesty." He shook his head. "No, they will not stay quiet long."

Ibrahim excused himself and quickly left, going off in search of Domovoi. He found the little hairy man under his favorite stairs. He lay curled up into a furry ball, and his bright eyes were dim.

"Eva is sick!" Ibrahim told him.

Domovoi nodded, listless. "Everything is bad now."

"It's that Likho! We have to do something about it! Stop the other thing from coming!" Ibrahim didn't know much about this Pyotr of the Russians. Maybe like the Sultan, the Tsar had done something bad to deserve this. But not Eva. Not the girl with watery blue eyes who had shared her pastry. She hadn't hurt anyone.

Domovoi sighed. "Too late for that. It's already here. Came in last night."

Ibrahim glared at him. "What? Where?"

Domovoi's eyes turned to the floor. "In the cellar."

It took more coaxing, but Ibrahim managed to get the house spirit to lead him to the cellar. The closer they came to it, the worse the bad feelings got. When they reached a long set of stone stairs Domovoi stopped and whimpered. Taking the lead, Ibrahim walked down into the dark.

The cellar was huge, like the house had a great big belly beneath. It was filled with old things: iron suits of armor, paintings and even swords. They cluttered up the space; things from long ago hidden in dust, cobwebs and gloom. It was the perfect place for a monster to hide.

Ibrahim saw it almost immediately. A large shape sat in the dark of the cellar, sprawled out among the old things. Its bright green scales shimmered and its body heaved when it breathed. It was gigantic. Monstrous! He counted one, two, no, three heads! Each looked like a snake with horns and had sharp teeth that poked out from mouths on long snouts. Grey smoke seeped from their flaring nostrils as they slept, and a rumble like a snore rose from their throats. He had heard of things like this before, from the Sultan's storytellers. This was a dragon!

"It looks very scary!" Domovoi squeaked behind him.

It did, Ibrahim agreed. He'd never seen anything so big. When an eye on one of those giant heads opened, it was all he could do to not run. The eye swam about to regard him, narrowing to a red slit on a bright yellow sun. A deep growl from its throat quickly woke the other heads. The three opened their eyes then lifted sinuous scaly necks to stare down at him.

"What is this?" the middle head rasped. "Who wakes us?"

Ibrahim swallowed, searching for his voice.

"I do," he called up.

The head on the left snarled, its eyes narrowing. "And who are you?"

Ibrahim faltered. That simple question seemed suddenly very hard.

"I'm Ibrahim," he said at last. "I've come to tell you that you have to leave. You're scaring people here, making them sick. I think a curse brought you, but you shouldn't be here. Please go away now. Go somewhere else."

The dragon glared at him with six red-on-yellow eyes for a moment, then laughed. It came grating and barking out of three different throats to make one unpleasant sound.

"Go away?" the middle head rasped. "Why should we go away? Do you know who we are?

"We are Zmey Gorynych, the great serpent!" the right head thundered. The dragon lifted itself up on two large back paws, and two smaller front ones

– each with black talons that raked on stone. "Our wings bring darkness!" the left head snarled. The monster unfurled two wings like a bat that plunged the cellar into a deeper gloom. "And our breath is fire!" hissed the middle head, orange flames licking the inside of its mouth. "We have come for this Tsar!" the right head rumbled. "The betrayer! The one who would change our lands!"

Ibrahim wasn't certain what kept him standing. His heart pounded fast. All he wanted to do was run. Somewhere, he found the courage to speak.

"But you're hurting everyone. You're hurting Eva. And I won't let you!" He reached out, and drew his sword. The broad curving blade came at his summons, gleaming gold in the dark as he held it high above his head. He hoped to at least frighten the dragon. But the monster only laughed, wisps of smoke escaping its throats.

"*You* would harm *us*?" the middle head rasped. "*You* would stand against *us*?"

"You are not from these lands," the left head growled.

"Everyone can see you are different," the right thundered. "That you don't belong."

"Look at your skin" the left sneered, "black like soot."

"Your nose is flat, and your hair crisp and tight," the right added.

"You are nothing more than a slave," the middle hissed.

"The Tsar's pet," the right mocked with rumbling laughter.

"The boy who does not even know his own name!" they bellowed as one.

Ibrahim felt himself falter again, and the too-big sword grew heavy in his hands.

"Yes," the middle head rasped. "What is your name boy? Where do you come from? Do you even know?"

"*We* know *our* name," the left head declared. "Zmey Gorynych! How can *you* with no name harm *us*?"

Ibrahim felt his hand tremble with the sword as those words reached inside and pulled at him. Why was it getting so heavy? Before him the dragon seemed to grow even larger, until it was his whole world, and those yellow eyes with red slits looked big enough to fall into.

"Go away little nameless boy, little slave," the three heads boomed together. "You are nobody! You are no one! Run away now, before we open up our jaws and eat you up!"

Ibrahim felt his sword grow too heavy – and he dropped it. The golden blade vanished before it hit the floor and he stumbled back. Before him the dragon stalked forward, taunting and laughing. He heard its thoughts in his head, and took them as his own. *Slave. No One. Nameless.* How could he fight this monster if he didn't even know his name?

"Bring back your sword!" someone pleaded.

Ibrahim looked to Domovoi. The house spirit cowered behind him but surprisingly hadn't run away.

"I can't," he stammered. He had stopped moving, too frightened now to do anything but stand there, and wait for the dragon. "I don't have a name. I'm just a slave. A boy who was stolen away. I don't even know who I am."

"But I know who you are!" Domovoi insisted. "You told me. You're the boy who comes from a faraway place. You're the boy who saved a sultan. You fought an ogre! You're the boy who came here from all the way across a sea. You're the boy sent to hunt mice for the Tsar. You're the boy who talks to spirits and carries a great golden sword...!"

Ibrahim listened as the talkative spirit told his tale. Had all of that happened to him? Had he really done all those things? He listened, and the words began to drown out the taunting laughter. Soon they were on his tongue and coming from his own lips. He felt the fear that made him numb ease away. Doubt shriveled inside him as his courage returned, filling up the emptiness. And he pulled his sword.

The blade came at his call, settling into his hands and almost singing with anticipation. He stared up at the dragon that now hovered in front him, so big it seemed to take up the entire cellar. It still laughed and sent its taunts. But Ibrahim was no longer listening.

With a yell, he lifted his sword at the head closest to him and brought it down with all his strength upon those scales. The blade bit through spirit flesh and bone to come clean through the other side. The dragon's neck wobbled momentarily where he had cut it and then the horned head slid away. It tumbled down, landing with a thunderous thud on the cellar floor. Those red-on-yellow eyes were turned up with a look of surprise and a long red tongue hung from its open mouth. The remaining heads howled their pain, and Ibrahim smiled. Sword in hand, he stepped forward.

"I am the boy who was stolen!" he cried out, swinging again at a paw sent his way. It came off beneath his blade, talons and all tumbling into the darkness.

"I am the boy who chopped off the ogre's head!" Another head roared at him with jaws opened wide, showing a hundred teeth. Ibrahim jumped as it came, bringing his sword down to cut through its thick neck. The head fell away and the dragon retreated now, as if to run. But Ibrahim wasn't finished.

"I am the boy who saw the Sultan cry!" he shouted. The dragon's last head sucked in air and then spewed a blast of bright orange flame at him that lit up the dark. Ibrahim dodged beneath the fire, feeling its heat on his back as he raced to hack off another paw. The dragon lurched off balance, pitching forward. Ibrahim jumped aside as it came crashing down in a heavy mass of green scales and spirit flesh. He quickly moved back in, bracing a foot on the dragon's neck and lifting his giant blade up above the remaining head.

"I am the boy with the golden sword!" Ibrahim proclaimed, as the red slit in that yellow eye stared up at him – afraid. "Today, I will be the boy who cut all the heads off the great Zmey Gorynych!" And with a final swipe he sent his blade through that scaly neck, until it struck stone – severing the last head of the dragon. Its monstrous body shuddered with tremors, and its wings folded in to cover it like a shroud. With a loud whoosh, it vanished into a green mist that swirled away to nothingness.

Ibrahim looked down, breathing heavy from the battle. Where the dragon had been there was now a tiny pale worm – with three tiny heads. It let out a squeal and began inching away. He brought a heel down on it, mashing hard and squishing out colorful goo that smeared the ground like a rainbow.

"You killed the dragon!" Domovoi yipped, jumping up and down in delight.

Ibrahim smiled. So he had.

It was later in the day that Ibrahim sat in the kitchens eating a pastry prepared by Eva's grandmother. The old woman was happy her daughter's fever had unexpectedly broken. She couldn't know he had anything to do with it, but she was giving out pastries all the same. These had cheese and sweet fruit jam in the middle.

The Tsar felt better as well, and was now eating so much food the cooks were kept busy preparing one meal after another. The Likho was gone from his back. Ibrahim had seen it shuffling through the halls – now a small, scrawny old woman with bony limbs and one big eye. It had glared at him but he waved his sword and the thing shrieked, fleeing the house. The gloom in the place had lifted and Domovoi claimed the other spirits were already returning, all of them talking about the strange new boy with the big golden sword.

As he sat eating, Spafarius No-Nose appeared. The man approached and sat down. He looked somewhat pleased and his white whiskers twitched as he eyed Ibrahim.

"So...did you catch your mouse?" he asked.

Ibrahim shoved a pastry whole into his mouth before answering.

"A worm," he replied.

Art by Patrick Thicklin

THE SHIP THAT BRINGS YOU HOME
CAMILLA ZHANG

1855
Chincha Islands, Peru

Before the living can even see it, they smell it: droppings from millions of birds piled over centuries on a treeless island. The stench is alien for Huang Achai. Even after months of breathing air polluted by salt, excrement, sweat, and death, his nostrils have never been so brutalized. From the hold, all he can do is look up and see bright strips of sky sear through the deck's floorboards.

Hope bucks beneath his feet. Achai and the other captives stand so close together that they sway like blades of grass in a breeze. Achai daydreams of such pleasantries, about visiting Keyuan in Boxia with his younger sister. He'd bribed a guard to let them in after saving a year's worth of apprentice wages from their father's shop. The memory of lavish ferns, blossoming trees, and ornate pavilions closes in on itself, like a morning glory bidding goodbye to the sun.

Achai would cry, but his tears were spent during the second week at sea, when he realized there was no chance of escape. To forget his despair, he thought of Yubing, the cousin who betrayed him into bondage – all to inherit the family afterlife shop. He'd lied to Achai about arranging a meeting between him and his betrothed, .

During the new moon of the Spring Festival, Achai waited for Huajing in front of Guangxiao Temple. Imagining the scent of her hair and what she might wear to their rendezvous, Achai did not hear Yubing approach him from behind. As soon as his cousin clamped a foul smelling cloth over his mouth, he lost consciousness.

Achai woke up with his hands and feet bound. He was in a large, stone cell, surrounded by other captives. The next day, they were marched into *Hope*'s hold. Achai yelled and demanded to see his father, who had some influence with the local magistrate. The White men made angry sounds he didn't understand, acting more like wolves than humans. When Achai opened his mouth to speak again, they snapped their whips at him.

In the ship's belly, many sobbed and begged to be let out. The White Wolves dragged one up and tied him to posts. They lashed at him with whips in front of everyone. From then on, no one did anything but whisper. Over the next few days, Achai's heart shriveled with every tear that flowed out in silence. Starving and weak, he mumbled a prayer for his family, that his sister was alright, that Yubing would at least care for his parents.

After ten days in the hold, Achai stopped praying. He could only listen.

In one corner were men who didn't seem so miserable. They had volunteered to be placed on this ship. They talked about how the gold mines of America would make them kings, that it would be worth suffering the shackles around their feet. Some of the men were soldiers, merchants, doctors, and scholars. One was even a small government official who complained about not being treated according to his rank. He was whipped after asking for water.

At first, the hold had been so tight one had to pee standing in place. Then, cholera claimed nearly a third of them. Every time a man collapsed dead, Achai would see a light mist hang about the body until it was thrown into the ocean without any funeral rites. Achai can still remember the wailings of their ghosts, lost, forever at sea and never at peace. He prayed for them to come back, to haunt the ship and kill the captain, but without gold spirit money for the Jade Emperor, a living man could not tear a ghost away from its old body.

Achai had longed for land. Now, he just hopes that they pass this foreign stench as quickly as possible. Above, he hears boots clomping on the deck and the crew calling to each other. Seagulls caw, but there is a louder sound, like babies giggling, only fast and manic. It is the tittering he imagines a small demon might make. The smell is overpowering now and Achai realizes that the true curse on his life is about to begin.

Hope slows as it approaches the docks and a wide plank is lowered into the hold. The crew starts yelling and motioning the captives to march up. One of them, a farmer called Zhang To-li, reaches the deck and runs to the ship's edge. With his feet shackled, he only makes it five paces before getting dragged back and beaten. The other captives dare not notice.

Achai gazes at the gray-brown cliffs in horror. The sky is overcast, not with clouds, but birds, whose childlike cackles overlap each other to create an endless siren.

A whip tears at Achai's back. He stumbles forward, but dares not fall. The crew member with the lash shouts something like "Ma wu tu!"

Thirty at a time, the captives are made to stand on a giant dock that's been secured to the island's cliffside. The White Wolves who inspect them are tawnier than the ones who caught Achai. They have brown and black hair and coarse mustaches. They wear beige linen and broad hats. They touch and probe the captives with canes and gloved fingers. They point and nod at some of Achai's countrymen. Papers and gold are exchanged. The crew herds Achai and twenty captives towards three large open tents, where more White Wolves are waiting for them. The others are marched back to the ship. Achai longs to follow them into the darkness of *Hope*'s heart.

Shackles clinking heavily around his ankles, he counts fifty paces from the dock to the tents. He wonders how fast he'd be able to run with untethered feet. Beyond the tents are a few blue and red cabins. Further away, near the foot of a gray mountain with rows of stairs carved into its face, are clusters of small, ramshackle hovels.

Under the tents' shade, Achai and the captives receive dirty, coarse tunics, crumbling straw hats, and thin trousers. As the White Wolves inspect him, a scribe stands close scribbling notes. Achai peers at the paper, fighting the urge to steal it. If only he could make some spirit money for *Hope*'s ghosts to move on from this world. It's what his father would have done. Even for farmers who couldn't afford regular spirit money, his father would work extra hours at night to make small, simple ones with just a dab of silver. He would give them away, sometimes for free, sometimes for just two snow peas.

A White wolf, darkened by the sun, and dressed in white linen and a white hat, approaches Achai. He points at him and says, "*Diego*." He repeats it again and points at Achai's chest, then at his mouth, sounding the name again, but slower. Sounds fumble out of Achai's mouth, none of which sound like "*Diego*."

"Mingzhi! *Diego*!" The man says, pointing at Achai, who finally understands.

"De ge?" Achai manages to mimic. The man dismisses him with a hand wave.

Achai is placed into a group of twenty. They are made to line up and follow a tall, muscular man with skin as black as ink. He is over a head taller than Achai and his body is nearly twice as wide. Achai has heard stories of these men, how they were ferocious and dumb, like bulls. After being caged in *Hope* for months, Achai now wonders if perhaps his people and theirs are not so dissimilar.

Achai marches, holding his "new" clothes, a chisel, and a wide brush. The pinching smell of ammonia stirs the water in his eyes. He sees other captive men with cloth tied around their mouths, digging and scraping at the guano-caked cliffs. Some of them look up at the new prisoners. Their eyes are grey and drained. They are phantoms trapped in starved, brittle bodies.

The ink-skinned man stops in front of a cluster of huts. He pushes each captive into a different one. Inside, straw mats cover the dirt floor completely. Achai steps over to one that seems empty and places his belongings down. Just as he is about to sit, the ink-skinned man comes in and bellows at him, yanking his arm hard. The ink-skinned man motions for him to gather his pick and brush. He then takes Achai by the arm the way an angry father might drag a rebellious child along the street.

The same group of twenty men is lined up outside the huts. They all carry the same tools. The ink-skinned man marches them back to the group of laborers they'd passed earlier. The laborers get up silently and approach the new ones. A man of about forty years walks toward Achai. Achai bows a little and introduces himself.

"I'm Yuan Guan," the older man replies and motions for Achai to follow him back to the cliffside. With eyes downcast he continues, "we call this place the Islands of Hell."

***

Achai drags a cart filled with sacks of guano to the docks. His open blisters burn and itch beneath the wooden handles. When he asked an ink-skinned man, Hu-An, for clean bandages, he was struck with the back of his hand. Achai had to tear a strip off his guano-stained shirt to wrap his hands.

Everything on the island is covered in the bird waste. And even his insides sting from the toxic dust.

The sun is beginning to set and Achai rushes, knowing that he needs to bring another load before dark. Dropping the bags down chutes that feed into the ships, he glances at the water below. Bloated, black-veined bodies bob against the shore. Even in death they are bound to this cursed place. Some fleshy blobs have made it to the boats further out, the ones that wait patiently for the guano. American, British, Spanish, they all flock here.

Within the first week of being on the Chinchas, Achai has seen others try to escape onto these boats. They are always brought back and publically tortured before being forced to work again. Yesterday, one of them collapsed into his fresh pile of guano, chisel and brush still in hand. Achai saw his final breath snake out of his mouth and melt into the air.

The only time he saw such cruelty was when Yubing caught a cricket and tore off its legs, one by one. After he pulled the last leg, Yubing watched it bleed out for a half hour. They were five at the time. Only months ago, Achai would have never believed one man could treat another like a cricket, but worse. More like a fly or maggot.

As Achai brings his last load to the docks, a guanay bird lands on his cart. He stares at its red-rimmed eyes, wishing that it and all its brethren would simply fall from the sky, dead. Then there would be no more guano, no more torture. They would get to go home, or at least, someplace better than here.

"There are other roads to freedom," the bird says without opening its long, thin beak. Its voice is syrupy and rich, like custard. Head tilted slightly, its pupils flash a jade light.

Achai flings his hands up in fright and jumps away from the cart. Sacks slide down and one of them opens, spilling precious guano all over the path. The guanay flaps its wings. Its white belly brushes over Achai's head before it takes off to the sky.

Yuan Guan is on his way down the cliff with a cart of his own. He sets it down gently and runs over to Achai. Together they scoop the fecal dust back into the bag with their bare hands. Hu-An spies them and stalks over.

"Hurry, hurry! Tie the bag up!" Yuan Guan stands quickly and waves with a smile at Hu-An. "Bu e ne, bu e ne," he says to Hu-An, who stops and narrows his eyes at them. Hu-An looks at Achai loading the fallen bags back on the cart.

"*No maiz.*" Hu-An spits and walks away. Yuan Guan's smile falls away from his face like a withered leaf. Achai runs to him and starts bowing, his hands clasped together.

"A thousand apologies, Yuan Xiansheng! It's my fault. I will give you my portion tomorrow, so you may have two!"

"Don't be foolish. If you don't eat two days in a row, you'll perish." Yuan Guan looks at the guanay in the sky. "And besides, we will all die here. It makes no difference if you give me your corn." Yuan Guan coughs and spits out greenish phlegm. He walks back to his cart. "Come on, let's go."

That evening, while everyone else is at the canteen, Achai folds one end of his sleeping mat over and draws a cake on the dirt underneath. His stomach heaves sharply. Achai doubles over for a minute, trying to subdue the pain. He straightens his back and looks at his drawing. He reaches over to the other end of the mat and scoops up red flakes: dried blood from tick bites. He sprinkles them over the cake.

Diao Mu, the older boy who sleeps next to Achai, returns to the hut early. He bends down by Achai's drawing and admires it for a while. He reaches into his trousers and takes out a boiled corn cob. He places it onto Achai's mat and smiles at him.

Achai gapes at the reddish kernels and raises his gaze. Diao Mu nods and extends his palm graciously. Achai grabs the corn and eats, barely chewing.

"You've been here only a week and already you're in trouble." Diao Mu's northern accent is strange to Achai. Diao Mu recognizes the confusion on Achai's face. "You need to be more careful," he continues slowly, studying the curve of Achai's lips as he chews.

"How long have you been here?" Achai swallows the last kernel.

"Almost a year now, I think. I can't remember really. Every day feels like an eternity." Diao Mu looks at his brown and callused hands. "Sometimes I wish I would just die. I see it happen to others, but they are usually already sick or weakened." His curved lips do not hide his sorrow. He takes a strand of hair in one hand and examines the greys. "I don't look it, but I'm barely eighteen. I was in the army, very handsome..." Diao Mu's look lingers on Achai, who, in comparison, is cleaner and smoother. "How old are you?"

"Sixteen." Achai looks down at his dirt and blood cake. His stomach lurches.

"Ah...How long is your contract for?"

"I never got a chance to look at it."

"I suppose it doesn't matter. No one survives even the five-year term. Most die within a year. I'm lucky I'm still alive." Diao Mu chuckles bitterly. "Well, not lucky. No one here is lucky."

"Thank you for the corn," Achai looks dumbly at Diao Mu's face, aging prematurely from the sun, light wrinkles filled with dirt, oil, and, no doubt, guano.

"It's fine. Hu-An gives me extra sometimes," Diao Mu cocks his head toward the hut's doorway. "If you give him some of your wages or other gifts, he lets you move a little slower too."

"What wages? Four *bei su* a month? They deduct everything. By the time they're done I have less than nothing."

"As I said, there are other gifts you can give." Diao Mu looks away, "but it's never enough to get even one day's rest. We are merely starved, caged birds with clipped wings."

Achai thinks he sees tears in Diao Mu's eyes, but before he can say anything, Diao Mu rises, blinking rapidly.

"Don't ever let them see you slow down," Diao Mu says softly and walks out of the hut.

***

Achai scrapes the hardened guano. His blisters have healed and callused over. The humidity makes the air viscous, so he takes off the cloth covering his mouth to breathe a little better. His nose is numb to the droppings now, but his lungs hurt all the same. The sunburn on his forearms is starting to peel. It flakes off into the dust pile at his feet. He wonders where his skin will end up, after it's packed with the guano, shipped off to some farm and eaten by worms.

He looks off at the cliffs. Hundreds of his countrymen dot the hand-carved steps and trails, like hungry flies on a rotten peach. The continuous sound of iron hitting and scraping against rock stings his ears. He tries to single out one pick-ax and count the strikes. The dry ground devours Achai's sweat, which dribbles down his limbs in small streams. His lips are cracked and bleeding. He prays that Hu-An will come around with corn water soon. He imagines tart plums to fool his dry tongue. He loses count of the pick-ax.

Achai packs the dust into a sack, seals it tightly, and piles it with five others. It is nearly two in the afternoon and he has another five to pack. He looks up at Yuan Guan, who is a dozen steps higher. He is excavating the newer deposits, in some ways more plentiful, but harder, as they have been baking in the sun for much longer. Yuan Guan only has three sacks and he will still have to have ten by the end of the day.

Yuan Guan coughs loudly into his shirt. Achai sees blood splatter against the browned cloth. Before he realizes that he is staring, the guanay from a month ago flaps his wings against Achai's face, a welcome breeze in an arid place.

"Your Sifu will not last much longer," the bird says without moving its beak.

Achai blinks very hard and opens his eyes again, waiting.

"Don't worry, young one. You are not dreaming." the bird sings, jade eyes flashing again.

"What are you?" Achai reaches a hand out. The bird flaps its wings at him. He falls back.

"Not a what." The bird hops and glares at Achai. "I was a man once. I was the first of us to die here. I've been seeking vengeance for over ten years."

"You're a Yingui.'" Achai feels every urge to run, but remembers he has nowhere to run to. All he can do is shiver in place.

"And even death is no respite. Not for those such as we."

"Why are you talking to me?"

"Because you're the first one to ever be open to our existence. We have had warriors, scholars, and peasants, but you are the first Mouh-si."

"My mother's father was a Mouh-si... He died before I was born. No one taught me."

"It is in your blood. Your family is far, but their reach is here, with you. Let that be some comfort," the bird smiles sadly.

A scream breaks through the day. Achai looks up and sees a man tumbling down a cliff. The scream is filled with rage, as if it wants to punish the gods in some way. The man's bones crunch against the ground and for a second, the picks and scrapes stop. Before a whip can crack, everyone returns to work.

A few months go by. At the canteen, the White Wolves hand out green, mottled, maggot-infested plantains. Achai peels one and is surprised to find the fruit bland, hard, and dry, like ash.

On his way back to the hut, he passes by the barred pig pen where the White Wolves chain those they wish to punish. Every week there is someone in there. Achai once saw three men squeezed together, bound and bleeding, hugging their knees, crying silently.

Achai sees Yuan Guan inside the pen, eyes fixated on the dirt. His shirt is torn and blood runs down his back. His feet are shackled together.

"Sifu! What happened?" Achai holds the bars.

"Don't call me that!" Yuan Guan barks. Achai flinches. Yuan Guan's eyes soften.

"I didn't make my quota today. I was off by two sacks." Yuan Guan looks at the ground and looks up again at Achai. "They will put you in here too if you don't leave soon."

Achai lets go of the bars and walks away, his heart sinking to his stomach.

When he gets back to the hut, he sees Diao Mu tearing a strip of cloth from his own shirt. He looks down at a swollen, purple ankle. Diao Mu is crying and cursing softly.

"The pain will go away." Achai tries to comfort him.

"Pain?" Diao Mu spits out a venomous snicker. "I'm not crying because of the pain. I'm crying because this is the beginning of my slow death. They will make me work on this ankle. It will fester and bloat, and become infected and then I will die in the pig pen. I have seen it happen to others...I'd rather die in battle, hard, and fast...with honor."

With honor. Those last words sounded more like stabs.

Achai does not know what to say, so he lies on his mat and turns away.

At night, Diao Mu inches close to Achai and places an arm over his chest.

"It gets lonely here." Diao Mu whispers despondently. His hand starts to go lower. Achai takes it and brings it up over his heart.

"I know, but sleep is its own blessing. Perhaps we'll dream of our families" Achai lets Diao Mu cusp his body. He has not felt warmth from another since he last hugged his sister almost a half a year ago.

***

The next morning, Achai wakes up to feet brushing against his face. He looks up and yelps. Diao Mu had stripped naked and tied his clothes together to hang himself on the thin rafters of the hut. The roof bends to his weight as Diao Mu releases his last breath. The guanay bird from yesterday titters from one of the beams. Achai starts calling for help.

Hu-An cuts Diao Mu down, annoyed by the inconvenience. In the dark corner of the hut, Achai sees a mist in the shape of a man. It waves at him before walking through the wall.

The sun is especially cruel that day. Most of the birds are at rest, too hot to fly. Achai sees Yuan Guan working on the higher cliffs again. Most of the blood on his shirt has dried, but some patches are freshly wet. Achai climbs up to join him.

They scrape together for a few hours without speaking. Yuan Guan winces every now and then, sucking the air through his rotting teeth.

"I was a teacher in Nantong." Yuan Guan punctures the silence. "It was a very small town and I did not make much." Yuan Guan brushes some dust into a sack. "An old acquaintance told me that a wealthy family in Macao needed a private tutor and that they would pay me in gold. It was a trick. He rowed me to the ships and put a knife to my neck. He forced me to sign a contract."

Yuan Guan looks up at Achai, eyes glistening.

"You are young and strong. You may survive this. If you do, please find my family. Tell them what happened."

Achai stares at Yuan Guan. For a moment he reminds him of his father.

"I will try," Achai says, hesitating with each word.

"Thank you." Yuan Guan looks back at his pile.

The few minutes that pass are thick and seem to stretch forever.

"Some of them are here because they were told they'd be working in America's gold mines. But this shit we collect? It is worth more than gold." Yuan Guan holds a pile of dust in his palm. "I wonder if farmers even know how many lives have been sacrificed for this."

"Those who eat crops from this dust, they are eating our souls." Achai says softly. Yuan Guan looks at him in surprise. Achai looks down and brushes his own pile of guano into a sack. "They are demons and do not even know it."

***

Weeks pass and Yuan Guan's body only weakens. The sun begins to set. Yuan Guan has gone down to the boats with his first load. Achai pushes himself harder to fill his thirteenth sack. Yuan Guan was only able to fill seven. Two guanay circle above Achai, providing some respite from the sun's glare, which is strong even as it settles on the horizon. He hears a light plop against his hat. He ignores the cawing of the guanay, even though anger burns through his cheeks and up to his ears.

"Demon birds," he mutters as he scrapes. They land next to him and he jumps back.

"We are not the demons here, but you knew that already." The jade-eyed one says.

"Achai, you were right. I did dream about my family." The smaller one seems to smile at him. "You know my own father sold me? I was the youngest son, after all. No use to him...and I spent too much time in the Opium dens."

Achai begins to shake.

"Diao Mu?" Achai manages to whisper.

"Yes," the small guanay bobs its head.

"What do you want from me?" Achai leans away from the birds.

"The same thing you want." Diao Mu steps closer to Achai. "To leave this place."

"What can I do? I have no talismans, no spirit money, no extra food to burn, no way to bury all the bodies in the ocean."

"Our contracts." Diao Mu hops closer. "Find them and burn them. We can help you."

"You two?" Achai scoffs. "What can two birds and one boy do?"

"Not just us," The jade-eyed one says, "All of us." Thousands of wings beat against the heavy atmosphere and take to the sky, drowning out the sun. A gun goes off, making the cloud of birds disperse.

Achai feels a slap against the back of his head. Yuan Guan stares at him sternly.

"Do you want to go a day without food again? Stop daydreaming." Yuan Guan's face is pale and sweaty.

"Sorry," Achai says, bowing slightly. He watches as Yuan Guan loads his cart with more sacks. His moves are slow and brittle, like that of an ninety-year-old man.

As Yuan Guan wheels his last load down. He looks like he is about to collapse. Achai rushes over to him.

"Please, let me help you take that down." Achai reaches for the handles of the cart.

"Are you mad? They will think I didn't fulfill my quota today!" Yuan Guan begins to cough uncontrollably, spitting out blood. He falls, gasping for air. Achai calls for help.

An ink-skinned man runs over and pushes Achai away, grabbing Yuan Guan and draping him over his shoulder as if he were a scarf. The ink-skinned man stalks over to the infirmary. Achai tries to follow him, but he holds up his palm and points to Yuan Guan's full cart and then points to the ships waiting in the bay. Achai nods and wheels Yuan Guan's cart to the docks.

***

After a few days, Achai asks around for Yuan Guan, but no one has any news. They shake their heads, saying that the White Wolves never waste any resources to save the likes of them.

"*Tu! No hablar!*" an ink-skinned man snarls. They never want *los Chinos* to talk in groups of three or more. Achai sulks away and back to his post.

Towards the end of the day, when Achai goes back up the cliff to get his last load of guano, three birds land on his cart.

"Yuan Xiansheng?" Achai whispers at the third bird. It has a longer neck than the others.

"Hello, young one." The third bird looks at Achai like his own father would.

"I'm ready for the next step. What do I do?" Achai asks all three.

"You are familiar with curse methods, are you not?" The jade-eyed bird sings.

293

"I don't know how to make talismans."

"There are simpler, more primal ways."

Achai looks to the sky, trying to recall any unusual memories.

"Once, for a whole week, my mother chanted the names of those she hated whenever she used her knife to cut something. Those people fell ill after that"

"The names of the night guards. None but us know them," sings the jade-eyed guanay.

"Say their names when you are chipping or digging at the cliffs." Diao Mu hops angrily.

"Say them for four days," Jade Eyes says, "Right now they wear gold. Only a small piece in their ears, but it is enough that we cannot touch them yet."

"After four days we shall return," Yuan Guan says.

***

"Mei Gui Le." Achai chants and scrapes. "Bei Dou." Scrape. "E Nan Tou." Scrape.

For the first time in months, eighteen hours pass like they are nothing. Achai even feels some strength return to his limbs.

When he takes his sacks down to the ships, he sees a guanay perched on each of the floating bodies in the water. Some of them have washed back ashore. There are guanay on those as well. They all look at him, waiting for a wall to break.

***

On the third day, Achai is just leaving his hut when Hu-An pulls him aside. He motions for him to follow as he walks toward the other end of the island, which is bare and unexcavated.

By the rocky beach, Achai sees a White wolf, the overseer, pacing around a large wooden crate. There is one other young countryman standing around, muttering to himself. It is Chen Fengji. While they share the same age, he has gone mad from the heat and suffering.

Hu-An pushes Achai toward the overseer, who is dressed in white linen and a straw hat.

"*Ah, Diego.*" The overseer scans Achai from head to toe. He gives a crowbar to Hu-An.

"*Juan, ábrelo,*" the overseer points to the crate.

With a creak and snap, Hu-An pries the cover off. Inside are thick, red sticks, larger than the ones Achai's family used to welcome the New Year.

"*Carlos* will show how to place these" the overseer tells Achai in broken Mandarin and points to the un-excavated rock face.

"Here, help me carry this," Fengji says to Achai. Together, they carry the dynamite to the base of the cliff. Splinters dig into Achai's fingers. A guanay follows them overhead. When they set the crate down, Jade Eyes lands and perches on the edge.

294

"As you climb up, take a couple sticks and hide them in your trousers," the bird's voice is calm, but stern.

"Qu! Qu!" Fengji shoos Jade Eyes, who makes no protest.

"You talk to the birds too?" Fengji takes a red bundle out of the crate and hands it to Achai. He then takes out a burlap sash and instructs Achai to wrap the red bundle in it. He ties the sash tightly over Achai's chest.

Fengji takes another bundle in his own hands and begins to unravel it. All the sticks are linked together with long wire.

"I talk to the birds too." He glares at Achai with wild eyes. "They are mean, always making fun of me." Fengji hisses at the ground.

Achai nods in silence. Fengji ties on his own sash and pulls out a red stick.

"You take that side. I will take this. Plant each stick in a deep crevice, like this one," Fengji points to a crack above them. "Make a stair-like pattern," he makes a zigzag shape with his finger.

Achai climbs up the cliff. Steps have not yet been carved into the side. He wishes that he were a monkey. It would be easier to crawl up these boulders. He looks at his hands and cannot recognize them. They look like an old man's, wrinkled and thin. His fingers are damp with sweat, but the guano gives the rocks a dry grip.

As he plants each red stick, he chants the names of the night guards. The higher he climbs, the thinner the atmosphere gets. His chest aches for more oxygen. His muscles shake and his feet begin to slip, but he does not look down. He hears the guanay cackling overhead. Once they sounded like demons, but now they are like the battlecries of heroes. Achai's limbs become lighter and springier. He pushes on.

When he has two pieces of dynamite left, he stops at a sloped area, where he can lean his body forward without falling. He rubs the wire against a sharp boulder, severing it. He tucks the red sticks into his underwear and begins to descend.

Fengji is already scrambling down the cliff, like a mountain goat. Achai carefully and slowly tries to retrace his path. The sun hits his head like a thousand bright arrows. He fights the urge to faint, heart knocking against his chest like a woodpecker. He looks up at the cloudless sky and squints, feeling his dry, burned skin stretch away from his ears.

The jade-eyed guanay flies under the sun. A cool breeze picks up, making Achai more alert and awake. He reaches the base of the cliff a few minutes after Fengji, who is running toward the overseer and Hu-An. The overseer motions Achai to hurry back. He jumps from a small precipice and begins to run. With each stride he mutters a night guard's name. He finally makes it back to the overseer, who holds a small red box with a lever sprouting out the top.

"Watch how we make heaven tremble," the overseer says in heavily accented Mandarin. He smirks at Achai and pushes the lever down.

The cliffside explodes in a cloud of guano dust and gunpowder. Broken boulders fly into the air. A high ringing pulsates in Achai's ears. He can hear nothing else. Fumes burn through his lungs as he coughs under his shirt. The back of his tongue tastes like mercury. The overseer laughs with an open jaw, as if he is about to eat everyone.

Hu-An motions Fengji and Achai to follow him back toward the huts. Another ink-skinned man is leading a large group of countrymen toward them. Hu-An and Fengji stare at the new faces, most likely just off a ship like *Hope*. Only fresh *coolies* have shackles around their feet. They don't know yet that the entire island is a shackle. Hu-An pushes Achai and Fengji toward the tool shed, where pick-axes lie in a large, tangled pile.

With the crowd, marching back to the newly demolished cliffside takes twice as long as it did the first time. Achai spends the rest of the day breaking steps into the side of the cliff. With each strike of the pick-ax, he chants the names. The dynamite in his trousers grates against his flesh and hangs heavily. Every now and then he has to adjust his waistband to ensure no one sees what he has.

***

On the fourth day, the night guards, *Miguel, Pedro*, and *Ernesto*, get ear infections and need to take out their golden studs. The guanay perch on the hut rooftops, waiting for the moon to rise. *Miguel, Pedro,* and *Ernesto* take their posts. The full moon reaches its peak and the guanay descend upon the guards, pecking out their eyes.

Achai wakes up to the sounds of supplicant shrieks. He runs out of the hut, the guanay are everywhere, but only the guards are screaming. Everyone else stands around, watching, unsure of what to do. Achai does not hesitate. He runs toward the canteen.

When he arrives, the main camp is in ruin. Huge, empty pots are overturned. Sacks of corn and yams are torn and spilling out. Some ink-skinned men are trying to whip the guanay back. A few White Wolves are shooting at the birds and cursing loudly in their crude tongue. No one notices Achai make his way into the overseer's office.

Inside, it is calm, as if the large hut is protected. An oil lamp glows on a desk, which is flanked by two cabinets. Achai scampers over to one and opens a drawer. Inside are hundreds of papers. Achai pulls one out. White wolf scrawls cover the paper like squirming lice. At the very bottom is a name he recognizes: Yuan Guan. Next to it is a golden seal embossed with a shield and crown.

Achai plants one stick of dynamite in each cabinet. They are still connected to each other by a long strand of wire. He takes the shade off the oil lamp and lights the wire in the middle. Dropping the lamp, he sprints out of the hut. Flames engulf the desk and the hut walls.

He runs for his life, past all the White Wolves and the ink-skinned men and the guanay. An explosion bursts from behind him. It is not large like the one from the cliffs, but it pushes him forward. Smoke and ash grab at him. His eyes begin to pinch. The White Wolves shout. Achai runs toward the shoreline, hoping to swim away from the island. Perhaps he can be a stowaway on one of the distant ships.

He hasn't been this close to the ocean since he left *Hope*'s hold. The salt air cleanses his lungs and leaves a sweet tang in the back of his throat. It's refreshing, almost delightful. Just as he reaches the rocky beach, a small shard of metal punctures his back. The breath is sucked out of his body. Falling on his face, Achai's cheekbones crack against a rock. Another piece of metal burrows into his neck, leaving him cold as winter.

His body is pinned to the ground, but he feels the lightness of Gravity's release. His soul begins to rise. He looks at the moon, which grows bigger and bigger, and while he no longer has a mouth, he smiles. He is pure peace, like a light summer breeze whistling through thick, glossy green leaves. He looks down and sees his own body. The White Wolves have surrounded it. They are kicking it and yelling, but they cannot touch him. Achai is free and bright with hope.

Achai looks at the clifftops. The guanay are all in flight. They look at him and sing, not with the tittering of birds but the voices of men. Silver ghosts float out of the feathered bodies and up to the clouds. The jade-eyed guanay flies close to Achai. It smiles. A spirit seeps out of its wings and its eyes flicker from jade to black. The birds fly back towards the island. Achai and the other spirits rise to the moon, merging to form a silvery ship.

All the white pinpricks of light in the night sky begin to swirl together. The Jade Emperor takes shape. Robed in shimmering crimson and gold, he is bigger than any mountain, as big as a planet. He takes the ghost ship in his hands and brings it up to his long, luxuriant, black beard. Smiling, his lips lets out a soft breath. Arced streaks of light envelop the ship as it moves across the world.

The moon slips under the horizon like a child under a blanket. Achai turns around to see the sun swell and warm his spirit. Below the ship is a shape he recognizes. Before his sister was born, his mother's older brother had taken him to a Westerner's exhibition. His uncle pointed to a map and ran his fingers around a border, telling him, "This is our nation. Look how big it is!"

The ship begins to lose its shape, scattering into thousands of individual ghosts. Achai waves at Yuan Guan and Diao Mu. They smile, bow slightly in thanks, and descend to the land below, fading like stars against the dawn. Achai lets the pull of the living world take him down. He sees Keyuan from above. It's a bright afternoon in fall. The leaves are turning orange and red. The mid-autumn festival will take over the city soon. He traces familiar streets, passing by food vendors. The savory, starchy steam that rises from large pots filled with rice porridge makes him ache with nostalgia. He wonders if he will ever taste again.

There, next to the mortuary is the family afterlife shop. Doors that used to be gray and chipped are now a newly painted light slate blue. On either side are wreaths of white and yellow chrysanthemums for sale. Above, on the store sign is his family's name, Huang. Pride and relief radiate through him. He floats above a threshold he's stepped over, even tripped over, so many times, times that now, could never be enough.

Inside, the shelves are lined with paper models of clothes, shoes, houses filled with furniture, palanquins, and other items the dead might want. There are replicas of gold and silver ingots and varieties of ghost money. Behind the counter, his father is teaching his twelve-year-old sister how to make gold spirit money. His hair has gone a chalky white and puffy pouches hang under his eyes. His sister has grown a few inches. She looks solemn, but healthy with thick, jet-black braids that drape down her neck.

His sister paints a thin coat of gold on bamboo paper, making sure the lines are smooth and perfect. She finishes and adds it to the row of gold spirit money drying in front of her. She plucks one from the other end of the row and picks up her black brush. She begins inscribing symbols for things the dead need in the afterlife: shoes, clothes, chopsticks, and the like.

His father and sister are standing in front of the door to the back office and workshop. On the mantel above them, Achai sees a tintype photo of himself. It had been taken on his sixteenth birthday, just months before he was abducted. Smoky sandalwood incense burns in front of what used to be his carefree brown eyes. Next to the incense is a bowl filled with bright, fragrant oranges, his favorite fruit. Achai floats closer. His sister glances up from her work and seems to recognize him. She stares for a long time.

"Awei," their father says, "are you alright?" Tears veil over her eyes. It has been too long since anyone looked at Achai with love. She opens a drawer and takes out a box of matches.

"What are you doing?" His father tries to grab his sister's hands, but she pulls away and lights the match, bringing its flame to the spirit money with the finished symbols.

"Goodbye, Daaih-lou. Look for the food offering tonight," she whispers. Achai, still invisible to his father, feels his form taking the shape of a man. New clothes and shoes wrap around his body. He puts needle, thread, chopsticks, and scissors into his pockets. Tears skim down to his sister's chin.

"Take care, Sai-mui." He hugs her goodbye. He looks to his stunned father, who is still gaping at his sister.

"Bah, goodbye." Achai puts a wispy hand on his father's shoulders and walks through the door to the back office.

His mother is sitting at the writing desk, filling in a ledger. She is about to make some calculations on the abacus in front of her. As he approaches, she looks up, gasps, and stands abruptly, knocking over her chair with a hollow clatter. His mother's eyes are wide and her mouth hangs open.

"Mah, leave the shop to Awei." Achai smiles and cups her cheek. "I'll make sure Yubing never touches what's ours." His mother lifts her hands and tries to hold him, but Achai is already dissolving, like the scent of jasmine on the wind.

Art by Anna D'Amico

FEAR OF THE DARK
DE ANA JONES

1920
South Central, Los Angeles, CA, USA

She woke to the waning sunlight and immediately shot out of bed to turn on the lamp in the corner of her room. She was glad she'd woken up when she did, because as she went to the window to close the curtains, the last of the orange light left the sky and the small yard behind the house was swallowed by the night. She shuddered as she saw the shadows outside of her window shift and bend, some scurrying across the yard while others flew off into the sky. Lisette told herself that those shadows were not monsters, that if she shined her light in the back she would see mice and owls playing in the dark.

Except there was that shadow.

In the middle of the yard was a shadow that was out of place. With all the scurrying in the dark the stillness of this shadow seemed odd, and slowly, what started off as a still spot in the moving darkness became a silhouette. Lisette watched as the figure began to form a face about where its head should be. Its eyes searched around the yard, looking over the scurrying shadows which made Lisette let out a little squeak. Instantly the eyes were on her and the shadowy figure opened up a grotesque black hole of a mouth.

"Lisette!" Momma called from in the living room. Lisette closed the curtains quickly and swallowed, hoping it would push her heartbeat back down into her chest. "Lisette come say 'hi' to Anita!"

A few moments passed before Lisette could remember who Anita was. She was the babysitter Momma had been talking about for weeks. She was going to be watching her and her sister tonight while Momma went out to see some musician from back home in Louisiana. He played Jazz, and Momma always said there wasn't any good Jazz music in California. Naw, momma always said you had to be in New York or New Orleans for that. Momma had lived in both places, but she said she preferred right here with her girls over any of those haughty places.

Lisette stood silently in the door frame on one side of her mother's room. On the other side of her mother's room was another open door that led to the living room where her mother, her sister and the new babysitter stood, three smiling figures bathed in light. Momma was a tall light-skinned woman, with hair that she kept straightened and pinned down close to her scalp. She stood poised in the living room, with one of her kitten-heeled feet angled outward. She wore a short dress that stopped high above her knees and was speckled with glittery gold colored fringe. The lamplight reflected off the fringe of the dress, making her look to Lisette like she was wearing the stars. Her sister,

Rosette was dark brown like her and wore sun yellow pajamas with her hair braided into tight cornrows like her own. There in the living room, that was where she wanted to be. However, darkness filled her mother's room, and without her sister near her the darkness frightened Lisette.

She opened her mouth to call her mother and her sister then shut it quickly when she thought she saw a flicker of movement out of the corner of her eye. She kept her eyes straight ahead towards the other side of her mother's room, afraid that if she looked into the darkness she'd see that shadowy face staring back at her. Lisette peered at the thin strips of light reflected off the floor that connected one of the doors of her mother's room to the other, not daring to look further into the room to her left, for fear of what she might see there. Instead she focused on how she would have to travel in the little path of light to get to the safety of her mother and sister.

There were two beams of light on the floor, one coming from the lamp in her room behind her, and the other coming from the living room. In the light she could see the swirled pattern on the wood floor from where Momma had washed and waxed it. She followed one of the swirls with her eyes as it looped back and forth, then suddenly vanished into the black shadowed space on the floor where the strips of light didn't touch. She shuddered followed with her eyes again up the one beam until she came to the spot where the two beams came to a point near her mother's closet to her right. If she kept in the light she would be safe, none of the scary things could catch her as long as she stayed away from the pyramid of darkness. She took a deep breath and after her mother called her again she began the tightrope walk in the light towards the other side.

Left foot. Right foot. One in front of the other she followed path of light until it became too thin for her feet to fit. She paused there on one foot, trying to decide if she could take another step or risk jumping across the darkness to the other strip of light. If she jumped and landed too early, she'd be momentarily in the dark. The thought of one of the monsters grabbing her made Lisette shiver, but she couldn't walk any further. She had to jump.

Lisette set both her feet back on the ground and bent her knees. After a quick beat she pushed herself off the ground and jumped as high and as hard into the air as she possibly could. As she reached the apex of her flight, Lisette felt something wrap around her ankle and before she knew it she fell onto her stomach into the shadow, just before the beam of light she'd been desperately trying to reach.

Lisette opened her mouth to scream but felt the air rush out of her as she hit the floor. For a quick moment she stared at the light in front of her, just out of her reach then down at herself drenched in shadows. Then she took a deep breath and let out a shrill scream.

"Hey girl!" She heard, then felt the grip on her ankle loosen. She looked back just in time to see a shadow bearing down on her and Lisette screamed even harder, kicking wildly at it.

"Hey girl, hush all that noise!" The shadow enveloped her, grabbing her around her waist, lifting her high off the ground and carrying her into the living room. Into the light. "I was just tryin' to scare you a little bit, you don't need to keep screamin'."

"Bobby!" Lisette's mother rushed to her and grabbed her out of the shadow's grip. Lisette clung desperately to her mother for a few moments, sobbing into her shoulder, thankful that the darkness didn't get her. When she finally calmed down she looked at the others in the room. She saw no shadow, only her mother, her sister, the new babysitter and her mother's boyfriend Bobby. They all looked back at Lisette with concern, except for Bobby. He looked worried.

"She's so scary," Bobby said, trying to brush Lisette's tiny footprints off of his dress shirt and leaning on the doorframe. He, like Momma, was dressed to the nines in pale-blue-and-now-footprint-stained dress shirt, dark grey slacks and dark suspenders. "I was only tryin' to scare her a little."

"Well you scared her a lot," Momma replied. "And I don't like when you frighten her like that."

Bobby dropped his head and when he lifted it again he smiled and held up his hands. He looked at Lisette, hands still in the air and apologized for scaring her. Lisette smiled — she could never say mad at Bobby too long, after all he was her boogeyman chaser when she needed him — and once she had calmed down a little more Momma sat her down on the floor.

"Lisette this is Anita." Momma said politely. "She's going to watch you and Rosette while Bobby and I go out tonight."

Lisette wiped the last of the tears from her eyes and looked at Anita. She was an older girl, not quite an adult as far as Lisette could tell, but close to it. Her skin was a medium brown, but still darker than her mother's, and she had dark black hair that came just past her shoulders in two braids that were fastened with bows.

Remembering her manners Lisette pulled her lips back into a weak smile and said "Hello, Miss Anita" so that her mother wouldn't be embarrassed. Anita grinned and said hello back to the girl before turning her attention back to her mother. Lisette then quickly searched the room to find her sister. She wasn't planning on being too far away from Rosette tonight.

"Don't let them stay up too late," Momma said. "If anything happens, Mrs. Parker next door has a telephone. You can call the drugstore on Central. Let me give you the extension."

Lisette watched quietly as her mother looked about the room for a pen and paper, all the while rambling instructions to Anita. After she'd found her pen and a spare scrap of paper she looked apologetically at the babysitter.

"I'm sorry," Momma said. "I'm not sure if you know, but Kid Ory is in town. I'm so excited to see him. I want to show Bobby what real Jazz music sounds like, and Ory is the bee's knees."

As Momma wrote down the extension, Lisette felt a tap on her shoulder. She quickly spun around and found herself face-to-face with Bobby, who had knelt down to speak to her.

"I didn't mean to scare you that bad, Liz." Bobby said. "Remember kid, all them shadows ain't really nothing, and you ain't gotta be scared of nothing in this house." He winked "Besides, you know I already chased all the bad things away anyway. I'm your boogeyman killer."

Bobby stood and grabbed his and Momma's coats as Momma came over and quickly kissed both the girls on their cheeks and said her goodbyes.

"You girls be dolls tonight, understand?" She said as they both made their way out the door. "And Anita please, don't let them leave the lights on all night!"

***

The three of them stayed up for a few hours doing various activities in the small living room. The girls liked Anita, because she knew a lot of games and asked them questions about how to and not to use things in the house unlike the other babysitters who just assumed that because they were little they didn't understand. At one point in the night, the three of them stood staring at Momma's gramophone. Momma's talk about Jazz had made all three of them curious, but the girls weren't allowed to touch the expensive machine and Anita wasn't sure how to work it, so instead they gently looked over Momma's records until they got bored with that too. Now they sat in the living room.

"Do you two want to play another game?" Anita asked.

Lisette drew in a long yawn and slumped onto her sister's shoulder on the couch. Rosette let out a quick snore, then jerked as the sound woke her up. Anita laughed at the two of them as she stood and began to walk over towards the floor lamp in the corner of the room.

"No, it looks as if it's lights out for you two."

Lisette sprang up, back rigid as she looked back and forth between the lamp, her sister and the babysitter.

"Please don't turn the lights off!"

Anita paused and for a moment Lisette was worried that she would ignore her plea and turn off the light anyway, but instead Anita turned her attention back to the girl.

"You're afraid of the dark?" Anita asked and Lisette nodded, looking down at her feet dangling off the side of the couch.

"She's a chicken." Rosette spoke up, rubbing her eye with one hand and stretching one long, thin, dark brown arm into the sky.

"No, I ain't!" was all Lisette could say back.

"Why are you scared of the dark?" When Lisette looked up, she saw that Anita had moved away from the lamp and had come closer to her.

"There are monsters," Lisette responded, looking down at her feet again. "In the shadows."

"Who told you that?"

"I seen 'em"

"You ain't seen nothing" Rosette piped up again. "Anyway we don't have to worry about the monsters, Lisette. We can make light!"

"Make light?" The babysitter raised her eyebrows and smiled in that way adults do when you ask them to play a game. Lisette knew she and her sister now had Anita's full attention. She smiled and looked up at the babysitter and nodded.

"Do you know any hand games?"

Anita shook her head.

The two girls shifted on the couch so they faced each other. Rosette held her hands out first, her palms facing each other and her fingers pointed straight at her twin. Lisette placed one hand between both of Rosette's and the other on the outside. They sandwiched their hands together and when they slid them apart, each pulling their hands towards their own body, the air buzzed around. They both clapped their own hands together and what started as a buzz became an explosion of energy around them. The whole room seemed to radiate with warmth and as they began to clap their hands together again and again the energy and warmth seemed to focus itself between them, just above their tiny hands.

Clap. Clap. Clap-clap. Clap. The more steady the rhythm went the heavier the buzz, until finally a small ball of light formed between the two girls. They clapped harder and faster and the light grew brighter.

Anita gasped, and Rosette missed one of the claps. The loss of rhythm made the light dim. Another missed clap and the light got even dimmer until finally Rosette became frustrated and stopped clapping all together. The ball of light disappeared, and the buzzing energy that radiated from it and the two girls stopped just as quickly, leaving an empty, quiet space in it's stead. Anita stared at the girls in disbelief, and Lisette looked down at her feet again. This was usually why the other babysitters left.

"That was beautiful." Anita said. "Where did you learn to do that?"

"We just do." Rosette responded. "We've always done it."

Anita kneeled quietly in her space in front of the couch. Lisette watched as her eyebrows furrowed and unfurrowed as if she was thinking about something very important, but hadn't thought of the words. Finally Anita spoke up and asked, "What do you use it for?"

"The monsters don't like light." Lisette responded.

Rosette let out an exasperated sigh, "There are no monsters," she said. "It's just fun."

"Can you do it with anyone else, besides each other?"

The two girls looked at one another, then back at Anita. Rosette shrugged, and Lisette looked back down at her dangling feet.

"Have you ever tried?"

They both shook their heads.

Anita held out both of her hands to Lisette and waited for the girl to sandwich hers in between her palms.

"If we're going to keep the monsters away, you're going to need someone else to be able to help you make light."

***

After much trying, they didn't have any luck. They'd tried going as fast as they could, as slow as they could. They tried adding rhymes and riddles but to no avail. No matter how hard they tried, Anita couldn't make the ball of light with either of the girls. They found that after a while, if the girls made a strong enough light it wouldn't fade when they stopped clapping, and as long as the two stayed close to one another the light would shine bright and steady. If they got too far away from one another the light would slowly fade. Anita could even keep the light near her with no problem as long as both the girls were near, but she couldn't help make it.

"What does it feel like?" Anita asked as the three of them sat around the last light the girls had made.

"Bees." Rosette said.

"A lot of bees. Crawling from my chest to my fingers."

"Does it hurt?"

The two girls looked at each other and shook their heads.

Anita sighed and reached out for the glowing ball and touched it with the tip of her fingers. She smiled and looked at the girls.

"It doesn't feel like bees at all. It feels like - " She stopped as if she couldn't quite think of the words she wanted to say. Rosette laughed.

"I've never touched it before!" She said reaching her hand out.

"You said it felt like bees," Anita responded.

"That's what it feels like to MAKE it, not to touch it." Rosette let her fingertips touch the glowing ball and smiled a wide and bright smile. "It feels like being wrapped in a blanket at Christmas."

Lisette looked skeptically at Rosette out of the corner of her eye, but when she turned to look at her babysitter, Anita was nodding and hummed a small "yeah" in agreement. Lisette reached out herself then, and when her fingertips hit the tiny sun she smiled as well.

"It feels when Momma makes dinner for us." She said. "Or like when Bobby goes outside to scare away the Boogeyman."

"It feels," Anita finally added. "It feels safe."

Finally all three of them became too tired to play with the ball of light anymore and Anita insisted on shuffling them off to bed. At her insistence the ball faded slowly.

"Come on," Anita said after their last frustrating attempt. "We better get to sleep before your mother gets home."

Lisette watched Anita get up and begin to walk towards the lamp before pausing and turning to look at her. Anita smiled at the girl.

"Let's get you in your room first before I turn off the lights in here." She said.

Lisette and Rosette got up from their spots on the couch and filed behind Anita like two little ducks, but when they got to the entrance to their mother's room, Lisette grabbed hold of Anita's dress before she could walk in.

"Wait!" Lisette yelled. "You can't go in the dark either! You're not a grown up!"

Anita paused, then held out a hand for the girl to take hold of.

"Hold my hand tight, ok?" Anita said to Lisette. "Rosette you get her other hand, that way if anything grabs one of us, the other two will be able to pull us back to the light."

"I'm not scared!" Rosette responded and crossed her arms, refusing to take her sister's hand.

Anita frowned at Rosette, but said no more. Instead she tightened her grip on Lisette's hand then turned and took her first step into the room.

Lisette closed her eyes tightly in fear and only moved forward when she felt Anita gently pull her forward. She took one step, then another, expecting to feel the grip of the shadow monsters around her ankle at each step. After a few steps she felt a rush of wind to her right and heard something scuttle quickly past her. She yelped and closed her eyes tighter, only feeling calmer when she felt her sister grab hold of her empty hand.

Lisette knew they had reached the other end of the room when she could see the light from her room through her eyelids. She relaxed and opened her eyes to see her sister and Anita staring wide eyed at her. It was then that Lisette realized that she wasn't holding onto her sister's hand. Slowly she turned and found herself staring into the bright white eyes of a grinning shadow monster.

Before she could scream, Anita yanked the girl all the way into the light of the room. The shadow monster let go of the girl and stood at the edge of the light, staring at the three of them. It was a blob of inky black, but not shiny like liquid. It was a black cloud, a floating shape just barely noticeable in the dark, with bright white eyes and menacingly sharp white teeth. While it said nothing, it's mouth moved at the three, sending threats and curses in the silence.

"It's ugly!" Rosette yelped. "Keep it away!"

The monster looked at Rosette and mouthed it's silent curses at her. Slowly, the darkness of their mother's room began to creep into theirs, and the shadow monster moved slowly forward with it. Anita pushed the younger girls behind her.

Inch by inch the shadow creeped into the room, and inch by inch the girls backed towards the lamp until finally there was nothing but the wall behind them and the floor lamp next to them. Anita reached out, and grabbed the long stem of the lamp and held it out in front of her towards the shadow. It moved it's silent mouth again, more violently this time than before and the light of the lamp flickered and died out. There was a loud crash as the lamp hit the floor and the girls felt a rush of air. Lisette screamed and clung to her sister who clung on just as hard.

After a moment Lisette called for their babysitter, but heard no response. Then, remembering what happened in her mother's room Lisette looked at her sister.

"Rosette, is that you?"

"Yeah, are you, you?"

Lisette nodded, then whimpered out a yes when she realized her sister couldn't see her.

The two sat in silence, waiting for the shadow monster to attack again. In the dark Lisette felt invisible hands grab at her ankles and her arms, and she gripped tighter to her sister scared afraid that she might get dragged away too.

"Anita!" Rosette called this time. "Anita where are you?"

"She's in the dark." Lisette responded. "They Shadow Monster got her."

"She has to come back!" Rosette cried.

"She can't, she doesn't know how to make light!" Lisette responded.

"Then we have to go get her," Rosette said. "Momma's gonna be real mad if she comes back and nobody is here."

Rosette made a motion to stand but Lisette grabbed her arm and pulled her back onto the ground. After a moment, Lisette took another deep breath and grabbed her sister's hands, sandwiching them between hers. As they slid them apart, Lisette felt the air buzz between them and watched the little ball of light grow with the rhythm of their hands. As light slowly began to fill the dark room, Lisette felt her fear slowly melt away and after a short while they had a full little sun between them. Her sister was right, as long as they could make light they had no reason to be scared.

When they were certain it was strong enough the girls stood and looked about them in the room as the ball of light hovered between them. Inside their radius of light the two of them were almost glowing in their yellow pajamas. Outside of their light was nothing but shadow and Lisette was glad after looking around to find that these were normal grey shadows, not the unbreakable blackness of the Shadow Monster. All except for the doorway, which seemed like a dark and still square on the other side of the room.

Lisette could feel her sister shiver next to her, and reached out a hand and grabbed her twin's.

"Momma said if we needed anything we should use Mrs. Parker's phone next door." Lisette told her sister. "If we can get next door we can call Momma and she can help us find Anita."

"But we don't know the extension!" Rosette replied. "Momma wrote it down but it's all the way in the living room."

The two girls looked at the unbreakable shadow in the doorway and shuddered. Lisette reached out and grabbed her sister's hand.

"We'll hold hands like Anita said," Lisette said. "That way it can't get us."

As the two girls walked towards the doorway Lisette tried her best to see into her mother's room but only succeeded in seeing the matte inky blackness. When they entered the room the darkness pressed against the light that surrounded the two girls. Lisette could feel the pressure of it but when she looked over her shoulder, hoping to escape back into the grey of her room she saw that the still shadows had now filled that up to.

"Look!" Lisette felt her sister tugging at her hand. "Anita's on the bed!"

Lisette looked toward the deeper part of the room, off to the left, where earlier she'd be so afraid of the normal grey shadows. Sure enough, a body lay on her mother's bed, on it's side. Rosette held on to her sister as she walked closer to the body, pulling Lissette with her.

"Wait!" Lisette tried to stop her sister, but Rosette already had her momentum up and if Lisette stopped walking, she could find herself out of the safety of their little sun. "What if it's not Anita."

"Of course it's Anita." Rosette responded. "Who else could it be?"

The idea of the Shadow Monster laying in her mother's bed flashed across Lisette's mind. In a panic she dug her bare heels into the floor and pulled her arm back as hard as she could. Rosette was unwavered, and quickly slipped her hand from her sister's grasp and walked out of the safety of the light towards the bed. Lisette stifled a scream when her sister slipped into the darkness, and watched as Rosette's silhouette climbed onto the bed and searched around. After a moment, Lisette heard her sister let out a disappointed huff.

"They're just clothes." Rosette whined. "Momma brought in the wash–"
There was silence.

Lisette squinted hard at the darkness trying and see what happened. Instead of the silhouette of her sister sitting on the bed, Lisette saw what still looked like a human shaped shadow laying on the bed, only now there was a child sized hole in the middle.

"Rosette?" Lisette called out towards the bed but heard no response. Slowly she walked towards the bed until she was close enough for the little light to catch the pile of clothes her sister had mistaken for Anita. Her sister was nowhere to be found.

"Rosette!"

There was no response. Now the Shadow Monster had Rosette too.

The little light dimmed slightly and Lisette backed slowly away from the bed. She wanted to cry, but if she started crying now she would never find Anita and Rosette. Lisette took a deep breath and held back the tears that were stinging the corners of her eyes. Then she turned to the door that led into the living room. She was going to find that extension and call Momma herself.

When she walked into the living room she looked over on the couch to see if she could see any other silhouettes. She saw nothing, but noticed there was a soft whirring sound coming from the other end of the room. She turned and saw the turntable of her mother's gramophone spinning and spinning and spinning. She gasped when the needle fell slowly onto the record.

Slowly the music play began to play, heavy, dark. It wasn't at all like the Jazz her mother liked. Momma's music was joyous, with horns that would flit between notes like hummingbirds through flowers. This music was sad and slow. It seeped into Lisette's skin and weighed on her heart so heavy she thought it would stop, and just when she thought she couldn't take any more, a deeper and heavier voice began to sing out from the speaker.

I got your sister
And the babysitter too
But to eat my fill
I'm gonna get you

Lisette shivered as her little light dimmed and the darkness tried to push in closer to her. The heavy voice sung it's little chorus over and over again. Tears began to well up again behind Lisette's eyes and it was harder this time for her to fight them. She brought both of her hands up to her face to wipe them again and when she blinked them clear she noticed two shapes on either side of the gramophone stand.

Lisette paused.

She didn't want to get her hopes up. Rosette had mistaken the figure in Momma's room for Anita and had gotten swallowed in the darkness because of it. Lisette didn't want to make the same mistake as her sister.

She watched the two shapes, looking back and forth between them not quite sure what to do when she noticed one of them moving. It was a slight movement, the slow rise and fall of what could be shoulders. One of the shapes was breathing!

Lisette looked about the room, trying to see if there was any sign of the Shadow Monster and saw nothing. She took a deep breath and walked towards the gramophone.

I got your sister
And the babysitter too

Lisette pushed the taunting chorus to the back of her mind and tried to ignore it as it grew louder. She felt chills move up her back and when her and her light reached the gramophone there was nothing.

Gonna have me a stew
Gonna feast all night
Gonna boil you up
When you lose that light

The chorus changed and Lisette couldn't hold back her tears this time. She wanted to drop wholly onto the floor and have a tantrum, but the idea of it brought thoughts of her Momma scolding her and instinctively her back straightened and she tried to wipe the tears from her face before finally deciding her crying couldn't be helped. She then sat where she had stood in front of the gramophone with her knees pulled up to her chin.

Her light was fading, and it was fading fast. She hadn't been able to find her babysitter or her sister. She wasn't sure how much longer the light would last, but she was positive that without her sister she wouldn't be able to make another one. Soon she would be swallowed by the dark as well.

Lisette reached out and grabbed the little sun and pulled it close to her. The feel of the light calmed her and Lisette wiped the last of the tears from her eyes. Anita was right, the light did feel safe, and she could almost feel the warmth in her hands from her and her sister's hand games.

Gonna eat my fill
Gnaw down to your bones
Then I'll get a second course
When your momma comes home

Lisette looked up and just beyond the dying shield of her little light was the Shadow Monster. He seemed more in focus now, instead of just a moving black cloud. He stared at her, grinning and running his black tongue across his stark white teeth. Lisette would have shivered if she wasn't holding onto her last bit of light as tight as she could.

Gonna eat my fill
Gonna gnaw on your bones

As the light faded and the shield around her began to get smaller and smaller the Shadow Monster leaned closer and closer to Lisette until he was just inches from her face. There he stared at her and Lisette stared back unsure of what to do.

She should have been afraid, she knew this, but maybe it was the little light that kept her from wanting to scream. Instead of panic she felt calm as she stared into the shadowed face. She saw nothing there, no nose or cheekbones, just a blank black canvas. Suddenly her curiosity got the best of her and she reached out with one hand to touch the Monster's face.

She felt nothing.

"You ain't scary." Lisette's voice sounded strange to her, all wet and bubbly from crying. "You ain't scary at all. You're nothing!"

The Shadow Monster's grin fell from it's nothing face, and instead it frowned.

"You just make everything seem scary," Lisette sneered. "You hide things, but you can't really hurt nobody. You're just nothing, and I ain't gotta be scared of nothing in this house. You bring my sister back. You bring Anita back. They don't belong to you."

Although she hadn't notice, the eerie chorus from the gramophone had stopped. It wasn't until she saw the Shadow Monster's ghastly mouth moving again, yelling silent curses like it had done earlier to her sister, that she had noticed the absence of the music and the soft whirring of the turntable.

The absolute blackness in the room began to fade, and soon there was only the silhouette. It stared menacingly at Lisette and she looked down at the dying light in her hand as it burnt out. Instantly the Shadow Monster was on her, reaching out for her with its smoke hands and grabbing hold of her arms. It made a move like it was going to snatch her up but Lisette didn't budge. Instead she looked up at it and sneered again.

"I ain't scared of you."

Just as quickly as it had quickly as it had appeared, the Shadow Monster was gone and suddenly the room was bright again. Lisette looked around her, thinking that maybe Anita and Rosette had made their own light, but instead she found Anita and Rosette asleep on the couch. She turned back and looked at the gramophone which hadn't been touched. Everything in the house was back to normal. Lisette stood from her spot on the floor and walked over to the couch.

Anita woke gasping for air, and when she saw Lisette, she quickly reached out and pulled the little girl into a tight hug.

"Are you ok?" She asked after a while. "Are you scared?"

"No," Lisette responded. "There's nothing to be scared of."

Anita looked the girl over and then looked over at Rosette who was still sleep on the couch. When she turned back to Lisette she smiled and mouthed a low 'thank you.'

"It's already way past your bedtime." Anita said as Lisette let out a long full mouthed yawn. She stood and scooped Rosette off the other side of the couch and slung her over her shoulder.

"Do you want me to get the light?" Lisette asked, making her way over towards the living room lamp. Anita shook her head vigorously.

"I'll risk your mom getting upset about the lights this one time." Anita responded, then she stood and made her way to the entrance to Momma's room. Once there she paused and leaned slightly forward to survey the darkness.

"We'll hold hands," Lisette said, reaching out for Anita's free hand. "If the monster's show up I'll bring you to safety."

"I know you will." Anita said and grabbed the little girl's hand. The two of them stepped into the grey of Momma's room.

AUTHOR BIOGRAPHIEJ

Jessi Cole Jackson lives in the prettiest part of New Jersey. By day she builds costumes for a Tony Award-winning theatre. By night she studies Children's Literature at Hollins University. Somewhere in between, she writes. Her fiction can be found at *Crossed Genres Magazine, InterGalatic Medicine Show,* and *Cast of Wonders.* You can read more about her sometimes exciting (but mostly just normal) life at jessicolejackson.com.

Jaymee Goh writes fiction, poetry, and academese. Currently a PhD Candidate at the University of California, Riverside, she has been published in *Science Fiction Studies, Strange Horizons* and *Stone Telling.* She recently co-edited *The Sea is Ours: Tales of Steampunk Southeast Asia* (Rosarium Publishing).

K.T. Katzmann lives in Florida, surrounded by Cthulhu idols and crazy people. He's working on the second novel in his series featuring a Jewish vampire and a Bigfoot who fall in love while working for the NYPD. Despite all this, he is somehow still allowed to teach children.

He counts among his greatest influences the works of H.P.Lovecraft, Douglas Adams, and Roger Zelazny, and is thankful for years of boring public school classes which provided him with plenty of time to read them all.

He can be found at @iwritemonsters on Twitter, iwritemonsters on Tumblr, and www.iwritemonsters.com. He is, obviously, a bit of an obsessive.

Momtaza Mehri is a poet currently in conversation with biomedicine, inheritance and her brand of transnational baggage. Her work has been featured and is forthcoming in *Puerto Del Sol, Elsewhere Lit, Sukoon, Bone Banquet, VINYL* and *Poetry International.* She is a fellow of The Complete Works national programme and has been shortlisted for the 2016 Brunel African Poetry Prize. Her chapbook *sugah.lump.prayer* will be published as part of the New Generation African Poets series. She co-edits the digital platform Diaspora Drama and contributes to a variety of international zines. She is a believer in speculative fiction and its imagining of better worlds.

Daniel Brewer is a previously unpublished author. A resident of Western Massachusetts, he frequently volunteers at his local public access station, having informal training as a cameraman, sound technician, and director. After dropping out of public school at age twelve, he did things such as theater, fly airplanes, and play video games. Nowadays when he isn't a media volunteer, he bounces around from project to project. Projects such as a web series where Daniel was a sound grip, or on a research team as a mongoose surgical assistant. Daniel has loved writing since he was in elementary school, and has at last overcome his reservations about submitting his work for publication.

AUTHOR BIOGRAPHIES

Sioban Krzywicki is a trans woman living in MA with her wife and 4 cats. Her days are spent fighting with databases and much of the rest of her time goes to helping run Readercon. "Trenches" is Sioban's first published story.

A.J. Odasso's poetry has appeared in a number of strange and wonderful publications, including *Sybil's Garage, Mythic Delirium, Jabberwocky, Cabinet des Fées, Midnight Echo, Not One of Us, Dreams & Nightmares, Goblin Fruit, Strange Horizons, Stone Telling, Farrago's Wainscot, Through the Gate, Liminality, inkscrawl, Battersea Review,* and *SWAMP* (just to name a few). Her début collection, *Lost Books* (Flipped Eye Publishing, 2010), was nominated for the 2010 London New Poetry Award and for the 2011 Forward Prize, and was also a finalist for the 2011 People's Book Prize. Her second collection with Flipped Eye, *The Dishonesty of Dreams*, was released in August of 2014. Her two chapbooks, *Devil's Road Down* and *Wanderlust*, are available from Maverick Duck Press. She serves as Senior Poetry Editor at *Strange Horizons* magazine and holds degrees from Wellesley College, University of York (UK), and Boston University.

Alec Austin enjoys fantasy fiction which draws on the complexity of actual history and cultures. He's a game designer, media scholar, former nuclear reactor operator, and an alumnus of Clarion West and Viable Paradise. Alec's prior work has appeared in *Analog, Beneath Ceaseless Skies*, and *Strange Horizons*, among other venues. Some of his ancestors served in the Xiang Army. He's @AlecAustin on Twitter.

A former US Marine, **Michael Ezell** lives in California with his lovely wife of 28 years. His fiction has appeared in the anthologies *Girl at the End of the World, Vol. 2, Fantasy for Good*, and *Beyond the Stars: At Galaxy's Edge*, as well as *On Spec Magazine*.

Warren Bull is an award-winning author with more than fifty short stories in publication. He is the author three novels: *Abraham Lincoln for the Defense, Abraham Lincoln: Death in the Moonlight* and *Heartland*. His short story collections are: *Murder Manhattan Style, Killer Eulogy and Other Stories* and *No Happy Endings*. He is an active member of Mystery Writers of America and a lifetime member of Sisters in Crime with no hope of parole. He blogs on Fridays on the Writers Who Kill blog. His website is www.WarrenBull.com.

Erik Jensen is a professor of ancient Mediterranean history at Salem State University in Salem, Massachusetts. His scholarly work concentrates on cross-cultural interactions in antiquity. It was his love of fantasy that first inspired him to study history; now his love of history inspires his fantasy writing. "How I Saved Athens from the Stone Monsters" is his first published work of fiction. Erik and his wife Eppu blog about history, fantasy, science fiction, and other fascinating things at co-geeking.com.

J.M. Templet lives and works in Baton Rouge. She graduated from LSU several years ago and earned the Matt Clark prize in short fiction there. She then got her graduate degree in Library Science from TWU.

She has previously been published in *Triggerfish, Counterexample Poetics, Marathon Literary Review, Strong Verse, Dig, Crossed Genres,* and *Fae Fatales.* J.M. won third place in the 2016 St. Louis Writer's Guild Short Story Contest.

Imani Josey is a writer, dancer and fitness professional from Chicago, Illinois. After graduating Howard University, Imani received her Master of Science in Communication from Northwestern. Sometime during all of that studying, she danced professionally for the Chicago Bulls as a (Luvabulls) cheerleader, and won the title of Miss Chicago for the Miss America Organization.

Imani's one-act play Grace was produced by Pegasus Players Theatre Chicago after winning the 19th Annual Young Playwrights Festival.

Imani hasn't penned any plays since, turning her sights to fiction instead. She now spends the majority of her time working on back story and teaching Dance Fitness classes.

You'll probably catch her sending chapters to her beloved beta readers or choreographing new moves with her American bulldog Thor.

Peter Medeiros has most recently published or has speculative work forthcoming in *SQ Magazine, Spark: A Creative Anthology, Strange Horizons,* and *Mirror Dance.*

Peter received his MFA in Creative Writing from Emerson College, where he currently teaches college composition and research writing. He's from Worcester, Massachusetts and currently lives in Somerville, MA.

Thom Dunn is a writer and rock/folk musician of various stringed things. He is currently a staff writer for Upworthy, as well as a Playwriting Fellow at the Huntington Theatre Company in Boston, and his plays have been performed across the country from New York to Hollywood to Alaska. He has also published comic books with Grayhaven Comics and Ninth Art Press; essays, criticisms, and other vaguely-non-fictional ramblings for Quirk Books, Dark Horse Comics, and Tor.com; and, poetry in *Asimov's* and others. A graduate of the Clarion Writer's Workshop at UCSD and Emerson College, Thom enjoys Oxford commas, metaphysics, and romantic clichés (especially when they involve whiskey), and firmly believes that Journey's "Don't Stop Believing" is the single greatest atrocity ever committed against mankind. You can follow his thrilling adventures online at thomdunn.net, on Twitter @thomdunn, or at facebook.com/thomdunnwrites.

E.C. Myers was assembled in the U.S. from Korean and German parts and raised by a single mother and the public library in Yonkers, New York. He is the author of numerous short stories and four young adult books: the Andre Norton Award–winning *Fair Coin*, *Quantum Coin*, *The Silence of Six*, and *Against All Silence*. E.C. currently lives with his wife, son, and three doofy pets in Pennsylvania. You can find traces of him all over the internet, but especially at http://ecmyers.net and on Twitter: @ecmyers.

Kate McCane grew up in Australia, where she began telling stories at a very young age, and soon afterwards started writing them down. She loves the stage, and received a degree in Theater from the University of Alberta in Edmonton, Canada, which is also where she learnt to speak German, a language she loves, and where work at a living history museum rekindled her interest in the past. While performing and writing are her passion, translation from German to English is currently what pays the bills. She has loved all things fantastic from a very young age, and thinks Social Justice Warrior is a compliment, not an insult (although she's personally always preferred Rogues). She moved to Berlin in 2007, where she currently lives with one partner, two computers, three cats, and more books than can reasonably be counted.

Nitra Wisdom is a queer femme mermaid and Mama of two, currently living in Atlanta and working toward the day when she can retire to her little blue house off the coast of the Atlantic. Until then, she fills her time with hiking trips, long talks with her Granny, Netflix and rants about gentrification. She has written book reviews and author interviews for Elixher Magazine, and plans to release a collection of short stories and personal essays when she overcomes her fear of inadequacy. You can find her lurking and retweeting at @BlkSiren.

J.S. Hawthorne was raised largely in Western Massachusetts but lives near New York City now. An avowed fan of video games, Dungeons & Dragons, and films of all genres and eras, Hawthorne is a lawyer by day, but spends all available free time engaged in the pursuit of fantastical stories, whether writing or consuming them. Previous published stories are mostly confined to convention books, and are probably pretty hard to find nowadays, but one can find Hawthorne on Twitter: @jshawthorn3.

P. Djéli Clark is a historian and occasional speculative fiction writer. His short SFF stories have appeared in *Daily Science Fiction*, *Every Day Fiction*, *Heroic Fantasy Quarterly*, Tor.com and several print anthologies including *Griots I & II*, *Steamfunk* and *Myriad Lands*. You can read his ramblings on SFF, diversity and more at his blog The Disgruntled Haradrim (pdjeliclark.com). He also tweets stuff: @pdjeliclark.

New York City native **Camilla Zhang** is a writer with a background in comics. She has been published in educational comics publication *Reading with Pictures* and is a runner-up in Top Cow's 2015 Talent Hunt. Her passions include diversity, feminist, and overall equality issues, Asian American culture, and sexual identity. In her spare time she enjoys spooning her cat, Captain McNugget, collaging, dancing, and singing karaoke. She is an overall positive person, but is relentless about the struggle against hate, bigotry, and violence. This is Camilla's first official prose publication.

De Ana Jones is a blogger and podcaster from Southern California who in elementary school learned that the stories in her head were easier to keep track of on paper. She currently likes to talk about nerdy things on the Nerdgasm Noire podcast and is a self-proclaimed Professional Smartass on twitter as @NaniCoolJ. She also has a blog NerdyGirlSwag.com. This is her first published work.

EDITOR BIOGRAPHIES

Mikki Kendall is a writer of comics, speculative fiction and non-fiction. Her non-fiction work often deals with issues of feminism and race, and can be found in The Guardian, Washington Post, Salon, NPR's Code Switch, Hood Feminism, and many other places. Her fiction can be found in Revelator Magazine, Torquere Press, and occasionally appears on her website. Someday she will unleash all of her stories. In the meantime she enjoys editing the work of others. She only works this hard because her kids eat more than any three superheros.

Mikki is the Co-founder of Hood Feminism.com. She can also be found at MikkiKendall.com.

Chesya Burke has written and published nearly a hundred fiction pieces and articles within the genres of science fiction, fantasy, noir and horror. Her story collection, *Let's Play White*, is being taught in universities around the country. In addition, Burke wrote several articles for the African American National Biography in 2008, and Burke's novel, *THE STRANGE CRIMES OF LITTLE AFRICA*, debuted in Dec 2015. Poet Nikki Giovanni compared her writing to that of Octavia Butler and Toni Morrison, and Samuel Delany called her "a formidable new master of the macabre."

Burke's thesis was on the comic book character Storm from the X-MEN, and her comic, *Shiv*, is scheduled to debut in 2017.

Burke is currently pursuing her PhD in English at University of Florida. She's Co-Chair of the Board of Directors of Charis Books and More, one of the oldest feminist book stores in the country.

For more information, check out Chesya at www.chesyaburke.com.